# THE
# GALLAGHER
# PLACE

*Praise for*
# THE GALLAGHER PLACE

"Gothic and twisty! Don't miss it."
—LISA UNGER, author of *Secluded Cabin Sleeps Six*

"A spellbinding mystery of buried secrets and family ties, set in Rip Van Winkle's Hudson River Valley. In page after chilling page, the revelations pile up in this shocking debut that resonates with the emotional weight of loss—and the even darker truths that can lie beneath it. Julie Doar is a promising new voice."
—LLOYD DEVEREUX RICHARDS,
author of *Stone Maidens*

"A beautifully written slow-burn mystery about a woman haunted by the disappearance of her childhood best friend. Everyone is holding a secret, and the ending is a true shocker!"
—SARAH PEKKANEN, author of *House of Glass*

"Haunting and atmospheric, *The Gallagher Place* is a pulse-quickening ride through a beautiful but threatening landscape that will keep you turning pages late into the night. I loved it!"
—KATIE SISE, author of *The Vacation Rental*

"This modern-day Hudson Valley Gothic, complete with fog-covered fields, class conflicts, and ancient folklore, will keep you guessing until the final pages. Your heart will ache—and pound—when you discover the real wolf in sheep's clothing."
—SARAH SAWYER, author of *The Undercurrent*

# THE
# GALLAGHER
# PLACE

A NOVEL

## JULIE DOAR

ZIBBY PUBLISHING
NEW YORK

*This novel contains sensitive subject matter pertaining to animal harm.
Please read with care.*

*The Gallagher Place: A Novel*

Copyright © 2025 by Julie Doar

ZIBBY, Zibby Publishing, colophon, and associated logos are trademarks and/or registered trademarks of Zibby Media LLC.

Library of Congress Control Number: 2025930784
Paperback ISBN: 979-8-9923770-0-2
eBook ISBN: 979-8-9923770-1-9

Book design by Neuwirth and Associates
Cover design by Danielle Christopher
Cover art © Roberto Moiola / Sysaworld / Movement via Getty Images

www.zibbymedia.com

Printed in the United States of America

10 9 8 7 6 5 4 3 2 1

*For my parents*

# PROLOGUE

**Saturday, June 6, 1998**

Marlowe hissed as the tip of her pencil snapped. She cast it aside and shoved at her sketch, lifting her head to look out at the cloudless night. From her room, she had a view of the wide front yard and the red barn across the street. She bit down hard on her lip as she stared at the solid structure darkened by shadows.

Her bedroom door was open, and she could hear voices downstairs. Her father's somber murmur, her mother's quick response. She was supposed to be sleeping. As if that were possible. She had been up all night. Her whole family had been up, crisscrossing their acres of land, searching. A heavy exhaustion had settled over her, but she felt like she would never sleep again.

Marlowe grabbed a new pencil from the expensive drawing set she'd been given for her sixteenth birthday and flipped to a new page in her sketchbook. The charcoal tip flew over the thick, creamy stock. She had sketched the single birch tree in her front yard a hundred times, gradually layering light and dark strokes for the texture of the bark—more black than you would think—with sharp flicks to angle the serrated curve of a leaf. It was a simple one-point perspective that she'd mastered. But she'd yet to produce a sketch of the woods that captured what it felt like to stand among the dizzying trees.

Her heavy pencil strokes filled the page. She drew tree after tree in rapid succession, the woods becoming an impenetrable wall of black. The forest surrounding her family's country home often gave her a feeling she couldn't place, like there was something just out of frame, like a taunt that dared her to look closer. She felt it every time she heard a twig snap or the faint sound of footsteps in the layers upon layers of fallen leaves. Even the thought of it made the back of her neck prickle.

"It's just your imagination," her older brother, Nate, always explained. "We're the only ones out here," he would say. He didn't understand her frustration.

She ripped the drawing out of her sketchbook and threw it onto the pile in her trash can. It was no use; she would never be able to capture the feeling correctly. Not now.

Instead, she forced her trembling fingers into a firm grip and etched out the first few lines of the old barn, its doors wide open. It didn't matter that she couldn't see the details at this time of night; she knew from memory exactly what it looked like—its walls becoming a little more warped with every snowfall, every windy autumn, and every summer's round of hay loaded into the loft.

She slanted her pencil to shade in the yawning darkness within the barn, and farther back, near the ladder, she tried for a shape. Broad but sloping shoulders, legs and boots shrouded in shadow. A nameless figure tucked away in the corner of the barn. She imagined him stalking through the open doors, over the hayfield, and into the thickest part of the woods. Marlowe felt a sob rattle in her chest as she took a breath, and fresh tears fell onto the page, watering down the pencil marks, making everything blurry and gray.

It didn't matter. She couldn't even attempt to sketch the stranger's face, because she had never seen him.

But he wasn't in her head. He was out there. He had to be.

# FRIDAY

**NOVEMBER 23, 2018**

# ONE

Marlowe woke to the tread of feet in the kitchen and the muffled chatter of her nieces. Slowly opening her eyes, she glanced out the transom window above her bed, where a cloud bank scattered the late autumn sun and the frozen lawn glowed faintly. She guessed it was well past eight, the breakfast hour her mother, Glory, insisted upon seven days a week. The house was in full swing above her basement bedroom, which she'd taken over in her twenties, when her nieces encroached on her childhood room upstairs. She didn't mind retreating—she preferred her privacy, especially during these annual Fisher family holiday weeks at the Gray House.

Pleased that her head had only a dull ache and no searing pain, Marlowe swung her legs over the side of the bed. Last night, along with her brothers, Nate and Henry, she had stayed up until the small hours, cracking open bottles of wine and trading old stories. That was the routine this time of year, when they were all back under one roof at their cherished upstate home. She had been visiting the country house in Dutchess County since she was five years old. Memories from their childhood weekends fleeing New York City and running wild always felt fresher around the holidays, probably because Nate and Henry had their own kids now and came back only for special occasions.

Although she kept an apartment on the Upper West Side, Marlowe had spent increasingly more time in the country over the past few years. She was used to the silence now, and it made weeks like this one feel loud and overwhelming. Marlowe tried to be a kind and attentive aunt, but she often found herself counting down the hours until it would be quiet again.

She ran back through what she remembered of the previous night—the Thanksgiving meal that hadn't changed since she was a child, the wine by the fire—but she winced as she recalled her nieces bounding down from their baths in matching pajamas, looking cherubic as they hugged their parents good night. Nate had glanced at Marlowe with concern, and Henry had actually reached out and patted her hand. She could read their minds: *How awful to be a single woman in her thirties without any prospect of children on the horizon.* Marlowe's only response was to take a large gulp of chardonnay. Never mind that Marlowe had plenty to fill her life. She had friends and her painting and her travels and her burgeoning career as an illustrator. Despite her brothers' fears that Marlowe must feel left behind, thirty-six was hardly ancient. And she had always been patient. Better to wait forever than settle for less than what she wanted. Although not even she could say exactly what that was.

Marlowe tiptoed over to the French doors that opened to a small back patio, flinching with every step across the cold floorboards. She pushed the sheer curtain aside and peered out at the grass tipped with frost and the silent sentinels of apple trees, drab and colorless now that their riotous autumn was ending. All the apples had fallen into patches of brown leaves and rotted in sweet-smelling clumps. Even with the doors closed, she caught the scent of bonfires in the November air. The Fisher men had made a massive one yesterday, filled with all the dead branches Henry was so diligent about collecting. Marlowe wondered if her younger brother would ever love practising law as much as he loved his time-honored exercise of picking up sticks.

Once she was dressed, Marlowe ran a brush through her dark hair before heading upstairs. Crossing the spacious living room, she felt a flicker of relief as the empty kitchen came into view. Of course, it was spotless. An hour earlier, the children had probably turned the countertop into a chaotic, sticky land mine, but Marlowe's mother had already swept in behind them to clean up the mess. Holiday or not, Glory never left a single dish unwashed before bed or after a meal.

It was also Glory's habit to rise at five every morning and brew a massive pot of coffee. It was nearly nine. The coffee would be cold. Marlowe poured herself a cup anyway, just as the side door off the kitchen opened and Nate strode in, a pile of logs in his arms.

"Mom and Dad are in town getting the papers." Nate spoke as he unloaded the logs. He brushed off his coat, always in motion and poised for action. "Walk?"

Marlowe nodded and set her mug down on the counter.

Nate grinned, his eyes crinkling up. Nothing seemed to make him happier than rallying his siblings for a walk, as if it was a pleasant surprise and not something they had done hundreds of times. That was the charm of her older brother. His smile could convince you that a river runs uphill.

Henry entered with another armful of logs. Marlowe noted he moved slower than he used to after a late night.

"Marlowe is in," Nate said to Henry. "Come for a walk with us?"

"Just us three?" Henry smiled. "Sneaking off to the Bend for old times' sake."

It was a joke now that they were adults, but the Bend had once been their most cherished secret. As children, they were forbidden to swim without parental supervision. They swam anyway and vowed never to tell.

Nate led them to the door, and Marlowe buttoned up her coat as they stepped out into the frigid cold. She followed her brothers across the wide front lawn, the grass flat and faded to a yellowish green. She glanced back at her home. Even with its boxy proportions, the Gray House stood elegant and alluring. The sky was overcast to match the house's somber tone, but the Gray House was far from drab. The shutters were painted dark green, contrasting its namesake clapboard color. It was cozy, yet regal, and lovingly maintained by regular visits from a house cleaner, painters who applied a fresh coat every other spring, and a fleet of lawn mowers in the summer, all arranged long ago and directed by Enzo, the wizened Italian handyman who'd become like a second father to Marlowe and the boys.

At the road, Nate paused to look at an oak tree, musing that it might be diseased. It was a habit he had picked up from their father, who believed he had a preternatural ability to spot a rotting tree long before anyone else might notice the symptoms of decay.

"We might have to cut her down." Nate patted the trunk with his gloved hand, and Henry nodded along. Henry didn't claim to have the same skill, but he never missed an opportunity to fool around with heavy equipment. During summer weekends, the Weedwacker was practically glued to his arm.

"I'd bet fifty dollars that tree is still fine by next summer," Marlowe said.

Nate simply sighed and shook his head as they continued walking by a copse of young pines and crossed to the other side of the road, where they passed the empty red Gallagher barn. After their father purchased the Gray House, they'd spent nearly every weekend of their childhoods upstate, watching the Gallagher brothers tend to their herd and mow their hayfields. A ragged wood fence still separated the barn from the gently sloping pastures, but no livestock roamed now that the farmers were gone. Marlowe, Nate, and Henry walked through the open gate toward the other side of the field. Their boots crunched over the frostbitten grass and hardened lumps of dirt. The field had to be mowed every few weeks in the summer now that the cows no longer grazed.

The gradual incline met with a hill that climbed steadily into an overlook—one of their favorite spots on the property—that they called the Rise. There was an old queen oak at its crest; inert branches arched up from the trunk before drooping toward the icy ground. It took them almost twenty minutes to get from their house to the tree. How fast had they run that distance in their youth, with their nimble legs and relentless hearts? Fifteen minutes? Ten?

Marlowe clenched her fists in her pockets. She had her jacket collar pulled up against a bitter wind.

"It hasn't been this cold at Thanksgiving for a long time," Henry said. "Even with that snowstorm five years ago, it wasn't this *cold*."

"Can't handle it, little brother? You must be spending too much time in that fancy law office of yours," Nate ribbed.

Marlowe laughed. She wondered what she and her brothers were, if not three people with shared memories of an array of holidays and the weather that accompanied each one.

From the top of the Rise, Marlowe could make out the slate-shingled roof of the house and a few of the upstairs windows. Mere steps beyond the house were the garden and the apple orchard, ending at the foot of the north hayfield on its steep hill. The field and the orchard were surrounded by the woods, carved up by old footpaths and loosely mortared stone walls—a perfect playground orbiting the warm sun of the Gray House. A few wisps of green grass and some orange leaves clinging to barren branches provided the only color except for the faded red of the barn. Yet in any season the view was idyllic, like a storybook farm from the olden days, when life was simple and people were good. Marlowe knew this was an illusion, but like the illustrations she painted for children's books, the deception was a lovely one.

Marlowe looked to her brothers, who smiled broadly as they turned their backs on the barn and the house and headed down the other side of the Rise, toward the wooded gully. They traversed a thicket of trees and underbrush to reach the narrow valley carved from a dried-out streambed. After climbing out, they found themselves on the western edge of the Flats—another field, which was wider, more unkempt, and distinguished by a maze of birch trees, weeds, and brambles guarding their trunks. The Flats rolled in gentle hillocks, their northern side lined by the swamplands. At the northeast corner of the Flats, the Bean River emerged from the murky pools and gnarled trees of the bog. The river cut steadily across the Flats from north to south, about a hundred yards from where Marlowe stood with her brothers. This land had never been a pasture or planted with any crops. It was too uneven and rocky. But it was beautiful—not quite wilderness but not tamed either.

The tall grass, once lush and green in the summer, had turned a soft yellow hue by November. Somehow, this made the field look even more lovely. The trees grew dense near the winding Bean River. As a child, Marlowe had imagined the name came from an actual legume, or perhaps the river's shape resembled one. Maybe beans had once been cultivated along its banks. In truth, the name traced back to a family who had lived near the river long ago, though no one could quite recall exactly when, or who they were.

With what felt like an ancient instinct, Marlowe turned her head away from the swamp and toward the mythical Bend, hidden among the trees in the southeast corner of the Flats, where the river turned at a right angle and the water widened into their old swimming hole.

"Might be a good day for a dip, Mar," Henry joked.

Marlowe shook her head. "I'm ready to go back."

She cursed herself for not eating breakfast before the walk. The freezing cold and the exertion were making her woozy. She was starting to crave the armchair by the fire.

"Come on, we have to at least get to the Bend," Nate said.

Marlowe huffed a few more steps and then stopped to take in the scene. Her eyes froze on a black shape near one of the solitary trees about three hundred feet away.

"Is that a tent?" Henry had spotted it as well.

"Must be a deer hunter," Nate said.

Marlowe's father occasionally granted hunting leases to some of the locals in exchange for a chest freezer full of venison, which kept the Fishers well fed throughout the year. It was a quiet exchange that tied the family to the rhythms of the land, even in their absence. Marlowe rarely saw or heard from the hunters. She had spotted their blinds and perches in the woods her whole life, but the men themselves came and went in the silent predawn hours, their presence more imagined than real. They had a few wire seats rigged up in tree crowns with ladders, and there were some lean-tos as well, but a tent was unusual. Not one like this, with its bent poles and sagging canvas top.

Nate moved first, and Henry a second later. He wasn't wearing a hat, and the rims of his ears had turned bright red. Part of Marlowe wanted to turn and run home on the spot, but she'd never once let her brothers venture without her.

As they approached the tent, the silence turned heavy. Marlowe didn't hear any rustle or movement from inside, and the front was zipped up almost all the way.

Henry let out a small chuckle, but it lacked any real mirth. "Well, let's see what's inside."

He reached out and yanked hard on the zipper so that the flap fell open at once.

Marlowe clapped her hand over her mouth as Henry reared backward, his shoulder colliding with her chest.

Had the body been arranged differently, it wouldn't have been so bad. If the thick boots and mud-splattered pants had fallen out first. But it was a man's misshapen head that appeared at the opening, one vacant eye staring straight up at Marlowe. He was wearing the type of camo jacket local hunters donned, with brown leaf patterns.

In one swift, sharp movement, Nate turned his entire body to the side, but Marlowe couldn't look away from the matted hair twisted over the indent in the man's forehead where his head had been bashed in, where the white of his skull gleamed.

"Jesus, who *is* that?" Henry had taken several steps back.

Nate tugged on Marlowe's arm. "We need to go."

Marlowe didn't let him lead her away. She reached out and nudged the flap lower.

"Don't touch anything." Nate's grip on her arm tightened.

Henry pulled out his phone and held it up in the air. "There's never any service out here—I can't get a signal."

"We need to get back to the house." Nate took off in ground-eating strides, and Henry followed, matching the pace.

Marlowe tasted bile on the back of her tongue. She swallowed hard and ran after her brothers.

# TWO

Nate made the call.

Seated in the armchair by the fire, Marlowe watched her brother pace back and forth across the red-patterned rug in the living room.

"A male, hard to say the age," Nate said. "Yes, on our property, just off Bean River Road . . . We didn't get too close . . . Yes, that's right. Fisher."

Nate's wife, Stephanie, sat on the bottom step of the old staircase, elbows propped on her long legs, her rich blond hair pulled back in a ponytail with a pink hair tie. She glanced at Marlowe.

"Who opened the tent?" she asked.

"Henry did," Marlowe said.

A barely audible hum slid through Stephanie's lips, which Marlowe clocked as mild dissension. Stephanie had an easy elegance and never neglected a chance to pass judgment. She appeared to relish this even more in the company of Marlowe, who was still bundled in her shabby barn coat. Stephanie adjusted her chic oversized cashmere turtleneck over her leggings. Despite childbirth and the long years since her college athletic career, she still maintained her figure.

"And what did you say the guy looked like?"

"I don't know. He was wearing a hunting jacket," Marlowe said. "But he was a mess. I mean, it was hard to really tell anything about him."

"So you didn't recognize him?"

"No," said Marlowe, turning back to the fire to politely signal that she was done with the exchange.

Stephanie stood up. "I think I'll put on some tea," she said, betraying the age-old instinct: Tragedy strikes; a wife fills the kettle. Marlowe watched her cross the room and pass through the arched entryway to the kitchen. Huddled around the kitchen island, Henry was whispering the story to his wife, Constance, who held the baby, Frankie, against her shoulder as she listened. She drew in a long, uneven breath as the weight of Henry's words settled unhappily on her face. Nate's daughters, Kat and Dolly, were fighting over a blueberry scone, blissfully ignorant of the discovery that had left the rest of the family somber and mired in their own quiet suspicions.

Marlowe held her hands to the flame and then pulled the heat into her chest. Every time she blinked, she saw the man's bloodied head contrasted with the stark whites of his eyes, the scruff along his jaw matted with crimson.

Nate cleared his throat and pushed the phone closer to his ear. He was listening intently.

"It did look violent," he said at last. "Yes, it did."

Nate hung up and declared that the police were on their way. Marlowe lifted her head to meet his gaze.

"He couldn't have been dead long," Marlowe whispered.

Nate stared blankly, as if he hadn't heard her. The crunch of car wheels on gravel jolted him out of the trance, and then Nate was bolting for the side door that opened onto the driveway. Frank and Glory were back. Marlowe followed closely behind but only watched from the window as Nate murmured something to their father. Frank had shrunk in recent years, his shoulders dipping forward in a hunch, and his skin was dry and deeply wrinkled. Where Nate's dark hair was thick and healthy, gleaming beneath the cold sun, Frank's white tufts of thin hair added to his appearance of frailty.

Marlowe watched as her father's eyes widened and he reached a pale hand toward Glory's arm. A moment later, Nate and Frank took off at a slow, steady pace in the direction of the barn.

The kitchen door swung open, and Glory entered, decked out in a spotless beige barn jacket and a plaid scarf. Her white-streaked hair was piled atop her head and secured with a black clip. "Nate took Frank out to see it," she said, her mouth set in a thin line.

Marlowe nodded. "We called the police. They're on their way."

Glory paused, looking Marlowe over in her disheveled state. "You've had a shock. Maybe you should go lie down."

Laughter, inappropriate as it was, bubbled in Marlowe's throat.

"I'm not tired," Marlowe said. "I want to be here when the police arrive."

"Darling, it looks like you didn't get much sleep last night. I'll come and get you if you're needed."

Her mother was every inch the pragmatist, and when she was faced with strife, she put the dead weight to bed first so things could get done.

Marlowe convinced herself that she wasn't following an order by turning on her heels and padding down to the basement, but she felt like a child. Marlowe was never considered a useful member of the family. Quiet, artistic maybe, occasionally sarcastic, but never useful.

She shut herself in her bathroom and shrugged off her coat, letting it fall to the tile floor. It was then that she noticed her trembling hands. She yanked open her medicine cabinet, looking for the familiar label, not finding it, and then slamming it shut. The house cleaner who came once a week sometimes moved things around. Glory too. Marlowe could never be sure who the culprit was.

Marlowe had meant to rest for only a moment, but when she sat down on her bed fully clothed, the soft pull of sleep overtook her. She awoke thirty minutes later to the low hum of a car in the driveway and the sound of a murmured conversation just outside her window.

Sitting up, she rubbed her eyes and listened for another minute before heading back upstairs. In the kitchen, Glory was at one end of the massive wooden table custom-made from repurposed barn doors, her hands wrapped around a mug. Stephanie was beside her, absently swirling tea in her cup, while Constance leaned against the counter, her arms crossed, her eyes darting toward the window every so often. A singsongy melody drifted in from the den; the children had been placed in front of a television program.

Their silence gave Marlowe the sense that the three women had been talking about her.

Glory glanced up as Marlowe entered. "The police are here," she said softly. "Henry took them out to join Frank and Nate in the field."

"Did you speak to them yet?"

"The police? No, Henry met them outside," Glory said. "Feeling better?"

"Yes, I'm fine."

Marlowe surveyed the straight line of Glory's back. She was over sixty but still moved as well as she had twenty years ago. It had to do with her childhood on a farm. There was something in her that was as all-enduring as dirt.

On the other hand, Marlowe's father had been waning for years. She had concerns about his walking all the way out to where they'd found the body. He had heart trouble and lung trouble and sugar trouble. He hated growing old and helpless. He despised needing help to get up and down stairs, and he resented being unable to walk wherever he wanted on his own land.

It must be strange, Marlowe mused, for Glory to know for certain she was going to outlive her husband, likely by many years.

Marlowe pushed the thought aside and then quickly grabbed her coat as she headed for the door.

"Where are you going?" Glory asked.

Marlowe shut the door behind her. She didn't have to explain to her mother why she had a right to go wherever her brothers went. For the second time that day, Marlowe crossed the street and walked through the old Gallagher property.

Marlowe's breath shortened as she trudged over the Rise and down into the gully, faster than she'd gone before.

There was no massive crowd, no white tent that Marlowe had expected. For now, there were just two policemen cordoning off the area with stakes and yellow tape. One of them was taking photos, not of the tent but of the ground and the landscape. Another was talking to Nate and Frank and taking notes. No one had approached the tent yet; it seemed they were waiting for the experts.

Marlowe drew to a stop beside Henry, where he stood scanning the tent and the police officers. Pale light pooled in uneven patches along the banks of the river. The water levels were low, but she could still hear the faint trickling.

"Detectives are on their way," Henry said.

"Do they know who it is?" Marlowe asked.

"Dad recognized him," Henry said. "He's a Gallagher cousin."

Marlowe's brows shot up. The Gallagher brothers had owned the barn and fields across the street from the Gray House when the Fishers first bought it. All three Gallaghers had been single and childless. It was part of their tragedy. When they passed, Frank purchased the land, extending his own property to its current size. Marlowe was a teenager at the time, but she had never heard of any other Gallaghers.

"Or a great-nephew." Henry shoved his hands deeper into his coat pockets and shook his head. "Cousin once removed. Something like that. He came to talk to Dad a few years ago about buying some of the land back."

Marlowe had never heard Frank talk of anyone approaching him about the Gallagher land. She glanced over at her father, who appeared to be watching the water move. The skin of his face had taken on a purplish hue. It was a miracle he had been able to walk all the way out here. Crises gave people strength.

"Did you know about this?" Marlowe asked.

"What, about the land?"

"That a Gallagher had come back wanting to buy some of it."

"Dad must have mentioned it to me when it happened, but there wasn't much of a conversation. He'd never sell."

Henry seemed to be avoiding Marlowe's gaze.

"Did Dad give him permission to hunt here?"

"Doubt it." A cautious smile, of all things, came to Henry's lips. "Think about it, Marlowe. Does that seem like something Dad would do?"

No, their father wouldn't have liked anyone pestering him about selling his land. And he certainly wouldn't have rewarded that with a hunting lease.

"Even if he had permission, it's odd to be hunting the morning after Thanksgiving," Marlowe said.

Henry shrugged. "Some people find it relaxing."

Marlowe had never fired a rifle herself, and she didn't have any desire to do so. Over the years, she'd seen plenty of trophy antlers displayed in various establishments around Dutchess County. The elegantly curved tines reaching out, the blackness of the tips revealing the number of years the animal had lived in the wild. She didn't care how big its antlers were or how majestic they appeared tacked up on the wall; a deer was still a deer.

# THREE

*Harmon Gallagher.* Marlowe turned the name of the dead man over in her head like a shard of glass she had discovered on the ground. Something that should fit into a shattered windowpane, if only she could find the other pieces.

It had been hours since they'd returned to the house, and Frank had given everyone the news. The body belonged to Harmon Gallagher. A local police officer had been dispatched to Harmon's mother's house just one town over; this wasn't the kind of news given over the phone. She claimed she hadn't seen him since the previous day at Thanksgiving dinner. He usually went out before dawn to hunt this time of year, and she'd figured that had been the case. A photograph confirmed it was him. Once she identified the body in person, it would be official.

Marlowe would have liked to spend the day in the Flats, watching for any movements and aberrations in the land that could explain such a horrific incident, but the family was told by the police to stay in the house, so as not to accidentally destroy any evidence. Their own footprints already covered the scene.

By now, the family had scattered throughout the house, taking refuge in the privacy of their rooms while they waited for the homicide detectives to arrive. Only Marlowe and her mother sat by the fire in the living room, Glory in her red armchair and Marlowe cross-legged on the floor with her chin propped on her hand.

"You have work to do?" Glory asked.

Marlowe had steady illustration work, but her focus dissipated the moment they'd found that body.

"There's always work," she said. "But how am I supposed to get my mind off something like this?"

"I thought I taught you the powers of compartmentalization. Discipline, sweetheart."

"You didn't see it," Marlowe said. "It was bloody."

"Lots of things are bloody," her mother said. "It's none of our concern. The professionals are going to handle it."

"But it's our property."

"No," Glory said. "It's my property. Mine and Frank's."

How could she forget? Frank and Glory owned the land. It wasn't Marlowe's. It wasn't Nate's or Henry's. Nothing was set in stone. The matter of future ownership was always held over them. Frank still hadn't devised a plan for the inheritance.

Marlowe studied her mother's placid brow, her steely comportment. All of it was a result of having been raised on a farm in the country, milking cows and picking corn and even helping slaughter pigs. Despite her designer clothes and tasteful gold earrings, Glory had grown up accustomed to blood and death. But surely Glory had thoughts. She couldn't possibly be sitting in that chair, devoting all her attention to the *New York Times* Arts and Leisure section. Not when the air was so weighted with uncertainty. Marlowe wanted to shake her, pry open the vault that was her mother's mind, to hear something—anything—that revealed the deep currents running beneath the surface. But Glory remained a locked door. Her response to crisis was for her daughter to busy herself with a sketch pad.

Marlowe's mind whirred as she reluctantly descended back into the basement. Her best theory, based on what little she knew, was that two hunters had gotten into some sort of fight, and it had turned ugly.

She looked at her sketchbook, pencils, and watercolors strewn over her drafting table, but work felt futile in a moment like this. Still, she was restless. Stepping through the French doors that led to the back patio, she settled onto the stone bench against the side of the house, watching as the light began to change. This was a peaceful place to admire the garden, the orchard, and the silent woods atop the hill. A retreat from the city. That was what this Hudson Valley house was supposed to be: a wholesome family sanctuary to escape the crowded city life and the bittersweet pain of growing up too fast. A haven, her father sometimes called it. If that was the case, why did bad things still happen? It made the magic of the Gray House feel like a broken promise. Even so, she loved this place more than any other.

Her mother sometimes snuck a cigarette on this little bench, among the foxgloves, tiger lilies, and hostas. For once, Marlowe wished she were a smoker so she could partake in a minor vice. What she really wanted was a drink. There was a bottle hidden deep in her closet, somewhere Glory wouldn't find it when she poked around, but Marlowe didn't go get it; she had to stay sharp for whatever was to come. She shouldn't be nervous. Marlowe hadn't done anything wrong. She never had, and yet a feeling of guilt crept up on her as the sky behind the apple orchard turned pink, then violet, then dusky blue, then black.

She was stepping back inside when Nate appeared at her bedroom door.

"The detectives are upstairs," he said. "They want to talk to us. All of us."

Marlowe was tempted to click her heels and salute. Yes, sir. Whatever you say, Captain. That was what Nate wanted. To be in charge. To be the commander in chief. He wanted to be the honorable and good-natured leader of their merry band.

Marlowe followed Nate up the stairs to the large living room.

The detectives, a man and a woman, stood in the middle of the living room in black coats over their button-downs and slacks. The man was tall and groomed, in a well-tailored coat; his dark hair was neatly combed away from his face, highlighting his smooth olive complexion. The woman, by contrast, had a short, stocky build. Her hair was scraped back, and she had circles under her eyes. She had made no attempt to brighten her complexion with makeup or even a friendly smile. Their ages were hard to place, but neither of them looked over forty. The man had a calmness to him, but the woman, Marlowe noticed, was jiggling change in her pocket.

The family wordlessly settled into the available couches and armchairs in the living room, inviting the detectives to have a seat too. Henry carried in two extra chairs from the kitchen and placed them near Stephanie. Frank and Glory were opposite them on one of the tufted leather couches. Kat and Dolly perched on the wide first step of the staircase, and Constance held little Frankie in her arms. Two armchairs had been left empty for Nate and Marlowe.

The man cleared his throat. "I'm Ben Vance, and this is my partner, Ariel Mintz."

The woman gave a respectful nod.

"We're up from Poughkeepsie," Ben said. "Unfortunately, this event has been deemed a homicide." He let that linger for a moment. It was a shock to no one. Harmon Gallagher hadn't bashed his own head in. Not inside that tent, anyway.

"Is everyone in the house present here?" Ben asked.

Frank spoke up. "Our longtime caretaker, Enzo, is upstairs in bed. He is suffering from the early stages of dementia, and after yesterday's Thanksgiving festivities, he's spent most of the day resting." The detectives quickly glanced at each other and nodded.

"Okay, then, we're here to inform you that we are launching a full investigation. The time of death is yet to be confirmed, but it's important we have an accurate timeline of your movements last night and this morning," Ben continued. "I'm going to ask some questions, together at first, and then I'd like to take your individual statements."

Everyone nodded, and Frank spoke. "We understand. We'll help in any way we can."

"At this point, we have an official ID on the body. Mrs. Gallagher was able to come to the station to confirm that the victim is, in fact, her only son, Harmon Gallagher," Ben said.

Constance's mouth parted, and she gripped Frankie tighter, her face a crumpled image of maternal pity, but she was the only one who reacted. The rest of the clan sat in silence. Marlowe watched Ben's hooded eyes flick from person to person. The more she looked at him, the younger he seemed. His black wool coat and stubble along his jawline seemed like carefully curated choices to counteract his youth. The caps of his dress shoes were coated in mud from hiking out to the river, but that was the only hint of anything out of the scope of his control.

Ariel Mintz had a similar pattern on her flat lace-up boots. She barely came up to Ben's shoulder without a heel. Her plain face and an ill-fitting blazer made her a study in understatement. Marlowe wondered how this unlikely pair had gotten stuck investigating a lone hunter's death way out in the sticks. Maybe part of an early promotion meant slumming it for a few years in Poughkeepsie before moving on to bigger cases and better pay in the city. She could practically read their minds as Ben and Ariel studied them: *Stone-cold rich white people.*

"Had any of you interacted with the victim before?" Ben asked, scanning the room. "See him in town, conversations at the store—that type of thing."

"I spoke with him a few times," Frank said.

Ben turned his head, giving Frank his attention.

"The first time was about three years ago. I couldn't say the exact date. He called me because he wanted to discuss buying some of our property. He had some relation to the family who used to live across the street from us. A second or third cousin, I think."

"And what did you tell him?"

"I told him I wasn't selling. He was pushing for a meeting, but I said it was a hard no."

Marlowe kept her head down. Until Henry mentioned it a few hours ago, she hadn't heard about any of this—not about the call, the cousin, or an offer from a Gallagher to buy back some of the land. Then again, it wasn't unusual. Secrets weren't premeditated in this family so much as habitual. The conversations left unfinished and details innocently falling through the cracks of their separate, busy lives, though Marlowe always felt slightly less busy than everyone else.

"Did he call just that one time?" Ben asked.

Ben was the one speaking, but Marlowe couldn't keep from examining his partner instead. Ariel sat with her eyes trained on a blank page in her notepad, pen at the ready, but she wasn't taking notes.

"No, he called several times." Frank sighed, his throat pushing against his tight collar. He may have been in the waning years of his life, but he'd left not a single button undone, and his maroon sweater was smooth and spotless. "He called my office in the city every few weeks. I'm semiretired, so I'm not there often, but he kept leaving messages with my secretary. After the fourth or fifth call, he got testy with her. Frightened the poor thing."

"What did he say?" Ben asked. "Specifics would be helpful."

Frank's white eyebrows drew together, a deep line splitting his forehead. Marlowe knew that look. It was the face he gave his children when they interrupted him.

"I couldn't say word for word," Frank said. "I believe he raised his voice, accused her of not passing on the message. I figured it was best to give him another call."

"And you did?"

"Yes," Frank said. "I once again made it clear that I wasn't selling. And to be blunt, I doubted he had the money to buy the land in the first place."

"You think he was just trying to harass you, then? Get a rise out of you?" Ben asked, as if he truly valued Frank's opinion on the matter, as if Frank's words would be instrumental.

Frank considered his answer. "I can't guess at his motives, but it seems his family's history meant a great deal to him. I didn't know the man, not really."

"What made you think he didn't have the money?" Ben kept his tone upbeat, almost childlike in its curiosity.

"I looked him up after the first call," Frank admitted. "He was living with his mother and working odd jobs, from what I could tell. If he had the kind of money to buy that much property, he must have come by it in some odd way. But like I said, we didn't get that far. I wasn't selling."

Marlowe chewed on her lower lip. Her father was all but accusing Harmon of dabbling in shady activities.

"What land specifically was he interested in?" Ben asked.

"The farm across the street," Frank said. "As I said, Harmon appeared to be related to the three Gallagher brothers who once owned it."

"Not far from where he was found," Ariel interjected. This caught the attention of the rest of the family, who seemed attuned to the new speaker in a way they hadn't been with Ben.

"Near there, yes. I presume you've been out there already. From the road all the way back to across the river once belonged to the Gallaghers. It now belongs to me," Frank said.

Marlowe watched Ben and his partner exchange a look, and Ariel's eyes fell back to her blank notepad.

"Dave Gallagher, the youngest brother, passed on in '97," Frank continued after an uncomfortable pause. "Another cousin inherited the land. Caroline Rodine. She sold it to me. She was no farmer."

"But Harmon was?"

Frank shook his head. "Not that I know of. He was just another young man who felt something was owed to him."

Ben bobbed his head at this information. "So how did you let him down, finally?"

"I met him in town for a drink last winter," Frank said. "And I told him, in so many words, stop calling. It was never going to happen. He got frustrated, but I told him to pick a fight elsewhere."

"Where in town?"

"Vera's."

"We'll need the exact date for that meeting," Ben said.

Frank nodded. "I understand. I'll have to check my daybook."

"And you never saw or heard from him again?"

"He called again in the spring, but I didn't call back," Frank said. "That was the last I heard from him. I saw someone walking in the woods around that time, and I figured it was him. Can't say for certain."

"Why didn't you call the police?" Ben asked.

"I don't know," Frank said. "I guess I pitied him."

Marlowe studied her father as he spoke. The carefully measured pauses. The friendly lean toward his interlocutor, hands clasped. These weren't simply answers; Frank was performing his own morals and sense of justice. He had not given the detectives facts. He had given them a story. A truthful story. But a story nonetheless.

Ben broke eye contact with Frank and slowly regarded the rest of the group.

"Okay, thank you, sir. If it's all right, we'll take your individual statements now. It's standard procedure." Ben smiled. "It will be more comfortable here than at the station. Is there a room we could use for that?"

"The study," Frank said. "It's just down the hall."

Both detectives stood up. Ben and Ariel traded a look of recognition. She uttered one word: "Henry."

"We'd like to talk to Henry first," Ben confirmed.

Marlowe examined Ariel Mintz with renewed interest. Her face remained blank under her tightly pulled-back hair, but it suddenly became clear that she was the one with the plan. They looked over at Henry, who hadn't moved from his chair.

"We understand this is an inconvenience," Ben said. "We really do appreciate your help."

"Of course," Henry said, standing up.

Frank plastered an unruffled smile on his face, but he remained seated. Glory stood up and led the detectives toward the study. Henry patted Constance's shoulder once as he followed.

The rest of the family busied themselves around the kitchen and living room. Stephanie walked to the refrigerator and began heating up some leftovers while Glory told the kids to set the table. Constance put the baby in his high chair.

Marlowe kept her eye on the clock. She was waiting for someone to make sense of what had just happened. For Frank to give the family a quiet reminder to keep any explanations simple, to answer only what they were asked.

No one spoke. Nate sat in sullen silence, as if frustrated with his own thoughts: Why wasn't he the one called first by the detectives? Or perhaps he was thinking, like Marlowe, of the last time they were questioned in this house, one by one, all those years ago.

# FOUR

By the time Henry emerged from the study, Nate was pacing in the living room. Marlowe knew it was driving him crazy to have his younger brother get the first word. "What did they ask?" Nate had all but pinned his brother to the wall of the kitchen.

"Just stuff about the family and the landscape of the farm," Henry said, nudging his brother a few steps backward. "They had me draw a map."

A footfall announced Ariel's arrival in the kitchen.

"Marlowe," she said. "We'd like to speak with you now, if you don't mind."

Everyone turned to Marlowe.

"Of course," she said, following Ariel back through the living room to the study.

Marlowe sank slowly into one of the matching armchairs in front of her father's desk, but she did not allow herself to lean back. She didn't often come in here anymore, and memories of all the times she had retreated to this dark-paneled room to read or draw as a girl flooded her.

"We'd like you to tell us about this morning," Ben said. "In your own words."

Marlowe nodded. "I was in my bedroom until around nine. Nate and Henry and I went out for a walk, just the three of us. It's something we often do on family holidays: we hike to a spot on a river where we went swimming when we were younger. But before we got there, we spotted the tent. And, well, you know the rest."

"And how long did it take you to walk from the house to where you saw the tent?" Ariel asked.

"About half an hour," Marlowe said. "It's more than a mile."

"Almost two, your brother said." Ariel folded her arms and smiled with her lips pressed together. Friendly or cross, Marlowe couldn't tell.

"I guess it's hard to say, because of the hill. If you run it, you can do it faster." She wanted to be useful, but she had nothing to add besides a pointless observation. "We used to run all over this land when we were kids."

"Of course," Ben said. "Your father bought the property when you were a child, right?"

"Yes, the Gray House when I was five," Marlowe said.

"And then the Gallagher land?" Ariel asked. "How old were you then?"

"I was in ninth grade," Marlowe said. "Fifteen."

"Lucky," Ariel said. "To have all this as a kid."

Marlowe had long since accepted the tacit bitterness toward her family's wealth. She was certain the detectives looked at her and saw nothing but a stiff snob. Marlowe had learned that instead of resenting her own cold brand of beauty and the judgment it prompted in others, she could use it. She had been born with money, a straight nose, thick hair, and willowy limbs. But she had not been granted a winning personality in addition. She wasn't warm or bubbly, and she was never charming. All Marlowe had was her composure.

"Yes," Marlowe said. "I'm very lucky."

"Do you remember the Gallaghers much? Harmon's relatives?"

"Yes."

There was a pause, and Marlowe stared over Ariel's shoulder, at the black night framed in the window. Marlowe didn't try to fill the silence. Anything she said about the Gallaghers would surely sound fake. To her, they had been like characters in a storybook, the three farmer brothers tending to their cows. But Marlowe *had* known them, and Ben and Ariel had not.

"Sad, what happened to the three of them, dying so close together. Your brother told us the long and short of it," Ariel said. "Must have been pretty difficult for Harmon."

The admission surprised Marlowe. Henry hadn't mentioned anything about this line of inquiry, and she didn't know why he would volunteer that information.

"I didn't know the Gallaghers had other relatives nearby," Marlowe said. It was true enough. She had always thought of the Gallagher brothers as alone, except for each other.

"I guess Harmon preferred it that way," Ariel said. "Until he didn't."

"How do you mean?"

"Harmon reached out to your father, but did he ever reach out to you?" Ariel asked.

"No," Marlowe said. "I'd never heard his name before today."

"How often are you up here?" Ariel asked, each question following quickly after the previous one. She was making up for her silence in front of the group. Ben had a passive bearing now, leaning back in his chair and flipping through his notes, as though completely at ease with Ariel taking the lead. They had a kind of shorthand that was indecipherable to Marlowe. How nice it was to know someone else so completely, to read a whole speech in the tilt of their head, the raising of their brows.

"I'm here for a week or two out of every month," Marlowe said. "Sometimes longer in December or in the summer."

"What do you do for work?" Ariel asked.

"I'm an illustrator," Marlowe said. "Mostly children's books. I can work from here or the city."

"Ah, anything I would know?" Ben asked.

Marlowe cocked her head. "I don't know. Do you have kids?"

Ariel's chuckle was brief but genuine, and it relaxed Marlowe somewhat.

"No, not yet," Ben said, and then paused. His mind seemed to go elsewhere.

Ariel collected the reins once again. "Last night, you had dinner with your family, and then what?"

"I stayed up talking with my brothers," Marlowe said. "I went to bed around eleven, maybe a bit later."

"And you didn't hear anything? See anything?" Ariel asked.

"No." Marlowe shook her head. "Nothing unusual. Just some coyotes howling around two. I woke up for a few seconds, but I didn't get out of bed."

"What about since you've been back from the city? Have you seen or interacted with anyone besides your family?"

"Not that I can think of," Marlowe said. "There are hunters with permission to come and go in the early hours, but I'm typically not around to see that. And I've only run into neighbors on the road."

"Who?"

"Charlie Beacon. He's out with his dogs often," Marlowe said. "There's a weekender family at the top of the road too. The Hopewells. They sometimes take walks with their three young daughters."

The Hopewells had the second-largest Dutch colonial house on the road, the first being the Fishers'. Marlowe thought their renovations looked out of place, far too shiny. But Frank and Glory had fully embraced Mrs. Hopewell, who was British and charismatic and always threw a Boxing Day party.

"And who lives on the property across the river?" Ariel asked. "I'm a bit turned around. GPS isn't very strong out here."

Marlowe nodded in acknowledgment. "Sarah and Bob Chase have a house on that land. I couldn't say exactly where the property line is, but my dad would know."

"Thank you. We'll be talking to your neighbors tomorrow," Ariel said. "Harmon's friends and family as well." She paused and made a point of refocusing her attention on Marlowe. "It's awful what happened. But don't worry, we'll piece it together."

She wasn't sure exactly what her face had betrayed to Ariel, but for a moment Marlowe felt like they were the only ones in the room.

"Thank you, Marlowe, that's all." Ariel and Ben stood. They looked absurd together; Ariel was so much shorter. Marlowe could hear her mother's voice in her head: *A woman of that height ought to wear heels, if she wants to play at a career.*

Marlowe nodded and rocked herself up from the chair, pulling down the hem of her sweater as she rose. She smiled, as if to thank the detectives for their time spent in the comfort of her own home, and reached for the door handle.

"Oh, before you go, I wanted to ask you one more thing." Ben's voice came from behind her, as if this incidental thought had just occurred to him.

"Of course, anything." Marlowe looked over her shoulder, her fingers still resting on the brass knob.

"A girl went missing around here a while back. Isn't that right?"

The question felt almost inevitable. It had been carving its path toward her since they saw that tent, like the river finding its twisted way through the swamp and flowing out to the basin, relentless in its own course. But the shock of it still caused Marlowe to stagger. Her hand tightened around the handle, and then she let go, turning all the way around to see Ben and Ariel, their chins raised, more engaged than they'd been at any point before.

"Yes, that's right."

Ariel and Ben waited. It was going to hurt to say the name, but she forced her mouth to form the sounds.

"Nora Miller," Marlowe said, finally. "She lived up the road."

"And you were close?" Ariel pressed.

"We were best friends."

# FIVE

They cracked the tops on their cans of Sprite. The sound echoed loudly through the old barn, and Nora's soda fizzed over. She giggled and jerked back, trying to avoid getting it all over herself.

"Shhhhhh." Marlowe was stifling her own giggles. "They'll *hear* you."

"Don't worry," Nora said, drying the can with a handful of hay and leaning back against a bale so her straight yellow hair fanned out over her shoulders. "The coast is clear. Tom drove off in the truck, and Leroy and Dave are out mending the fence in the cow field today."

"Right, I knew that," Marlowe said. It was her first weekend back in the country since the start of seventh grade in September— one of the longest stretches she'd been away—and she was out of sync with the rhythm of the place.

They were up in the hayloft of the Gallagher barn, across the road from the Gray House. Marlowe and Nora knew every nook and cranny of the loft. They had claimed it as their secret spot at the beginning of summer and had been sneaking up the ladder for months now. They'd gotten so good at it that they could each climb the ladder one-handed, gripping a blanket or cans of soda and snacks in the other. It wasn't a comfortable place. The air was musty, often making Nora's blue eyes turn red and itchy. Plus, the hay was scratchy and impossible to sit on while wearing shorts.

But it was secret. A hidden place of their own. Nora and Marlowe liked to climb over the wall of hay and perch in a little room they had made for themselves by shifting and stacking the square bales. They'd spent countless hours whispering up there, away from the prying ears of Marlowe's brothers.

As a bonus, the loft made a great place to spy on people. If the girls hovered around the opening that looked down into the stables for long enough, they would inevitably see a Gallagher brother pass below. Sometimes the girls made cooing sounds as if they were birds, and once or twice a Gallagher paused and looked up, too slow to catch the girls pulling away from the trapdoor, stifling their laughter.

Once they had watched silently from above as Nate and Henry snuck into the barn to use the knife sharpener, a heavy ceramic wheel located against the far wall, next to a row of old pitchforks and rakes. Ever since helping the Gallagher brothers with baling the hay, Nate considered himself the expert on farm equipment. With a pompous air, Nate pulled a kitchen knife out of his pocket and passed it to Henry before sitting down on the rusted seat, pressing his foot against the pedal, and forcing the creaking gears into motion. Henry gripped the knife and held it against the wheel as Nate pumped. The girls, lying on their bellies with only their faces peering over the ledge, were unimpressed, until a burst of red sparks flew upward, and they instinctively pulled back into the protection of their secret hay-bale room. They were careful never to get caught by the farmers or Marlowe's brothers. They knew the moment Nate and Henry found out about the hideaway, it would stop being fun.

Marlowe inhaled the muted scent of cow manure in the barn and relaxed next to Nora, their legs folded before them, knees lightly touching through the thick denim of their jeans. Marlowe glanced over at her friend and felt a familiar surge of joy. How many middle school girls could say they had a best friend, a *real* best friend?

They'd been best friends since they were five years old, when Marlowe's dad took her down the road to meet the neighbors. Nora had plummeted out of a tree right in front of Marlowe, giving her a grin that showed off a missing tooth. It seemed unfair that they didn't attend the same school, but Marlowe had been coming up to the Gray House almost every weekend since her father bought the place, and the girls were inseparable whenever they were together.

"Did you already have Ag Day at school?" Marlowe asked.

"Oh God, it was so dumb this year. The Future Farmers of America kids got new jackets and were showing them off," Nora scoffed. "And everyone at school had to make these crazy creatures out of gourds—like little vegetable monsters—and put them on display to be judged."

"Sounds kinda fun." Ag Day took up a whole weekend, and Marlowe's family had gone the year before. Marlowe found the endless rows of pumpkins and the cow shows endearing, but she understood Nora was too used to it. "Did you get a ribbon this year?"

"No, but you would have won for sure, with all your art skills."

Marlowe shook her head. "Not really my style."

"Like I said, it was dumb. I wish I went to school in the city with you. It's *so* boring here."

"I wish we went to the same school too." The gleaming wood floors and ancient austere desks of Marlowe's Manhattan private school flashed through her mind, but she couldn't picture Nora in the plaid skirt and blazer. Nora belonged here, in her baggy jeans and oversized crewneck sweaters, having adventures. "But the city isn't what you think it is. This is *our* place. It's more fun here."

Nora finished her soda and flattened the can under her foot. She pushed her hair back out of her face, and Marlowe momentarily wondered if she wasn't going to agree.

"I guess you're right," Nora said, swiveling around to face Marlowe as she pulled two silver tubes out of her pocket. "I almost forgot to tell you—I got these from a girl in my homeroom."

Marlowe gasped in excitement when she saw the mascara and lip gloss. Her own mother would have confiscated the makeup, but Nora's parents never cared.

"Let's test it." Nora handed the mascara to Marlowe and unscrewed the shimmering gloss. "Another thing," Nora continued, "this really cute boy joined the baseball team this year. His name is Sean. *All* the girls are going to watch the games now."

"What about you? Do you like him?" Marlowe nudged her playfully.

Sometimes they used Nora's pocketknife to carve the names of their crushes on a wooden rafter, like a spell to summon luck, but their crushes never lasted long.

"Maybe." Nora dabbed the peachy gloss on her bottom lip. "He asked for my number, but I haven't given it to him yet."

A slight queasy feeling bubbled in Marlowe's stomach. She'd felt it before, when a man on the subway had looked at her for too long. Her mother said it was because she was almost thirteen. She didn't feel ready to flirt with boys. In the fifth grade, she and Nora had vowed they wouldn't date until high school, because middle school romances were childish and short-lived. Unless Nora had changed her mind.

Marlowe fiddled with the mascara wand and forced a laugh. "Who needs boys when we have each other, anyway?"

# SATURDAY

**NOVEMBER 24, 2018**

# SIX

A new tension had bloomed in the house overnight. The coffee had been brewed as usual, and the children were playing as if nothing had changed, but something had. A man had been killed on their property. What's more, Nora had been evoked, the memory of that horrible night unleashed from its box.

Marlowe went upstairs to get a cup of coffee but quickly excused herself, claiming she had a work deadline. In reality, she spent the entire morning nursing a single cup of coffee while searching the Internet for anything she could find about Harmon Gallagher.

He was twenty-three. His social media pages were already flooded with overwrought comments mourning the tragedy of his death. Marlowe studied his profile picture online—he grinned warmly beneath a camo ball cap, caught mid-laugh at a backyard barbecue. He was broad-shouldered and had a solid build—the kind of person who probably wouldn't go down easily without a fight . . .

At last, Marlowe rose from her computer and walked over to the large drafting table in the far corner of the room. Her next project was for a client she had worked with before, who wanted Marlowe's trademark: whimsical rustic scenes. Friendly animals. Innocent children. In art school, Marlowe had dreamed of gallery shows and groundbreaking pieces, but it was hard to gain any recognition in the art world. It took guts to break through.

There at the drafting table, she opened her sketchbook to a new page, waiting for the right images to come. She usually felt free to work out her ideas and impressions in this room. She began to outline a face and a wave of untidy hair. She filled the background with dark strokes. A locked room, with only one window. A narrow bed. She returned to the face. Marlowe dropped her pencil when she got to the pointed nose, the delicate eyebrows. She knew whose face she was sketching. And she couldn't bring herself to continue.

She tore her eyes away from her drawing, casting a glance out the French doors. The morning had already faded to a wintry afternoon. All too soon, the day would dim into evening. Marlowe gave up on the pretense of productivity and headed upstairs, empty coffee mug in hand.

Henry was seated in front of the fire next to Enzo. She crossed into the kitchen and rinsed her mug, placing it carefully in the dishwasher, before joining them.

"Marlowe." Enzo blinked up at her from behind his thick spectacles. "There you are."

Enzo pronounced Marlowe's name the same way he pronounced Merlot, as if he were offering a taste of his favorite wine. His voice had become gravelly over the years, and his speech had slowed, but his Italian accent was as thick as ever and carried the same warmth. It was nice to see him rested and returned to his place in the family room. Stocky and bald except for the squares of silver hair at his temples, he had a bent posture from the many years of hard, honest work he'd provided to their family.

Marlowe gave him a tight-lipped smile as she sat on the hearth, her back to the flames. "Where is everyone?"

"Stephanie and Constance took the kids to that ice-skating rink in Salisbury," Henry said.

Marlowe nodded absently. That was the plan, she recalled. Of course, everyone was moving as usual.

"Mom went to town for groceries," Henry said. "Nate and Dad are in the study."

"Has there been any news?" Marlowe asked.

Henry sighed and closed the book he was reading. "Neighbors have been calling," he said. "The detectives have visited just about everyone on the road, asking their questions. No one knows anything."

"Well, I doubt anyone was taking a stroll that far from the road at that hour," Marlowe said.

"Terrible thing." Enzo shook his head, and Marlowe watched his pale, sagging skin pull at his neck. He was bundled up in a knit sweater that consumed his shrunken limbs. He had once been able to hoist her and Henry up, one under each arm, and carry them out of the kitchen when they were getting in the way.

He had always seemed to quietly favor Marlowe, or at least it felt that way when she was young. During summers in the country, Enzo told Glory and Frank that their daughter was the responsible child. It embarrassed Marlowe at the time. Being the good girl was tantamount to being a coward.

"They talked to Damen Miller. Charlie saw their car there this morning when he was out walking his dogs, and came by to let us know," Henry murmured, rubbing his fingers against the woven blanket tossed over the armchair. "Nothing out of the ordinary, though. I'm sure they're going to have to talk to all the neighbors."

Henry worked for a blue-chip law firm in Manhattan, but he had done a few years at the DA's office right out of law school. He knew how these things unfolded. Nora's father was just another name on the list of locals.

"I hope they don't upset him," Marlowe said.

Many years had passed since she'd last spoken to Damen, but she used to visit often, bringing baked goods, and then casseroles when Jennifer got sick. Increasingly, her presence had seemed to distress him. Marlowe understood—she had lost the appearance of the sixteen-year-old girl who was best friends with his daughter. The reality was shocking even to Marlowe, who had never considered what it would be like to mature without Nora by her side. Damen stopped answering her calls altogether after Jennifer passed.

Henry shook his head. "They're just stirring up pointless grief."

Marlowe leaned against the edge of the mantel, feeling the heat of the fire radiate through her shirt. She thought back to some of the outlandish theories she had heard about Nora. Most of that noise had died down, even if the crackpot blogs still found a reason to post occasionally. The twisted conspiracy theorists couldn't resist a salacious cold case. As for Damen, if he had theories of his own, he never shared them with anyone, and he had grown even more silent with age. Marlowe had not told her family that Ariel and Ben had asked about Nora, and none of them had shared the details of their interviews with her.

"It must have been a dispute among hunters." Marlowe brought herself back to the present. "Late at night."

"That's what I would guess." Henry slid his finger between the pages of his book, a historical tome about the Vikings, but he did not open it.

"These hunters are not playing with toys," Enzo said abruptly and then took in a deep breath, his sunken chest rising and falling. "Do not go looking for that bear."

Henry's shoulders slumped, and Marlowe bit her lip.

"Enzo," Henry said. "That was a long time ago."

"A hunter clipped that bear's leg. I didn't believe it the first time we heard the story. And then I saw for myself. After that I couldn't keep you kids out of the woods, looking for him. Only Marlowe knew nothing good would come of it."

Enzo reached out and placed his hand on Marlowe's knee. She kept her face turned toward the fire, unable to return the warm gesture. It unnerved her when Enzo slipped out of time. It was unclear how much he understood about what had taken place yesterday. His dementia was progressing steadily—some days he seemed acutely afflicted by it, but occasionally he appeared more lucid than ever.

Marlowe could remember all the afternoons she and her brothers spent huddled around Enzo as he told one of his famous yarns. Over the years, they became more adept at sensing his embellishments, but they still hung on his every word.

He seemed poised to begin another one at any moment, nodding slowly up and down. It was his signature way of conjuring a story from his boundless vault of memories.

"What did you say this hunter's name was?" Enzo stared penetratingly until Marlowe met his gaze.

"Harmon," she whispered. "Harmon Gallagher."

Enzo hummed in recognition. "I remember when you moved down into that basement bedroom. Converted from that dreadful cellar just after your parents bought the place. And, of course, you remember that I was the first one who lived down there after the first renovation."

"How could I forget?" Marlowe chuckled. The recollection seemed irrelevant but harmless enough.

"And many more improvements came after that. The master bedroom annex, front porch. A big, beautiful kitchen. But the bones of this old house . . ." Enzo trailed off, looking up at the patinaed trusses and then the slate mantel of the fireplace. "Those have stood here unchanged for over a century. Something to take great pride in, but also a reminder of those who came first."

Marlowe froze. Not so irrelevant. Hearing the name of the deceased had drawn him back to the history of this place. After all, the Gray House had been a part of the original Gallagher farm. The land had been divided down the middle decades ago, separating the Gray House from the farm across the road. The Gallagher ancestors had dwelled in the house long before Marlowe or Enzo for that matter.

"Mysterious lot, all of them," Enzo continued. "But that girl still gives me a chill."

"Which girl?" Marlowe felt a shudder of anticipation.

"The Gallagher girl," Enzo said.

She had expected her friend's name to slip through Enzo's cracked lips. But he meant another girl—a local myth Marlowe vaguely recalled her father talking about years ago. She wasn't sure if the story was true or just part of the local lore bandied about by dubious real estate agents.

Marlowe and Henry remained quiet, allowing Enzo to continue his meandering story. "The Gallaghers who lived in this house, great-grandparents to those brothers, had a beautiful daughter. The prettiest farm girl in the county. But this daughter harbored a rebellious streak. Her mother tried to keep her tethered to her chores around the fields and in the house, but the Gallagher daughter was always running off. The house was too confining for her, or so it goes."

Enzo raised his brows upward. He was beginning to take some liberties, add in his customary drama, but the reflections on the house as some sort of prison rattled Marlowe.

"And where would she go?" Marlowe asked, trying to keep Enzo engaged and cogent. His stories always made the listener desperate for answers, even if she knew he was lying.

"Her favorite spot was at the top of the North Field, where the land rises and the grass grows tall and green. And out of sight from the house, you know. From her perch, she could look out at the house and the barn and, beyond that, deep into the valley. The Gallagher daughter sat up there every season. In the summer, she was cushioned by the waving grasses, and in the winter, she sat on a snowbank like it was her throne. She weathered the rain in the spring and the cool wind of autumn. That was her favorite, which got her in even more trouble, as fall was the busiest time for a valley farmer. She left the cows unfed and the kitchen dishes unwashed and the bread burning at the hearth. And then one day, out in the hedgerow, she started to hear voices whispering from the woods behind her. She came back home that night with stories that turned her parents' hearts to stone. They were convinced the poor girl was going insane or, worse, had been visited by a demon."

Henry shifted in his chair, and Marlowe's gaze dropped to the floor. Neither of them spoke, but the air between them tightened.

Enzo continued: "She was confined to her bedroom, where the visions and whispers got worse until she went completely mad. Everyone murmured stories about the crazy girl at the Gallagher house. They said that on certain nights, you could hear her screaming. After that—well, that kind of story casts a long shadow on a family."

Enzo fell back against the cushion, eyes wide and glassy like some ancient soothsayer's. It was an odd tale that didn't really have an ending. He just seemed to run out of things to say, and the story petered out. A girl was locked in her room and went mad. She didn't die, but everyone else had to live with it.

"Don't tell the kids that story," Henry said. "They'll be too scared of ghosts to sleep."

Enzo wrinkled his brow. "That story is not about hauntings," he said. "There's a different lesson: Never lock up a child. When a girl wants to run free, let her. If she encounters strange things, it is better that she is free."

Marlowe imagined what the Gallagher girl might have looked like, sketching her in her mind. A great-aunt to the Gallagher brothers would have been born in the 1800s and covered head to toe in drab, modest clothing. She would have weary eyes threaded with red veins and mirrored with tears. Long unkempt tresses of strawberry-blond hair. Thin, baleful lips.

Down the hall, the heavy mahogany doors of the study swung open, and Nate and Frank emerged. Nate was frowning, but Marlowe's father wore a look of utter calm, as if he had just woken up from a restorative nap.

Frank grinned at the trio in front of the hearth.

"Better get more logs, Nate," Frank said. "Keep it roaring for us."

Neither of the men offered an explanation about what they had been discussing, and Henry didn't seem to be curious. He probably already knew. Marlowe was left to her own imagination, as usual.

# SEVEN

The fire in the living room had burned down to smoldering embers by the time the side door flew open and Stephanie and Constance herded the kids inside. Their cheeks were flushed from their ice-skating excursion, and their voices tumbled over each other in fits of laughter and whining. Stephanie peeled off Kat's coat and sent her bounding after Dolly, then floated into the kitchen with the ease of someone who had staked her claim long ago. She was now the one who started to pull materials out to assemble dinner—another of the ceaseless attempts at currying favor with her mother-in-law, who Stephanie once joked had ice in her veins. Constance trotted in with a market bag in one arm. Glory followed, Frankie on her hip, and settled down in a chair near Marlowe to bounce her grandson on her lap. Both the wives got to work chopping vegetables and murmuring instructions, while the girls were occupied at the table with their crayons. It amazed Marlowe how normal they were all acting.

From the moment Henry brought Constance to the Gray House for a weekend, Marlowe had found her winsome and pleasant enough. Stephanie, however, had gotten under Marlowe's skin early. She was pretty sure Stephanie had taken an instant dislike to her as well. It had taken years for their chilly relationship to thaw. There was one time, about a month before Nate and Stephanie's wedding, when Marlowe ran into her at Grand Central Station. They were both taking the 6:02 Metro-North upstate and had arrived at the station with time to kill.

"Should we grab something to eat?" Stephanie had asked haltingly. She didn't know how to talk to Marlowe when Nate wasn't around to lead the conversation.

Marlowe suggested the oyster bar. She adored its sleek chairs and elegant old New York feel.

Stephanie relaxed once they were seated, and considered the sparkling arches above them. "So pretty."

"It's one of my favorite places," Marlowe said. "I've been meeting Frank here for years."

"That's sweet," Stephanie said. "It must be nice to be his only daughter."

Marlowe bristled at the implication she was spoiled, and then ran through possible conversation topics—their respective jobs, Stephanie's soon-to-be husband, Dutchess County—but Marlowe was bored of all that.

"So, do you really think you and Nate will go through with the wedding?" Marlowe raised her dark eyebrows in a moment of rare bluntness.

To her delight, Stephanie laughed. "Sometimes I think of calling it off, especially when your parents get involved with the planning."

"They are merciless," Marlowe said. "But it's the first wedding in the family."

Stephanie rolled her eyes. "They act like it's the first wedding *ever*."

For once, they talked as friends and not soon-to-be in-laws.

"Oh God, I feel like I'll never live up to your mother." Stephanie took a long sip of her drink, a pink concoction with a lethal amount of gin. "I'll never be as smart or as competent or run such a perfect household."

"Trust me, I've long since come to terms with that." Marlowe flashed a sly grin over her martini. The evening began to feel like one shared between friends gossiping and commiserating about the eccentric cast of characters in their lives.

The two of them were well and truly drunk by the time they got on the train, giggling together like schoolgirls. But when they pulled into the station and saw Nate there, waiting, everything instantly transformed to the way it had been before. Marlowe was reminded that Stephanie would always be Nate's wife before her friend.

Stephanie's eyes flicked up from the pot of boiling potatoes and met Marlowe's. She shot her a quick, impersonal smile and Marlowe returned the favor. She wished she could tell Nora about her sister-in-law. Better yet, Marlowe wished Nora were here to trade knowing glances. She would have hated Stephanie. People like Nora didn't suffer phoniness or groveling.

Marlowe considered what her best friend's response would have been to Harmon Gallagher. She would have given Marlowe the confidence she sought to walk into Frank's office and ask him what the hell was going on. Why was Nora's name being brought up by the detectives?

A man had been killed in the darkness, only a mile from the house, in the field that Marlowe could navigate with her eyes closed, near the river with a current she could feel in her bones. There was no gate around the land, no moat. Anyone could drive up the road or hide out in the barn. Break a window or open the doors to Marlowe's basement room; she rarely locked them. Or someone could wait in the woods until one of them went on a walk. It would be easy. It *had* been easy for Harmon to be caught, alone and vulnerable, the sounds of the fight stifled by the babbling river, his shouts drowned out by the coyotes. Marlowe was on edge, and so was her family, but they were hiding it. They were whispering their concerns behind closed doors. Why?

Everyone rushed into the kitchen at the sound of Glory clanging the antique dinner bell that hung above the counter, and took their seats at the table. Stephanie set down a golden-brown roast chicken, potatoes, and one of Constance's salads, to which Constance had added too many bitter greens for Marlowe's liking. Kat and Dolly chattered the whole time about their day at the rink and how they wanted to be figure skaters.

"Oh, Marlowe had this outfit, remember?" Frank smiled at Marlowe. "The velvet skirt and jacket you used to wear at Bryant Park."

"I want a skirt!" Kat practically bounced out of her seat.

"Put it in your letter to Santa," Stephanie said.

Nate smiled. He was spoiling Kat, but Marlowe doubted she would turn out rotten. Nate bragged to anyone who would listen that at eight years old, his daughter was already classified as an advanced child and whizzed through the chapter books she checked out of the library. He would hold fast to high standards, and Kat would spend her life determined to never fall short.

"I beat Kat in every race," Dolly said. "Except when I wiped out."

Dolly cackled with her mouth open, revealing her chewed-up chicken.

Children were the center of their own universe, and their unwavering belief consumed everyone else. It was so easy to talk of nothing but them.

Glory speared a potato and held it in front of her. "A bit firm this time, Stephanie," she said. "And what's that, rosemary?"

"Rosemary, yes." Stephanie forced a smile. "And I guess I pulled them out a little early. There's always a trick when you're not in your own kitchen."

"Tastes fine to me, hon," Nate chimed in with a mouthful. "Lots to be grateful for around this table."

The stilted exchange caused Enzo to perk up. "That's right, Nate," he said. "Having a wonderful meal with family like this is what gives meaning to life." Glory immediately softened. Enzo had a special gift for playing peacemaker and putting the Fisher matriarch at ease. Marlowe pushed food around on her plate, eager for the meal and her family's playacting to end. There were questions she needed to ask as soon as the children were out of earshot.

After the dishes had been washed and cleared, the kids went off to watch a movie with Stephanie and Constance. Frank and Glory drifted up to their room. Henry helped Enzo up the old staircase to his bedroom and then returned to the kitchen.

Only then was it silent. Nate walked over to the cabinet and pulled out the scotch and three glasses. Marlowe instinctively grabbed a tray of ice cubes out of the freezer and filled each glass halfway.

Each with a scotch in hand, they walked to the living room. Henry sat in the same armchair he'd been in that afternoon, Marlowe in the one Enzo had claimed earlier. Nate dragged a chair over from the table and set it close to the fireplace.

Marlowe took a long drink, savoring the burn in her throat. "What was going on earlier in the study?"

"We're considering how to deal with this," Nate said. "It's nothing to worry about; we just know how people will dig up old rumors."

"Rumors about what?" Marlowe asked.

"The Gallaghers. Us." Nate waved his hand. "Harmon might have been more disturbed than we realized. We think he was sending us anonymous threats."

"What?" Marlowe blinked in surprise and turned to Henry, who didn't look shocked.

"Stephanie got these messages sent to her work email," Nate said. "She didn't think too much of them at the time, but then a few notes came to the house."

"What did they say?" Marlowe was almost lunging at Nate for an answer.

"You'll pay for what you've done." Nate frowned as he recited the phrase. For half a second, Marlowe thought he was speaking directly to her, and she recoiled before realizing Nate was quoting Harmon. "He sent one that said, 'Your house will burn with you and your family in it.'"

"He put that in an *email*?"

The past twenty-four hours rattled and shifted. What had looked like bad luck—Harmon being in the wrong place at the wrong time—now turned sour with intention. He had been out there for a reason. He'd been sitting in the darkness, plotting against Marlowe's family, and someone had gone out and found him there. Confronted his vitriolic anger.

"He wasn't exactly a mastermind," Nate remarked. "We still aren't one hundred percent sure that it was him, but that's what we assumed. He was unhappy and reckless, not a real threat. We figured it would all blow over with a little time."

"I got a letter too," Henry said. "Vague threats, blackmail."

Marlowe nearly dropped her glass.

"Blackmailing with what information?" Marlowe jerked her head back and forth between her brothers.

"He was just trying to scare us, Mar." Nate spoke as if he had it all sorted out and almost found it boring. If it was an act of superiority, it was a good one. He had always possessed that talent. "He wanted the land, but Dad wouldn't sell. So maybe he figured the threat of arson or vandalism would spook us into leaving. Mom and Dad got some strange emails too."

"I didn't." Marlowe sounded plaintive. A surprising feeling of jealousy started to well up. She had been at the center of this house and its stories for years, and yet everyone was being contacted except for her.

"It was nothing," Nate said brusquely. "We told the detectives about it today. Now it's on them to piece together the extent of his lunacy. He probably picked fights with a lot of people around here."

Marlowe recalled the friendly smile from the photo online. What if Harmon hadn't picked fights with anyone else, just the Fishers? It would look bad that her family hadn't mentioned anything about anonymous threats the day before or reported them when they originally occurred. Marlowe had watched enough crime dramas to understand that something like this could establish a motive. That explained the hours in the study. Nate and Frank had been putting the whole story together, wrapped up with clear reasoning, before handing it over to the detectives.

"What did he mean by saying we'll pay for what we've done?" Marlowe asked.

"Who knows?" Nate said. "The guy was a loon."

"Was he talking about Nora?" Marlowe knew this was dangerous territory, but she had to ask. "Did he say something about her?"

Nate sighed. "Not everything is about Nora."

"Remember how Brierley questioned us? Half of the county thought we were involved somehow. Is that what Harmon thought too?"

Nate clenched his jaw, and Marlowe knew she'd hit a nerve.

"We were questioned," Henry said. "But we didn't do it. You *know* that, Marlowe; you were there. We were all there. This guy Harmon only invoked Nora to pick at old wounds, to scare us. But we had nothing to do with what happened."

"I know." Marlowe took another sip of scotch. "But someone did."

"Someone did." Nate's eyes were dark pools. "I will never forget that."

Nate stood up and hung his head. Nora had been Marlowe's best friend, but they had all been a unit back then. A team. Nate was the oldest. The leader. Marlowe worried for a second he was going to cry. Henry's tears were normal; his eyes welled up at almost every movie. But she hadn't seen Nate cry in ages. He walked to the sink and dumped the rest of his drink.

"I'm going to sleep," he announced.

Marlowe and Henry watched Nate stalk up the stairs and heard his heavy bedroom door close. Marlowe turned back to Henry, her fingers tightening around her glass.

"Why was he out there?" Marlowe asked. "And who would have followed him there to kill him?"

"We can't guess," Henry said. "We don't know him at all."

"Nate's acting like he does." Marlowe raised her brows at Henry, trying to awaken the old habit of the younger siblings muttering about the know-it-all eldest.

"Nate's upset—you know how much he loves the Flats." Henry stared down at the glimmering gold liquid. "He had that plan to build a house there."

Nate's daydream had slipped her mind amid the drama, but he had been scheming for a few years to craft a gravel driveway along the south edge of the cow field and into the Flats. The house would be designed for him, Stephanie, Kat, and Dolly, built with his own money. Nate would have to pick a new spot. Harmon owned the Flats now. In death, he had accomplished a fragment of his ambition.

"It's a cruel joke," Marlowe murmured. "For him to die where he wanted to live, and so violently."

"Well, it will all come out," Henry said. "And I think we'll see Harmon made choices that probably got him killed."

"Henry, that's insensitive."

"We're in the privacy of our own home." Henry shrugged. "And I've seen enough crimes to know that they rarely happen to people who don't go looking for trouble."

Henry would never have said such a thing as a boy. He used to be the gentlest of them all. But then, he was entitled to his opinion. And what did Marlowe know of crime and punishment, cocooned in her soft life?

Henry shook his head, no longer in the mood to theorize. He stood up to wash his glass and then disappeared up the stairs after Nate. Once she was alone, Marlowe grabbed the bottle of scotch, unscrewed the cap in two quick twists, and refilled her glass.

She sat down in the silent kitchen and drank it as slowly as she could. Nora had not gone looking for trouble. She was an exception to Henry's bitter rule. Marlowe thought of Stephanie receiving that email. *You'll pay for what you've done.* Had she known it referenced Nora? Had Nate told her about the night a girl vanished into thin air? The days of questions and searching that followed? He wouldn't talk about any of it with Marlowe, but a wife kept secrets a sister was never granted. The fire popped a few times before dimming for the night.

In her mind's eye, she saw an image of Harmon's broad shoulders hunched over a desk, writing out his threats. He would have been a toddler when Nora disappeared. A quiet rage began to simmer just underneath her skin. He had no right to bring Nora into this. It was maddening how casually he'd poked at Marlowe's greatest agony, and all so he could grasp at land that wasn't his, had *never* been his.

# EIGHT

**THE BEND**
**Saturday, July 1, 1995**

"Let's go back in," Nora said. "I'm hot again."

Marlowe opened her eyes and rolled onto her stomach, propping herself up on her elbows. They were in their swimsuits, lounging on towels spread atop a flat rock embedded in the bank of the Bean River. Marlowe smiled as Henry cannonballed off the rock on the far bank, sending a silver burst of water into the air.

Tom Gallagher had revealed the swimming hole to them the summer before, as a reward after they helped load hay into the barn. The narrow river took a sharp left turn here, and the current slowed just enough to create a wide pool, ideal for swimming—the Bend in the Bean, Tom called it. He told them it was where he and his brothers used to swim as kids after a long day of working on the farm.

Marlowe remembered that day in vivid detail. She'd torn off her sweaty outer layer and jumped in, her body cutting through the summer humidity and finding relief in the soft motion of the river. Nothing felt more delicious than cool water against tender skin, sunburned after hours of hoisting hay bales. A few days later, Tom hung a rope swing from a branch that arched over the river. That was all the invitation they needed to keep going back.

This summer, they hadn't hesitated to claim the Bend as their own. Marlowe and her brothers had been upstate since school let out, and they had gone swimming every day. Enzo stayed with them at the Gray House all week while their parents carried on with their usual responsibilities in the city, joining them only on weekends. Marlowe, her brothers, and Nora were blissfully free to spend endless hours on their own.

Nate swung out on the rope, twisting his body as he released it over the deepest part of the swimming hole. His flip went crooked midair, and he landed on his side with a smack.

"Ha!" Nora was up, her green one-piece flashing by Marlowe as she splashed into the water and caught the rope, her arm stretching up as she dragged it back to the bank. Marlowe pushed herself to her knees and watched as Nora swung out and let go, arching into a graceless but neat dive. She was smiling when her head popped back up.

Neither Marlowe nor Nora could manage even a sloppy flip like Nate, but they were both proud of their diving abilities.

The summer had fallen into a near-perfect routine, and it seemed to stretch on forever before them, the drudgery of middle school far out of sight. Nora slept over every other night. They spent their days swimming at the Bend and romping through the woods and fields, returning in the early evening to the hearty meals Enzo prepared at the house, his old opera music playing in the background. Enzo took care of everything—the laundry, the groceries, and cooking. They only had to fulfill their quota of chores and swear off sibling fighting for Frank and Glory to let them stay at the Gray House all summer long.

Nora was practically a fourth sibling. Her mother worked long hours as a nurse, and her father was often preoccupied with business at his auto shop in town. Her presence was never questioned at the table, her place setting always laid out. Marlowe had a weeklong tennis camp scheduled in August, and in a few weeks, some of Nate's friends from the city would be up, but for the most part, the summer belonged entirely to the four of them.

"I'm coming in too!" Marlowe cried, getting to her feet and adjusting the new black swimsuit Glory had purchased for her. She dove in headfirst and came up next to Nora. Henry launched backward and kicked a spray of water into their faces. They squealed and returned fire, splashing him as hard as they could. Nate joined forces with Henry, bombarding the girls with such an onslaught that they screamed for a truce.

By the time they headed back to the Gray House, they were starving. They ambled home along the path Tom had shown them, cutting along the edge of the Flats and between the smaller cow field and the southernmost hayfield, the afternoon bleeding into a long, warm evening. Fresh beads of sweat were forming on their brows as they reached the road.

"Do you think we could convince Enzo to take us for ice cream in town after dinner?" Marlowe wondered.

"You read my mind," Nora said.

"Mom!" Henry yelled, suddenly running ahead. The rest of them looked up to see Glory sitting in an Adirondack chair on the front lawn. Marlowe had forgotten her parents were coming up that day for the long Fourth of July weekend.

Marlowe, Nate, and Nora quickened their pace, waving hello.

"Where've you been?" Glory squinted up at them as she wrapped Henry in a hug. "Your hair's wet."

"We were swimming," Marlowe said. "At the Bend in the Bean." Her stomach dropped when she saw how her mother's smile transformed into a cold frown. Beside her, Nora pressed her knuckles against her top lip.

"You went swimming alone?" Glory rose to her feet and fixed her glare on Nate. "Do you have any idea how dangerous that is?"

"Mom, it's not even that deep," Nate said. "Tom showed us the best spot."

"Is that right? Tom showed you?" Glory nodded once. "Did you tell Enzo where you were going?"

Marlowe bent her head. They hadn't specifically told Enzo about going swimming. She knew better than to point out that Enzo had surely noticed their wet hair and their swimsuits hanging up to dry in the bathroom every night but hadn't bothered to ask them about it.

"So you lied," Glory scolded.

"We didn't lie!" Henry protested. "It's just *swimming*."

"Go inside, all of you. It's time to set the table for dinner," Glory said. "We'll discuss this more later."

In the doorway, Nora tutted at Henry.

"You should've put a shirt on," she whispered. "You made it *obvious*."

Their father, oblivious to what Glory had just discovered, greeted them all with a hug and told them they would go see the fireworks on the Fourth. Nora bounced up and down in excitement, while Nate and Henry only smiled, still feeling the sting of their mother's words.

In the kitchen, Marlowe slowly circled the large wooden table, carefully placing down forks and napkins, as Enzo chopped vine-ripened tomatoes for the salad.

"Your mother is just concerned," Enzo said. "The river is dangerous—incidents happen, even in the shallow water."

"You could have *told* us she would get upset," Marlowe mumbled.

Enzo chuckled. "Don't worry, Marlowe. It will be all right." It was just about time to eat when Glory stalked back into the house from across the street.

"I don't know what Tom Gallagher was thinking," Glory said as they sat down at the table, "I gave him an earful for encouraging you children to swim unsupervised."

"I hope you left the poor man alive." Frank laughed. "He doesn't have kids, you know. He probably didn't realize."

"I'm not a kid anymore; I'm almost sixteen." Nate slouched in his chair. "Anyway, Tom swam all the time when *he* was a kid. If it's such a big deal, I can get lifeguard training. Will that make everyone feel better?"

Glory laid down her fork. "You're not swimming out there ever again, unless Enzo is present. And that's final."

A sense of relief spread across the room. Glory wouldn't make them return to the city or stay inside the Gray House for the rest of the summer, as Marlowe had feared. This was just one more rule. And Tom had ended up bearing the brunt of her mother's fury.

After dinner, as Enzo sliced into a strawberry-rhubarb pie, there was a tap at the front door. Tom Gallagher stood in the yard, his faded green hat pushed up above his damp sun-weathered brow. An iron tractor tire rim sat aloft on three bricks on the grass behind him. Frank reached out his hand, and Tom shook it in his own leathery paw and nodded at Glory before pointing at the tire rim.

"Makes the best firepit," Tom said. "Figured the kids would like it."

Glory thanked him with genuine glee, recognizing the gift as an apology. She said she remembered her father having the same thing behind his house. Marlowe was reminded that Tom had known Glory as a child. Her mother's family had owned a nearby dairy farm, and Glory's father knew the Gallaghers, running into them at least a few times a year at livestock and farm equipment auctions. Glory would forgive Tom for his part in the crime.

Enzo told Henry that the next day, he would show them how to build a fire and would go into town to pick up some good chocolate for s'mores.

That night, while Marlowe and Nora sat cross-legged on their twin beds, Nate and Henry tiptoed into the girls' room.

"We'll obviously still swim," Nate declared. "We just have to stick together and make sure that Enzo doesn't find out." The Bend was too good a place to give up, and the four of them nodded in agreement. In somber tones, each of them vowed never to tell. It was a simple promise to make: If any of them were in danger, they would save each other.

# SUNDAY

## NOVEMBER 25, 2018

# NINE

Marlowe carried Kat's bag to the car, her niece trotting beside her, the pink pom-pom on her hat bobbing with each step. Her younger niece, Dolly, was already complaining about having to go back to school the next day. Nate and Stephanie were driving home to Hartford, and Henry and Constance were heading to the city. They would return next weekend, and the moment school let out for winter break, they'd all be back in the Gray House for the holidays—just like always.

Marlowe heaved the bag into the trunk. Stephanie rounded the car and adjusted the placement before quickly hugging Marlowe goodbye. Nate followed her with a longer hug and a few reassuring pats on the back.

"Don't worry, this will be over soon," he said.

Nate and Stephanie pulled away with the girls, while Constance was still buckling little Frankie into his car seat. Marlowe turned to Henry and gave him a brief embrace.

"Take care of Enzo," Henry said. "I'll be back later this week, as soon as I can get away from the office."

Increasingly, Henry reminded Marlowe and Nate that they all needed to look out for the old man. He had lived on his own in

Queens since moving to New York in his thirties, but after being hired by the Fishers, he spent most of his time with them, until he grew too old to work. Enzo visited the Gray House only during holidays now, and Henry worried that Queens was a harsh exile.

"Enzo will be fine," Marlowe reassured him. "I'll see you soon."

And then they were gone. The Gray House was quiet except for Glory digging out the Christmas decorations and Frank puttering from room to room with a book. Enzo stayed in his room, resting.

Marlowe retreated to the basement. Instead of opening her sketchbooks, which would have been the sensible thing to do, she went online to check the local news. A more recent article about Harmon's death had been posted, but it offered no new information. Still, she lingered over a line in the third paragraph: *Harmon leaves behind a grieving mother, Layla Gallagher.* Of course, she knew that Harmon's mother had identified his body, but in her initial shock, Marlowe hadn't given much consideration to who Layla was in relation to the Gallagher brothers. Marlowe read the line again, anticipating a ring of familiarity. She had never heard the Gallagher brothers mention Layla, and couldn't recall ever seeing a woman visit their property. Without thinking, Marlowe opened a new tab and typed Layla's name into the search bar.

Layla had lost her husband, Peter Gallagher, five years earlier. The cause of death was referred to as an unspecified illness in the short obituary. His friends called him Pete, and he had worked at a Tractor Supply Co. store a few towns over—a fact that was also unfamiliar to her, though she knew of the store. Harmon was Pete and Layla's only child. How abandoned she must feel now. All alone, just as Marlowe assumed the Gallagher brothers had been.

Tom, Dave, and Leroy's house had been bare when Frank ordered it torn down. Had Frank known that besides an empty house, the brothers had left people behind as well? Who was Pete to them precisely? Had they shared a great-grandparent? He wasn't the relative who had inherited the property and sold it. Marlowe wanted to ask her father, but she knew her questions would upset him. He would tell her, as Nate had, not to worry about it. To get some rest. To work on her painting.

Marlowe paused with her hands hovering over her keyboard. Her half-hearted searches were fruitless. Tom, Dave, and Leroy had parents, and those parents must have had siblings. So Pete Gallagher was a possible cousin. Or second cousin. He would have been far younger, Marlowe thought. She pressed her fingers to her eyes as she realized she didn't even have a guess at the Gallagher brothers' ages. When she was a child, they had already looked old, but not decrepit—that was as much as she remembered.

Everything else she recalled felt flimsy, as if it couldn't be trusted.

The Gallaghers had been nothing but kind to Marlowe and her siblings, even when they had been running wild all over their land. But they were strange. Perhaps stranger than she'd realized as a child. The way Leroy never talked but only stared—even Tom's friendliness was warping in her mind. Why was he always showing them places on his land, giving them little gifts, asking about their games? As for Dave, she and Nora, with their overactive imaginations, had made up stories about him harboring a secret broken heart based on a rumor Nora's father had told her about a long-ago engagement that was called off without explanation. They romanticized his past, crafting a tale of young lovers torn apart by cruel parents and interfering siblings, even searching the desk in the tiny barn office for hidden love letters that might have contained years of pining for a girl whose family didn't approve of him. But what if the source of the rumor hadn't been tragic, but sordid instead?

With a huff of frustration, Marlowe stood up and reached for her coat. She tugged on her boots and slipped out through the basement doors. A glance up at the windows as she rounded the corner of the house told her no one was looking out. Both her father and Enzo napped around midday, and Glory was probably taking advantage of the silence to read. Marlowe slowed after she crossed the road. She thought to go toward the Rise, perhaps head all the way out to the Flats once again, looking for what Harmon had hoped to find there in the darkness. But she stopped at the barn and placed one hand on the door, the paint faded and dull beneath her fingers. She had left too quickly to put on gloves, and the rough splintered wood dug into the bare skin of her palm.

Just above her was the dim loft where she and Nora had played. They had watched the Gallagher brothers push open the heavy sliding doors over and over with ease. Leroy was lean, almost scrawny, but Dave and Tom had larger, protruding bellies, markers of their age and poor diets. Beneath their thick coats and worn flannel shirts, all three of them had been strong. Tom would sometimes pat Marlowe or Nora on the head when they were little, and his touch was always gentle. She shook Dave's work-worn hand once and was startled by his almost effeminate grip. Leroy had never touched her. Whether he was ill at ease around children or people in general, he steered clear of them. And yet Marlowe had seen him, countless times, tenderly patting the soft necks of his cows as he led them in from the fields.

She put her back to the barn and crossed the road again, but at a diagonal toward the path that led upward along the side of the North Field and eventually into the woods above. The trek up the hill was steep but short, and the view from the top was Marlowe's favorite. She headed up there almost every day when she was at the Gray House, to think about a project or to daydream. When friends or fellow artists she knew from grad school visited her, she always took them up to admire the vista of rolling hills, the farms in the distance, and the blue outline of the Catskill Mountains.

At the top, she took in the stunning view of the house and fields below her, but her mind was too busy to appreciate it. Instead, she wondered what the Gallagher girl had been running away from all those years ago.

Marlowe kept walking to the edge of the field, following the path into the woods. She used to brag to visitors at this point on a tour, pointing out the moss-covered stone walls that cut straight lines through the trees. One of them stretched a few yards away from the path Marlowe trod, the rocks scattered in places, the top of the wall dipping in height, but the gray stone enduring.

"This is old land," she would say. "Land with a history."

Once upon a time, those stone walls had a purpose. They were built to separate properties or to keep the cows to certain tracts of land. There was something beautiful and ancient about them.

During her time studying abroad in college and while traveling the world, she had witnessed firsthand the age of many European structures; some were centuries older than anything in America. Yet when she stood before Stonehenge and, later, the terra-cotta soldiers of China, her thoughts had inevitably drifted back to the stone walls.

She enjoyed taking archeology in college. In one class, the professor showed a series of slides depicting little statues carved by people who had roamed the earth long before recorded history. He stopped on a stone effigy of a woman, bare-chested and with hands outstretched. There was a wolf beside her, snout tipped up, as if it was about to suckle on her breast. Her features had been worn away by time, until her face had become a smooth oval.

"Any guesses who this is?" The professor's eyes twinkled in a way that signaled it might be a trick question.

Students raised their hands and chirped out their theories. *Artemis, the goddess of the hunt. Maybe Hera. Perhaps a representation of the mother wolf that raised Romulus and Remus before they founded Rome.*

The professor acknowledged that Artemis was a good guess, but then he revealed that the statue dated back a good three centuries before Greek mythology took root, when the oral stories were ever shifting, when people whispered tales that were lost or altered before they could be recorded. The little stone goddess—she was something else, something later goddesses were molded after.

"The Mother Goddess," the professor said. "An ancient figure that appears across early civilizations in various forms."

He took off his glasses as he continued. "Think of the Christian origin of man—where Adam was shaped in God's image, and then Eve was made in man's image, out of Adam's rib. The people who carved this statue did not believe that. Women were not made in man's image or God's image. They were made in *her* image. The Mother Goddess, the origin of all life."

And in that classroom, so far away from the woods by the Gray House, Marlowe blinked up at the picture projected on the screen and wondered why it looked so familiar. Wondered why she felt she had unearthed something similar, running about as a child.

Marlowe stepped off the path and placed one boot atop a rock. Not a pagan carving, just a stone, moved into place by a humble farmer. It felt like more. As children, they had always searched for deeper meaning to add intrigue to their adventures. She shivered as she recalled the stories her brothers and Nora made up to scare each other, about a villainous stranger lurking in the woods.

The wall Marlowe stood by stretched westward as far as she could see. The barren branches seemed to point the way. Marlowe hadn't followed their directions since she was a girl, but she knew if she kept walking, she would reach the old abandoned car. They had found it as teenagers. It had likely been left by a previous tenant, but charred logs nearby had been enough for them to conjure a character camping out in the woods.

They called him Mr. Babel. Nora had come up with the name, inspired by the biblical story of the Tower of Babel, which had stuck with her since Sunday school. She'd claimed Mr. Babel spoke to snakes and came out of the woods at night to peer into the windows of the Gray House.

Marlowe had added her own details: Mr. Babel had no fear of getting caught; he had lethal aim with his shotgun and knew the land, with all its hiding spots, like the back of his hand.

Even now, Nate and Henry told stories about him to their children, but their tales were tamer. Mr. Babel had transformed into a genial hermit hiding treasure in the woods. That wasn't how he had started out, though. In fact, there was a time when Marlowe truly feared Mr. Babel. She'd even thought she had spotted him once or twice, weaving among the trees, a grizzled beard covering his face, dead squirrels tossed over his shoulder.

All at once, a smile tugged at the corners of Marlowe's mouth, and tears threatened to well in her eyes. She wasn't sure whether to laugh or cry at the memory of Nora's dramatics.

Marlowe moved back to the path. The abandoned car was still a long ways off, and she doubted there would still be any sign of a fire. Mr. Babel was a myth; by the time Nora disappeared, Marlowe was certain of that. The woods weren't even that vast—a few miles in any direction and a walker could hit a road or someone's backyard. It wasn't a true wilderness, and there were no monsters hiding behind the thick tree trunks.

But there had been Gallaghers. Marlowe confronted that fact as she emerged into the field, the ground brown and dull. Another

Gallagher, camping out, just as Harmon had done mere nights ago.

Only this other Gallagher was far more secretive. He had picked a hidden spot up in the woods. He had not reached out to them. Had he been watching them? And, if so, for how long?

# TEN

The laptop screen flickered before the search results populated one by one in rapid succession. Marlowe scanned each link and snippet before pushing the laptop toward her father, sitting next to her at the kitchen table. Marlowe was tired and peckish after her long walk and wanted to rest in her room until dinner was ready, but Frank had asked her to do an online search for background information on the detectives after they'd called to say they would be stopping by on Monday to discuss Harmon's threats in more detail.

Ariel Mintz and Ben Vance had both attended the police academy and served in uniform. Judging from the dates she could find, they were promoted quickly. Other than their basic credentials as homicide detectives, that was all Marlowe could find. She recalled Ariel's sharp gaze, her no-nonsense attitude. Marlowe wondered what it would be like to take in the world and make definitive judgments about it so easily. The harder Marlowe looked at people and places, the more confused she became.

"I wonder why Poughkeepsie," Marlowe mused. "You would think if they were good enough to be promoted so young, they would perhaps go to a bigger city."

"Never assume your own ambitions exist in others," Frank said, folding his hands together and resting them on his stomach.

"You should call that judge upstate. You know, Lydia Freeman's husband. Bill. See if he's crossed paths with them before and has anything useful to share," Glory said without looking up from the salad spinner.

"Good idea," Frank said.

Frank and Glory believed in research. They never so much as attended a dinner without discovering the crucial details about the guests. Who had accomplished what. Who was useful or interesting or well connected. Marlowe wondered what kind of value they would assign her if she weren't their daughter and they were to research her.

"Did you speak to the Hopewells or any of the other neighbors yet?" Marlowe asked. "I'm curious what the detectives have been asking."

"Yes, Todd Hopewell and I spoke briefly. They asked him about the brothers, the land, dates of purchase," Frank said. "As if that poor young man, Harmon, had anything to do with what was between me and Tom. Not that the Hopewells would know—they're still new around here."

Frank had always maintained that he and Tom, the oldest and most approachable of the brothers, had an agreement of sorts: Frank never hassled the farmer, but Tom was aware that Frank would make a fair offer to whoever inherited the property.

"Marlowe, are you going back to the city before Christmas?" Glory asked, changing the subject as she rounded the counter with a pitcher of water. "For Paige's party?"

Marlowe's friend Paige from college and her husband threw an annual holiday party in their Cobble Hill brownstone. Marlowe had fond memories from her twenties, before Paige had kids, when she and Marlowe used to invent special cocktails laden with gin and cranberry juice and decorated with sprigs of thyme. They liked to get tipsy and gossip about other guests at the parties they attended together. They'd lived in the same dorm and become friends chatting in each other's rooms late at night, Marlowe's shyness eased by Paige's reliable supply of cheap alcohol. After Nora, it hadn't been easy for Marlowe to connect, and she never had a bevy of girlfriends.

She still appreciated Paige, but Marlowe wasn't looking forward to the holiday party this year. Paige would likely retire early to put her toddler to bed. The year before, Marlowe was left on her own to make small talk with Paige's husband's friends, all of them couples with high-flying careers and children starting school at Packer or Chapin. Everyone in the room had a partner and plans. She had retreated to a corner, feeling stilted and untethered.

"I'm not sure." Marlowe glanced away from Glory. "Maybe."

"You need to let me know so I can plan out groceries and meals," Glory said. "And get the house cleaner in while you're gone."

Marlowe nodded. She was too used to Glory's ways to point out that the amount Marlowe ate couldn't possibly put a dent in the well-stocked kitchen. Nor did she balk at having to run her comings and goings by her mother. Dancing to Glory's tune was part of staying at the Gray House.

In fact, Marlowe had come to take comfort in the assurance that Glory would take care of everything. If Marlowe got caught up in a project and didn't have time to do laundry, Glory would get it done. If Marlowe forgot to buy a new dress for a family wedding, Glory acquired options. When Marlowe was traveling and a flight got canceled at the last minute, Glory was her first call. She oversaw Marlowe's move into her apartment and read Marlowe's contracts with her keen eye. Her mother was so confident and capable that Marlowe had grown to accept her control.

"Dad." Marlowe leaned toward her father, pulling him out of his reverie on old law contacts. "Did Todd say if they asked him about

Nora? They asked me, and Henry mentioned they went to Damen."

Frank furrowed his brow and shook his head. "He didn't say. Why would they? What would Todd know, anyway?"

The Hopewells were recent additions to the area. But Marlowe had the sense that Ariel was thorough. If she was going to ask about Nora, she would ask everyone, if only to hear about the rumors. Obviously, Harmon had been aware of the rumors himself; he'd referenced them in his threats. Marlowe was suddenly mad with curiosity: What did Harmon think he knew? Could his information, gleaned from his own relatives perhaps, have a fragment of truth? And would the detectives bother to find out?

"Marlowe, go up and see if Enzo wants to come down for dinner," Glory said. "And then set the table."

Marlowe rose and drifted up the staircase. It had been two days. Ariel and Ben would have more information on Harmon and his family than she did by now. If Marlowe cooperated with them, they might share what they'd found out with her.

Twenty years ago, the detective in charge of Nora's case, John Brierley, had told her nothing. He was short and balding, and it was clear he took no enjoyment from the long hikes over uneven terrain that the search required. He was in no shape for it, but he never complained; Marlowe could give him that. Despite his bulbous nose, sweaty appearance, and blunt manner of speech, Brierley managed to put Nora's parents at ease. Marlowe, too, felt tremendous faith in him at one point.

She'd last seen Brierley in the fall of her junior year of high school. Marlowe was with the Millers in their living room when Brierley arrived to give them yet another hollow update. When he left, Marlowe followed him out, with the intention of walking home before the sun set. Her eyes were cast down, scanning the ground as she walked, forever looking for traces of her friend. A piece of her shirt. The imprint of her shoe. A strand of blond hair. I hoping that maybe Nora herself would pop out from behind a tree, laughing and explaining it was all an elaborate trick.

Brierley had paused by his car door and called out to her.

"Miss Fisher, you should know that at this point, we're assuming that she ran away." Brierley always called her Miss Fisher.

"She didn't run away." Marlowe had been repeating that same phrase for months, as Brierley dug up every negative comment or passing grievance against Nora he could find, trying to piece together a possible reason for her to flee. When Brierley asked if Nora's father ever hit her, she'd answered through heaving sobs. Nora wasn't abused; she would have told Marlowe something like that. They'd changed together a thousand times, and Marlowe had never seen any marks. There was simply no reason for her to run.

He looked at her more pointedly then. "Miss Fisher," he said. "The only way you're going to survive this is if you start telling yourself she ran away."

Then he got into his car and left.

Marlowe decided, however, that Ariel Mintz was no Brierley. As she returned downstairs to report that Enzo was dozing, and began circling the table, placing the plates and glasses, she thought of Ariel's somber face and direct manner, her rough edges and sharp teeth. She pictured Ariel at work, grinding through the long days in uniform, eager to be moved up to detective status. Marlowe didn't possess that kind of grit or confidence, but she didn't begrudge it in Ariel, or in Ben, for that matter. They were hungry, whereas Brierley had been tired, his energy drained by a case that simply didn't make sense.

They would be back tomorrow. Frank and Glory would brace themselves behind all the intel they could hoard. But what armor did Marlowe have to guard against the memories of Nora, once carefully contained, now flooding back to her?

# ELEVEN

**THE BRAND**
**Saturday, September 23, 1995**

A blanket of clouds stretched over the afternoon sky, casting a shadow over the valley. It had rained all week, and there was still some residual dampness hanging in the air.

Marlowe and Nora were alone in the house, while the adults were off shopping for a new piece of furniture in a nearby town. The two of them were sprawled languidly across the twin beds in Marlowe's room, more often called the "girls' room," because Nora slept over most weekends. Henry and Nate shared the "boys' room" down the hall.

A little while ago, the boys had lit out to work on their weekend project: a lean-to fort made of sticks and fallen branches in the woods behind the Gray House. Marlowe and Nora had been told in no uncertain terms that they would be banned forever if they weren't going to participate in the work of gathering and building. "You don't get to enjoy it if you're too lazy to help build it," Nate had said.

Nora traced the soft, raised edges of the embroidered daisies covering the quilt on the bed. "I'm bored," she said, rolling over onto her back and peering out the window toward the red barn across the street. Marlowe looked up from her sketchbook. She knew

Nora got bored more easily than she did, but then, Nora always had a remedy for her boredom; an idea was brewing.

"Let's go pet the Gallaghers' cows."

"Pet them?" Marlowe laughed at the thought.

Cows were foreign beasts, and besides, they belonged to the Gallagher brothers. Playing around in the hayloft was one thing, but interfering with the cows was something different. Just as Marlowe knew not to touch the paperwork strewn about her father's desk, she also knew not to mess with the Gallaghers' dairy cows.

"I bet you've never touched one," Nora said. "Cows aren't scary, trust me. You could even ride one if I give you a leg up."

"People don't ride cows." Marlowe was resistant, but she could already feel the corners of her mouth curling into a smile. Nora was going to convince her; she always did.

"Come on, let's go. It's not raining anymore, and we can't let the boys have all the fun."

Giggling mischievously, the girls ran down the stairs, pulled on their galoshes, and headed out to the pasture. The Gallaghers were nowhere in sight, and their old green truck was gone, which meant they were probably in town, purchasing supplies.

The field was so saturated their boots sank up to the ankles in the mud, making loud squelching noises. They only giggled more and clasped hands to keep their balance as they trudged in the direction of the lingering herd.

Marlowe grew hesitant as they drew near. The cows seemed bigger up close. One of the black-and-white heifers plodded right toward her, and Marlowe steadied herself and slowly lifted her hand to pet its nose. The cow huffed through its wide nostrils—its breath was warm and slightly damp on Marlowe's fingers. Feeling brave, she stepped closer and gently slid her hand along its smooth, muscular neck.

The cows remained placid as the two girls wended among them, patting their rumps and stroking their velvety soft ears.

"I thought farmers always branded their cattle, like in the Old West," Marlowe said. "Right here on their flanks."

"No brands on these," Nora said.

"Guess the Gallaghers aren't scared of cow thieves."

Nora's eyes lit up, the way they did when she had a spectacular idea. "We should brand them!"

Marlowe raised her brows. "You mean like with a hot iron? We can't do that."

"No, no, you could *design* the mark," Nora said. "You could sketch something cool, and then we could paint it on."

"I don't know. They're not *our* cows." But even as she spoke, Marlowe was dreaming up possible designs.

"The Gallaghers won't care; we're not hurting them. Anyway, nothing ever happens around here—they'll probably think it's hilarious," Nora said.

That was all the urging Marlowe needed. The girls ran back to the Gray House, where Marlowe dug out her art supplies. Nora leaned on her elbows and grinned over Marlowe's shoulder as Marlowe started to sketch. Some of Marlowe's school friends in the city teased her about how serious she was about art, or worse, they seemed to resent the attention she got for her drawings and watercolors. Lately, she'd become more guarded about drawing at school, but she didn't need to pretend she wasn't talented around Nora, who would brag to her parents or anyone who would listen: "You should *see* how good Marlowe is!" It was one of the reasons Marlowe couldn't wait for weekends in the country, where she could be herself.

"It's perfect!" Nora said, as Marlowe put down her charcoal pencil. She'd sketched a simple circle, about the width of a hand, with an infinity sign in the center. Intersecting the middle of the sign was a rudimentary tree, its branches stretching up to the top of the circle, with thinner lines at the bottom to indicate roots.

"I thought about doing a lion or something like that, but I think this will be easier to paint," Marlowe said.

"I agree," Nora said. "I'm the branches, and you're the roots."

Marlowe flushed with pleasure. That was exactly what she had intended; somehow, Nora always knew. They understood each other so well.

They took the sketch and walked up the road to Nora's house, where they grabbed a can of bright blue paint and some brushes from the garage and headed back to the pasture, so delighted with their plan that the mud and distance were hardly a bother.

"How many city blocks do you think we've walked?" Nora asked as they plodded by the southern hayfield and the Gray House came back into sight. This was a game they played. Nora was obsessed with hearing about the city and liked to guess at the number of blocks they would have walked if they were in New York instead of trampling through woods and fields.

"Maybe forty—I feel like we could have walked from our apartment on East Seventy-Fourth all the way to the Empire State Building by now," Marlowe said, though it was hard to judge. Blocks were flat, and no distance in the country was ever on even terrain.

Luck was on their side that afternoon. The Gallagher brothers were still off-site when the girls entered the cow field.

Nora picked out a lazy-looking cow and patted its neck, whispering soothing things in its ear, while Marlowe dipped the brush into the thick blue paint and began to work her magic. The heifer didn't seem to notice or mind as Marlowe made quick brushstrokes over its coat, making sure to angle the brush in the direction of the cow's bristles.

The blue paint glistened against the cow's white flank. Even with the rudimentary brush, the etching of the tree intersected with the infinity sign was clear as day. Nora squealed with glee when she saw, and grabbed her own brush.

They were meticulous in their mission. They didn't miss a single cow.

When they were done, the whole herd of milk cows bore Nora and Marlowe's brand, shining bright and blue on their black-and-white bodies.

The girls turned and ran back to the Gray House, the dripping brushes dangling from their hands. Even from across the road, the circles were still visible. They hurriedly washed the brushes in the sink before hiding them with the empty paint pail in the back of Marlowe's closet and then threw themselves onto their twin beds as if they'd never moved.

Later that evening, after the Fishers had returned home with a new set of living room chairs, the family gathered for dinner. Nora stayed, as she always did, confidently taking her usual place next to Marlowe at the dining table.

"Tom Gallagher's up in arms," Frank announced. "Someone's been messing with his cows."

Nora and Marlowe gave each other a quick sidelong glance but stayed silent. They'd become good at that, communicating with their eyes.

"What happened?" Glory asked. "Don't tell me there are a bunch of hooligans out tipping?"

"Someone painted brands on the cows, made a crazy symbol with a tree," Frank explained. "I'm sure it was someone's idea of a joke, but Tom was yammering on about Wiccan nonsense. Devil worshipping, if you can believe it."

Nora cast her eyes down at the table, and Marlowe tugged on a lock of her hair so as not to laugh.

Glory chuckled. "Those old men sure do spook easily. I suppose they should just count themselves lucky that cow tipping has gone out of style."

"It wasn't any of you who messed with those cows, was it?" Frank asked.

He surveyed the children with eagle eyes, and they all shook their heads vehemently.

If Marlowe had a sheepish tilt to her mouth, or Nora had a twinkle in her eye, no one noticed. They would never be the suspects. Pranks were a boy's domain.

"Let me remind you, those cows and fields are not for fun for the Gallaghers," Frank said. "It's their livelihood."

Everyone nodded, and the issue was forgotten as they dug into their meal.

Marlowe clasped Nora's hand under the table. The cow prank didn't feel like a crime. If the Gallaghers were silly enough to cry witches or satanism, that was hardly Marlowe and Nora's fault. It was their secret. Their own brand. Harmless mischief just between them, tying them closer together.

# MONDAY

**NOVEMBER 26, 2018**

# TWELVE

It started to snow right before the detectives arrived. The flurries were intermittent and wouldn't stick, but an early snow seemed foretelling. Of what, Marlowe didn't know, but to her, something about this place—the land, with its cycles and weather—always seemed to hold special knowledge.

Glory welcomed the detectives to seats at the kitchen table. Frank and Glory sat next to each other, Marlowe near her mother, facing Ariel and Ben.

"We're pleased to inform you that we've made some headway on the case," Ben announced. "We just have a few more questions for you."

"I'm grateful for it," Frank said. "All of this happening on our land has unsettled us, to say the least."

Ben nodded. "We can confirm that Harmon Gallagher was killed at some point between midnight and three in the morning on November 23. The initial coroner's report states the cause of death as blunt force trauma to the back and top of the head."

"And you have suspects?" Frank asked.

"I can't say at this time. We're still gathering information," Ben said. "We have officially traced those threats you sent in back to Harmon, and we'd like to go over the details again, Mr. Fisher."

"Certainly. Shall we talk in the study?"

"That would be great, thank you." Ben stood up and followed Frank, but this time Ariel lingered.

"I'd like to get a better sense of the property," Ariel said. "Marlowe, would you mind showing me where the old Gallagher house used to be?"

"All right." Marlowe had expected, even hoped for, this kind of chance, but still she was hit by a ripple of shock at being so neatly singled out. Ariel didn't waste time. Marlowe glanced at her mother, who wasn't looking at either of them.

"Thank you, I appreciate it. And the guest you told us about on Friday, Enzo Marino." Ariel turned to Glory. "Is he still in the house?"

"Yes, of course he is." Glory looked confused. "He went upstairs for a nap shortly before you arrived."

"We'd like to speak to him, if he's able, when we're back," Ariel said. "Neighbors all recalled he was here full-time every summer; he must know this area as well as you."

"Perhaps even better," Glory said. "I'll see if he's up to it."

Ariel stood in silence while Marlowe pulled on her coat, hat, and gloves.

Their footsteps were muffled by the dusting of snow as they traversed the lawn. Marlowe cleared her throat and pointed toward the chestnut tree as she crossed the road.

"The Gallagher Place was beneath the tree," she said. "Over there by that hydrangea bush. And there was a small milk barn beside the bigger barn; you can still see the foundations." They paused where Marlowe estimated one of the cornerstones of the house had been.

"After it was torn down, the grass was replanted. It was just a modest farmhouse, smaller than the Gray House. I remember it was painted dark green."

Ariel nodded and then tipped her head back, peering up at the arching boughs of the chestnut.

"The brothers didn't spend much time inside," Marlowe continued. "They were always in the barn or the fields, trying to keep things up. The farm slipped more out of their hands each year."

They continued tramping over the slippery grass, and Marlowe pointed out where the earth rose in a lump. "There was a cellar there. It's filled in now, but there was a trapdoor in the house that once led down into it."

"How do you know so much about the place?" Ariel asked.

"We explored the empty house before it was demolished." Marlowe didn't clarify whom "we" meant, but it had been the four of them as usual, including Nora. "There wasn't much to see after they died. It was a simple place to begin with. The cellar was the only exciting thing. It was pitch black down there, and the stone walls were cold and slick. It felt old, far older than the house itself."

"The house was torn down right after your father bought the land, is that right?" Ariel paused, and Marlowe nodded her confirmation.

Marlowe couldn't tell what Ariel was after with this line of questioning. The ground began to feel flimsy beneath her feet, as if it might crumble and send her and Ariel tumbling into the ancient pit. And she hated to admit to herself that she felt the dull beginnings of a craving for a glass of wine taking form.

"Leroy died first, yes?" Ariel looked up as a flurry hit her cheek and melted. "Then Tom shortly after, and then Dave. Here, on the farm, right?"

"Yes," Marlowe said.

"Pretty strange, don't you think? All of them passing within two years of each other?"

"Strange things happen all the time," Marlowe said.

"Funny," Ariel said. "Your father said the same thing."

"It was more sad than anything else." Marlowe's instinct was to defend the Gallaghers. Who was Ariel to judge how their lives had ended?

"You mourned them?"

"I was a teenager; I barely understood it," Marlowe said. "But those men were kind to me and my brothers, even when they didn't have to be."

"So they were fond of you?" Ariel asked.

"We were probably annoying, running around playing in their fields and barns," Marlowe admitted. "But they never seemed angry. They told us we could play on their land, even encouraged us to, as long as we didn't mess with their operation."

"Your father says he was on good terms with them, that they even knew he planned to buy the land from whoever inherited," Ariel said. "He says he had their blessing."

Ariel's voice was tinged with cynicism, as if to imply that a blessing had to be given, rather than claimed.

"As far as I know. But like I said, I was just a teenager. I didn't have much insight into those things."

"I wonder what set Harmon off, in that case," Ariel said, walking toward the barn. "Why he decided to start sending those messages so many years after the property had passed hands."

"I don't get it either."

Ariel paused and took in a long breath. Her mouth softened, as if even she was soothed by the beauty of the land, just as Marlowe always was.

"One of the threats mentioned Nora Miller by name, and a few others referenced her indirectly," Ariel said. "Could you tell me more about her?"

The question struck Marlowe like a shot of freezing air in her lungs. Everyone—Nate, Henry, her parents—had downplayed Harmon's words, too scared that Marlowe couldn't handle it, but she had been correct. The threats were about Nora, and Ariel was taking them seriously.

"She was my best friend. We met when we were five. She lived just down the road."

Ariel waited for her to continue. She wanted more. Marlowe's gut twisted with apprehension. Her brothers could never wait out her silences, but Ariel was practiced at this, and her curiosity seemed to grant her all the patience in the world.

"When she vanished, it was awful." If they were inside, Marlowe might have been able to stymie the emotion, but her eyes were already watering in the cold, and the barn blurred into a red smear, the white fields blending into the gray sky. "We couldn't find her. Couldn't find anything."

"I looked over the old notes. June 5, 1998. About a year after your father purchased this land. The house would have been gone by then." Ariel nodded at the empty square of grass, as if she was trying to anchor Marlowe to the ground, tether her to the present. Marlowe hadn't realized the panic settling over her until Ariel pulled her back. It was jarring that Ariel could see her so well.

"So you're familiar with the details," Marlowe said.

Ariel shrugged. "I've been wanting to hear your version."

Marlowe had no version. She had only her memory, as useless as it was, but she had nothing to hide, no matter what the rumor mill or the bloggers had to say.

"Summer had just started, and Nora was at our place," Marlowe said. "Nate had some friends from college over, and Henry had a friend up for the weekend as well. We were up late, laughing and drinking in the kitchen. Nothing crazy. Nora and I tried the beer but we didn't like it. We were just tagging along with Nate. It was exciting to be included with the older boys. Around midnight, Nora went to take out the trash, and she never came back."

Marlowe swallowed hard, pushing down the images of Nora cackling at a story Nate and his college friends were telling, of her own smile as she sipped the vile-tasting beer. The kitchen floor hadn't been redone yet—it was still the faded orange linoleum. They had been outside all day. Nora's cheeks were tinted pink from the sun. The stifling heat of summer hadn't set in, and chilly night air wafted through the open windows.

"We looked for her in the pitch black," Marlowe said. "And the next day the search party started."

"And your parents?" Ariel asked.

"They were asleep, but we woke up them and Enzo when we couldn't find her," Marlowe said. "They called Nora's parents."

Marlowe's voice wavered when she thought of Damen and Jennifer Miller, confused and desperate. Nora spent every spare second of her life at the Gray House when Marlowe's family was in town. She loved it. She loved the Fishers. It was supposed to be safe. Good for her, even.

Ariel looked over her shoulder, toward the trash bins by the road, tucked beneath the copse of pine trees.

"How long before you noticed she hadn't returned?" Ariel tilted her head, like a bird eyeing a fat worm.

"No more than ten minutes," Marlowe said. "I'm sure that's in the reports from back then. I went over everything a million times with the detective, John Brierley."

Ariel nodded. Marlowe could tell she already knew his name, had read and internalized whatever Brierley had written about Nora and Marlowe, had weighed his thoughts and impressions against her own. They stood side by side, both facing the Gallagher barn, backs to the road. Ariel stepped forward and turned to look at the Gray House. "Nora Miller vanished mere yards from this house. Harmon Gallagher was killed just over a mile from it, after sending threats to half your family, claiming he knew what they had done to Nora and the Gallagher brothers. I know all this is hard for your family, and you especially but the circumstances are puzzling. You have to grant me that much." Marlowe remained silent, listening with as much patience as she could.

"Ben and I have talked to your neighbors, Harmon's family and friends, as well as other locals. We've been asking about Harmon and this place, but no one seems to be able to explain the Gallaghers without bringing up the Fishers." Ariel's tone was clipped and frank.

Marlowe huffed. "If you're going where I think you're going with this, then you're wrong."

Ariel held up a hand, a conciliatory gesture. "I'm just explaining our progress. I can see that you're already aware of the rumors that your family was involved in Nora's disappearance. We're not making any assumptions. But what we want to know is if Harmon was inspired to write those threats based on general rumors, or something more specific, possibly passed to him from a relative."

Marlowe hesitated for only a heartbeat before she took the opening Ariel was offering. "The Gallagher brothers were dead before Nora went missing. Anyway, I looked up Harmon and his father, Peter Gallagher. I'm not sure how they were related to Tom, Dave, and Leroy, but I know they couldn't have been close."

"Why do you say that?" Ariel's question rang with curiosity, not judgment. It gave Marlowe confidence.

"From the age of five onward, I spent all summer and every holiday here," Marlowe said. "I never saw any family visit those brothers on Thanksgiving or Christmas Day. Not once. No cousins came to help out with the hay. *We* helped. I'm not saying that makes us their family, but they asked Nate, and it was fun for us, and they had no one else. If any relatives were poking around here after the brothers died, they didn't make themselves known to us. It would have been too little, too late, anyway."

"So you're saying it's very unlikely that Harmon could have known anything about Nora at all," Ariel mused. "Or even if he thought he knew something, it couldn't have been based on first-hand knowledge from a relative."

The tension was dissolving between them. Marlowe suddenly felt as if she were Ariel's partner and they were bouncing ideas off each other, crafting and comparing theories, the way she and Nora had once composed pretend histories for Dave Gallagher's lost love or Mr. Babel.

"I just keep wondering how often Harmon camped out around here without us knowing about it," Marlowe said. "And if other Gallagher cousins might have been doing that."

"Back when Nora vanished." Ariel finished the thought for her. This was the part the detective loved, Marlowe could tell by the way she nodded, her nose twitching, as if she were catching the scent. That pulled Marlowe up short. Ariel was a hunter, and Marlowe didn't yet know Ariel's preferred prey.

"We spoke to Damen Miller," Ariel continued. "He claims he didn't know Harmon Gallagher and was surprised when we asked if Harmon or anyone else had ever approached him about Nora. But Damen also told us he doesn't think he's ever known the whole truth of what happened that night he lost his daughter."

"From us, you mean. Did he say that? Does he think I would have lied to him?" Marlowe frowned. Damen deserved her sympathy, but she felt only annoyance.

"You don't strike me as a liar," Ariel said. "But if you did, you were a minor and it was twenty years ago. You wouldn't be culpable."

Marlowe went still, and the detective held her gaze. This was what Ariel had intended to ask her all along. It wasn't about the Gallaghers or Harmon. Ariel wanted to see if Marlowe would change her story about Nora. If Marlowe would react to Damen's insinuation.

"I didn't lie about anything, and neither did anyone in my family," Marlowe said. "I don't know why Harmon Gallagher was bringing up Nora, and I don't know why he was out in that field. But I want you to find the answers. I'll tell you everything I can. About the Gallaghers and about Nora."

"I appreciate that." Ariel flashed a gentle smile, and Marlowe's shoulders loosened with relief. Ariel believed her. "It's a muddled situation. Nora's case has a lot of dead ends; that's what I've gleaned from Brierley's notes." Ariel paused. "Do you know that one local actually suggested that a wolf got her? As if this were the seventeenth century and packs of wolves still roamed the woods."

Ariel chuckled, but Marlowe remained stone-faced. She couldn't act casual. Not about Nora.

"And another lady who lived in town, she thought that Nora might have been a changeling," Ariel said. "That the witches or elves or whatever came and claimed her back. She was an old woman, probably a little off her rocker, but still."

"This region is old." Marlowe tried not to reveal that at one time she had been seduced by similar theories. "The old stories about this place. Some people haven't let them go, I guess."

"Tell me about it," Ariel said. "My mom lives in Kinderhook, near Ichabod Crane High School. Their mascot is literally the Headless Horseman."

The snowflakes whirled down in dizzying spirals. Damp clumps clung to the grass. The Gray House's windows glowed across the street, beckoning them, as if to say, *Come back here, to where it's warm and safe.* Glory had put the wreath up on the front door.

"Marlowe." Ariel's voice had a dry rasp to it. "What do you think happened to Nora?"

"I don't know," Marlowe said. "At the time, I thought someone from her school or someone local had taken her. Maybe some sort of stalker. Someone who was never suspected or looked at closely. Maybe he got her in his car and drove away before Nate and I went out looking for her."

"Interesting you say *he*."

"But Brierley thought she ran away." Marlowe shook her head. "He didn't explore every option, and he didn't have all the tech and the forensics that exist today. He had a few bloodhounds that never caught a real trail, and that was it."

Marlowe didn't know she was still angry about it, but standing under that chestnut tree, where the Gallagher house once stood, she found some of the rage that had filled her teenage heart. Brierley had never *listened* to her. Marlowe had told him the truth, and he hadn't believed her. He hadn't even sufficiently questioned her. He had spent most of his time grilling Nate and then Henry, hammering him with questions until he cried. He'd gone so far as to collect DNA samples from the men in the house—a desperate attempt to reassure a restless community that he was doing everything he could to bring a local girl home. They'd all obliged voluntarily, but it didn't matter. No tangible evidence was ever found.

"All that stuff the bio experts can tell us, that's useful, sure. But the way we solve a case isn't through forensics. It's through talking to people, asking questions, until something or someone sticks out. Something doesn't add up. The forensics and DNA and all that—that's just for the judge, jury, and executioner. It's important. But it's not how we catch them." Ariel took a long breath before continuing. "So that's why we're talking to you, and Harmon's family and friends, over and over. That's why I'm asking about Nora; there's a connection there. I have a hunch that some long-forgotten detail might lead us to answers about Harmon, and if we're good enough detectives, it could also lead us to answers about Nora."

Marlowe stared at Ariel in stunned silence. She almost felt pity for the woman and her hubris. Ariel believed she was going to figure it all out—the mess that no one had untangled for decades. She thought she was that good.

Still, a foolish hope glimmered to life in her heart.

"You want to know what happened, right?" Ariel pulled her hands out of her pockets and adjusted her gloves.

Marlowe's head spun at the possibility. What would it feel like to finally know? Would it bring her any peace? Would she want vengeance? Or would this whole affair be another disappointment, possibly more of a torment than the initial tragedy? She had a sudden need to lie down, to breathe, to be alone.

"I want Nora back." Marlowe turned and started walking back toward the Gray House at a faster pace than before. Ariel had to scurry to catch up.

As Marlowe's boots smacked the pavement of the road, Ariel tapped her elbow. Marlowe's arm jerked at the physical contact.

"Why don't you think she ran away?" Ariel asked. "At her age—it seems like the most reasonable explanation."

Marlowe's words were heavy in her throat, but she forced them out. "If she had run away, she would have taken me with her."

# THIRTEEN

Ariel and Marlowe both slowed as they approached the Gray House. Their conversation had sparked thoughts and feelings in Marlowe, but she was tired, as if digging around in her past was a physical exertion. She stopped before the porch steps, gathering herself before climbing them. Above her head, each thin branch of the birch tree held a layer of pristine snow. As a child, Marlowe once asked her mother why the white of the birch tree changed colors from season to season. She knew now that the bark didn't change at all; it was only the angle of the sun that cast a different light on its branches. It was not magic, simply the inevitable turning of the earth.

Two figures passed by the front window on their way to the living room. Enzo, hunched and wobbling; Glory, her arm firm around his.

"There's Enzo. He's awake." Marlowe gave Ariel an apologetic look. "I have to warn you, though, he might not have much to say. His mind's been going."

"I'm curious about this Enzo Marino," Ariel said, lingering on the porch steps.

Marlowe quirked her lips. "You mean Enzo *Marino*?" Like the rest of her family, she put an extreme emphasis on the second syllable. "What about him?"

"What's he doing here?" Ariel asked. "He's not related to your family. He was, what, a handyman? A groundskeeper?"

"More than that," Marlowe said. "He did a little bit of everything for us. He was born in Italy but moved all around Europe, working in kitchens and vineyards and doing carpentry. He ended up in Queens in the eighties."

"Is that when your family met him?" Ariel asked.

"That's right, he came to install a door at our apartment in the city. When my mother learned about his background, she asked him to do a few more odd jobs and, eventually, to help her cook for a dinner party. And then it just seemed like he was always around. He started watching us as kids, cooking our meals. He was the one who oversaw the renovations at the Gray House and babysat us all summer. We never had a nanny, but I guess Enzo was something close to that."

It was an odd situation, but once people met Enzo, it made sense. All his experience and charm had suited the Fishers, and he adapted to their changing needs, year after year.

"Well, it seems like that work is over now, and even if something needed fixing, he's a bit old for that. Why keep him around?"

"Loyalty, I guess." Marlowe shrugged, moving toward the door. "And perhaps some pity. He has no one else. No family, no children. It's a sad way to go, all alone."

Marlowe and Ariel entered the house, bringing with them a draft of icy air. Glory snapped to attention as Ariel shed her coat, folded it over one arm, and walked over to Enzo's seat.

"Hello," Enzo said. "Have we met?"

Ariel didn't answer but simply studied him for a few uncomfortable moments. Marlowe had the urge to step between her and Enzo.

"I'm Detective Ariel Mintz," she said at last.

Down the hall, the study door swung open, and Ben and Frank emerged.

"We have a few more questions for all of you," Ben stated.

"Go ahead." Frank settled into the armchair. Glory perched on the edge of the hearth, and Marlowe sat beside her.

"Now that Mr. Fisher and I have looked over the threats"—Ben nodded at Frank—"we'd like to hear from the rest of you about your relationship with the three Gallagher brothers. Were there any tensions? Any disagreements?"

"I grew up in this area, and my own father was Tom Gallagher's good friend," Glory said. "They were good men, and we were happy neighbors. The issue was never with *that* generation."

Glory was adept at playing up her farm-girl background when it served her and then quickly tucking it away, far out of sight.

"There was no feud, no bad blood whatsoever," Frank added.

"So these threats Harmon sent—none of you believe they originated with the brothers across the street?" Ariel asked.

"Not at all," Frank said.

"Enzo." Ben narrowed his eyes and turned his head, suddenly shifting his attention. "Did you have much interaction with the Gallaghers?"

"They are dead," Enzo whispered. "All of them. Very sad."

"But when they were alive?"

"Some say sadness like that is in the blood." Enzo sighed and stared at the fire.

"And what about Nora Miller?" Ariel asked. "Do you recall how the Gallaghers felt about her?" She didn't seem to direct the questions at anyone in particular but simply threw them out toward the fire for consideration.

If she was hoping for a dramatic reaction, she didn't get one. Frank and Glory regarded her with puzzled yet sympathetic expressions, as if Ariel were a child mispronouncing a word. Enzo's gaze remained distant.

"She was their neighbor as well," Frank said, finally. "Harmon only mentioned her to pick at an old wound in our community, nothing more."

"This all came from Harmon's imagination, then?" Ben asked. "No story he might have heard from relatives?"

"The Gallaghers we knew wouldn't have spread stories like that," Glory said. "They were decent men."

"Of course." Ben nodded.

The detectives rose, bid everyone farewell, and headed for the door.

"I don't think they know what they're doing at all," Frank grumbled, watching their car pulling out of the driveway.

That was her father's endless refrain. *They don't know what they're doing.* He said the same thing about the headmaster of the school where Henry had gotten bad grades, and about the restaurants that took too long with his order. Frank was the epitome of responsibility. The rest of the world was incompetent.

"Well, let's stay calm; there's no need to fuss." Glory didn't show any frustration, merely resignation. "They'll get over this morbid curiosity about Nora soon enough."

"This is Damen Miller's doing," Frank spat. "He's lost his mind all by himself in that house. He's let it consume him, let it drive him to make senseless accusations. It's given him an audience in those detectives."

"You think they told Damen about Harmon's threats?" It seemed to Marlowe that would be crossing a line, perhaps sharing too much with someone not directly involved in Harmon's death.

"Maybe not," Frank said. "I bet they let him ramble. But only fools would take grief and gossip as facts."

Without a word, Glory headed to the kitchen. Marlowe followed and watched as her mother pulled out onions and carrots and began to chop them up at the counter. Glory peeled potatoes and dumped them into boiling water. Mashed potatoes were Marlowe's favorite, and Glory always made them the first night Marlowe was home after a long trip—or sometimes as a quiet apology after they'd bickered over something.

"These questions about Nora," Marlowe said. "And Harmon—"

"They're absurd," Glory said, setting down the knife and stepping forward to hug Marlowe. Glory rubbed her hands up and down Marlowe's arms before letting go. "Don't let them get to you."

Marlowe nodded and brushed at her damp cheeks.

"Go pull yourself together," Glory whispered.

Marlowe turned and headed downstairs. She couldn't explain to her mother that Ariel's questions had felt not like badgering, but more like faith, as if Nora's disappearance and Harmon's death were nothing more than a challenging puzzle that, somehow, Ariel believed Marlowe could solve.

In her bathroom, she turned on the sink and splashed cold water on her face. She straightened to face the mirror. She had long ago learned to look at her features with the detached eye of an artist. In graduate school they had taught her how to paint a self-portrait. How to know yourself so completely and yet remove yourself enough to render your own likeness honestly. For once Marlowe didn't cast an indifferent eye over the crow's feet or the lines around her mouth or the way the skin along her jaw seemed to sag in profile.

What would Nora look like now? Over the years, Marlowe would sometimes imagine conversations with her friend. She would picture Nora older, more mature, as if she had grown up along with Marlowe and was still around to dole out friendly counsel. At first, it had been easy to imagine Nora's advice. There were times in high school and college when Marlowe was able to carry out full conversations in her head.

"I love my art classes, but maybe I should do prelaw," Marlowe would wonder aloud. Frank had high expectations for all his children, and she often worried she wasn't hitting the mark.

"Are you kidding me?" Nora answered. "Your soul will shrivel up and die if you become a lawyer. You're too good to stop making art."

She remembered crossing the quad on a crisp autumn evening, after her first boyfriend told her she needed to open up more. He wanted to talk about their future but claimed Marlowe kept pulling away.

"It's not me; he's the boring one," Marlowe confessed to her imagined friend. "He was easy to talk to when we first started dating, but I can't help but feel like there must be more out there, someone more exciting."

"You're twenty!" Nora cried out. "Get rid of him and live a little."

Later, it became harder to imagine what Nora would say to Marlowe's grown-up problems. How to befriend her sisters-in-law. If she wanted kids or not. Whether she should continue illustrating children's books or consider other artistic pursuits. Eventually, she stopped summoning Nora in her mind.

Marlowe studied her face in the mirror. She closed her eyes and tried to conjure Nora again, not as she would be at thirty-six, but as she once was. Her youthful face appeared in an instant. Her unbrushed blond hair fell about her shoulders, and she gave Marlowe a sly smile. Nora raised her brows at her in the mirror, and her blue eyes danced. She was eager to hear the latest news and weigh in.

"They're asking about you," Marlowe whispered.

Nora had a way of lifting her chin and sticking her pert nose up in the air, as if she didn't care what anyone said—her opinion was the only one that mattered. She tossed her head and leaned forward, as if they were gossiping in the hayloft. "Let them talk."

Marlowe's eyes flew open. *That* Nora wasn't real. She was gone.

Nora's ghost was forever on the brink of sixteen, and when Marlowe looked in the mirror again, she was somehow shocked that she was now twenty years older.

A sudden sadness poured through her veins, weighing down her limbs. Staring into her own eyes, she recognized something old and familiar. Heartbreak. Nora had been her best friend. They'd shared every delightful little secret with each other. But Nora had kept one secret to herself. She'd never divulged where she went that night. And she'd left no clues.

Or if she had, Marlowe simply hadn't been clever enough to follow the trail. Maybe Ariel Mintz was.

When she returned to the kitchen, Frank was back in his study, and Glory had taken Enzo upstairs. Marlowe took the opportunity to open the fridge and slip her fingers around the bottle of white wine that had been opened for dinner the night before. She poured what remained into a mug, then sat by the fire. The shakiness drained out of her fingers, and the riot of emotions began to ebb. Marlowe sighed. Now she could think.

A week after Nora vanished, Enzo had pulled Marlowe aside. It was past eight, but given the time of year, the sun was still up and the tiger lilies outside the kitchen window were swaying in a gentle evening breeze.

"Marlowe, dear Marlowe, how many times have you cried today?" Enzo asked. "Have you slept at all?"

Marlowe glared at him. She could not tell her family how much she dreaded going to bed. Every night, instead of sleeping, Marlowe pictured Nora locked up in a cold basement. She pictured her friend losing weight and growing hopeless. She pictured a faceless man doing awful things to her. And in the darkest hour of each night, Marlowe faced the truth: It should have been her. Marlowe wished with every bone in her body that she'd been the one who had been taken.

If Nora had been left behind, she would have been far better at handling the panic and seeking the truth. She would have demanded that Brierley do more than just slump his shoulders as he trudged around pointing out that it was hard to determine anything without a body, without any sightings of a car, without drops of blood. Nora would see whatever Marlowe had been missing all these years. Marlowe was useless; she was trying her hardest, and she couldn't do anything to help. To her unskilled eye, it was as if Nora had been swallowed up by the night, and Marlowe was too stupid and timid to save her friend. As penance for failing Nora, Marlowe would torture herself by imagining, in extreme detail, a man grasping Marlowe's arms until they were mottled with bruises, tying her up in some basement, abusing her. For the brief periods when Marlowe did sleep, the visions came to life in her dreams. She wept when she woke to find she was still in the Gray House.

"Pain is part of life," Enzo said. "But sometimes it must be numbed."

Then Enzo pulled a bottle of red wine from behind the bread box and poured some into a tumbler.

"Swallow what you can, Marlowe," Enzo said. "It will help you sleep."

Marlowe took the glass and choked on the first sip.

"Just swallow as much as you can, that's a good Marlowe. Then clean the glass and put it away, yes?" Enzo patted her head.

It took her a few minutes, but Marlowe managed to drink it all. For the first time since Nora had vanished, the sharp pain loosened its grip. Marlowe could finally hear herself think. It was a good thing, she realized. She would never find Nora if she let her emotions drown out her thoughts. That night she slept, and she did not dream.

All these years later, Marlowe was well practiced. She gulped the wine and waited, running through everything Ariel had said earlier that day. The detective had not dismissed Marlowe. She had listened. She had not argued when Marlowe claimed Nora couldn't have run away. That was something different. Marlowe reached for that and held tight.

She wasn't a child anymore. She knew exactly how to navigate her fears and emotions. She didn't have to torture herself by composing her own nightmares. Instead, Marlowe could do it right this time.

A log cracked, and the dancing flames seemed to burn away Marlowe's fears. She took a sip of her wine. "This is a second chance," Marlowe whispered.

She could just make out the reply: "It's fate," Nora whispered back.

# FOURTEEN

**THE SLED**
**Thursday, December 28, 1995**

The toboggan veered to the right. Through the spray of powdery snow, Marlowe saw the grove of apple trees ahead. She screamed and launched herself sideways, flipping the sled and sending everyone careening headfirst into a deep bank of snow.

Marlowe rolled over and wiped the snow out of her eyes. Her face was so frozen she could hardly feel her cheeks.

Nate jumped up and stomped his feet to dislodge the clumps of snow clinging to his pants and jacket. "Enough is enough, Marlowe!" he yelled. "Just stay on the sled!"

They had been doing runs on the sloped North Field all day, trying to navigate the wooden toboggan down the steep hill with all four of them aboard.

Nora staggered back up the hill behind Marlowe, her blue knit hat covered in a layer of snow, her cheeks bright red. "Seriously, Marlowe, that was our best run yet." She grinned.

"But if we crash into one of those apple trees, we'll all break our necks and die! Mom said that happened to someone she knew growing up." Marlowe groaned.

Henry threw his arms out toward the orchard at the bottom of the hill. "They're a thousand yards away!"

Marlowe balled her ice-cold fingers inside her mittens and peered down the slope. Henry had a point. From where they had crashed halfway down the hill, the snow-covered branches were minuscule.

"Don't worry, Mar, we'll have time to jump off closer to the bottom," Nate said. "Trust me."

"Okay, fine, but I don't see why I have to be so close to the front," Marlowe said. "It's too scary, and I'm taller than Henry. I should sit behind him."

"Just close your eyes!" Nora advised.

"Henry and I have to be in the back," Nate said. "The sled has to be anchored."

Earlier that morning their father had given them scientific counsel on the physics of sledding: The heavier riders had to sit in the back, with the smallest person up front, feet jammed firmly beneath the curved prow. That meant Nora sat up front, which she didn't mind at all. The faster the sled went, the more she squealed with joy. Marlowe had a few inches on Henry, but she was skinnier, according to Nate's calculations, so she was in the second position, with a full view of any dangerous obstacles in their path as they hurtled down the slope. Henry, on the other hand, was tucked safely between his older siblings, blissfully unaware of the panic Marlowe felt as the sled went racing over the slick, icy powder straight toward the trees.

At the top of the hill, they paused at the hedgerow to catch their breath. Behind them, the woods were hushed and still, while below them, the land unfolded its pristine pearly skirts. Six fresh inches of snow had fallen overnight, and the white was broken only by the vivid red of the Gallagher barn and the green pine trees by the road. Though the hill was on the Fishers' property, Frank let the Gallagher brothers use the slanted field, as well as the smaller field to the south of the Gray House, for hay in the summertime. "For tax-break reasons," he'd told his children, "Actively farmed land receives exemptions." The even layer of cut hay left covering the ground after the harvest every season made the winter sledding conditions all the better.

A puff of smoke emerged from the Gray House's chimney. Marlowe wanted to get in a good run as much as they all did, but soon she would start to yearn for hot chocolate by the fire. She longed to spread out her new acrylics on the kitchen table and try to capture the snowy scene on paper. Ivory paint mixed with something else to capture the glistening sparkle of the snow, she mused.

Nate settled down into the back, the toes of his boots locked against the small ridge, and Henry threw himself between Nate's legs. Marlowe took her own place, rolling her eyes as Henry jammed his knees into her sides and gripped the back of her coat in his fists. That was part of the problem. Without any sides to the sleigh, Henry was the only thing keeping her on. Nora scooted backward against Marlowe's chest, and Marlowe wrapped her arm around her friend's torso.

"Ready?" Nate called from the back.

"Wait." Nora wrapped her hands up in the looped rope and then nodded. "Ready!"

"Prow to the garden!" Nate shouted as he wiggled the sled loose, pointing it downhill.

"Yes, Captain!" Henry shrieked in excitement.

The sledding had reawakened the childish games of pretend they used to play, where they were treasure hunters aboard a stolen pirate ship. Marlowe and Nora would be high schoolers in the next year and had left such games behind, and Nate was certainly too old, but at twelve, Henry was still clinging to his childhood. It was going to have claw marks when he finally let go.

Henry could have this day. They all could, she supposed.

"Man the sails!" she yelled, laughing and squeezing her eyes shut as tightly as possible.

"Full speed ahead!" Nate shouted the command as he pushed them off. The toboggan inched down the slope and then picked up speed, going faster and faster.

"Lean portside!" Nate hollered, and they all leaned to the left. Marlowe whimpered as her shoulder dropped almost parallel to the snow, and then screamed as Henry pulled her back to the center. She cried out again as they hit a bump, and opened her eyes, immediately catching a blizzard of icy powder in the face as they whizzed downhill. They held on to each other's coats, leaning left and then right, trying not to tip over.

Nate was shouting at them to hold the course; they were bound straight as an arrow toward Glory's garden and the flat patio to the side of the house. They just had to dodge the small green garden shed.

They were going too fast, but Marlowe knew it was too late to bail. She clenched her eyes shut again and screamed. Nora, having at last reached the limits of her daring, shrieked as well. Marlowe was pretty sure she heard a fearful yelp escape from Nate as they shot over the bottom of the hill and flew through the garden, missing the shed by just a few feet. The sled clipped a snow-covered bush and finally slowed down to a glide between the house and the orchard.

As it drew to a stop, they all tumbled off. Marlowe leapt up, exhilarated that she had survived. Nora rolled around in the snow, laughing, and Nate pumped his fist in the air.

"That was it," he said. "The perfect run!"

Henry tried to stand up but toppled over like a puppy in the snow. He was quivering from the adrenaline rush.

"Come on, young one, let me help you up," Nora teased, hooking her arm under his and hauling him upright. Henry's chubby, wind-chapped cheeks burned redder. But Nora smiled and patted him on the back, and he wrapped her in one of his sweet, brotherly hugs.

They celebrated with grilled cheese sandwiches and hot chocolates before Nate wandered off to his room with a book, and Henry sprawled out on his stomach in the living room to do a jigsaw puzzle. When it was time for Nora to return home, Marlowe bundled up in order to walk part of the way with her, as she always did, stealing a few extra moments of alone time together. Near the road, Nora tugged Marlowe toward the Gallagher barn.

"Quick," Nora whispered.

Marlowe didn't hesitate to follow; the hayloft was their favorite place to trade stories about school and share secrets. Tom and Dave Gallagher had been scarce that holiday season, mourning the loss of their brother Leroy, so she didn't fear getting caught as they ran under the boughs of the chestnut tree and snuck through the small opening between the barn's old doors, which hung slightly askew.

As they slipped into the barn, Marlowe shivered at the memory of the last time they'd seen Leroy. She remembered it being the first weekend in November, mere days before Leroy's death. She and Nora had spent all Sunday afternoon in the loft, swapping stories about their separate Halloweens and giggling. When the setting sun was casting only a dim light and the air was almost unbearably chilly, Marlowe knew it was time to run back to the Gray House for the drive back to the city. Still, they lay on their stomachs for another minute together before peering through the hay drop. Leroy emerged from the office and moved through the barn aisle, his bowlegged stride causing him to sway as he moved.

"Hello? Anyone there?" he asked. Crouched behind the bales, Marlowe and Nora turned to each other and clapped their hands over their mouths, eyes gleaming with mischievous delight. A girlish whisper or footstep was easily written off as a mouse or a squirrel in the rafters, or the old bones of the barn creaking in the wind. Leroy walked on.

Marlowe now fixed her gaze on Nora's blue coat, so vivid and real in the moment. They scrambled up the ladder and climbed over the bales until they were perched in their spot.

"I have to tell you something," Nora said. "I couldn't in the house, in case Henry or Nate were spying."

Marlowe nodded in understanding. They had suffered a disastrous humiliation in September, when they shared detailed descriptions of their respective crushes, unaware that Nate was listening outside the door. He and Henry still chanted the names whenever they wanted to get a rise out of Marlowe or Nora.

"I got my period!" Nora whispered.

"When?" Marlowe almost jumped off the hay bale. "*Now?*"

"No, it was two weeks ago, but I couldn't tell you over the phone!" Nora shook her head. "It didn't hurt as much as I thought, and it lasted four days. My mom made me use a pad, but I hated it, and I told her I want to try tampons next time."

"Oh my God." Marlowe leaned back against a bale, stunned by all the information.

"Thirteen is a good age to get it," Nora said, with all the wisdom of a newly flowered woman. "Not too old, not too young."

"My mom didn't get hers until she was sixteen." Marlowe sighed. "I'll probably be waiting forever like a freak."

"Well, that's the thing," Nora said. "No one really has to know; I thought everyone would be able to tell I got it, but it's not like that."

"Good." Marlowe nodded, relieved that Nora had been the one to go first. Though Marlowe was five months older and a few inches taller, Nora was braver.

As Nora recounted her momentous four days, Marlowe's mind began to wobble around this new imbalance between them. She decided it was a good thing: With a guide like Nora, she knew she would be ready to take the leap into womanhood too. They climbed down the ladder and stepped into the orange light glinting through the windows, when inspiration struck.

Marlowe dashed over to the neat row of pitchforks, hoes, and shovels leaning against the wall near the knife-sharpening wheel.

"Let's move them," Marlowe whispered. "Just a bit—to commemorate this day."

Nora caught on at once. "Of course!"

Marlowe flipped every shovel so the blades were facing up, and Nora moved a row of empty milk pails from one side of the aisle to the other, then she tipped over a bucket of dried yellow corn kernels, scattering them across the floor.

"It will look like the wind did it," she said.

"Exactly!"

Their hearts racing with all the thrills of the day, they dashed through the barn doors, sprinted across the smaller cow pen, and disappeared behind the thick row of trees that bordered the Gallagher property.

Huge crystalline snowflakes were swirling down again. Nora held out her tongue and caught one. In no time, their footprints would disappear without a trace.

The girls weaved through the trees and came out onto the road. If anyone spotted them now, they would appear to be the picture of innocence, as pure as freshly fallen snow.

# TUESDAY

**NOVEMBER 27, 2018**

# FIFTEEN

It wasn't a long walk, but she had to drive. Marlowe told her parents she was going to town to run some errands—pulling away in her blue Toyota RAV4 was a necessary part of the deceit. She passed the weekenders' houses, which had grown larger every year, their expansions and renovations signaling money and permanence. But in between those were the older homes, humble and unadorned, their owners holding fast to a bygone way of life as they watched their town change around them.

The Miller house had never been much to look at, bordering on dingy, but there was a time when a lived-in warmth made it feel welcoming. Now it was weathered and left to decay. One more thing Marlowe had to feel guilty about.

She noticed the old Ford F-150 still in the front yard as she eased onto the shoulder next to the Millers' mailbox. The truck's paint had faded to a dull salmon color, but its broad grill still resembled a rakish grin. The front porch of the house looked like it could collapse on itself at any moment. A layer of dirt and grime crept up from the ground onto the exterior walls. Beside the house, among the scant patches of snow, Marlowe spotted a pile of branches that Mr. Miller, an old man now, must have spent all afternoon gathering.

She tapped on the glass panes of the front door and then leaned over to squint through the window. She could see into the hall, which was lined with Damen's boots, a few pieces of car equipment, and—she could hardly believe it—Nora's dirty Converse sneakers.

There was a stirring from within, and then Damen's stooped frame appeared.

He opened the door and regarded Marlowe with a cool gaze.

"Hello, Mr. Miller." Marlowe forced a smile.

"Marlowe." Damen opened the door wider and led Marlowe down the hall and into the cramped kitchen. A few mugs and dishes were piled in the sink. Through the door to the living room, Marlowe could see a corner of the lumpy brown couch, a coat tossed over the arm.

Marlowe set a Tupperware container of brownies on the counter. Damen looked puzzled by the gesture, as if the paper-thin facade of kindness was beneath her.

"I know it's been a while, but I just wanted to check in with you, what with the unfortunate news of the last couple days," Marlowe said; she saw no point in beating around the bush.

Damen raised his shaggy head, and instead of looking him in the eye, Marlowe gazed at the gray hair that hung behind his ear, and his belly straining against his flannel shirt. He seemed a lifetime away from the neat, well-mannered mechanic he once was.

"Tragic," he said, considering his words. "But if you're here to talk about Nora, I'm not interested. I know better than to get my hopes up."

"Well, let's talk about you instead. How have you been?" Marlowe suddenly felt stupid. She and Damen hadn't spoken in ages, and the detectives' line of questioning made that painfully clear.

Damen threw his arms wide, gesturing around the kitchen, indicating the state of it. "I've been alone," he said curtly.

She could picture his nightly routine: a frozen meal, a cheap beer, and whatever swill was on TV. Or maybe he sat in silence, muttering to himself.

Marlowe hung her head, staring at the chipped linoleum. She felt like bolting out the front door at that very moment but found the resolve to try again. "The detective who spoke to me, Ariel Mintz, she seemed competent. And she believes this Gallagher situation could lead to answers about Nora."

"I only want justice," Damen said. "Is that too much to ask?" He gazed out the window. When the glass was that dirty, it made the whole countryside appear stained. "And, anyway, I mostly talked with the other one. Vance."

Marlowe waited for him to continue, but he just kept staring. As awkward as the conversation was, she needed to know what he thought about Harmon—and any theories he was harboring that he might have shared with Ben Vance.

"Well, what do you think happened to Harmon Gallagher?"

"Those dogs ran straight toward that barn," Damen said. "I always remembered that."

"The bloodhounds," Marlowe said.

"They were brought in the day after, right before the larger search party started. The police claimed it was best to give the dogs a go, before a load of people stomped all over the land and confused the scent. You remember that?"

"I remember." She had the specific memory of Damen holding out Nora's pillowcase to the dog handlers. It was the greatest moment of hope she'd felt since Nora vanished. Here was something finite and scientific. These dogs had been trained. They would track her. They could detect things humans could not. After sniffing the pillowcase, they ran toward the trash bins and circled the area, and then one of the hounds lifted his snout to the air and howled. As a unit, they tore across the street, looped around to the open barn doors, and dashed up and down the aisle, pausing to sniff, occasionally running outside and then back in again.

"But it amounted to nothing," Damen said. "There wasn't a damn thing in that barn."

He continued staring out the window, eyes glassy, like an old sage waiting for a revelation. And then his lolling head snapped to attention.

"Tell me, Marlowe," he said. "How much time did you two spend in that loft?"

"I've already told you this," she said.

"Tell me again." He smiled placidly. "I'm getting old."

"A lot." Marlowe twisted her hands together. "We started when we were twelve. We used to go up there every weekend."

"What did you do?"

"We just talked." Marlowe chewed her bottom lip. "Sometimes spied on the Gallagher brothers when they were still around."

It had been embarrassing to confess to their childish tricks in front of Detective Brierley all those years ago, and it wasn't any easier now.

"Did your brothers know about this? Did they ever hang out with her up there?"

"It was *our* place."

"Of course it was."

All the hours they spent up there, running down the aisle, scraping their knees on the rough rungs of the ladder. Skin, hair, blood, secrets. They had sprinkled pieces of themselves all over that barn.

"You and your family," Damen said, his voice turned low. "Messing around on land that wasn't yours." Marlowe tensed at the throb of fury in his words. "Stirring up trouble with those Gallaghers, getting Nora caught up in it. And if that boy knew something, now he's dead too."

Marlowe had her answer now. Damen had told a deluded, jumbled version of this story to Ariel and Ben. Her chest tightened, but she pushed back: "The Gallaghers wouldn't have done anything to Nora. They were never angry with us."

Damen scoffed. "You were just a kid."

"Mr. Miller." Marlowe was treading on dangerous ground, confronting him like this. "What exactly do you think happened?"

He grunted and turned his body away from the question, shaking his head. Marlowe's pulse hammered against her throat.

"I don't know," he said at last. "But someone does."

He kept her sneakers waiting for her in the hall, but he was beyond hoping that his daughter would return. That loss had hardened in his mind. What still haunted him was that he didn't know why.

"I wonder what Nora would look like," Damen said. "Sometimes I see you, Marlowe, and it's as if you've barely aged. It's only when I look at the old pictures that I see all the changes."

He believed she had changed for the worse. He didn't have to spell it out for her. In the beginning, when they grieved together, Damen would tell Marlowe lots of things. His favorite stories about Nora, and she would share hers. Jennifer would join in with anecdotes.

"I bet she would have looked just like Jennifer," Marlowe said.

Damen flinched, and Marlowe felt a jolt of anxiety.

"I'm sorry." She reached out her hand but stopped it in the middle of the counter. "This is hard for you, I know."

Damen straightened up and swung his head back toward her. "Tell the detectives everything this time. Tell them everything."

It was Marlowe's turn to wince.

"I will. I have." She refused to suggest that maybe he was the one who had hidden something.

"I'd better go." Marlowe turned back toward the hall.

Damen followed her to the front door.

She walked down the steps, past the pile of cordwood that reached her shoulder. If the wind blew north that night, she'd be able to smell the smoke from Damen's fire. Damen stood in the doorway as she pulled away, and Marlowe wondered if he was thinking of another car and another day; she wondered if he cursed the moment her father pulled up to introduce himself to the neighbors, with Marlowe in the back seat.

She hadn't been gone long enough to complete any errands, so she pulled over before the road curved home. The memory of the bloodhounds was dulled and warped by time and nerves and, possibly, the couple of drinks she had every evening. In this case, how different was she from Damen, really? Images of those chaotic days started rushing in as Marlowe sat on the soft shoulder of the road. The hounds on point. Henry kneeling beside one that the handler said he could pet. Marlowe heard him whispering into the dog's soft spotted ear: *You'll find her, you'll find her.* The inconsolable tears that began each day at dusk—the moment Marlowe realized her friend would be gone for another night.

# SIXTEEN

The afternoon stretched on with Marlowe anticipating a knock at the front door from the detectives. She pictured Damen Miller digging out their card from where he had shoved it in a drawer, dialing their number as her car vanished from sight. He would tell them the Fisher daughter was bothering him—that the family was acting strange. He knew they were hiding something.

Her parents weren't acting strange at all. They sat down for a quiet dinner. Enzo stayed upstairs. He was sleeping almost fifteen hours a day, like a cat. Marlowe picked at the shepherd's pie. It was her dad's favorite. Back when Glory was a young, overwhelmed wife, Enzo had taught her how to cook dishes far more elegant than the simple fare she'd grown up with. Though Glory was wealthy enough that she didn't need to cook for herself, she wanted to be a talented hostess to impress the New York elite Frank moved with—a social class to which she was determined to seamlessly belong.

Marlowe crumpled the napkin in her lap and then took a quick sip of wine.

"Dad," Marlowe said. "Did you know you were going to buy the Gallagher property when Leroy died?"

"Marlowe." Her father's head jerked back, his fork suspended in the air.

"I just don't understand Harmon's threats," Marlowe said. "Or this so-called feud."

"There was no feud." Frank set his fork down and folded his hands together, speaking slowly, as if he were explaining something to a child. "Harmon was disturbed."

"They all were," Glory whispered. "But at least Leroy, Tom, and Dave did their best."

Leroy's best was a rope wrapped around a rafter. When she was young, Marlowe had thought it was such a horrific avenue. It happened in November of 1995, when the Fishers were in the city. Glory and Frank didn't believe in watering things down for their children. It was important that Marlowe and her brothers knew the truth of the world.

"He hung himself in the barn," Frank had said.

Marlowe's shock was mirrored in Nate's face. She remembered Henry's gasp, and repeatedly asking, "Why would Leroy do that? Why was he so sad?"

"Suicide is a weakness of character," Frank had said. "There are other ways to deal with one's illnesses." His pragmatism often teetered on the edge of callousness, and Marlowe had learned long ago that his sense of compassion had limits, especially when it came to matters of personal suffering.

"It's a shame," Frank had continued. "Leroy could have gotten help."

Thinking back, Marlowe could recall Leroy's sadness. It was palpable. She had seen it with her own eyes, felt it in his silences. Even before his death, he had already been a ghost. She wished she understood where all this sadness started.

Marlowe blinked, pushing away the memory, and the dim light of the dining room came back into focus. The clink of silverware, the scrape of Glory's chair. Frank reached for his glass and took a long sip, his expression unchanged.

"Nobody planned for it," he said. "But I let Dave know that I was there to help after Tom also went. He needed the money, but he wasn't ready to sell."

It wasn't long—a mere four months—after Leroy's suicide that Tom Gallagher swallowed enough pills to join his brother in eternal rest. Once again, Frank and Glory told their children. Frank seemed at a loss for how to explain it. Leroy was always silent and sad, but Tom was so steady. He did the hay in the summer, took the cows out, brought them back in. Climbed up on his tractor, climbed down. He made it through one last winter and, at the brink of spring, gave up.

Marlowe didn't like thinking of it now. Tom was different from Leroy. Tom had talked to them when they were kids, joked that Marlowe would be taller than her mother, chuckled over their games, and shown them the Bend.

There was no point in pressing Frank any further. It didn't matter why or when he decided to buy the Gallagher land. It wasn't a crime to want something. Frank Fisher hadn't done anything nefarious. He had simply waited them out.

After helping Glory clear the dishes, Frank headed to his study. Marlowe pulled a stool out from the island, facing the sink. It had taken years of plotting, but Glory and Frank eventually knocked out the back wall of the original kitchen, expanding it to twice its size. They were able to fit a double-top stove, all the cabinet space Glory could possibly want, and the island with a cavernous farmhouse sink. Glory was bent over it, the sleeves of her button-down rolled up, hot suds up to her elbows. If Marlowe tried to help, Glory would nudge her aside. Only Glory knew how to do it right. Only Glory knew exactly how to load the sleek German dishwasher that she had spent months researching before commissioning an extravagant overseas freight service to deliver and install the unit.

As Marlowe watched Glory scrub, her mind drifted back to an earlier version of her mother, before the farm, before Frank, before all of this.

Glory ran away once. At twenty, tired of scraping by on a struggling farm, she boarded a train to New York with a carpet bag. She took a typing course, shared an apartment with three other girls, and became a secretary. It was 1976, and the city was both thrilling and dangerous. She used to joke that she didn't even know she had legs until she arrived in Manhattan.

Glory kept a framed photo in her closet of her and her roommates, arms slung around each other, dressed for work on a city sidewalk. In it, Glory wore a plaid skirt with a matching blazer and a crisp white blouse—clothes her mother never let her wear on the farm.

Frank had told the story of their meeting enough times that Marlowe could picture it. He was a successful lawyer, and she was the secretary who could type three times faster than anyone else in the office.

Glory wasn't a great beauty, she didn't come from an esteemed family, and she wasn't particularly well read or sophisticated. But she was sharp, efficient, and had a certain world-weariness that set her apart. Frank grew up in Boston, courting girls from well-heeled families like his own. At Princeton, he took out girls from Smith and Bryn Mawr on the weekends. Girls who played golf or squash and could quote poetry and owned beautiful hats.

He didn't realize it until he met Glory, but she was exactly what he had been looking for.

"She walks tall," he'd say. Whenever he described her, he always quoted Catullus—the line about a statuesque woman who, for all her elegance, lacks a grain of salt. "Glory," Frank liked to say, "was salt of the earth."

Glory claimed her mother had told her once, "You'll never be beautiful, so be smart instead."

Marlowe wondered if, when Glory met Frank—handsome, rich, and twelve years older—that voice was echoing in her head. *Be smart, Glory. Be smart.*

They married within a year. Frank's career took off. By the time Nate was born, they were discussing a country home. It was Glory who wanted something near where she grew up—not too close, but within driving distance. Not for her family. She visited them, of course, but Marlowe knew that wasn't the reason. She hated the farm enough to leave, but something had always pulled her back. She loved the land, but she wanted it on her own terms. She didn't let it slip away from her like the other dairy farmers did. She wasn't capable of such resignation.

Marlowe watched the sponge raking across the pan, held fast in Glory's red-fingered grip. She ran the water scalding hot, always barehanded.

"Mom." Her voice cut through the silence. "What did Harmon say? What was he threatening?"

"Nothing." Glory rinsed the pan and set it aside, reaching for the next dish. "He was pretending he knew something, but there weren't any specifics."

"Do you think that Brierley missed something back then?" The question had been bouncing through Marlowe's head all day. "Something important."

"That man missed many things," Glory said. "Or else he would have found her, wouldn't he?"

Glory no doubt believed that if she were a detective in charge of the case, she would manage it with perfect precision. She bent to set the dish in the rack, then closed the dishwasher door with a smooth, practiced motion.

"This isn't good for you, Marlowe," Glory said. "Dwelling on all this."

"I'm not *dwelling*." Marlowe slid her finger over the condensation on her glass. "Someone has been killed. Don't you think we should be talking about it? The detectives seem pretty interested in what we have to say."

"And so we will answer them—and that's it."

"But Nora—" Marlowe stopped, unsure how to finish the sentence.

"I hate speaking about that night. It's not just because of what happened to her, but because of what it did to you." Glory shook her head. "I am the lucky one; I got to keep my daughter. I don't have the right to complain, and yet I watched you fall apart and for a moment I thought I was going to lose you too. It broke you, Marlowe. Don't think I didn't see every crack. Don't think I didn't wish every day I could somehow bear the pain for you."

Her mother folded a floral dishrag into a neat rectangle and hung it on the oven handle. Marlowe had seen Glory cry only once, when looking at an old photo of her father years after he died. But Glory had untold depth. Marlowe knew it was there.

"I survived," Marlowe said. "I put myself back together. Maybe not perfectly, but I did."

"But that girl," Glory continued, a pained expression contorting her face. "I don't know what was happening with her, but I was concerned—about Nora's path, but also the road she might lead you down."

"What do you mean?" A defensive urge pinched at Marlowe's throat. Nora wasn't a bad influence with loose morals. Her parents should have known that. They had watched Nora as a child.

"I know what it's like to grow up out here. How small everything can feel." Glory released a heavy sigh. "And for some young people, that feeling—being trapped—it gets to them. They rebel. Pick up vices. Act recklessly."

"You think Nora was upset with her life?" Marlowe's stomach tightened at the insinuation that Nora had gotten involved with drugs or bad people. "We were only teenagers. We were happy."

Glory studied her face and then rounded the counter and placed her hand, warm and slightly damp, on Marlowe's cheek. "Go to sleep. This will be over soon."

# SEVENTEEN

## THE BIRTH
## Sunday, March 31, 1996

Marlowe, Nora, and Henry sat around the dining table in the Gray House with their textbooks propped open. Homework: a dull but necessary activity on Sunday afternoons. Marlowe was holding her yellow highlighter poised over a slim copy of *Romeo and Juliet* when Glory appeared in the wide archway to the kitchen, jacket in hand.

"Girls, there's something to see over mountain. Marlowe, you can finish reading on the train back to the city," Glory said as she slipped into her coat and began to button it up the front. "Let's go."

"Thank God." Nora flipped her history textbook closed. "I can't read any more dates and names."

Henry started to rise, but Glory shook her head.

"You have a math test tomorrow, Henry," Glory said. "You need all the studying time you can get."

Nora tittered at Henry's indignant face, and Marlowe shot him a smug look. Henry was awful at math, and Glory had his syllabus and test dates memorized. No son of hers was going to fail pre-algebra. That very weekend, Nate had stayed behind in the city for an SAT prep course. Marlowe received weekly reminders from Glory that next year, when she started high school, her grades couldn't slip.

"Over mountain" was Glory's home turf, a few towns over. The girls didn't know exactly where they were going or what they were about to see, but they didn't care. No one ever asked Glory too many questions. Marlowe and Nora were happy to chat away in the back seat of the car, their schoolwork already long forgotten. They paid little attention to the scenery as they drove through town and turned onto a tree-lined road that twisted through the countryside. At the top of the pass, the landscape opened up to reveal a patchwork of fields and pastures dotted with horses and cows. Every now and then Glory nodded at a run-down farm and recited the family's name with bits of old gossip.

"The Smiths," she said as they passed a small house at the bottom of a hill. "Oldest son was an addict."

"That way takes you to the Taylor place," she said at a fork in the road. "My brother dated a Taylor way back when. He broke hearts before he gained all that weight."

"Bob Martin had a heart attack decades ago," Glory said, as they passed an abandoned pole barn. "Son was away in the army when it happened."

Marlowe and Nora nodded but did not respond. They were accustomed to Glory's cynical catalog of life's disappointments.

At last, the car rumbled over a graded gravel lane toward a simple whitewashed farmhouse with a gray barn behind it. Marlowe and Nora, their interest now growing, spied a couple of girls wandering in and out of the house, tending to various chores. They wore long dresses and bonnets.

"I think they must be Mennonites," Nora whispered. "You know, those religious people who don't believe women should wear pants. They're probably not even allowed to watch TV." Glory brought the car to a halt alongside a wooden fence and got out just as an overalled farmer with a bright red beard approached.

"Hello, Ernie. What's the status?" Glory asked the farmer. Marlowe was confused. She'd never met or seen this man before, but her mother's connections to people in the valley never failed to surprise her. Glory was an encyclopedia of old gossip, but she never seemed to talk to anyone local. It was sometimes easy to forget she was from the area.

Ernie scratched his head. "Just got her out of the barn. I'm about to use the truck." He gestured for them to follow him through the muddy field. Marlowe stepped forward, wading through a puddle of spring rain, and tugged gently on Glory's sleeve.

"What's this about, Mom?" she asked.

"You'll see."

She and Nora walked next to each other, their arms grazing. They could hear moaning sounds as they rounded the corner of the barn and craned their necks to see a large brown heifer. Marlowe took another step closer. It was then that she noticed the tiny delicate hoof, black as onyx, sticking out of the heifer's hindquarters and the blood staining the cow's back legs.

"It's giving birth," Nora said, with sudden understanding. Marlowe scrunched up her nose. She and her brothers had learned about how children were made at a young age. They had asked, and Glory had answered, with all the clinical forthrightness of a girl who grew up on a farm. Still, Marlowe hadn't known that cows gave birth standing up. She had never witnessed any of the Gallagher cows giving birth.

Glory turned to look at them. "The calf is breach."

Ernie tied a piece of rope to the calf's foot. Then he tied the other end to the back of a faded green truck. He got behind the wheel and turned on the engine. He moved slowly, so very slowly. Too slow, Marlowe thought, at first. He needed to accelerate forward faster and just yank the baby out, as quick as he could. The mother let out a moan, low and agonizing, and Marlowe realized Ernie was trying to be gentle for the heifer's sake. He was giving the mother's body the time to open up a little more, if she could.

Marlowe clutched Nora's hand and fixed her eyes on the calf's little hoof. Strangely, she itched to sketch the distinct cloven shape.

They all watched as the baby's second hoof slipped out and then its body dropped in a wet bundle. Nora let out a small gasp, equal parts shock and delight, but Marlowe stood silent and still.

He was tiny and precious and damp.

The heifer cried out in pain, and only then did she slump over, her knees and the heft of her stomach hitting the muddy ground with a damp thwacking sound.

On the drive back to the Gray House, Glory surveyed the girls in the rearview mirror as she kept both hands firmly on the wheel.

"That's the type of thing girls need to see," Glory said.

Marlowe turned to see Nora raise one brow. Of course Glory would believe in scare tactics as birth control. She needn't have bothered, Marlowe thought, rolling her eyes; neither she nor Nora were interested in dating.

"Any questions?" Glory asked.

Marlowe thought of the poor heifer's bloodstained legs, but she was too afraid to ask if it would survive.

# WEDNESDAY

## NOVEMBER 28, 2018

# EIGHTEEN

When Henry stepped through the front door early on Wednesday morning, Glory had just put the bacon on. She stood at the stove, prim in her turtleneck, wielding a spatula like a baton, while Frank nursed his mug of coffee at the head of the table.

"Smells great, Mom," Henry said, taking a seat beside his father, as if he hadn't been away. Across the table, Marlowe cracked open a can of seltzer and winced at the sound. She had woken up with dry skin and chapped lips. Winter air and heaters had always plagued her.

"An old friend from the DA reached out to a contact in Poughkeepsie," Henry said, stirring milk into his coffee. "They're pursuing Harmon's harebrained intimidation schemes, but they have other suspects. Harmon was tied up with some dodgy people and owed money. They're tracking down alibis, following protocol."

"As I thought," Frank said.

"My friend couldn't get any details, but looks like it'll blow over soon enough," Henry said.

"Did he say anything about Ariel or Ben?" Marlowe wanted to know the detectives' reputation. If they were good, or at least better than Brierley.

"They're lightweights, eager to prove themselves," Henry said and shrugged.

"Well, they can prove themselves by wrapping this up quickly so we can enjoy the holidays," Glory said. "I was thinking of getting a tree this week and decorating when the kids are all here."

Marlowe was happy to excuse herself from the empty conversation about Christmas and children and gifts to help Henry carry breakfast up to Enzo. Clutching his mug of coffee, she leaned against the doorframe of Enzo's bedroom while he smiled up at the surprise visitor. Henry fussed over propping him up with pillows.

If anyone would be willing to talk about Nora, it would be Henry. He had felt it deeply when Nora disappeared. For over a month, Marlowe had seen him tearing up over breakfast while their mother patted his back.

"The detectives think it could be connected to Nora," Marlowe murmured. "Did your friend hear anything about that?"

Henry turned to Marlowe with an expression she knew all too well: pity.

"What could they possibly find?" Henry asked. "It was so long ago."

"They could find lots of things." Marlowe heard how she sounded like a defensive child. "Ariel Mintz said they can find things just by asking around; you know Brierley didn't question a ton of people besides us. And they have better technology now."

Henry shrugged. "The sergeant will only entertain an investigation like this for so long. He's not going to waste resources on a wild-goose chase."

"What if Damen said something misleading to them?"

"Marlowe." Henry sighed and then seemed to lose his train of thought.

"Maybe it's worth hearing him out."

"Leave that poor man alone," Henry said firmly. "After all this time, I'm sure he just wants some closure, like we all do. But I don't suspect it's coming."

He sat in the chair beside Enzo's bed and watched as the old man lifted a spoonful of eggs to his mouth. Henry was beginning to sound like Nate—playacting as the voice of reason.

"It's not about him," Marlowe said. "It's about Nora, who deserves closure."

"You're generous to her in memory," Henry said. A faint smile came to him then. "Don't you remember how it bothered you that she always had to be the center of attention? You were like her sidekick, helping her get ready for dates, going along with all her plans."

"You're oversimplifying things, as usual."

"Come on, Marlowe. She always went after what she wanted. She was—bolder."

"And I was more cautious, fine. But that doesn't mean we weren't equals."

"I remember homecoming. You spent hours doing her hair," Henry said.

"And I remember Nora praising me when she looked in the mirror. The way her body relaxed, and how grateful she was to have me with her."

"You didn't even go to the dance."

"I don't expect you to know what that time is like for a teenage girl," Marlowe said with some defiance.

"So you don't think she was more concerned about making a good impression on Sean Hastings?"

"He was just a casual boyfriend. I was her best friend. She came running home to tell me about the dance afterward. Honestly, I think she enjoyed telling me about homecoming more than the dance itself."

"You really believe that?" His tone was not accusatory; it had an air of genuine curiosity.

"We had different personalities," Marlowe said. "That didn't lessen our friendship."

"You were different; you were never nasty, Mar, but she could be." Henry frowned. "Cruel, almost."

Marlowe was puzzled as to why he would bring this up. Nora was gone, but it seemed like he was still harboring a grudge.

"Not to you, never to you," Henry said. "But she used to tease me."

"We all teased you, Henry."

"Not like her." Henry's brows drew together, and despite the hint of gray in his hair, Marlowe saw the little boy again, crying over his cereal. "Her words always had a bite to them. She made me feel like she wanted to push me out and replace me. I always thought she was envious. Because I was a Fisher, and she wasn't."

"I remember how she teased," Marlowe said. "But I also remember other things. She listened to you when Nate and I brushed you aside. You used to hug her all the time when you were younger."

Henry swallowed. The grooves on his forehead were as deep as tire tracks in spring mud. Marlowe couldn't believe this had once been that chubby-cheeked boy.

"I think you loved her just as much as I did," Marlowe whispered. "I think you were as heartbroken as me when she was gone. And you thought of all her flaws over and over to get through the pain."

Marlowe had nearly forgotten that Enzo was in the room with them, struggling over his plate of eggs. He seemed tuned out of their conversation, but even in his old age, he was still alert to the tension between them. Henry adjusted his blanket, and Enzo blinked his watery blue eyes and peered up at the siblings.

144

"You must take care of each other," Enzo said. "Out in those woods, collecting stones."

Marlowe bit her lip as Henry's shoulders slumped lower. Enzo was parroting phrases of the past, thinking about that last summer they had all been together. Their father had envisioned the stone wall built over on the newly purchased Gallagher property. He wanted it to line the northern edge of the Flats, where the river emerged from the swamp. And Enzo announced that they would be the ones to build it. Nate lit up at the idea and instantly started musing about where they would find the best rocks.

"It is not easy to build a stone wall; it takes much time," Enzo said.

And it did take a lot of time. Marlowe couldn't say for certain, but it felt like the whole summer had been dedicated to that stone wall. It was still there, serving no real purpose, but vaguely marking the far side of the Flats.

Marlowe glanced over at Enzo's pale, shriveled face, wondering if he would talk more about their project. He just blinked a few times, heaved a tremendous sigh, and then slouched back into his pillows. Marlowe watched as Henry reached out and patted Enzo's hand. She dreaded the day when breathing would become a labor.

Like Marlowe, Enzo was surrounded by a family, old friends, but he was alone in the way that mattered most. He had no partner. No love. The hair on the back of Marlowe's neck stood up, and she turned toward the window above the bed, the one that faced the road. The Gallagher brothers had each other, but that hadn't been enough. Not even for Tom. Beneath his cheerful facade, his soul had lived in isolation.

Maybe they hadn't died of suicide or sickness. They had simply died of loneliness.

# NINETEEN

Ariel and Ben arrived after lunch, while Glory and Frank were in town picking up more wreaths for the exterior walls. Marlowe was hunched over her desk, sketching for a client, when Henry came down for her. She wasn't happy with her preliminary work. The story she was meant to illustrate took place in a woodland where rustic pixies, perched high in the trees, defended their home from invading crows. But her pencil had wandered of its own accord, tracing something far darker—a twisted rope dangling from a barn rafter, a man suspended above the ground. Even after all these years, she could still render Leroy's bow-legged stance with unsettling precision.

"As I said," Henry murmured as they ascended the staircase. "Covering their bases."

Ariel and Ben stood in the living room with their black coats still on. Ariel had a large yellow envelope tucked under her arm.

"We won't stay long," Ben said. "We just came to give an update."

Henry seemed gratified to be one step ahead of the detectives, with his contact in Poughkeepsie.

"It seems Harmon Gallagher had a detailed plan to harass your family, whether to get you to sell or out of pure spite," Ben said.

"We've spoken to his friends and family members, looked through his computer and belongings. The threats were just the beginning. We can assume he was planning vandalism, possibly arson."

"We'll need to speak to your brother Nate and his wife." Ariel followed up Ben's remarks. "Considering the threats directly concerning their children."

"What?" Marlowe jerked her head toward Henry. "No one said that he mentioned the children."

Ariel and Ben bowed their heads solemnly.

"They're in Hartford," Henry said. "But they'll be up this weekend."

"You're sure no one noticed any strange occurrences the week leading up to Harmon's death?" Ben asked.

"No." Henry's answer was immediate. "We didn't connect the threats to discovering his body, and we assumed they were one-offs that would stop if we ignored them."

Except for Marlowe, who'd assumed nothing, because she'd known nothing.

"Of course." Ben glanced at Ariel, then hesitated, as if weighing his next words. "You should know that we've also reopened Nora Miller's case on a provisional basis due to a recent connection with Harmon's murder investigation."

"What connection?" Marlowe's voice cut through the tension. This caught everyone in the room off guard, and the three others stared quizzically at her. "I mean, don't we have a right to know?"

"I'm sorry," Ariel said in a conciliatory tone. "This is an ongoing investigation, which means we're not at liberty to share every detail at this time."

"Rest assured, we wouldn't reopen Nora Miller's case without cause," Ben said hastily. "There are a number of small things, inconsistencies in the original investigation. Enough to suggest that we wouldn't be doing our jobs if we didn't take another, more careful look."

"So, what? You think whoever killed Harmon—" She stopped short. "I just want to be helpful."

Henry, silent until now, gave a slow, ponderous nod.

"I hope you find whoever is responsible for Harmon's death and Nora's disappearance soon," he said. "And if you don't find answers, I hope we can find peace." It sounded like a line Henry had jotted down beforehand, like something he wanted to use in court for a closing statement. Do not seek answers; seek peace.

"Bringing peace to this community is our goal, Mr. Fisher," Ariel added.

Ben moved to go, and Henry jumped up, eager to show him out. But Ariel hung back for a moment as the men filed out through the kitchen. She didn't move closer, but something about the way she held herself—hips squared, head invitingly tilted—suggested patience. Understanding.

"Are you all right, Marlowe?"

Marlowe fought the urge to scoff. As if Ariel cared about her well-being.

"I want to know what happened to Nora," Marlowe said. "I want to believe you'll figure it out. But it hurts. That's all."

Ariel nodded, pursing her lips. The show of compassion seemed genuine, not like anything Marlowe had seen from her before. She studied Marlowe in a way that felt less like an interrogation.

"It's not easy," Ariel said. "Losing someone close like that. The pain is one thing, but it can also make you question your life. What you hold to be true." She exhaled, almost like she was drawing from her own experience.

The words settled over Marlowe like a weighted blanket. They were a comfort.

Ariel let the moment stretch just long enough before shifting gears, her voice still measured.

"I was looking through Brierley's notes. He mentioned that you and Nora liked to play tricks on the Gallaghers. He assumed they were pranks. No details, though."

"I don't think I gave him details," Marlowe said. "But we did play these small pranks, moving things around. The brothers always seemed too busy to notice, and they didn't mind us in the barn or running around the fields, as long as we kept out of their way. Nora and I played in the loft a lot."

"Play" didn't feel like the right word. They had mostly talked, but Marlowe didn't want to dig up the nuances of her friendship and lay it out for Ariel to pick apart. The pranks were childish but never malicious.

Ariel didn't push the issue. Instead, she switched tacks.

"What do you remember about Dave Gallagher's death?"

"I was fourteen when it happened," Marlowe started. "He died of cancer."

It was a half-truth, but it was what everyone said, out of respect for Dave.

Ariel's expression was unchanged. "Right. And then your father bought the land from Caroline Rodine. His cousin."

Marlowe shrugged. "I guess. If I ever heard her name before this week, I don't remember."

"The sale upset some of the Gallaghers," Ariel said. "Did you know that?"

"No," Marlowe admitted. "I didn't hear about any of that."

Ariel hummed thoughtfully, as if deciding how much more she wanted to say. "They cleared out the house before the sale, took some personal effects and heirlooms. Pete Gallagher—Harmon's father—ended up with Dave's journal."

Marlowe was struck by a sudden flush of heat in her face. She could feel herself beginning to sweat, but it was cooled instantly by a draft coming from a kitchen window.

If she noticed Marlowe's discomfort, Ariel didn't show it.

"Seems like he passed it on to Harmon, who kept it in his room."

A stoic farmer who kept a journal. Marlowe shouldn't have been surprised.

Ariel pulled a yellow envelope from under her arm and held it out. "Photocopies. Dave's journal, along with some of Harmon's threats, since it seems you missed those."

Marlowe took the envelope, which wasn't thick enough to contain a whole journal. Clearly, Ariel had edited the entries down to just what she wanted to share.

"Dave noticed your tricks," Ariel said, offhandedly. "And I think they inspired Harmon. He told his friends he was planning something to spook your family. Spray paint symbols on the barn and house, destroy some property."

Symbols.

The brand.

Marlowe's breath hitched. She and Nora had made it up—an infinity symbol intersected by a tree, drawn on the cows with blue paint. Once. Then again. She never told Brierley about that. It hadn't been relevant—a harmless prank that meant nothing. It was too private to share with a middle-aged man who wouldn't have understood.

Her fingers twitched; she half expected the feel of dried mud beneath her nails. A ghost sensation, but still real. Her mind scrambled for purchase on the memory. She lifted her gaze to find Ariel watching her. Not in the way of interrogators, but like a woman who understood. Like she already knew. Marlowe had the sudden, sickening feeling that everything was already laid out and neatly recorded in Ariel's mind. Dates. Names. Secrets.

"So this is the connection?" Marlowe asked. "The reason the case has been reopened?"

Ariel gave a slow nod. "Among other things."

"So Harmon might have really known something?" Marlowe asked. "His threats weren't shots in the dark?"

"Take a look." Ariel spoke casually over her shoulder as she reached for the door. "Call me if anything jogs your memory."

Then Ariel was gone, leaving Marlowe holding the envelope, her stomach in knots.

# TWENTY

Dave Gallagher's handwriting was manic. His letters were well formed but not always evenly spaced. Sometimes words bunched together, the pen or ink dark against the page. He dated every entry, and as Marlowe flipped through the photocopied pages, she could see that Ariel had included only the last year of his life: the summer and fall of 1996 in the first few pages, and then his final winter. That was her freshman year of high school, just after Tom died, when Dave was left alone on the farm.

Hidden in her basement, Marlowe felt deeply unsettled holding the account of a life unraveling in real time, knowing exactly where it led. The scrawled entries, the growing paranoia—a handful of phrases jumped out to indicate that Dave had been lost in his grief, and his writings were an attempt at comfort, a way to make sense of things no one else could see. But she couldn't concentrate on them for long. She skipped ahead to when, years later, someone else had been reading those same words as a call to arms.

Harmon's threats were all typed up on a single page with dates and notes about whom he sent them to. He wasn't just lashing out indiscriminately; he'd done his research. As Marlowe had figured, he'd emailed Stephanie about Kat and Dolly: *Someone will take care of your daughters the same way they took care of Nora Miller.*

There was another that Nate had received: *That house will burn, with you and your children inside.*

Marlowe couldn't believe Nate hadn't taken these directly to the police. She would have. So why had Nate hesitated? And how on earth could they tell the detectives Harmon wasn't the first person to come to mind after discovering that body? Marlowe began to see why her father and Nate needed to discuss the threats before handing them over to the detectives. These emails—they established a motive for the Fishers.

According to the documents Ariel shared with Marlowe, Harmon had mailed three letters to the Gray House concerning the Gallaghers. One in February read: *I know what you did to me. —Dave Gallagher.* The next one was mailed in March with the same line but signed by Tom Gallagher. The final one had been sent from Leroy the first week of November. The letters lined up with the months of their deaths. Deaths that Harmon seemed to think the Fishers had orchestrated. Harmon had a flair for the dramatic, but his logic was absurd. No one made Leroy reach for the rope. Tom had hoarded those pills himself. And Dave . . . Marlowe hesitated. She had to admit, Dave was the one that never made sense.

The emails sent to Henry and Frank repeated the same few phrases.

*I know what you did to Dave, what you did to Tom. You can't kill us all . . .*

*Greed is a sin.*

*Leave this house, or I'll tell what happened to Nora.*

A fourth letter was mailed to the Gray House in June.

*They're going to find me. —Nora.*

Marlowe was upstate at the time, which meant that Frank or Glory had tucked this envelope away without a word. It might have been meant for her. Ariel didn't include the recipient line or envelope for that one.

Had there been tension in the air one week ago, when the family was gathered for Thanksgiving? All Marlowe could remember was being overwhelmed by the shrieks of the children and the endless revolutions around the kitchen by Stephanie, Constance, and Glory.

What was Harmon keeping in that tent? A can of gasoline? A box of matches? Marlowe paced across her bedroom floor, her heart slamming into her chest. She threw the poisonous threats aside, cursing Ariel for handing them over without any more context.

Ben's decision to take another round of exterior photos suddenly made sense. He was trying to locate the door someone could have slipped out of to get at Harmon in that field. He had threatened to hurt the children, and he had put on a good front of possessing vital information. This went beyond what Henry classified as the detectives "covering their bases."

Marlowe's head spun as she turned back to her desk. The journal entries. Ariel had given them to her for a reason. She couldn't ignore them.

Marlowe sat down and began to read.

Most entries were short and consisted of fragmented sentences.

*Hot day. Fields need rain.*

*Walked out to the Flats, thought of Father.*

*Hottest day of the year so far.*

Marlowe stiffened when an entry dated from July mentioned her family.

*Fisher boys helped unload the hay. Older one tried to hand back the cash I gave him. It made me angry, as if I need charity. We have our land. My land. But he's just a boy. I can be patient with him. The girls messed around in the barn while we worked, making up some dance.*

*Sometimes I hear a strange singing, when I'm atop the Rise or passing the barn. No words I can make out, just soft fragments of melody.*

*Wind in the leaves, some might say, but I don't think so. Mother always said witches hum, while they spin their curses.*

Marlowe looked up, staring hard at the wall. Could that have been them? She and Nora had made up a game while walking through the woods, where one of them came up with lyrics and a melody and the other had to write another verse with a shared theme—typically some girly love song.

Dave must have known it was them. Then again, when they branded the cows with paint, Tom should have realized the most obvious culprits, yet he had told her father it looked like Wiccan rituals. They had laughed over that, Marlowe remembered.

She continued tracing her finger down the inked lines. The August pages were dense with his familiar complaints—missing cow leads, misplaced tools, the burdensome heat. There was a suggestion that someone might have been toying with him, but he'd always resort to blaming his aging mind. Then he got more pointed:

*Frank Fisher wants to buy. He'd do it tomorrow; I get the feeling. Told Tom as much, and mentioned it again to me today. When I go, he can have it. I don't care, and I doubt it'll bring him peace. Those boys of his are trouble. Born too lucky to ever be careful. And the daughter—she's sheltered and timid, but she'll put them through hell one day, I'd wager. Innocence like that ends badly. As for her friend, Leroy used to call her a changeling. I used to think it was a joke, but maybe Leroy saw more than I ever did.*

He hadn't even called Marlowe by her name. To him, she had been just another sheltered girl, destined for corruption, her fate so familiar, he was almost bored by it. And he said Nora was a *changeling*. A fae child swapped at birth, forced upon unsuspecting parents. Marlowe had told Ariel people out here still believed in the old myths, but seeing it in Dave's own hand was different. Maybe

Harmon had seen this as proof, a justification for whatever he'd planned to do. And Frank had wanted the land; that much was clear.

She flipped the page to find that Dave's thoughts had turned inward toward the end of the summer.

*I sometimes wonder what the point is. The corn is high as it's ever been, the cows are healthy, but what's it all for? I'll be 53 this spring, but I feel ancient. My parents are gone. My brothers are gone. A blue heron stopped at the river this afternoon. There's only me to see it.*

Then, in September:

*I heard those voices again, coming from the loft. I tried to ignore them, but they kept coming—clear as a bell. And then they said my name. I've heard them over the years, but now they're calling me, whatever they are.*

Marlowe's blood ran cold. All those afternoons lying on their stomachs in the loft, she and Nora stifling giggles. Dave had never reacted besides a momentary stiffening of his shoulders, a sidelong glance. They'd assumed he hadn't noticed. But that was all wrong.

*This place is haunted. This morning, I found the milk cans moved. All stacked on the back table. And I swear, last week, I latched the gate. Something unhooked it. Something is out there, trying to tell me something.*

How many times had they moved those milk cans? Had Nora done things on her own when Marlowe was in the city? Or had Dave started seeing things that weren't there? She flipped to the entry she knew was coming: the October night she and Nora had snuck out after homecoming.

*They've marked the barn. Mud from the pasture. I washed it out. Had to use the shovel to scrape it off. But now I wonder—who have I angered by scouring off the mark? And how will they retaliate?*

Dave sketched it in the margin, the symbol Marlowe had dreamed up as a child, the twisted tree rising from the infinity sign, a circle around it, With his shaking hand, it looked sinister. Not like a prank, but like its own kind of wordless threat. He continued:

*Tom was upset by the brands on the cows. He didn't like the missing tools, but this would have been worse for him. It's getting worse. And I wonder if he ever knew. I wonder if he saw where this was headed. The voices called Leroy, and then they called Tom. Now I think they're calling me.*

Marlowe clenched her jaw. She and Nora hadn't done many pranks that fall besides the brand. Had they? There were a few Sunday afternoons spent in the loft; that was it. But Dave kept recording mysterious events through October and November.

*I woke up past midnight, and when I looked out the window, I saw strange figures dancing on the lawn.*

*Coal stove running well this fall, but my bones stay cold. Wish Tom were here. I worry some cursed wind, the same kind that blew open the loft door last night, will start a fire in the house, and I'll sleep through it. I worry over it, and I crave it.*

*They scratched that symbol into a fence post. This one I can't wash off. It's a warning, clear as day.*

And then—

*Evening time. The cows were riled again. Something walks among them, when I turn my back. I saw the changeling creeping out of the Gray House. Fishers aren't here. She's up to something. I ought to tell Frank, but I reckon he knows.*

Marlowe checked the date and then searched it on her phone. November 12: a Tuesday. She had been in the city. Nora had no reason to be lurking about.

The entries started waning but became increasingly frantic.

*I hear them. Every time I walk through the barn, I hear them.*

*The drawers of my office desk were all pulled out this morning. They're looking for something.*

*It's not my farm anymore. Maybe it never was.*

Finally, the last entry, February 1997, the week he died:

*Thaw came early this year. Unless we're in for one more frost.*

Marlowe let the papers fall from her hands. Outside, the gnarled apple trees stood sentry beyond the garden. She wanted to scream that it wasn't their fault. But it had started when he heard Marlowe and Nora. He had been forced to endure their laughter, their tricks. A man teetering on the edge, pushed over by childish games. It was worse than she remembered. Nora had gotten bored during the weeks Marlowe stayed in the city, and carried on without her.

Dave's final months had been plagued by these hallucinations. Pete Gallagher had discovered this after finding Dave's journal. Harmon had known too. The Gallaghers had been angry. And why shouldn't they have been? Dave, Tom, and Leroy had been driven to the brink of psychosis.

Marlowe stared down at the photocopied pages. There was a reason Harmon had kept that journal. It was evidence. Proof that evil things were passing between these two families. Marlowe closed her eyes and flattened her shaking hands on the desk. It was her fault. She had stirred all this up. She and Nora had unwittingly cast the first stone in this feud. And Nora had gone running out there into the dark, where vengeance lay in wait.

Marlowe thought back to that winter, the damp cold curling into the walls of the house as it always did, the kitchen still warm with Glory's cooking, Nora rolling her red ball of yarn across the table. How she had teased Nora about the scarf she was knitting for Sean. They were waiting for the brownies to finish baking when her father burst in from his walk, hat askew, chest heaving.

"Call Charlie Beacon," he said to Glory. "Dave Gallagher is passed out in the cow pasture."

They watched from the window as Frank and their neighbor Charlie hauled Dave into the car, slipping on ice and nearly dropping him. That night, she and Nora crept to the top of the old staircase to eavesdrop on Frank and Glory.

"He had lung cancer," Frank said. "Sick for a year and never got treatment. He just let himself go."

Marlowe thought of Dave trudging through the ice and slush, facing the rise that blocked the Bean River, the sky streaked with pink and lavender behind him. Alone. Without his brothers, without anyone left to anchor him. One brother died in the barn; one in the house; the last Gallagher brother died in the field.

# TWENTY-ONE

**THE HOMECOMING**
**Saturday, October 26, 1996**

Marlowe slid the gold pin into Nora's smooth yellow hair. Nora grinned and bounced her head excitedly at her reflection in the mirror.

"Hold still," Marlowe said. "Just a few finishing touches."

She had labored over Nora's twisted bun, carefully pinning her locks just so. Nora insisted she had to wear her hair up for the dance. They had been in Nora's bedroom for hours, doing face masks, plotting hairstyles, and debating the best makeup to match the lavender dress Nora had picked out at the Kingston Mall.

Marlowe moved from where she knelt on the bed, and stood in front of Nora, carefully pulling a strand out of the pin, letting it frame her face.

"You're a genius with hair." Nora sighed.

Marlowe smiled. She had learned to French braid at seven, and ever since then she had been the expert in the hair department, whereas Nora was hopeless. She only ever managed to pull her straight hair into a ponytail.

Nora hunched over as she slipped her feet into her silver heels.

"You're *sure* those won't make you taller than him?" Marlowe had never been invited to a dance herself, but she was committed to following every rule on this momentous occasion.

"Positive." Nora tapped her finger on the glossy page of the year-book, open to Sean Hastings's freshman picture.

"He's gotten taller since last year," Nora added.

They paraded downstairs, where Nora's parents were waiting for her to make her entrance. Mrs. Miller cooed over her daughter and snapped photos, while Mr. Miller appeared to be feigning indifference. But he broke into a smile when Marlowe and Nora posed as if they were waltzing together.

The women bundled into the Millers' pickup, and Mrs. Miller dropped Marlowe off at home before driving Nora the rest of the way to the high school.

"Have an amazing time!" Marlowe waved from the front door.

She entered the house and found her brothers playing chess in the living room. "All dressed up with nowhere to go," Nate teased. Marlowe felt heat rise in her cheeks, remembering that she'd also applied some eyeshadow and rose-colored lipstick to herself when Nora was getting ready.

"Shut up, asshole!" she hissed, running up to her room. Nora was coming back to the Gray House right after the dance for a sleepover, but it seemed impossible to wait three hours to hear about how it all went. Though she wasn't interested in any of the boys at her own school, Marlowe now felt a mix of hope and terror at the thought that a boy might ask her to the winter formal in December.

By the time the doorbell rang, it was almost eleven, and Marlowe had abandoned the loneliness of her room to watch a movie in the library with her brothers. She bolted up to greet Nora, who was still in her dress and heels. The hair spray hadn't managed to hold Nora's slippery locks, and chunks of hair had come loose from her bun. Despite the messy hair, her face was lit with a pretty glow, and she looked slender and fairy-like in the flowing dress.

"It was amazing," Nora declared as she hugged Marlowe.

"How many times did you fall over in those shoes?" Nate shouted from his chair.

Henry cackled, but Nora waved off the teasing as Glory and Frank rose from the couch.

"Oh, you look beautiful." Glory lightly touched one of the gold hairpins, and Marlowe realized that she had taken them from her mother's room without asking. "I hope you took pictures."

"Stop this!" Frank grabbed Nora's head in his hands, the same way he embraced Nate after a good soccer game, and then wrapped his arm around Marlowe's shoulders. He had long since given Nora the same affectionate greetings he used with his own children. "You girls are growing up too fast."

Marlowe rolled her eyes and dragged Nora upstairs. She demanded a play-by-play of the night as they changed into pajamas and brushed their hair. They analyzed every second in furtive whispers, pausing only when they heard Nate and Henry passing by on their way to the boys' room.

As soon as there was silence in the hall, Nora picked up where she had left off, her slow dance with Sean.

"He kissed me," Nora whispered, once they were curled up in bed. "We walked out to the hallway because it was hot in the gym, and then it was quiet, like there was nothing left to say. I felt awkward, but then he kissed me, and it wasn't awkward anymore."

"Your *first* kiss." Marlowe sighed. "What was it like?"

In answer, Nora grinned and flopped back against her pillows, kicking her feet beneath the covers.

"I don't think I can sleep," Nora said. "Not tonight."

Marlowe sat up, inspired by Nora to take action. She pointed at the clock. It was past midnight.

"Everyone's asleep," Marlowe whispered. "Let's sneak out."

Nora tumbled off the twin bed and pulled her gray sweatshirt over her tank top and plaid pajama pants. Marlowe slid to the floor, yanked on her sneakers, then quietly opened the window and prized out the screen. It was a short jump to the roof of the front porch, and from there an easy climb down the railing post. At the bottom, they scampered across the damp grass of the front lawn.

The moon was bright and full, a good omen.

"I can see almost as well as during the daytime," Marlowe gasped.

"It's magical, like fairies lighting our way," Nora said.

When it was just the two of them, they pretended the woods around the house were magical; they were girls having trouble letting go of fairy tales.

Though they hadn't planned to go to the loft that night, they silently flitted toward the old red barn, both of them instinctually drawn to the same spot—their secret place.

The grassy, rolling hillocks of the cow pasture rippled with silver under the full moon. Marlowe tipped her head back and peered wide-eyed at the blanket of stars spread out over the inky sky. They looked so close, as if Marlowe might be able to reach out and pluck one. The unusual brightness of the night had transformed the familiar landscape into something mystical. The barn loomed with more power. The rough surface of the wooden fence, the dark outline of the tree atop the Rise, the gray stone of the milk barn—it all seemed touched with magic.

Earlier that day, they'd seen Dave Gallagher move in steady lines between the fields and the barn. The last Gallagher. The cow herd had thinned out, more than half of it sold off. He could manage only a few wagons of hay bales on his own.

The cows were silent now, most of them sleeping in the pastures, their white spots glowing in the moonlight.

"Remember our brand?" Marlowe asked.

"Yes." Nora's eyes lit up. "Should we do it again, to mark this night?"

Marlowe nodded. Adrenaline at their sneaking out in the middle of the night bled easily into creativity. Instead of paint, Nora suggested mud from the pasture.

They scooped up huge wads of claggy earth and carried it into the center of the barn, just below their loft, where they began to lay out the design on a large scale. They had to run back to the pasture several times to get more. It reeked of cow manure, but they didn't care.

When they were done, they stepped back to observe their handiwork: a circle, five feet in circumference, intersected by an infinity sign and a strangely human-like tree stretching its branches overhead. It appeared almost like a sculpture crafted out of lumps of mud.

A dark stain marred the front of Nora's sweatshirt. Mud was lodged deep beneath Marlowe's fingernails. But it was worth it. The brand looked so perfect in the shadowy light of the barn that it sent a shiver down Marlowe's spine.

They ran fleet-footed and silent back to the house, daring to walk straight through the front door and creeping up the old staircase. The house was sleeping like the dead. They washed off in the upstairs bathroom and donned fresh sets of pajamas before falling into their beds, exhausted but gleeful.

Marlowe looked over at Nora, who was already softly snoring, and thought to herself that she had never been so happy.

# THURSDAY

## NOVEMBER 29, 2018

# TWENTY-TWO

The road toward the Museum of Rhinebeck History twisted through the countryside, passing farmlands, then stately houses, then more fields. Marlowe had to stop at frequent four-way intersections, all of them named after old local families. Herman Corners. Jackson Corners. She took the curving road slowly as she headed west, gripping the steering wheel tighter. Every thought and every memory that popped into her head was now askew and grainy, as if someone had tiptoed through her mind and scratched at her old files with a knife, slicing off details, blurring the dates, knocking conversations off-kilter.

The night before, after trying and failing to sleep, she continued a fevered search on the Internet for information about Pete and Harmon Gallagher. She couldn't find anything beyond a bare-bones obituary for Pete, and that was no longer enough. Marlowe started searching for local museums and libraries, anywhere that might have records. Buried underneath results advertising Washington Irving's home and the historic Victorian mansions that lined the Hudson, she found the website for a local farm museum that housed photos and records for historic Hudson Valley families.

The museum was tucked away in an old building on a side street, behind a bookshop and across from a clothing store, its windows dressed with wicker furniture and soft cashmere sweaters. Marlowe was the only visitor. She meandered through the main room, trying to put on a show of examining the antique plow in its glass case and the photos of old farmsteads. After only fifteen minutes, she approached the woman at the desk who had sold her the entry ticket.

"I just moved to the area," Marlowe said. "I'm so curious about the local farmers—I was wondering if you had any old archives."

"Yes, we do." The older woman nodded. "Jeanine can show you—let me get her from the office."

Jeanine was a gray-haired woman in a heavy-gauge cardigan who peered out at Marlowe from behind her glasses with renewed purpose when Marlowe expressed interest in the museum's records. She led Marlowe to the archive room. It was narrow and dusty, with tall shelves and a pristine long wooden table that had a set of white microfiber gloves on top. Jeanine spread out a map of the county, labeled with old names and spidery ancient property lines.

Marlowe found Bean River Road and tapped a spot on the map.

"That's near the Pulvers," Jeanine said. "They had one of the biggest operations."

The name was familiar. Marlowe had driven by their massive barns, up on top of the mountain behind the Gray House.

"How long were they in the area?" Marlowe asked. "I'm curious about all the farmhouses built in the late nineteenth century."

"Well, a lot of those houses are gone or renovated beyond recognition," Jeanine said. "But so many do remain, and most have a striking history, which is what I just *love* about this area. Some of these farming families go back to the 1700s, back when apple orchards were one of the main industries."

Marlowe thought of the orchard behind the Gray House. The

biggest tree had a thick trunk, stout enough to fit several grown men. Its branches bent low to the ground, like a matron with thick hooped skirts. One of the trees had been struck by lightning a few winters ago and had to be taken down. Another one had withered and died. One of them was so old and gnarled and bent that Marlowe thought of it as the grandfather of the orchard.

"I didn't know that," Marlowe said, hoping to sell her ignorance. "When did dairy farming start?"

"Nineteenth century," Jeanine said. "The wet, swampy marshes create ideal grazing pastures. Obviously not *in* the swamps, but the water travels overground and underground; that's what makes it so green up here."

Marlowe nodded and looked back to the map. She got the feeling Jeanine was passionate enough to go on an environmental history tangent if Marlowe didn't redirect.

"I'd love to see some family trees," Marlowe said. "Do you have records for all the properties around here? I live closer to town, but I'm interested in the history of the older homes in the area."

"I have them organized by geography." Jeanine squinted at the map, mumbled a coordinate, and then turned to the shelves, pulling out a hardcover book.

"Here." Jeanine opened the book. "The Pulvers."

Jeanine flipped through the pages, reading names aloud. The third one was "Gallagher."

"I've heard that name," Marlowe said.

"Yes," Jeanine said and sighed. "It was in the local news recently. Someone from the family was killed. That type of thing never happens up here. People leave the city to get away from all that—that's why my husband and I moved up here."

Jeanine shook her head as she examined the list of births and deaths.

"Old family," she said. "They were around awhile, but the farm went down with most of the others in the eighties."

It had been a slow death, Marlowe thought to herself. Jeanine wouldn't have known all the details of how those three old brothers held on a few years longer.

"Oh, Victoria Gallagher." Jeanine smiled as she tapped on the name. The note accompanying it was brief: *Born 1875, married William Pulver 1896, died 1898.*

"Victoria was interesting, and a bit of a local legend," she said. "Nothing as big as the Headless Horseman or Captain Kidd, but rumors said she went a little mad as a teenager. That's what they always said back then about odd girls. She might have been put on trial as a witch a few centuries earlier."

The Gallagher daughter. The one who sat up in the hedgerow until she saw demons and was locked away. Marlowe didn't know she was married, let alone to a neighbor.

"What happened to her?" Marlowe asked. "She died so young."

"Likely childbirth," Jeanine said, turning the page. "If you run into any Pulvers, you can ask if she's haunting them. Most of the old houses come with a ghost story or two."

Marlowe tried to conceal a chuckle at the dark irony of Jeanine's comment, and she forced herself to remain impassive when she saw the square, faded ink on the next page: *Tom Gallagher b. 1935. Leroy Gallagher b. 1938. Dave Gallagher b. 1945.*

Notices of their deaths were not included. The records likely hadn't been updated in decades. Jeanine flipped another page, revealing a small pencil sketch that made Marlowe's heart drop. It was the Gray House, as it had once been, long before Marlowe was born: smaller, and without a front porch, but it was unmistakable, like seeing a photo of her dad in high school—thick, dark hair, his youthful smile wide and carefree. The antique front door, two windows on either side. The stone chimney. Where the thin birch trees now stood there was an old oak tree that must have died and been harvested for firewood. The clapboard of the house was etched with a light hand. The artist wasn't particularly skilled, and the sketch was far from refined, but it was a true rendering.

"I just love the architecture of the farmhouses." Jeanine brushed her wrinkled hand over the sketch, and Marlowe nearly swatted it away. "When weekenders buy them and turn them too boxy and smooth and modern or, worse, build *new*, it's just a travesty."

"There's construction near me, and the neighbors are upset. It's on a hill, and they've cut down a bunch of trees." The false story fell easily from her mouth. "When you have a great view, you're ruining someone else's."

"Exactly." Jeanine glanced up. "I have a whole book of photos and sketches of barns."

Jeanine was off, moving from shelf to shelf. Marlowe sank into the chair at the table.

"Do you mind if I just flip through these for a bit?" Marlowe asked.

"Oh, of course." Jeanine smiled. "I just get lost in these old records sometimes."

Jeanine pulled down a few more books and then, at last, left Marlowe alone. Marlowe flipped back to the Gallagher records and quickly took pictures of every page. There was an old map as well, and some black-and-white aerial shots. It was all muddled, and she had no sense of the landscape from a bird's-eye view, but she could study it and perhaps find a familiar road.

She made a show of flipping through the old barn pictures and then returned to the sketch of the Gray House. There were a few scribbled lines in the corner: *The Gallagher Place, July 1934.* The drawing was unsigned but dedicated to a Robert Gallagher. She turned back to the page of the Gallagher extended family and rifled through her purse for a notebook and pen. After snapping a picture of the page, she jotted down the names in a slapdash family tree. She wanted it on paper so she could distinguish the repeated names and see the generations lined up.

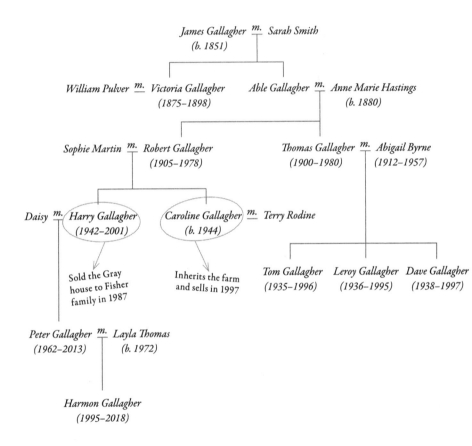

The records went back to 1851, starting with Victoria's parents, and then tracked through the generations. It appeared that Robert was one of Victoria's nephews, born in 1905. If he had been in possession of the sketch, Marlowe reasoned that he must have been the one who lived in the Gray House at the time. He had a son named Harry and a daughter named Caroline. *Caroline Rodine*, née Gallagher. Marlowe shuddered. This was who had sold Frank Fisher the property after Dave had died.

Continuing on the opposite page was a lineage of Robert's older brother, Thomas. He had a wife, Abigail, and three sons, Tom Jr., Leroy, and Dave.

There it was: Robert Gallagher with his children on one side of the street, Thomas and Abigail and their sons on the other. A farm split between two brothers. Cousins growing up together. Caroline didn't sell off an inheritance from a distant relative. She sold what was left of her childhood home, long after she had left it.

The final entry was for Harry's only child, Peter Gallagher, born in 1962.

Marlowe lifted her fingers, counting out the years she had been too hesitant to calculate before. If Peter was born in 1962, he would have been in his mid-twenties when Frank Fisher purchased the Gray House.

Marlowe slipped out of the archival room, avoiding any notice from Jeanine, and walked outside to her car. She turned on the ignition and cracked a window, taking in the cold air, and then went back to her phone to search for another obituary. Harry Gallagher had died in 2001, at fifty-nine, of an unspecified illness. He had watched, from wherever he ended up after the sale of his land, as all his cousins died. He had seen his sister sell the last of the property to Frank Fisher. Had Harry found Dave's journal, or was his son, Pete, the only one who had helped clear out the house?

Marlowe closed her eyes, trying to picture Pete as a boy. His bachelor cousins would have taught him to stack hay and sharpen blades on the stone wheel. A lump rose in her throat. Pete wasn't a weekend visitor. He had, in fact, woken up in the Gray House every morning of his childhood. He had known every winding path through the woods, climbed every apple tree. He must have loved it, maybe even more than she did. And maybe he had assumed he would inherit it.

Instead, he watched as the debts piled up and the farm slipped away.

That was the difference between the Fishers and the Gallaghers. The Fishers didn't depend on the land; the farmers did. They were at the mercy of the land and its many betrayals. There was never a perfect season. Rain ruined the hay. Cows got sick. Foxes ate the chickens. Maybe Harry Gallagher had suffered a few difficult years. Or maybe he just didn't want to struggle anymore. In any case, his loss was his son, Pete's, loss too.

Had Pete come back after his side of the family lost the land? Wandered old woods, mooned about in the fields. Marlowe knew she would have. If the Gray House were taken from her, she wouldn't be able to stay away.

One last time, Marlowe counted out the years. In 1998, the night Nora disappeared, Pete Gallagher would have been thirty-six years old. Marlowe's age now. He would have had a toddler, Harmon, but no farm. Her father had mentioned that Caroline had been willing to sell despite family pressure to hold on. She imagined that Pete had been among those dissenting voices. He would have been old enough to be angry about how things had panned out. Young enough to do something about it.

And if he had the journal—if he had pieced it together—he might have known. He might have known the Fisher children had blood on their hands, and might have seen an opportunity for revenge. No one wanted to live where a tragedy occurred. And if the Fishers looked guilty, all the better. The more Marlowe thought about it, the more she saw the logic. The roads spreading out from the Gray House formed a web tattooed in her brain. Where had Pete been all those years? She thought of the abandoned car she'd found with her brothers. A figure watching from the tree line, keeping an eye on the Gallagher Place.

Marlowe shoved the piece of paper back into her purse and hurled it to the passenger seat. There wasn't time to wait for the detectives to come to her. She pulled out of the parking spot and headed for Route 9, south toward Poughkeepsie.

# TWENTY-THREE

Marlowe gave her name at the front desk of the police station, and within ten minutes, Ariel appeared.

"Marlowe, is something wrong?" Ariel asked. "Or did you just want to talk?"

"No, sorry. Nothing's wrong. I just wanted to talk, if that's okay." Marlowe felt silly now, facing Ariel in the drab lobby, pretending she drove all the way here just to chat.

But Ariel didn't miss a beat. "Should we go grab coffee? There's a café round the corner, and I'm not ready to take you into a full-on interrogation room." Ariel smiled, her teeth as small and white as pearls. "Yet."

Marlowe didn't laugh at the joke, but she did let Ariel lead her a few blocks away. They ordered drips and found a corner table. Around them, a few people worked on laptops, puddles forming beneath their chairs as slush melted from their boots. The café was comfortable and quiet, with just enough background noise to keep their conversation private.

"I wanted to ask about Nora's case," Marlowe said at last.

Ariel raised her brows. "You know I can't tell you everything."

"I read the file you gave me. If Pete had that journal, he might have known about the tricks we played as kids. He might have been upset."

Ariel looked momentarily surprised by Marlowe's blunt approach. Marlowe was surprised too.

"And are you upset?" Ariel asked.

"Yes, I am." Marlowe met her gaze. "I had no idea he was so distressed."

She couldn't bring herself to say Dave's name. It was the latest in a long line of insults.

"You've been in the dark about a lot of things," Ariel said. "The details of the sale, the Gallagher relatives. Even Harmon's threats seemed to catch you off guard."

If Ariel meant to wound her pride, it was a wasted effort. Marlowe had lost any sense of pride the moment she read Dave's journal.

"None of it was on purpose," Marlowe said. "But Pete might have thought it was. Maybe he wanted revenge. Damen Miller said something about Nora being caught in a feud between families. He thinks we're hiding something, but we're not." She hesitated. "And never have been."

"When did you speak to Damen Miller?" Ariel asked, puzzled.

Marlowe shook her head, not realizing she hadn't shared details of their conversation with anyone yet. She felt a sudden chill after the admission.

"A couple days ago," she said, waving off the question and trying to remain calm. In truth, she wanted to stop Ariel's investigation from taking Damen's theories too seriously. His logic was tangled in grief. No matter how aggressive Harmon's threats had been, she couldn't picture any of the Fishers answering with violence. There were plenty of legal ways to deal with someone like Harmon, things her family was well versed in.

"Well, you shouldn't be talking to him," Ariel said. "That's not going to end well."

"Nora spent every second she could with my family," Marlowe blurted out. "Every weekend, she was with us from Friday to Sunday night. Every summer, she basically moved in. I never thought that was strange when I was a kid. But it is, isn't it? I always thought the Millers were nice. So why was she always trying to get away from them?"

Marlowe pressed her lips together. She sounded desperate, grasping at something she had no proof of. But hadn't she always been a part of this investigation? If anyone's theory deserved to be heard, it was hers.

Ariel folded her small hands together on the table. "Are you trying to turn this back on Damen?"

"No, I'm not accusing anyone," Marlowe said. "You gave me those journals, and I'm telling you what I think."

Ariel tilted her head slightly, considering. Then she took a long sip of her coffee and wiped her mouth with the back of her hand.

"I had a best friend too, when I was fifteen," Ariel said suddenly. "Carol Smith. We did everything together."

Marlowe frowned, suspicious of Ariel's motives in sharing this information. "And what happened to her?"

"We drifted apart. No big fight, just different colleges, different lives. We used to catch up now and then, but eventually, even that faded." Her face was inscrutable. "Still, I remember what it was like. At one point in time, that girl and what we had was my whole life."

Marlowe turned her coffee cup in her hands. "Is that supposed to comfort me? That Nora was taken before we drifted apart?"

Ariel studied her for a beat. "Look, Marlowe, it's not like we think you killed your best friend. But I do think you feel guilty. Maybe not for something you did, but something you didn't do. Something you didn't say."

Marlowe's fingers tightened around the cup. She wasn't a suspect. They had to stop treating her like one. It was a waste of time. "I told you, I'll tell you anything. I want to know—"

"I know how siblings can be." Ariel cut her off gently. "Through thick and thin, they protect each other."

"*Nora* protected me." Marlowe leaned forward, her voice low. "If you're so focused on siblings, you should know that Nora was like my sister. To my brothers as well. She was one of us."

Ariel held her gaze for a long moment before nodding. "I know."

Marlowe exhaled and leaned back. She didn't want to lose her temper or get emotional, not with Ariel.

"Dave Gallagher was suffering in silence from depression. A lot of men do," Ariel said, crossing her arms. Then she added, almost offhandedly, "I hate it up here, you know. I grew up in Brooklyn. I'm not used to all these empty roadsides and vanishing towns."

"If you hate it, why are you here?"

"My mom moved upstate for a little house in the country. She spent her life savings on it. Then got sick," Ariel said. "So. Here I am."

"I'm sorry about your mother."

"People hold you back; it's an old story." Ariel shrugged. "Maybe you were lucky to lose someone early."

Marlowe recoiled. The words were cruel. But then she caught the glint in Ariel's eyes. It was a test. She was hoping to elicit something from Marlowe.

"Maybe you'll get lucky soon too," Marlowe said flatly.

Ariel cracked a smile, shaking her head. "Maybe. I wouldn't mind leaving. This whole area is just a string of ghost towns." She glanced around the café. "I gave you those journal pages because if you want to get to the bottom of this, you need to think back and realize you're not a kid anymore," Ariel said. "What was really going on with Nora that year?"

Marlowe had a thousand answers. They ran free all summer on the Gallagher land. Nora was dating Sean, passing along all the lessons learned in a first relationship. Everyone kept saying they were growing up fast, but it felt like nothing was changing at all.

Ariel didn't push. She just scraped back her chair and stood up. "Come with me. I'm going to give you something."

At the station, Marlowe sat in a plastic chair for nearly half an hour, debating whether to ask more about Pete Gallagher. But pulling out her messy family tree and floating her half-baked theory—that Pete had lurked around the land as in some ghost story—felt ridiculous. She needed something more concrete.

Finally, Ariel returned to the waiting area, another big yellow envelope in her hand. This one was so full it couldn't be clasped.

"These are Brierley's old notes. More photocopies." She handed them over, and Marlowe almost dropped the envelope in shock. "It's not every interview, just his notes on what he was thinking."

"This is confidential," Marlowe said. "I tried to get these before, but the department wouldn't release them."

"I know," Ariel said. "But I want you to read them. Then tell me what you think."

Marlowe could only stare in astonishment.

"You know what the sergeant says about me?" Ariel lifted one dark brow. "He says I'm an 'agent of chaos.' That I chase leads on instinct, not reason."

"I can see that," Marlowe said dryly.

"It works for me." Ariel shoved her hands into her pockets and leaned forward. "We're close to wrapping up Harmon's case. And Nora—whatever Harmon might have known—my gut tells me we're close to that as well."

A trickle of cold dread ran down Marlowe's spine.

"Brierley. He wasn't dumb," Ariel said as she walked Marlowe to the doors. "He made some sharp observations."

"His observations didn't help," Marlowe said.

"Maybe he was just missing a piece," Ariel said.

# TWENTY-FOUR

As Marlowe walked across the driveway, she shoved the bottle of gin she'd picked up deeper into her purse, along with Brierley's notes. She was prepared to field questions about how she'd managed to shop all day long without making any purchases. But when she entered the house, nobody cared to ask. Ariel thought upstate locals had been turned to ghosts, but Marlowe was a ghost in her own home, slipping down the steps and into the basement.

Marlowe threw Brierley's envelope on top of Dave's journal entries on her desk. Ariel was dropping breadcrumbs, handing Marlowe riddle after riddle, like a troll under a bridge. And Marlowe had no power to resist the questions, no choice but to follow the trail.

She unscrewed the gin and splashed it into the cup of iced lemonade she had grabbed from the kitchen. Marlowe knew these notes were going to be about her, and she had to brace herself.

For over a year after Nora's disappearance, Marlowe had existed in a state of agony. It was more than sadness. Marlowe didn't know how to live without Nora leading the way. She couldn't make friends, definitely couldn't talk to boys, and she lost all sense of what she wanted or what she was good at. Nate saved her, of that Marlowe was certain.

She was seventeen, and it was August. More than a year since Nora. It was a scorching hot day in the city. Nate found Marlowe curled in a chair in the living room, idly sketching in her notebook.

"Marlowe, get dressed." Nate rapped his knuckles on the table.

Marlowe blinked down at her striped pajama shorts and baggy T-shirt. "I am dressed."

"To go out." Nate grinned. "I'm taking you out tonight."

Marlowe shook her head. She didn't want to go out. She didn't want to feel shy and awkward around Nate's boisterous friends. She didn't want to watch Nate laugh and joke and gleam with his electric energy. She wanted to stay tucked away, wrapped in her cocoon of silence. She was shy before Nora disappeared. Now, Marlowe was socially inept.

But Nate didn't take no for an answer. And deep down, Marlowe was flattered, as every younger sister is when her older brother demands her company. Of course she wanted to tag along when he looked her straight in the eye and begged her to.

Nate led Marlowe through the streets toward the subway, the lazy air pressing down atop them. As they stepped down the stairs into the train station, Marlowe felt the wave of heat rise up to claim her, and she thought of the descent into hell. She thought maybe this was how Dante felt when Virgil took him by the hand to show him each ring of the inferno.

They took the subway to a pub Nate knew of with a rooftop sitting area. Marlowe perched on a bench and looked out over the hazy city, while Nate carried up beers for the both of them. The glasses were ice cold and coated with condensing liquid.

They sat and talked about school and old friends. Nate reminisced about when their great-aunt Eliza babysat the three of them while their parents traveled. Eliza meant to treat them to sparkling apple juice, but she had served them glasses of real champagne by accident.

It was a story Marlowe knew well, but no one told it like Nate.

After one beer, Marlowe felt bursts of joy streaming through her veins. She was so happy she had agreed to come out with him. As Nate gave her a second, he announced that a few of his friends from school were going to meet them there. Marlowe was not scared or miffed. She was ecstatic at this news. When she went to the bathroom, she ogled at her own reflection. Her cheeks were flushed, and strands were falling out of her ponytail in a disheveled way she found attractive.

Drinking, she decided, made her pretty.

When Nate's friends arrived, Marlowe found it easy to laugh and joke with them. She talked to one guy for a long time as he peppered her with questions, fact-checking stories Nate had told him. Marlowe shook her head at Nate's exaggerations and gave wry responses, her lips twisted in a smile. She was a different girl. More clever, more eloquent, more everything.

The group walked to another bar, feeling like they owned the streets of Manhattan, and then to a third, where they danced a bit.

Later, Marlowe tumbled into bed, feeling happy and full with the pizza Nate got for them on the way home. She reflected to herself that maybe the taste of beer wasn't so bad after all. One just had to get used to it.

Her parents made her go to therapy after Nora, but Marlowe could take or leave the sessions. She didn't hate them, and she didn't resist, but therapy didn't save her. It was Nate who got her excited about life again. It was Nate and those pints of beer that made her laugh again.

Marlowe was still grateful for that.

She took a long gulp of her drink and let it settle her. She had survived this once. How could some old notes hurt her after all this time?

Brierley's scrawl was slanted, his letters crammed together but mostly legible. As she read, she wasn't surprised to see that throughout the investigation, he had clung to one central theory. She'd felt his suspicion that summer. The way he kept circling back to Nate and Henry, and how Luke, Mike, and Liam, the boys' friends, had been dragged in for questioning again and again.

It was clear from the notes that Brierley had been convinced the teenagers were lying, covering something up. If any of them broke, he figured it would be Henry's friend Liam. Brierley actually called him "the weak link."

But he still considered other theories.

With missing children, a detective always looks at the parents first. He noted potential logistics: They could have driven out to the property, taken her, then returned home in time to answer the Fishers' frantic calls. But there was no history of abuse in the Miller house, no criminal record. Nothing in the house when it was searched. No sign of a struggle.

A sigh of relief escaped Marlowe when she read Brierley's final verdict: *No evidence of domestic tension; no signs of abuse.*

The Fisher parents were considered too. But everyone knew they were asleep upstairs when it happened. And the idea of a family-wide conspiracy was dismissed outright. Far too outlandish.

Then there was what he called "the stranger theory." A person completely unknown to the Fishers and the Millers who could have swept in and kidnapped Nora at the opportune moment. But the notes on this theory were thin, and Brierley seemed unconvinced by it.

How would a random kidnapper know the details of their movements, with Nora taking the trash out at that precise moment? Crimes of opportunity happened, but this one would have required intense preparation. A well-timed approach. If someone had taken Nora, they'd moved quickly. And they'd silenced her instantly, because no one heard a scream.

Brierley had sketched out a rough map. A square for the Gray House, a line for the road. Beneath it, he jotted down a note about Frank purchasing the land from Caroline Rodine. A short list of names followed: Tom, Leroy, and Dave. And then, scrawled in his handwriting, Marlowe's own words from an interview.

*Marlowe and Nora: pranksters, played around in barn, moved things. Farmers liked the kids. Some cousins bitter after sale, dislike Fishers, but no real connection.*

In light of Dave's journals, she and Ariel both knew that wasn't true. "Bitter" didn't even begin to cover it. Not for Pete. Not for Harmon.

On the next page, dated June 9—four days after Nora vanished—Brierley's notes seemed to be more carefully composed, neater, as if he was thinking more deliberately.

*I question the trash story. The way they tell it, it's off.*

Of course it was off. Nate had been more than tipsy. Luke and Mike full-on drunk. The rest of them—Marlowe, Henry, Liam—were racked with fear.

She saw why Brierley harbored doubt. If a story doesn't make sense, a detective has no choice but to assume someone is lying. And teenagers? They're complicated, emotional, and impulsive. The center of their universe, as Brierley saw it, was the handsome and charismatic Nate Fisher. Brierley had written one note about Nate after his first meeting: *too charming.*

Farther down: *Nate and Nora romance? Marlowe, Henry, friends, and all parents say no.*

Marlowe chewed the inside of her cheek. Brierley's bleak assessment suggested a worst-case situation. Nora was young, and Nate may have taken advantage. His charming demeanor might conceal a violent streak. Maybe he manipulated her, hurt her. And then, as if tripping over a land mine, Marlowe saw the explosive question at the bottom of the page.

*Was Nora pregnant?*

It took a moment for her to regain her composure—to remember she had already been down this road. It was a dead-end question. Without a body, they'd never know. And if she was, she certainly hadn't told anyone. Her parents insisted she was not sexually active, but Brierley noted that didn't mean much.

She read the paraphrase of her own words shortly after: *Marlowe says no, certain Nora was a virgin. But the only possibility would have been Sean.*

Marlowe's stomach turned. Nate and Stephanie were planning to come for the weekend. If she asked him point-blank—had anything ever happened between him and Nora—would he tell her the truth? Would she even know if he was lying?

The first thing Brierley wrote about Nora was telling. He scribbled: *Nora Miller, age 15. Pretty.*

Marlowe clenched her jaw and grabbed the stack of Dave's journal entries. What did he write about Nora? "The changeling was *up to something.*" To Dave and Brierley, a pretty teenage girl had to be up to something scandalous. She had to be trouble.

That seemed to be why Brierley focused on Nate. Not Marlowe and Nora's bond, which was the only connection that actually mattered. Instead, he wrote about "an intensity" between Marlowe and Nora. He said that Marlowe wouldn't have been able to physically overpower Nora. But she could have had help, and this could have taken place long before midnight. Those teenagers had hours to come up with a cover story.

Then he wrote: *If Marlowe found out about Nate and Nora, what would she have done? And what would her brothers do to cover for her?*

Maybe, if she was in Brierley's shoes, she would have asked the same questions. But she wasn't him. She had seen Nora take out the trash. Heard the silence when they screamed her name. He could have his doubts, but Marlowe knew what had happened. And it didn't make sense, unless you knew about Pete Gallagher clinging to Dave's journals, feeding his anger over the Fishers' greed and entitlement. Marlowe and Nora's cruelty.

She wanted to scoff and roll her eyes at the suggestion that something had happened between Nora and Nate. She might have if she had read these notes a week ago. But Ariel was right. She wasn't a kid anymore. Nora snuck into the barn and played tricks without her. What else might Nora have done without her knowing?

Marlowe forced herself to consider it, tracing back to that final spring and the dawn of summer. They had been up for Memorial Day. Nate was out of school, and he built a massive bonfire. But how many summer nights had they sat around a fire? How many weekends had they set off into the woods or lounged by the Bend?

She struggled to remember the specifics of that holiday weekend. Was there a conversation between Nate and Nora? Did they slink into another room while Marlowe was distracted? Not for the first time, she wished she had kept some sort of diary. Marlowe always thought there were some things she would remember forever. It was shocking how many names that once rolled off her tongue with ease now escaped her entirely. How many events she saw photos of but never could recall happening.

She didn't know. She wanted to scream at the failings of her memory.

Most of all, she wanted to dig up Brierley from the grave and give him a shake and ask him what, specifically, he had meant when he wrote what he did.

Marlowe forced herself to continue with his notes. There, at the top of the following page, a name she never expected to see.

*Mr. Babel.*

Her breath hitched. She had forgotten until now, but Brierley had asked her about Mr. Babel. A throwaway question. And she had laughed it off. "Oh, he's just made up. We tell stories about him. He's not real."

That was all he got from her, and then he moved on.

Evidently, Nate and Henry had told a different story, one that Marlowe had never heard. Henry swore he'd seen a man in the woods, camping out and hunting small game. He saw him once pulling a dead rabbit from a trap. And Nate similarly claimed Mr. Babel was real but kept to himself.

A quote from Nate jumped out at her:

*We're not friends with him. We've just seen him. Two or three times.*

It appeared that Brierley invoked Marlowe during the exchange, because Nate made a point of mentioning that she didn't think Mr. Babel was real, before ending with a line that chilled her:

*Marlowe and Nora have their secrets, and we have ours.*

Marlowe raised her head, pulse thrumming in her ears. She couldn't believe it.

Brierley shared her confusion, having written: *The boys are leading me on wild-goose hunts after "Babel," and Marlowe is blind.*

It made sense why Brierley had suspected them. Why bring up some phantom lurking in the woods unless they were trying to misdirect? It may as well have been a confession.

Marlowe didn't see guilt. She saw fear. Of course, Nate and Henry might have their secrets, but if they had actually seen Mr. Babel, if he was real, they would have been falling over themselves to share that information. Unless they were hiding something.

Her eyes flicked back to the crumpled notes she had made at the museum. Pete Gallagher's name glared up at her. He would have known every inch of that property. Nate and Henry claimed they'd seen something a few times. But he could have been out there every night, watching them all. Waiting.

When she finished, Marlowe collected the notes. She knew why Ariel had given them to her—just in case Marlowe had evidence that might fit. But she didn't. The only evidence she had was the story that Brierley found so unbelievable, he had come up with soap opera plotlines to explain it.

Marlowe closed her eyes.

It had been a long time since she had pictured it in detail. She used to run it over in her head again and again, searching for clues she may have missed.

In her mind, it played like a movie: Nora stepping out onto the lawn, her wellies squishing against the damp grass. It had been a sunny day, but the earth was always damp—because of the swamplands and marshes, as Jeanine said.

Nora shivers faintly; she's wearing only a T-shirt and jeans, and the June nights can be brisk. But she walks on. The light from the house illuminates half the lawn with a yellow square. Beyond that, Nora can see only the outlines of the pines and the trash bins. But that's enough. She knows the property. How many times has she taken out the trash at night? Just as much as Marlowe had.

She pushes one of the bins open and tosses the bag in with a little huff. As the lid snaps closed, Nora hears something. Her attacker's car (and there had to be a car, unless he'd been clever enough to find a hiding spot before they searched) couldn't have been too close. Nora wouldn't have ventured farther. She would have turned around.

So her attacker approached on foot, and Nora would have heard something. A footfall or a rustling sound from the trees.

Nate liked to play jokes. He did it all the time. They all did. When Marlowe or Nora were outside at night, Nate sometimes jumped out from behind a bush to scare them. And they'd often returned the favor. It always worked, no matter how much you might expect it.

Marlowe imagines Nora hearing something but not panicking right away. She would have thought it was Nate.

There's a heavy silence, and Nora, who always had impeccable instincts, feels that prickle at the nape of her neck.

Then she's snatched from behind. That was what Marlowe had imagined the most. That's when Nora tries to scream, but before she can get the sound out, he drags her away. If he got an unconscious Nora into the thicket near the North Field, or into the old Gallagher barn, he could have hidden. Marlowe and Nate and the others never checked the thicket very well, or the woods. And they had poked about in the Gallagher barn, but it was so dark. Marlowe remembered Nate climbing up into the loft at one point, but just to have a cursory look with the flashlight. He didn't delve into every corner. Not that night.

The attacker had left with Nora before dawn, of that Marlowe was certain.

Whoever took Nora was good at hiding. It was not a nuanced psychological profile, but it was all Marlowe had up to this point. But now she had Dave's journals and Brierley's notes. Nate had told Brierley he had his secrets. They all had secrets. She had to stop looking for missing pieces out in the dark. She needed to consider the people who had been sitting in the house with her, hiding in plain sight.

She tightened her grip around the cold glass before gulping down the dregs.

Marlowe knew, even when she was a teenager, it was wrong to rely on drinking to ease her sorrow. She knew it would lead only to trouble. Her mother didn't drink at all, because she grew up with an addict for a brother. Glory told them that it was genetic. Alcoholism was in their blood, woven into their very DNA.

Marlowe tried everything to break the cycle of drinking. She tried traveling as far as she could; she tried therapy; she tried boyfriends. She hadn't tried marriage, but she would have for the right person.

Only one thing worked every time. There was only one true cure. Marlowe slowly rotated the empty glass in her hand.

It made her happy. She was better when she drank. She felt lighter and smarter and funnier. How could she turn away from that?

She'd had her share of misfires. There was the cousin's wedding when she was in college, at which she got glass after glass of white wine and didn't bother eating. The next morning, she was curled up around the toilet bowl, throwing up bright yellow bile that looked like the runny centers of sunny-side up eggs. There were a few nights out with colleagues, back when she was working as a paralegal in a New York office and wishing she could be a full-time painter instead. Nights when she couldn't remember how she got home. Mornings when she woke up to find vomit in her kitchen sink.

But over time, Marlowe learned to hone her craft. She learned to properly nurse a bottle of wine and to chug a glass of water between refills. She learned cocktails and hard alcohol before dinner, and then only beer or wine after. She learned that if she started with a drink at three or four in the afternoon, she could still be in bed well before midnight and up bright and early the next day.

Being a middle child taught Marlowe one thing: how to be sneaky. She knew how to snoop and how to identify the exact same type of wine her mother bought, so she could replace bottles that she emptied. She knew where to hide bottles. She knew that if she took the empty ones out early enough in the morning, before her coffee, no one would notice.

She had found her cure, and she knew how to get away with using it. How could there be anything truly wrong with that?

And none of it was Enzo or Nate's fault. He knew they were only trying to help her.

Because Ariel Mintz and John Brierley had been right about one thing: Siblings protect each other.

Marlowe had told Ariel that Nora was like a sister.

But like alcoholism, it came down to genetics. Blood. Either she was or she wasn't.

Nate could spend years teasing and deriding Marlowe. He could judge her and be furious at her. But when it really mattered, he would do anything to help her.

But Nora was not Nate's sister.

# TWENTY-FIVE

**THE CAR**
**Tuesday, July 8, 1997**

Marlowe tugged hard on the moss-covered rock lodged in the ground until she felt the dirt release it. She grunted as she caught her balance and then flipped the rock over, revealing its smooth underside.

"That one's pretty good," Nora said from where she stood atop the ancient stone wall.

The two of them had wandered deep into the woods, away from Nate and Henry, to hunt for the smoothest and flattest stones they could scavenge from the remnants of the old fieldstone walls that zigzagged the property.

Enzo had explained that the old walls had been built by colonial farmers, and Indigenous people before that, who had cleared the land of its abundance of glacial rock in order to farm it. Conveniently, they used the rocks to mark their property lines. The walls were still in good condition in many places, but Marlowe and her brothers frequently made unexpected discoveries of partial walls deep in the woods—ruins that must have dated back hundreds of years, now disguised by forest growth and long forgotten.

Their parents had challenged them to complete their own wall before the end of the season. Frank had picked out the spot, at the northern edge of the Flats, near where the Bean River spilled out of the swamp. Getting there from the Gray House required a long trek through the old Gallagher property along the outskirts of the swamp, but Marlowe and her brothers rarely shied away from a challenge set by their father. Besides, their father had recently finalized the purchase of the Gallagher farm. Dave, the last Gallagher brother, had passed on, and the abandoned barn, the fields devoid of cows, all the empty land across the street, called to them, as if it was lonely. Though the kids already knew the Gallagher property well, Nate said it was theirs now, so they should approach it with fresh eyes, exploring every inch anew.

But when Nate first came up with the idea of taking stones from the walls in the woods for the one they were building, Marlowe thought that would be cheating. It felt almost sacrilegious to pluck the flat, heavy stones off the old ruins, lugging them down to the appointed site of their new wall. Even so, Marlowe couldn't deny the convenience of the plan.

"It's not like we're destroying it completely," Nate reasoned. "We're just taking a few rocks."

Marlowe ran her hand along the cool hardness, inspecting the rock. She knew Nate wanted their wall to be perfect and would accept only the finest stones. She added her new find to the growing pile she and Nora were making in the woods. Nate and Henry would come find them soon enough with the wheelbarrow to ferry the stones down the side of the North Field and then across the road and onward to the building site.

The day was muggy. Though the thick trees blocked out the sun, Marlowe was coated with a layer of sweat. Nora's ponytail was limp, and she was breathing hard every time she lifted a rock.

"We need to go swimming after this," Nora grumbled.

"Let's just go now." Marlowe grinned over at her friend. "We don't *have* to follow Nate's orders all the time."

Nora smiled. "But you know he'll yell at us and tell us we're being lazy."

"Maybe I am lazy. It's too hot today."

Nora laughed, but she kept searching for rocks.

As annoying as Nate could be, it was fun to work together as a team. Nora balanced the power, so that Marlowe never felt outnumbered by her brothers. At the end of each long day of building the wall, they all laughed together round the dinner table and took stock of their progress. Peace reigned in the household.

Nate was headed to Princeton in the fall, and he had declared that he wanted the summer to be perfect. *Golden.* So far, Marlowe thought he couldn't complain. Since their parents came up only every other weekend, Enzo was the only adult supervision. Occasionally, Nate had friends up from the city, but most of the time, it was just the four of them: Nate and Henry and Marlowe and Nora. They were a posse of sorts, and Nate was the undisputed leader of the pack. Each morning over a breakfast of bacon and eggs that Enzo cooked up, Nate told them exactly what they were going to do that day.

Marlowe wandered into a small clearing, kicking dead leaves and ferns to the side as she scanned the ground.

Her eyes lit up when she saw several perfect rocks. "Nora, come over here—there's so many."

Nora scampered over, brushing aside the prickers that tugged at her shorts. "It's another wall!" It was decrepit and scant, but Nora was right. The bottom layer of another wall ran perpendicular to the one they had just been pillaging; it would have been undetectable if Marlowe hadn't been deliberately clearing the leaves.

Marlowe bent down to pick up a flat gray stone, but Nora tapped her shoulder. "Scouting trip—we have to see how far it goes. We'll bring the boys up here to collect rocks later, once we know."

Marlowe readily agreed. They tramped happily through the woods, veering into a section where they had never been before. That was what excited Marlowe about the land. She could spend a lifetime exploring it and still come across unseen tracts. The girls hopped from rock to rock, following the wall along the top of a gentle slope.

"Sean called me last night," Nora said, jolting Marlowe out of her musings. "He wants to hang out this weekend."

"But it's Henry's birthday this weekend." Henry was turning fourteen. Enzo was going to make barbecued ribs to honor the occasion, and Marlowe and Nora had promised to make a cake.

"I know, I told him that, but he didn't get it."

Marlowe breathed a sigh of relief, even as she observed Nora's furrowed brow. The summer had put a strain on Nora's relationship with Sean. They'd been going out for roughly nine months, since homecoming last year. During the school term, Nora ate lunch with Sean and his friends in the cafeteria and went to all his baseball games. They went to the movies together on Friday nights. But Nora still spent the majority of her weekends and, so far, all of the summer tromping through the woods with Marlowe and her brothers, an arrangement that suited Marlowe.

Nora confessed to Marlowe that she got bored with Sean sometimes. He never wanted to talk about books or traveling or college. He only ever wanted to talk about baseball and high school stuff. It made Marlowe feel good to know that she was still the more interesting, beloved person in Nora's life.

Nora jumped off the wall and turned to look at Marlowe over her shoulder. "I've actually been meaning to tell you something."

"What?" Marlowe stopped her skipping and sat on the wall. She could tell it was something serious from Nora's expression.

"The other night, after we went to the movies, Sean wanted to go all the way."

Marlowe gasped. "And you waited until *now* to tell me?"

"Nate and Henry are always around," Nora said. "Plus Enzo and your parents were up that weekend! I couldn't risk any of them finding out and telling my parents!"

"Did you . . . do it?" Marlowe asked.

Nora looked into her eyes before placing her hands on her hips and saying, "No, of course not!"

"Good. You should never let a boy force you into anything you don't want to do," Marlowe said, speaking with an authority she didn't have. She had still never been kissed. "So what happened after that?" Marlowe scratched at a mosquito bite on her thigh. It was turning red and swollen.

"Oh, nothing." Nora waved her hand, hopped up, and started walking again. Marlowe chased after her. She'd noticed that Nora had become less willing to go into detail about her dates with Sean recently. She claimed it was because they did the same things all the time; their relationship had become mundane. But Marlowe had her doubts. She had overheard girls at school comparing notes about how far they had gone with boys. Hands over the bra, under the bra, pants unbuttoned. She didn't know if Nora had done any of that stuff, but if she had, Marlowe hoped she would tell her, acting, as usual, as her most trusted guide in life. Though she had some friends at school in the city, none were as close to her as Nora was.

"I guess I should call things off with Sean, but we haven't even hit a year yet." Nora ran her hand over the trunk of a tree as she passed.

"Maybe it's just a phase," Marlowe said. "It will be nice to have a date for dances this fall and someone to hold hands with in the school hallway, won't it?"

"I don't know. Being with a guy isn't all it's cracked up to be, trust me," Nora said. "I mean, Sean never makes me laugh. He doesn't think like you and I do, like Nate or even Henry. All Sean cares about is baseball. Our school's team isn't even the best one in Dutchess County."

Marlowe lengthened her stride so they were side by side and threw her arm over Nora's shoulders. "Well, if the cons outweigh the pros." Without any practical experience herself, Marlowe could only parrot generic phrases when it came time to advise Nora. But it wasn't Marlowe's fault that no one asked her to dances. That the boys at school, especially the cute ones, made her tongue-tied with nervousness. Marlowe knew she wasn't ugly, but she also knew she wasn't considered fun. She was quiet and boring and wore her innocence stamped on her forehead. And no guy wanted an innocent girlfriend.

"There aren't any pros at all to the relationship," Nora burst out. "Even the stuff that's supposed to be a pro was weird."

"You'll know what to do when the time comes," Marlowe said.

Nora smiled, and they walked on, marveling at the length of the wall. The air seemed to crackle with sudden warning, and Nora halted and pointed into the pines. "What's that?"

There was a brown shape, twice Marlowe's height, several yards away, obscured by undergrowth and trees.

The hair on Marlowe's neck stood up. As they drew closer, they realized the shape was a rusty car; it looked like an automobile from the 1940s. There was something ominous about this latest discovery. Marlowe wondered how long the car had been sitting out in these woods unnoticed. *Decades?* The car held something bad, she just knew it, felt it somewhere deep in her bones.

"How did it get all the way up here?" Marlowe whispered.

"Maybe there was an old road," Nora said. "Look at it, it's been here for ages."

Marlowe reached out and gripped Nora's forearm. Her skin was surprisingly cold.

Nora gave Marlowe's fingers a squeeze. "Let's get closer, just a little."

With each step, their sneakers crunched in the leaves, a sound that seemed to echo through the woods. It was impossible to tell what color the car had been, it was so rusted over. The wheels were gone, and there seemed to be a bunch of debris and sticks inside.

Nora let out a little groan, a sound caught halfway between excitement and fear. "Oh, it's creepy."

Marlowe tore her eyes away from the car and to the surrounding area. She frowned as she saw the rim of an old tractor tire, the inside darkened with ashes. As Tom Gallagher had once told them, nothing made a better firepit than a metal tire rim. Marlowe reached down and touched the remnants of a charred log with a finger. It was not warm, but that was hardly a relief. The car might have been old, but the fire wasn't. The half-burnt log and ashes were recent.

"We should go." Marlowe's voice came out loud, piercing the quiet of the trees. "Something is wrong with this place."

A clattering caused Marlowe to jump out of her skin. She whirled to see Nora banging a stick against the door of the car. In two steps, Marlowe was at her friend's side. She yanked the stick out of Nora's grip.

"*Stop,*" Marlowe hissed. "We need to *go.*"

Nora's eyes widened at Marlowe's reaction. "What is it?"

"I can't explain, I just don't like this." Marlowe lifted her hand to her chest, where her heart had worked itself up to the pace of a hummingbird's wings.

Nora didn't laugh. She didn't question Marlowe's gut reaction. She simply let Marlowe take her hand, and together they ran all the way back to the edge of the woods, where Nate and Henry had been collecting near the top of the North Field. Marlowe knew then that she could trust Nora with anything.

By the time they reached Nate and Henry, they were panting.

"We found something," Marlowe said, her chest rising and falling sharply as she tried to catch her breath. "I think someone's living out there."

"What are you talking about? We know every inch of this place. No one is out there," Nate said.

Nate liked to swagger about as if he was the resident cartographer. He claimed to have explored every acre of the countryside. But he'd never come across that car before; none of them had.

"No, it's true. We found a car. It's old and abandoned and creepy," Nora added.

Marlowe raised her hands up to deliver the spooky part. "And there's a tire rim where someone made a fire."

Nate and Henry abandoned the wheelbarrow and the stones to follow the girls farther into the woods.

Nate moved at a rapid pace, and Henry's face turned red with exertion.

"You scared?" Nora asked Henry.

*"No."* He shot her a pointed glance.

"You'll be fine," Nora said. "Marlowe nearly fainted, but nothing bad actually happened."

"Yet!" Marlowe cried, suddenly annoyed at Nora's lightness. But she, too, was less scared now that all four of them were marching toward the rusty car together. There was power in numbers.

Henry was fascinated by the car. He loved any sort of machinery, and he instantly climbed through the window to investigate what remained of the steering wheel, as Nora stood by. She probably would have done that herself earlier, if Marlowe hadn't stopped her.

Nate and Marlowe stood above the tire rim.

"Could be a hunter." Nate poked at the charred log with a stick.

"I don't think hunters usually light fires. It would scare away the prey. Anyway, Dad doesn't give out permits for overnight use."

"So maybe someone's just camping out." Nate squinted through the trees. "This might not even be our property."

This suggestion surprised Marlowe. She had assumed that anywhere they could walk within a reasonable amount of time was on the Fisher property. But of course, that wasn't how it worked. So maybe this stretch of land belonged to a neighbor, one who liked to camp out by an old car that belonged to his or her grandparents. The thought settled her mind.

From a few yards away, Nora kicked at a glass bottle. Her bare suntanned leg was a blur in the air. "Or maybe it's a creepy old man. Who wears animal furs and hunts with a bow and arrow!"

Marlowe cracked a smile as Henry's ears perked up. He loved when Nora came up with stories.

"What's his name?" Henry asked.

It took barely a millisecond for Nora to respond. "Mr. Babel."

They all shivered at the delicious streak of fear the name induced, even Nate.

"Mr. Babel fled into the woods years ago, after his wife and children died," Nora declared.

"They perished in a fire!" Marlowe added, finally able to partake in the levity.

Nate rolled his eyes, but then he added, "I bet he's got an old shotgun, not some measly bow and arrow." He turned then, leading them all back toward the fresh pile of stones and the wheelbarrow they'd abandoned. He declared that they'd had enough rocks for the day—it was time to head across the street to the Flats. They talked of Mr. Babel the whole way back to the building site. Then they unloaded the rocks, and Marlowe beamed at the first few feet of the wall they'd built. It was so neat and tall and solid, nothing like the crumbling walls up in the woods.

They would build this one to last forever.

# FRIDAY

**NOVEMBER 30, 2018**

# TWENTY-SIX

Marlowe blinked against the hazy light filtering through her window, her head still heavy with sleep. She took a few slow breaths and then sat up too fast. The room tilted before settling back into frame. *Right*, she thought, *morning*.

She pressed her fingers to her temples, trying to recall when exactly she'd left her desk and lain down on her bed the night before, but the details were slipping from her mind like water through cupped hands.

Dragging herself to her desk, she pulled out a few fresh sheets of paper and gripped a pen. The day after reading Brierley's notes, she was going to start keeping some of her own. Ariel wasn't taking her theory about Pete seriously, which meant Marlowe would have to pursue it herself. She would have to be methodical, ruling out possibilities one by one. And she was going to have to consider something she'd avoided for years. Nora might have broken their oaths of secrecy. She might have told someone about their pranks. Or worse. She might have been seen by someone besides Dave, slipping in and out of places where she didn't belong.

Marlowe tapped the pen against the paper, forcing her thoughts into order. Her head ached, but if she wanted answers, she'd have to push through.

At the top of one page, Marlowe wrote: *Mr. Babel—Is he real? Is he Pete Gallagher?*

On the back she wrote: *Nate + Nora?*

She had a million questions, but they all boiled down to the three she had written so far. If she could figure those out, it would lead her to answers about Nora.

She lifted her pen and began to write out the names:

*Nate*
*Luke*
*Mike*
*Henry*
*Liam*

She looked down. The boys who had been in the kitchen with her the night Nora disappeared, and who might have known more than they'd told Brierley.

Her mind moved to the other rooms of the house. It was like a game of Clue. There was someone behind every door.

*Frank*
*Glory*
*Enzo*

There was also the yard, the road, the woods.

*Mr. Babel*
*Pete Gallagher*
*Harry Gallagher*
*Damen*
*Jennifer*

Marlowe set the pen down, rubbed her eyes, and glared at the list. She skipped over her family members. They had given her nothing the last twenty years, and she didn't expect them to come forth with some revelations now. But Luke, Liam, and Mike could be different.

Luke remained a close friend to Nate. He stood by his side as a groomsman at Nate and Stephanie's wedding, delivering a hilarious and heartfelt speech. Though he lived in Philadelphia, he made a point of visiting the Gray House with his family once a year.

As for Henry's friend Liam, Marlowe was fairly certain he still lived in New York. She pictured his round, bespectacled face and winced. Liam and Henry hadn't simply drifted apart; their friendship was shattered that summer. Marlowe could still hear echoes of Liam's parents on the phone with Frank and Glory, demanding to know why the detective wouldn't leave their son alone. After that, Liam never returned to the Gray House. By the time the next school year began, he had transferred elsewhere.

Pestering poor Liam had done Brierley no good. He was the most vulnerable, yet whatever Brierley had hoped to extract from him yielded nothing. So who should he have pursued instead?

Her eyes landed on Mike's name. A friend, but not very close. Marlowe remembered him pale and shamefaced and hungover the morning after Nora disappeared, climbing into Luke's car. They said they would just get out of everyone's way. They gladly gave Brierley all their information and fled to Luke's family's home in Connecticut. Marlowe remembered him all but fading from Nate's life after that. Last she heard, he had moved to Houston.

She pulled her laptop toward her and flipped it open. She searched "Mike Cameron Houston." It didn't take long to find him. He was an orthopedic surgeon. She looked at his photo on the

Texas Medical Center's website for a long time. His hair was thinner, and he had gained a bit of weight, but it was him.

Marlowe dashed off a quick email. She didn't go into detail—just said she would like to catch up. He would know what it was about, and she doubted he would respond.

As soon as she clicked Send, she drummed her fingers against the table, restless energy buzzing through her. She had been so sure she knew everything about Nora, but her memory had been playing tricks on her. Her testimony would never stand up in court.

Glancing over the list of names once more, Marlowe pushed back her chair, crossed the room, and grabbed her coat from the closet.

Nora's old friends from school were like phantoms now, nameless and faceless, but she did remember Nora's old boyfriend, Sean Hastings. Marlowe had almost been fond of him herself. She had craved romance, even if she had been too afraid to start one of her own. At least she could live vicariously through Nora.

They broke up after a year together, in a dramatic ordeal that Marlowe had to help Nora rehearse and reiterate to Sean on multiple occasions. Marlowe hadn't seen or spoken to him since, though she had kept tabs on him. It wasn't difficult—Sean had never gone far. Marlowe overheard from neighbors that he lived nearby with his wife, a hairstylist, and that he worked at the hardware store in town.

Outside the store, she squinted through the window but couldn't make out the man behind the register. The bell jingled as she stepped inside, and then she saw him. The long hair she remembered was now cropped short, dusted with gray. He was tall, still lean, dressed in a flannel shirt and jeans, arms stretched against the counter. She remembered how he used to shake out those sinewy arms before stepping onto the pitcher's mound. She had sat through enough games by Nora's side.

Sean recognized her immediately. "Marlowe, hi."

"Hi, Sean." She tried to smile, but it was more of a grimace. She glanced around the store. An employee was stocking shelves on the far wall. The rest was cluttered and disorganized. But locals knew their way around it.

Marlowe steadied herself, smoothing a gloved hand over her coat. She often wondered what it had been like for him. His first girlfriend, a girl he was in love with, vanishing seven months after she dumped him. He didn't have the greatest claim to tragedy; that belonged to Nora's parents. And, Marlowe liked to think, to her.

She had thought about reaching out before, but what comfort could they possibly offer each other?

Sean gave her a sad, lopsided smile. "I'm guessing you're not here for a screwdriver?"

"No." Marlowe shook her head. "You heard about the body."

"Yeah, everyone's heard." His dark eyes stayed locked on her. "The detectives came by. Asked about Nora."

She exhaled, relieved by his directness. She had no patience for subtlety. "They've reopened her case."

"That's what they told me. They asked me if I wanted her found." Sean bowed his head, but his voice harbored some quiet rage.

"That's a ridiculous question," Marlowe said. "Of course you do. Like I do. I realize we never really talked about it. But I know it must have been hard for you too."

Sean's expression hardened. "I wouldn't have welcomed you back then if you tried. Everyone knew Nora wouldn't have disappeared if not for your family."

The words were a slap across the face, but Marlowe didn't budge.

"I know the detectives were probably a bother, but I wanted to ask you a few things myself."

Sean glared. "Do you want my alibi? For the four-hundredth time?"

Marlowe recoiled slightly. His alibi had always been airtight. Out of town with his cousins, a dozen witnesses to prove it. She had never considered him a suspect, but others must have. The whispers could be deafening around here. Maybe that was why he blamed her family. The Fishers had power, connections. What couldn't they hide?

"I know it wasn't you," Marlowe said. "I know you were a good boyfriend to Nora. I always believed that."

"I doubt that."

She opened her mouth to protest, but he shook his head and held up a hand. "Nora always wanted more from me. I was always letting her down. But, hey, what teenage boy doesn't let people down? It's all water under the bridge."

"Sean, I know this is awkward, but I wouldn't ask if it wasn't important." Marlowe's cheeks were burning as she held his gaze. "Did you and Nora ever sleep together?"

His anger faltered, replaced by a stunned silence. He cleared his throat, dragging a hand across the counter. Then he looked up, and his shock turned to confusion. "How is it possible you don't know?" he said. "I thought Nora told you everything."

Marlowe bit the inside of her cheek, fighting the sting in her eyes. "I thought so too."

Whatever Sean saw in her face, it made his shoulders sag. "Twice," he murmured. "The fall before we broke up." He rubbed the back of his neck. She gripped the strap of her purse and nodded.

"Did she ever say anything about me? Or my family? Something that struck you as odd."

She was trying to disguise the real question: *Did Nora dump you because she wanted my older brother?*

Sean let out a dry chuckle. "Everything she said about your family was weird. She was *obsessed* with you guys. It seemed like her life didn't happen unless she was with you."

Marlowe had heard it before. The privileged Fishers, and Nora, their poor adopted daughter. But it wasn't like that. It never had been.

"I felt the same way about her," she admitted. "Nothing mattered as much as the two of us."

For a few weighted moments, neither Sean nor Marlowe had anything to say.

"I lied to the first detective," Sean said, finally. "Told him we never had sex. I was terrified."

"But this time?"

"I told them." His eyes darted to the window, as if he was hoping for a distraction.

"What else did they ask?"

"They asked me to describe Nora. So I did." With that, he pulled his computer keyboard in toward his stomach and shook the mouse to wake the monitor. "Look, I gotta get back to work," he said, gesturing at the screen. "End-of-year inventory."

"Right." She nodded. "Sorry to bother you. And thank you."

She hesitated before pulling a scrap of paper from her purse and jotting down her number.

"If you ever want to talk," she said, setting it on the counter. "You can call me." She swallowed hard. "I'm sorry, Sean."

He picked it up, sliding it somewhere underneath the counter, likely planning to throw it away as soon as she left. He would go home and tell his wife about the crazy lady who showed up at work, rehashing one of the most painful episodes of his youth.

As she turned toward the door, Sean called out, "Marlowe. Have a Merry Christmas."

Marlowe swung her head around. His smile was faint, tinged with remorse. She nodded again. "You too."

She didn't return to her car. Instead, she walked to the coffee shop and ordered a latte. The room was packed with weekenders and locals alike. Marlowe could easily distinguish between the two. The locals wore hoodies and muddy shoes, Carhartt jackets. The weekenders wore boots that held their shine, and tan or forest-green barn coats.

A tinny Christmas song echoed over the speakers. It was an older one. Sadder. No upbeat jingling of bells, just a melancholy croon mourning Christmases past.

Sipping her drink by the window, she turned over all the new information in her mind. Nora wasn't a virgin. She had slept with Sean and never told Marlowe. It didn't have to mean anything, but Marlowe couldn't imagine any scenario in which Nora wouldn't share such earth-shattering news with her.

Marlowe was never close enough with girls at her own school who might have swapped tales of their first times. In college, it was more of the same. Marlowe hung out with a studious group of coeds who were serious about academics.

Marlowe had envied the girls who spoke about sex so easily, who turned to their friends while brushing their teeth and said, *So, he tried this one thing in bed last night . . .*

She had never been that girl. But she had confided in the people she trusted most. When Marlowe lost her virginity her junior year to her first boyfriend, Nick (who didn't know she was a virgin), she told only her roommate, Paige. The two shared most meals together, and by junior year, Marlowe had warmed enough to open up about everything. She even told Paige about Nora one late night over a bottle of wine.

Marlowe finished her latte, the last lukewarm gulp heavy in her stomach. The crucial details Nora had withheld from Marlowe were beginning to pile up. In all her years mourning Nora, in all the time Marlowe had spent agonizing over what had happened, she'd rarely asked *why*. The answer always seemed obvious. People hurt teenage girls. People raped teenage girls. People took girls and locked them up and threw away the key.

For the first time, Marlowe wasn't sure that was it. Evidentially, Brierley didn't think it was that straightforward. Ariel and Ben didn't seem to think so either.

And yet, of all the secrets Nora had been keeping, Marlowe still didn't know which was the one that had put her life in danger.

# TWENTY-SEVEN

"Constance and the baby will be here soon," Glory announced when Marlowe returned home. "Stephanie and the girls, too," she added, placing a stack of plates on the kitchen counter. "Pizza for dinner."

"Not Nate?" Marlowe asked.

"He's staying in Hartford to work."

For a split second, Marlowe felt the familiar sting of paranoia. She was certain Nate was avoiding her. Keeping something closely guarded. She pushed the thought aside. He didn't know what she'd been up to: building old Gallagher family trees, flipping through weathered journals, confronting Nora's ex-boyfriend. She took a steadying breath and retreated to the basement to calm herself and refocus on what was factual.

The notes sprawled across the table. She stared at them, willing the pieces to connect. Jittery from too much espresso, she took a quick nip from the gin underneath her desk.

Nothing about Sean's comments suggested that Nora had been pining for Nate. He said Nora had been obsessed with the entire Fisher clan. Marlowe considered her part of the family. If Pete Gallagher had been watching, he might have seen Nora as a Fisher too. Targeting her would be an attack on the family that had taken everything from him. A family can't endure such hardship and remain in the same place. He would have known that.

Frank was right to call Harmon evil for threatening Kat and Dolly. If he had such violent inclinations, perhaps he got them from his father. Marlowe thought back to the fascination she'd had with epigenetics when she was considering a graduate degree in anthropology. The way the brain undergoes constant evolution due to trauma, and how that trauma could be passed down.

The threats Harmon had made, which her family had downplayed, suddenly felt more sinister. Why had they kept the specifics hidden from her? If Stephanie had received an email about someone threatening her daughters, she wouldn't have dismissed it. And if she had retaliated, wouldn't she have been justified?

Retaliation would have been out of the question for Constance, whose diminutive stature made her meek and doe-like. Stephanie, on the other hand, had broken every record in her college's lacrosse program. Nate had dragged them to his girlfriend's games, beaming with pride. Marlowe had a flash of Stephanie the college girl, with her long ponytail, calf muscles tensing as she sprinted over the grass, arms flexing as she yanked her lacrosse stick back and then hurled it forward.

And Harmon, while broad-shouldered, was no athlete. Marlowe wagered that beneath his hunting jacket, he had a perfectly average physique. He wouldn't have been able to outrun Stephanie. And if Stephanie had come at him with enough momentum, if she'd picked up a big enough rock . . .

A door slammed upstairs, pulling Marlowe to the present. High voices and rapid footsteps of the children rose and fell. It sounded like chaos, but it meant they were safe.

Still, the unease clung to her. The theories were just that— stories made up in the absence of truth. No one was giving her answers. At least Sean had, but she couldn't shake his cold gaze, looking at her as though she needed to be checked into a mental hospital. She yanked off her sweater and threw it on the floor in frustration.

Half an hour later, after a few gulps of gin, Marlowe made her way upstairs. Constance had arrived, and the kids clustered around the table, comparing their letters to Santa. Marlowe ruffled Kat's hair and lifted Frankie from his high chair, savoring the baby's warm weight as he nestled against her shoulder. Stephanie and Constance rose from their seats to greet Marlowe.

"Henry and your parents went to pick up the pizza," Constance said. "I'm going to start on a salad."

Stephanie sat down, and Marlowe took a seat across from her. There were so many things she wanted to ask her, but she aimed for lightness.

"How's work?"

"Busy," Stephanie replied, her attention on Kat's carefully folded letter. "But she's been my real project lately. Third grade's keeping us both on our toes."

"You've always been good at juggling it all."

"Well, you do what you can." Stephanie's gaze lifted briefly, her expression unreadable.

"Sometimes it's hard to keep everything in the air." Marlowe feared her evasions were apparent to Stephanie now, but she didn't miss a beat.

"You learn, though. Eventually," Stephanie said. Her lips curved into her trademark thin and mildly derisive smile.

A delicate pause lingered between them, provoking Marlowe to respond with a pointed comment about what Stephanie might have learned about her husband's past, but the front door burst open before she could.

"Did you see the news?" Henry's voice boomed from behind the pizza boxes. He set them down and pulled out his phone.

"What news?" Marlowe jumped up, and Frankie cried at being jostled.

"They made an arrest," Henry said.

Marlowe traded the baby to Henry for his phone, and he narrated as she read the news article.

"Rick Frasier. The police found bloody clothes at his house—no alibi for the night Harmon was killed. They say it's solid."

Gasps filled the room. Glory clasped her hands together, murmuring, "It's over. Thank the Lord."

Constance exhaled and clicked her tongue. Stephanie let out a long, dramatic sigh of relief.

Marlowe continued scanning the article. Rick Frasier had been hauled into the station earlier that day. Rick and Harmon had fought over money—a failed business venture of some kind. The details were murky. Rick had loaned Harmon cash, and the fallout was ugly.

"Overwhelming evidence," Henry said. "He'll be convicted. Might even plead guilty and take a plea bargain."

The house buzzed with tentative hope, but Marlowe knew it wasn't over. It was only beginning.

Ariel must have known they were close to an arrest when they spoke yesterday. She had given Marlowe Brierley's notes because she had to move fast if she was going to solve both cases. Marlowe set down the phone and accepted a plate that was handed to her.

Ariel wasn't going to stop, and she couldn't stop either.

# TWENTY-EIGHT

## THE SNAPPING TURTLE
### Sunday, August 24, 1997

The Bean River ran crisp and clear, except for one stretch that merged into a swamp just north of the Gallagher fields and barn. There, the river all but disappeared, becoming wide and shallow, its waters creeping through a quagmire of trees and grass and muddy puddles, before spilling out on the other side and once again finding its course through the Flats. The four of them set out that morning looking for a great new frontier, unknown and ripe for exploration.

In just a few days, Nate was leaving for college. For weeks now, he had been talking about the dorm he'd been assigned and the classes he was registered for and how much packing he still had to do.

But that afternoon, he didn't speak of it. As if even Nate could be nervous about the big changes to come.

Marlowe was relieved. Nora had recently become sulky whenever the subject of college came up.

"He'll go and he won't ever come back here anymore," Nora said to Marlowe the night before. "And then in a few years it'll be you. You'll leave too."

Marlowe reassured Nora it wouldn't be like that, but Marlowe couldn't deny that college students didn't leave campus every single weekend. And her father was already talking about the best art programs. In faraway states, and in other countries. It was awkward to share this with Nora, who had no clear plans. Her options were limited to the community college or maybe an in-state, four-year university, if she could get financial aid. Marlowe had taken to giving Nora small knickknacks from around the Gray House every so often so she could sell them to the pawnshop one town over. The cash would never be enough for college tuition, but it was something.

They marched past the Gallagher barn, but instead of climbing the Rise, they veered toward the soft mud along the edge of the swamp, cutting into the murky terrain when they were even with the gully. The sun was directly overhead, and the afternoon felt like it could stretch on forever.

Nate led them in a twisting trail along the scant solid ground and toward the site of a beaver dam they'd discovered earlier in the year.

"I'm sure it's still there," Nate assured them. "Beavers stick to one place."

"How do you know that? You watch a nature documentary or something?" Marlowe chided, getting a laugh out of Henry.

But sure enough, they soon reached the area where the water pooled around a thick dam, sturdy enough for them to walk across and continue exploring the wetlands on the other side.

Giant green ferns that reached up to Marlowe's waist, tangled reeds, and thick rows of cattails crowded in the shallow, cloudy water. Lily pads and duckweed blanketed the surfaces of every small pond. Marlowe was fascinated by how a place could produce so much vibrant green plant life while also containing so much sticky brown muck and so many gnarled branches.

She wanted to illustrate the wildness of the swamp, the way the trees were spaced out, unlike in the woods, each one staking a solitary claim to a patch of the marsh. Her fingers itched to depict how water pooled in every divot, but she didn't know how to begin such an endeavor. She had dozens of half-finished sketches of the Gray House and its surroundings scattered across her bedroom floor. The house itself was easy to replicate on paper, with its neat edges. But whenever she tried to draw the surrounding woods, the rolling field beyond the gully, or the Gallagher barn, they never came out right. She could capture the shape of the barn and the precise dimensions of the field well enough, but she couldn't capture what they were to her, the spirit of the landscape. Not entirely.

"Hey!" Nate's shout rang out from another pool up ahead.

Marlowe and Nora ran through the weeds to keep up, trying not to look down at their feet as they sloshed through the muck, for fear of seeing a snake or something else slimy and unsavory.

They pulled up short where Nate crouched down at the edge of the water, Henry standing tense behind him.

And then they saw it: a massive, hideous snapping turtle pulling itself through the mud.

Long ago, Tom Gallagher had warned them about snapping turtles. He had joked that they ought to be careful while swimming in the Bend—a snapper might swim up and bite off their little white toes. Marlowe had been scared at the time, but Nate had dismissed the stories of country children with missing fingers.

"Look at it." Henry turned toward the girls, keeping one eye on the snapper. "He's enormous."

His size was notable; the brown shell alone was over a foot wide, far bigger than any turtle Marlowe had ever seen before. And just as the stories claimed, his jaw was large and lethal. His spiked tail was leaving a line in the mud as the snapper dragged himself out of the water.

But it was his age that struck Marlowe most. She couldn't say how she could tell the snapping turtle was old, but she somehow knew that this one was ancient. It was something in the way he moved, as if every push of his clawed front legs required tremendous effort.

The snapper didn't look at them. He was done. Done with biting off toes and gulping down frogs. He was done with life.

Nate inched closer, and the snapper swung his head toward him, not to attack, but as if in some sort of obligatory gesture of toughness.

When it was clear that the snapping turtle was in no state to do any harm, Nate reached out and skimmed his hand over the shell and spiked tail.

"Don't," Marlowe said.

"Don't worry, he's too old to bite," Nate said.

"We should just leave it alone." Marlowe stepped backward. "To die."

Henry, emboldened by the fact that Nate had touched the turtle and suffered no consequences, bent down and wrapped his hand around the snapper's thick ash-colored tail. This the snapper could not abide. He turned and opened his gaping maw, making a strange, wheezing groan that sounded so much like an old man that it sent a frisson of panic through Marlowe's gut.

Henry wheeled backward, his foot slipping in the mud. He held tight to the one thing he could, the snapper's tail, as he crashed into the shallow water with a resounding splash, dragging the snapper in after him. Nora let out a cry when the snapper's soft belly caught on a stone that ripped into his flesh.

Henry released the tail, clambering through the reedy water, his eyes wide with fear as he tried to get away from the turtle.

It was Nora who reached out and grabbed Henry's hand and hauled him to his feet. Nora who didn't let go of his hand as Henry leaned against her shoulder, dripping swamp water down onto her shirt. Marlowe frowned in annoyance over her brother's antics. Henry had injured the turtle, and he was getting too old to cling like a baby to Nora for comfort.

Nate's eyes were fixed on the snapper, which was lying still, half in and half out of the water. Bright red blood oozed from beneath his body. He didn't strain; he just blinked up at the children, as if to ask, *What have you done?*

"Henry, you idiot." Nate's words were sharp, but no one disagreed. It was clear they were watching the turtle suck in his last heavy breath.

"I'm sorry." It sounded like Henry might cry, but his eyes were hollow and dry.

"It—it was dying anyway." Nora sounded only half convinced by her words.

Marlowe glared at Nate. "Why did you have to touch it? It could have died in peace."

They slipped away then, as quietly as they could. As if they didn't want the other creatures to hear what they had done.

They walked back through the trees, Henry's sopping-wet clothing making a squelching noise with his every step. Each of them exhaled as they approached the edge of the swamp and saw their stone wall up ahead, the pale green and gentle grasses of the Flats stretching beyond it.

"You're gonna have to check yourself for leeches, you know." Nora shook her head and smiled up at Henry. "I bet you're covered."

Henry made a sound of disgust and tore off his shirt to inspect himself. "I'm jumping in the Bend to wash off this muck," he said and took off jogging across the Flats.

They all followed, suddenly eager for a swim, a new adventure to erase the one they'd just had.

Henry ran straight into the river's crystal clear water, splashing it into the air as if trying to resurrect the levity of the day. Nate waded in after him, letting the water inch higher and higher. He was quiet, and Marlowe wondered if he was thinking that this could be the last swim of the summer. He'd return to the city the day after tomorrow to finish packing for college.

Marlowe lifted off her shirt and discarded her shorts. She and Nora wore their simple one-piece bathing suits underneath their clothes in the summer. One way or another, they always wound up swimming.

Nora shouted at Nate to pass her the rope. She let out a little squeal as she swung out and let go where it was deepest, her arms outstretched above her head.

For a moment, Marlowe stood still, watching the three of them. Nora and Henry twirled around each other like otters, their limbs flashing and rippling beneath the water. Nora dove beneath the surface, and a few seconds later Nate shouted and laughed as she grabbed his ankle, yanking him under. Nora popped up next to him.

They should have buried that snapping turtle, Marlowe thought. They shouldn't have just left him there to die in agony. They should have dug a hole and covered him with the mud he had lived in his whole life.

"Marlowe!" Nora's voice was clear as a bell, ringing out above the water. "Come in already!"

Marlowe sprinted toward the bank, splashing into the water at full speed. She ducked her head under, letting the pristine river water swallow her whole.

# SATURDAY

## DECEMBER 1, 2018

# TWENTY-NINE

Late into the night, in the quiet cocoon of the basement, Marlowe had sipped wine and skimmed news articles about Rick Frasier's arrest, the headlines blurring as she skipped from one to the next. In the most recent piece, a photo of Harmon Gallagher caught her off guard—an image she hadn't seen before. There was something in the tilt of his head, the way he angled it slightly as he smiled, that reminded her of Tom. He'd done the same thing, she realized, whenever he spoke to them. Somewhere between the third and fourth headline and the bottom of her glass, the decision took shape. She would go to the wake.

In the morning, she turned down Henry's invitation to get a Christmas tree with the kids and instead sipped coffee in the basement until noon. Then she dressed in a black sweater and slacks and drove to Harmon Gallagher's mother's house. The details had been in one of the articles she'd read.

On the way to the wake, she considered whether the Gallagher house might still be standing if Peter Gallagher had inherited the land instead of his aunt Caroline. Pete and Layla would have moved onto the old farm, and Harmon, a toddler then, would have spent his childhood there, walking the fields, tending cows, ducking in and out of the big red barn. Planting hay each spring, mowing in the summer, hauling bales up into the loft. Eventually, his skin would have become brown and weathered, his limbs wiry and strong with the resilience of old farmers. A quiet life, hard but honest.

Marlowe was certain Harmon would've chosen that over what had transpired—the debt, the desperation, the sudden end. Over being bludgeoned in the back of the head by Rick Frasier, who, according to one article, might have been bipolar—something his lawyers were already suggesting for leniency.

At a red light, Marlowe tightened her grip on the steering wheel, forcing herself to not think about other images in the article—the Gray House, tall and stately, looming in one frame, and Nora's sophomore yearbook photo in another. Nora's hair was straightened and brushed, her smile bright but strained, as though the photographer was moments from getting on her nerves.

It seemed like every few years, someone resurfaced a mystery of a bubbly teenage girl who disappeared without a trace. Marlowe lived in mortal dread of the day that someone made a true crime documentary about Nora. Or worse, a podcast.

At least one article stuck to the basics: *The site where Harmon Gallagher's body was found is also the location of another tragic event. In June 1998, local teenager Nora Miller disappeared after an evening with friends on the property.*

There was no mention of the Fishers or the suspected role they played. The comment section was less restrained, however.

Last night, she'd scrolled through every post, all the condolences for the Gallagher family, the exclamations of shock and horror at such violence in this quiet, beautiful part of the countryside, and the few posts by those with a rant against hunting regulations in the area.

But three specific comments had seared themselves into her mind, resurfacing now as she sat in the idling car.

*That girl was a travesty. I remember hearing about it and just knowing that some stuff got covered up. The so-called "friends" were rich, and we all know money can cover anything.*

Farther down: *I still pray for Nora. Something about that case never sat right. Hope someone gets to the bottom of it one day.*

And the final one: *Wait, they never found this girl? Not even the body?? Smells fishy to me.*

Marlowe bit her lower lip hard and hit the gas as the light turned green. She hated those people. Anonymous, gleeful in their speculation, reveling in the scandal. But today, she was going to get answers.

She pulled up to the small house, just past an old horse barn, and cut the engine. As she sat behind the wheel for a long moment, her breath became shallow and unsteady. She asked herself, Was she going to be brave, or was she going to run away?

She knew what Nora would do.

Buttoning her coat all the way up to her chin, Marlowe stepped quietly from the car, careful to close the door softly behind her.

She hoped it would be crowded. Crowds meant anonymity. But did Harmon have many friends? He seemed to be a bit of a loner.

When she opened the front door, relief washed over Marlowe. The narrow hallway and small living room were packed. People flock to tragedy like moths to a flame, and this was no exception. Harmon was young and he had been murdered, and everyone was curious.

Marlowe peeked into the living room and spotted a knot of older guests congregating around a heavyset woman—Harmon's mother, Layla. She clutched a mug and stared blankly, her swollen jowls marked with purple veins. Marlowe quickly turned toward the cramped kitchen, where the counter was laden with various dishes, most of them some variation of mac and cheese.

She grabbed a flimsy plate and scooped on a few carrot sticks and crackers, trying to look natural.

Everyone else formed tight circles, talking quietly, shoulders leaning in. Marlowe stood alone, acutely aware of how out of place she looked. She glanced toward the stairs, where people in Harmon's age range gathered. His old school friends or hunting buddies perhaps. She didn't want them; they were too young to know Pete and too ignorant to help. She needed someone older, someone who remembered.

Facing Layla felt impossible, so she abandoned the plate in the kitchen and slipped out the back door. The porch was small and weather-beaten. A thin layer of snow dusted the lawn, fresh from the morning. In a corner of the yard, a couple shared a cigarette, shifting their weight to stay warm. They gave her a curious glance before she rounded the side of the house, out of view.

"I'm sorry, excuse me," Marlowe said.

The woman glanced up, her age hitting Marlowe like a jolt of electricity. Deep wrinkles folded into her sagging skin, her features drawn inward toward a puckered mouth. She wore a bulky black wool coat, half unbuttoned, and a scarf in a sickly shade of puce. The cigarette between her fingers trembled, held as though it had been there forever.

"Are you all right in the cold?" Marlowe asked. "I can help you back inside."

"Oh no, I'm fine," the woman rasped, her voice like sandpaper. She raised the cigarette, as if to prove her vitality. At her age, Marlowe figured, what was the point of quitting?

The woman gestured to the chair across from her. "Sit. It's too damn crowded in there, isn't it?"

Marlowe sat down, relieved to keep her distance from the other smokers who had been eyeing her. This old woman seemed harmless—teetering on the edge of batty—and Marlowe doubted she would remember her in a few hours.

"Did you know Harmon?" the woman asked.

"No, not really," Marlowe said. "I know the Gallaghers. Tom Gallagher was friends with my father."

A version of the truth—something she was becoming quite good at.

"Ah, Tommy." The woman's yellowed teeth stretched into a grin. "My cousin. I'm Caroline. I was his favorite, you know."

Marlowe stilled. Caroline Rodine. The one who'd inherited the land and sold it to Frank. Her heart raced. She'd come looking for answers, and here they were. After so many dead ends and uncertainties, Marlowe was frightened by the potential.

"I think I heard him mention you once." It was a blatant lie, but Caroline beamed, probably the first time in years anyone had offered confirmation that she was anyone's favorite. Marlowe thought of the crumpled family tree in her purse. Caroline grew up in the Gray House. Tom Gallagher would have patted her head long before Marlowe was even born. The thought stirred something sour in her chest. Jealousy. She wanted the old man to belong solely to her childhood. And yet Caroline had been callous with his memory, selling all the brothers' land. In a way, Marlowe wondered if she was a better guardian of their legacy.

"He left me his land," Caroline said, nodding toward the fields beyond the house, as if they could see the old Gallagher land if they looked into the distance. "The land Harmon died on."

Marlowe leaned forward, matching Caroline's hushed tone. "Really?"

"Oh yes. And I sold it quick. I was married with children of my own to take care of. Knew no good would come of keeping it." Her eyes sparkled as she was likely remembering the tidy sum she'd made on the deal. "Harmon never knew Tom and his brothers, or he'd have stayed away."

"Oh?" Marlowe kept her voice even. "Why's that?"

"That farm was cursed," Caroline said.

Marlowe blinked. "Cursed?"

"All family farms are, one way or another, but ours, well, it was special," Caroline said. "Years and years ago, when the farm was thriving, a Gallagher married the wrong woman, I'll put it that way."

A shiver prickled Marlowe's neck.

"James Gallagher, my great-grandfather." Caroline spoke the name with pride. "He married a witch."

Marlowe couldn't speak, raising her eyebrows instead.

"Don't worry, dear, I know how I sound," Caroline said. "But when you're my age, you stop caring. And you've been around long enough to see a few things. Believe me, I've seen things. Everyone back then knew that his wife was a witch, and his daughter, Victoria, was one too."

Victoria Gallagher. The daughter obsessed with the hedgerow. Marlowe's head swam, and she felt like she might suddenly topple over in her chair.

"James didn't know what to do with her after her mother died," Caroline continued. "Victoria was beautiful but dangerous, and useless on top of that, which is even worse for a farmer's daughter. Made his life miserable, and she was just as unhappy. She spent her days locked up in her room, wandering the fields at night, riling up the cows, doing strange witchcraft in the barns. James beat her for it, but she'd just laugh and keep on."

Marlowe pictured the old house, lit up by a full moon, the window cracked open, a girl in a white nightgown slipping out and into the fields, just as she and Nora had once done.

"He shouldn't have beaten her." Caroline sighed. "Only made her worse. That's when she cursed the farm."

"What—what was the curse?" Marlowe's mouth had gone dry.

"Madness." Caroline lifted her cigarette for emphasis. "They married her off to some poor neighbor, and she poured her own madness into that land. Sealed it with blood, they say, muttering the curse on her deathbed. Childbirth gone wrong. No doctor. Bloody business." Caroline gave Marlowe a grave look. "Well, you already know what happened to Tom and his brothers."

Marlowe nodded, a heaviness in her chest. Three brothers, three tragic deaths—an aberration she sometimes forgot, since it had happened when she was young. But now, after reading Dave's journal, it all seemed darker. Sharper. A design crafted by a cruel hand.

"And then that girl in the nineties just disappeared into thin air," Caroline added. "I warned the man who bought the land from me to be careful. I told him all about Victoria Gallagher. But he didn't listen."

"You think that girl went mad?" Marlowe asked, feigning casual interest.

"Someone did," Caroline said, shrugging. "Someone took her, after all."

"A Gallagher?"

"Oh no, Tom and his brothers were gone by then. The land was sold to some rich city family, same one that bought my brother Harry's section years before. Harry was none too pleased, but I said better to part well and lucratively." She exhaled a long plume of smoke. "A curse is a curse. Can't argue with that, not with so many bad things happening on one patch of dirt. And now Harmon."

Marlowe blinked furiously. She always thought of what happened at the Gray House as her own personal tragedy, separate from the others. But now it felt like something much bigger—something that had been waiting there long before she and Nora ever crept into that barn.

"Harmon's father wasn't much better." Caroline's voice dropped to a true whisper now that she had shifted to more recent history. "My nephew, Pete—my brother's boy—was obsessed with that farm. I told him not to let Harmon linger around there, but Pete despised me. He never forgave me for selling."

A flicker of something approaching regret passed through her eyes. Marlowe wondered if she had ever reconsidered her hasty selling. Real or not, it was *her* family curse, after all. She was part of Victoria Gallagher's bloodline. Maybe she could've stayed, could've become the witch she seemed vaguely proud of having descended from. Instead, here she was: old, brittle, shivering on a back porch with nothing but the company of strangers and cigarette smoke.

"Was there anything wrong with Pete?" Marlowe treaded lightly. She couldn't exactly ask if he had been the type to lurk in the woods, hunt rabbits, and kidnap teenage girls.

Caroline lifted her head, and her eyes narrowed. She seemed to look again at Marlowe and see something other than an old family friend of Tom Gallagher's. For the first time, she seemed unsure.

"No, there was nothing wrong with Peter." The defensiveness in her voice was unmistakable. Gossiping was one thing, but this crossed a line. "He was passionate. Sad, maybe. Liked his drink too much—just like his father, Harry, who ran his share of the farm into the ground by the time Pete was grown." She paused, as if she could say more about Harry but chose not to. "If Harry and Pete were still alive, Harmon's death would've destroyed them." She crossed herself quickly, a gesture of faith layered over her belief in the occult.

"Of course," Marlowe said.

"It was that farm." Caroline flicked her cigarette ash. "Pete never let go of it, and neither did Harmon. They let their anger fester. Harry encouraged it. Thought anger made men strong."

Marlowe's hands balled into fists in her lap. An angry man, in a family with a history of addiction and madness. Her mind raced, but Caroline wasn't finished.

"I had to sell it." Caroline's voice cracked; the words were thin and fragile things. "I had to."

Guilt. It clung to her, as though all these years later she believed Harmon's death was somehow her fault. If she had been braver—if she had just hung on to the farm—none of this would have happened. Marlowe recognized that kind of guilt all too well. The corrosive kind that lingered for years.

"I'm sure you did." Marlowe stood up. "I should go. I'm so sorry for your loss."

Caroline's sunken eyes followed her. "What did you say your name was?"

"Alice." The old woman was sharper than Marlowe had first assumed. She wasn't giving her real name. "Lovely to talk to you."

Marlowe ducked around the side of the house, her heart thudding. The exchange had left her breathless, nerves buzzing. Old family rumors weren't proof, but they hinted at something darker. And Pete, angry and obsessed, lingering too long on cursed land. His culpability was becoming more plausible with every passing moment.

Marlowe jumped as Ben Vance and Ariel Mintz appeared on the porch. Both looked as out of place as she felt, but at least they belonged there, reminding everyone that Harmon's killer had been caught. Ben had even thrown on a tie. Ariel's frizzy hair hung loose, and she'd swiped on mauve lipstick, but the dark circles under her eyes remained.

"What are you doing here?" Ariel's voice was quiet but cold.

"I was about to leave," Marlowe said.

"Great." Ben smiled and jerked his head toward the road. "We'll walk you to your car."

Marlowe followed them in silence. At her car, Ariel crossed her arms. "Get anything good from Caroline Rodine?"

"I wanted to ask about Pete Gallagher," Marlowe admitted. "I keep thinking about Mr. Babel, if he could've been real."

"You sure you don't want to go back in there and hound the grieving mother about her deceased husband?" Ariel rolled her eyes. Her tone had turned sharper and less amicable than it had been in the previous days. "Not everything's some tangled mess. Sometimes it really is that simple." Whatever she wanted Marlowe to get out of Brierley's notes, it wasn't Mr. Babel.

"Pete was obsessed with the farm, just like Harmon," Marlowe pressed. "I thought maybe he hung around the woods. It would make sense that he was lurking on what used to be his family's land."

"He had no reason to hurt Nora," Ariel snapped. "He died years ago."

Ariel was no longer the patient conversationalist, coaxing out Marlowe's thoughts. With Harmon's murder solved, the detectives were running out of time. So was Marlowe.

"I know," Marlowe said. "But maybe he mistook Nora for someone else. Or he knew my family would be blamed and wanted to drive us out."

Marlowe's face flushed as the words tumbled out. The idea was wild, but Caroline had implied Pete was angry enough to do something reckless.

The detectives exchanged a look.

"Even if Brierley thought the Mr. Babel story was nonsense, he should have spoken to Pete," Marlowe said. "It was negligence."

"Pete Gallagher was a drunk." Ariel's voice snapped through the frigid air. "Like his father. Couldn't button his shirt, let alone kidnap a girl without getting caught."

Marlowe flinched, her back bumping up against her car. Ariel's eyes were blazing, but Ben placed a gentle hand on her elbow, and she clamped her mouth shut.

Ben gave Marlowe a tired smile. "We don't think you're foolish."

"I'm not foolish," she said flatly. Then she glanced at Ariel. She had believed in her, even as Ariel played with Marlowe's emotions. She still trusted in Ariel's intelligence, at least. "With the Nate thing—I don't know. I just can't see it."

"Is it possible, in your opinion, that they were romantically involved?" Ariel's low and steady way of speaking had returned, as if her outburst had never happened.

"Of course it's possible. But anything's possible."

Ariel hesitated but then simply said, "Well, we'll see you again."

Marlowe nodded. "I'm sure."

She slid into her car and started the engine but didn't drive off immediately. She watched them walk back to the house, heads bent in conversation.

They were being careful, guarded. They didn't trust her. Somewhere, her name was pinned to a board next to Nora's, with lines connecting her to Nate, to Henry—lines that couldn't be erased.

Marlowe finally pulled onto the road, Ariel's words echoing in her head: *Sometimes it really is that simple.*

Ben's fake reassurance, Ariel's sudden irritation and loss of patience with her—it was wearing her down. What was she doing running around chasing old rumors and shadows in the woods? Caroline's words were echoing in her head too: Pete wasn't a ghost back in 1998. Back then, he was a real man. And he had been angry.

# THIRTY

The sun was setting fast behind the red Gallagher barn, and the snow had turned to a sheet of ice on the front yard of the Gray House, gleaming beneath the onslaught of dusk.

Marlowe stepped inside the house and quickly hung up her coat. She was still mulling over what Ariel had said as she was leaving the wake. If the woods and hills really were haunted, as she had sometimes believed as a child, then wasn't that the simplest explanation?

"Marlowe!" Glory called from the living room, holding up a cardboard box. "How old were you when you made these?"

The tree was up in the corner of the living room, and Henry was putting on the lights with care as the girls circled around him. Dolly, her uncle's bumbling assistant, was tangled up in the excess strings of lights. The boxes of ornaments were spread across the floor. Kat was admiring her favorites, the ones with paintings of Victorian people dancing on the orbs, while Constance bounced Frankie on her knee and sorted through smaller glass ornaments. In the kitchen, Stephanie was pulling cookies out of the oven, setting them to cool. Enzo sat in the big armchair with pillows tucked on either side of him. He was half asleep, his head nodding. The room smelled richly of pine and cinnamon sugar.

Glory was holding the little dolls Marlowe had made from yarn. One was a cowboy, with brown boots and a tiny felt hat. Another was in a long scarlet ball gown with puffed sleeves. Marlowe lifted the third, a girl with yellow braids wearing simple blue overalls.

"Kat's age," Marlowe said. "Maybe a bit older."

"Such talent." Glory beamed.

"Marlowe has a gift." Enzo had stirred awake with a wavering smile. "But gifts must be honed."

Another phrase he was plucking from years ago, like a musician trying to play an old tune without sheet music.

"Another night of snow and we can dust off the toboggan," Henry said.

Dolly gasped with excitement. "I'll be in the front!"

"It's not as thrilling as you think," Marlowe said with a laugh. "I was always in the front, and I hated it."

"You were never in the front." Henry turned to her. A string of lights was draped over his arms.

"I thought I was." Marlowe frowned. "The snow was always hitting my face, and I would get scared because I could see when we were headed for the trees."

"You were too tall to be in the front." Henry paused, stopping himself from saying more. "We had some good snows back then; not sure we'll get the right conditions this year."

Marlowe mulled over Henry's contradiction. He hadn't needed to say her name—she remembered now. Those were Nora's blue mittens holding the looped twine in an iron grip at the front of the toboggan. If Nate were present, he would set the record straight. He'd loved those sledding days so much, he likely recalled every single run they ever made down the North Field.

"The snows were always better back then," Marlowe said, but they had already turned away from her, absorbed in their tasks again.

"Marlowe?" Her father's voice came from the study. "Is that you?"

Marlowe laid the doll on the table and walked down the hall.

"Hi, Dad, I was just out for a drive."

Frank was at his desk, sifting through papers.

He looked up at Marlowe leaning against the doorframe and smiled.

"They're praying for more snow out there, eh?" He chuckled and it sounded too close to a cough. "Remember how you used to sing 'White Christmas' over and over, because you thought you could conjure snow on Christmas Eve?"

"I remember." Frank used to pick her up and swing her around as she sang, raving that she was so clever to know all the words. He had been so tall and fit and strong. "Can I get you anything, Dad? A cup of tea?"

"I must really look weak if my Marlowe is offering to serve me." Frank grinned.

She smiled down at him in return. "Really, Dad, I'm going to make tea anyway."

"It's fine," Frank said. "I'm just fine, here in this house, surrounded by all of you. It's all I ever wanted."

Marlowe nodded and turned to leave the study, thinking how she'd always been sad for girls who didn't have fathers like hers.

Her father stopped her. "You love it here, don't you?" It was a common line of inquiry from Frank, as if he wanted validation that they belonged on this land and in this house.

"Yes, of course," she said.

He also seemed to want to know, the older he got, which of his children loved it the most. Frank was clear that he never wanted to divide up the land. It was supposed to remain whole. But Marlowe had a theory that one sibling was going to get more and outweigh the other two when it came to decisions about the property. One of them would have a head start on buying the others out, if it ever came to it.

"I've never been able to leave, not really," Marlowe said. "Or at least, whenever I leave, I always know I'll come back here, one way or another."

She supposed her brothers would say the same thing. The difference was, Marlowe didn't have anything else. And if that made her father pity her enough to give her the extra percentage, she would take it gladly.

"I know," Frank said with what looked like a twinge of sadness in his eye.

Marlowe leaned down and hugged her father before drifting out of the study and to the kitchen, empty now that Stephanie had joined the others by the tree. Marlowe didn't make a cup of tea. Instead, she poured two fingers of whiskey into a mug, then filled the rest with eggnog. She carried the mug past the revelry around the tree and down to the basement, where she opened her computer.

There was an email from Mike Cameron, Nate's old college buddy. She opened the message immediately.

Hello Marlowe,

Hope you are well. I can talk today. Let me know what time would work.

Best,
Mike

She quickly typed out a response, telling him that she was available now or anytime that afternoon, and she included her number.

Mike Cameron didn't keep her waiting long. Within ten minutes, her phone rang.

"Marlowe, hello." His voice was unrecognizable.

"Hi, Mike." Marlowe cradled the phone against her ear and set down the eggnog. "I know my email might have come out of the blue."

"It's about Nora, isn't it?" He got straight to the point. He hadn't been like that when he was young. She supposed a few decades in the medical field would do that to a person. "The detectives did reach out to me. I was glad to get your email, because I was feeling I should let someone in your family know."

"Know what?" Marlowe's throat went dry.

"I told them more this time," Mike said. "More than I said back then."

"That's good," she said. "That's—that's all I've wanted."

He must have heard some fear in her voice. "I'm not saying I know anything; there were just little things, really. Things I never said. Because I was young and Nate was my friend, and I honestly wanted to forget the whole thing."

"Can you start at the beginning?" Marlowe asked. "Can you tell me what you told them?"

Mike started on the drive up from the city, with Nate describing the weekend they were in for.

"It was clear he loved the place," Mike said. "He'd been raving about it for weeks. How we were going to take a long hike through the woods and maybe swim in the river if the weather was warm enough. The big dinners we would have."

The lost weekend.

"Nate talked about you guys too. And Nora. I was honestly curious to meet all of you." Mike paused and heaved a great sigh that sounded like the crackle of a radio when the channel hit a spot of static. "I've thought about that night a lot. I'm sure you know I was never close with Nate afterward. That we drifted. I guess I tried to forget, but I never could do it. That girl, disappearing—it stuck with me."

"It's not something we can ever forget." Marlowe's voice was low, barely audible.

"Yeah." Mike paused for a long second. "The thing is, I have three daughters now, and if it were one of my daughters . . ." Mike's voice trailed off as he considered the unimaginable. "Look, I wish I could go back and grab my idiot younger self by the neck and tell him to do more. To say more."

"To say what, specifically?" Marlowe was holding the phone so close to her ear that she felt it was going to leave an imprint on her cheek. She knew this was the moment Mike would tell her that Nate and Nora had been sleeping together.

"On the ride up there that Friday, Nate described the three of you. He'd mentioned his kid brother and little sister before," Mike said. "He told us Henry was a riot, and that his sister was solid. But in that car, that was the first time he mentioned Nora."

Marlowe was frozen in suspense, but a small part of her rankled at being reduced to "solid" by her older brother.

"Nate said the neighbor would be there, and he was tense about it," Mike said. "Look, I don't know all the details, but he implied she was clingy, always hanging around. Honestly, it just sounded like a typical neighbor situation to me, like something out of a sitcom. But then he claimed that she was a little thief. That's what he called her: 'a little thief.'"

Marlowe blinked. That was a secret.

"Nate wasn't mad or anything. He just seemed put off by it," Mike continued. "He didn't go into detail, but he said he knew she had stolen a ring from his mother's box, and some silver or something."

There had been a ring, yes, and a pendant. A paperweight from her father's office. Silver cuff links.

Small things. Things Marlowe had been quite certain her parents would never notice. Fallen behind a dresser drawer or misplaced somewhere. Left in the city, perhaps, or in a hotel room.

Marlowe helped Nora take them. Gave them to her. The Gray House had too much. Why shouldn't it go to Nora, who needed it?

There had been an older student with a car. Nora had cut some sort of deal. The guy drove to Albany or Poughkeepsie, to various pawnshops, and he and Nora split the cash.

It was for things she needed. School supplies. Clothes. Things that Marlowe just *had* easy access to.

Marlowe had seen the difference in their lives. She had seen how unfair it was. So she helped, but she never suspected that Nate had caught on to it.

"Is that all he said about her?" Marlowe asked.

"He called her tricky; I remember that," Mike said. "Sly. Manipulative. Said we should keep an eye on her. The way he described her, I thought we were going to meet some sort of red-eyed demon. But then we got there, and she was just a girl."

"And you never told Brierley this? Back when she first disappeared?"

"All Brierley asked was if Nate was sleeping with Nora, and I said no, full stop. Then I just repeated over and over that I didn't know anything."

"But was he sleeping with her?" Marlowe nearly whispered the question.

"No, I don't think so." There was a rustle on the other end. Mike was shifting and moving something. Marlowe pictured him in a plaid button-down shirt, eager to enjoy his day off. "I think he hated Nora. Not in a romance-gone-bad type of way. Just true resentment."

Marlowe furrowed her brow. Nate didn't hate Nora. He never had. They were friends, all of them. So why was Mike so certain?

"And that's what you told the detectives this time?" Marlowe asked. "Because you think Nate might have done something?"

"I told the detectives about the tension between Nate and Nora. Described the night, or what I remember. How she left. And the moment we realized something was wrong."

Just as Marlowe remembered it, save the minute details.

"So, I mean, we both know Nate was right there," Mike said. "And that's why I never said anything back then about what he really thought of Nora. But, like I said, it's haunted me ever since."

"I understand," Marlowe said. "Thank you for telling me."

"I know she meant a lot to you. Anyone could see that, even a stupid college kid," Mike said. "I told the detectives that as well."

Marlowe nodded, losing herself to the past, then forced herself to speak. "Yes. She did mean a lot to me."

"Anyway, good luck with everything." He didn't know how to end the conversation, but it was clear he was finished talking.

"What's your theory?" Marlowe pressed. "If you had to guess, what do you think happened? Who do you think took her?"

"I don't know your family," Mike said. "Really, I never truly knew any of you."

"But you must have a theory. Everyone does."

"Enzo." The name fell out of Mike's mouth, as if he had been waiting the whole phone call to say it. "I know he was your nanny or handyman, or whatever, and he was nice enough, but that's the guy I think of when I think of that night. And this time I told the detectives that."

Enzo. The one who had been on the premises, but not in the kitchen. The one who would have done anything for Marlowe and her family.

And he was obvious, wasn't he? To Mike—so removed from everything, so ignorant about the bonds that connected her family to outsiders like Enzo and Nora, satellite planets pulled into the fold—to Mike, Enzo made sense. To Marlowe—wrapped up in all the weekends spent with Enzo, all the long summers at the Gray

House—nothing made sense anymore.

Marlowe's children's book illustrations veered toward the whimsical—she couldn't help it, when they were all based, in one way or another, on the Gray House. The rolling hills, the hayfields, the red barn, the ever-burning hearth—they all lent themselves easily to stories set in fairy-tale lands populated by magical creatures: wood fairies, gnomes, elves. And in such places, there were always guardians, someone who lived in the eaves, who traded protection for porridge and chased foxes from henhouses, keeping the children safe and warm, behind glowing windows.

Enzo. He was the loyal protector. More than hired help, he was family. Enzo would have shooed the fox away, made sure the hens were fed, the children safe.

Marlowe had always known Enzo would never hurt them. She'd believed that included Nora, who should've been under his protection too.

After hanging up the phone, Marlowe forced herself to reconsider, to search the corners of her memory for Enzo, for any little thing she might have missed before. Enzo used to live in this very basement room. He'd been quiet over the last few days, saying the cold had seeped into his bones, and he'd spent most of his time tucked away in his bedroom or sitting in the armchair under several blankets.

The truth was, Marlowe knew next to nothing concrete about Enzo's life before them. Like any self-absorbed child, she never asked. He had a funny accent and told stories about Italian vineyards and Parisian streets, but she couldn't say whether these were facts or not. It was as if he'd simply appeared one day, summoned to care for her and her brothers.

Surely her parents had done their due diligence—background checks, references. But what could those reveal? Not the things that mattered. Not if Enzo had a taste for young women, if he'd once pursued a seventeen-year-old Italian girl or admired girls from park benches in Paris.

Marlowe stood in the center of the basement, the mug of eggnog in her hand. She drained it, the warmth cutting the chill in her chest. The room had been renovated fifteen years ago—new floors, windows, closets, a bigger bathroom. When Enzo didn't need it anymore, Marlowe moved in, turning his place into her own. Enzo retired to his tiny apartment in Queens. He was now a guest at the Gray House, relegated to the spare room upstairs.

Marlowe's stomach turned. While they'd been shouting Nora's name into the darkness, had she been right here all along?

Still, she couldn't think of a rational motive. Mike seemed to believe both Nate and Enzo had contempt for Nora. Enzo had, now and then, called Nora a hellion and chastised her impulsive nature. But Marlowe never thought there was any real malice in his voice.

Did Enzo know about the stealing? He might have blamed Nora, seen her as a bad influence on sweet, naïve Marlowe. She could almost hear his voice, sneering: *The little thief. That wicked girl.* He didn't know that Marlowe had basically given her those things.

It wouldn't have taken much. Enzo was strong back then. Years of carpentry and vineyard work kept him fit. The basement had the side door. He could have crossed the lawn, taken her inside without a sound.

Maybe he saw Nora as a threat. Or had it been something darker? A twisted desire. Had he imagined her and Nate together and wanted her for himself? Marlowe pressed her knuckles against her mouth, still damp from her last gulp.

Marlowe had always believed that someone from outside their

orbit had committed the crime. A stalker. A local weirdo. A stranger with a grudge. It had seemed like the most logical explanation at the time.

Had she been an idiot all along? A fool who couldn't follow a straight line. How many things could Marlowe simply miss? How many times could Marlowe ask a question, have a drink while she waited for the answer, only to get muddled all over again? But she was seeing clearly now, wasn't she?

Maybe the villain wasn't a fox in the briar. The villain was the one who was sworn to protect it.

# THIRTY-ONE

**BENDING BIRCHES**
**Saturday, February 21, 1998**

Marlowe and Nora trekked through the Flats, toward the stone wall they'd completed last summer.

It was Marlowe's sixteenth birthday, and Enzo was making steak au poivre and crispy potatoes, per her request. He vowed it would be better than anything she could order in a New York restaurant and then shooed them out for a walk to work up their appetites in the brisk winter air.

They perched for a moment on the stone wall, catching their breath. The wall already looked like it had been there forever, already seemed to have weathered many winters.

"So, I know you asked your parents for that travel easel this year. But now that we're alone, you can tell me your real birthday wish," Nora said, nudging Marlowe's shoulder with her own.

The two of them always shared their birthday wishes. Contrary to the rule about wishes not coming true when said out loud, Marlowe believed sharing with each other only made the wishes stronger.

"I'll tell you, but you have to promise not to laugh," Marlowe said. She could already feel herself starting to blush.

Nora feigned shock at the request. "Laugh? Me? Never."

"I want to be kissed." Marlowe buried her face in her hands. "It's pathetic, I know. But it would be even worse to turn sixteen and be *unkissed*! So that's what I want."

Nora sat cross-legged on top of the wall, and she leaned forward and touched Marlowe's knee.

"It's not pathetic or embarrassing at all," Nora said. "It means you have high standards and you're waiting for someone worthy."

Marlowe squeezed her friend's hand. No one else in the world could have made her feel so much better with so few words.

While they sat on the wall, Nora confessed to Marlowe about how much she hated school these days. Ever since she and Sean broke up, she didn't have any friends to hang out with.

"Everyone is stupid," Nora said as she wiggled atop the wall, the rock beneath her wobbling. "I hate the boring teachers, and I hate how everyone only cares about the next basketball or baseball game. I hate this whole town."

Marlowe hummed in sympathy. "I don't have many friends at my school either. No one like you."

"But you're in the *city*—you have so much to do outside of school." Nora slouched, her entire body deflating. "I'm only happy when you guys are up here."

"It will be summer in a few months." Marlowe linked her arm through Nora's. "And I'll be at the Gray House the whole time. We just have to wait until summer."

"Let's not wait!" Nora hoisted herself down off the wall. "Let's jump in now."

"Jump in the river?" Marlowe glanced at the ice clinging to the edge of the nearby bank.

"I heard it's good for your metabolism! I think they call it cold plunging." Nora was practically bouncing on her toes. "Come on, let's go to the Bend! A birthday plunge!"

"You're crazy, but okay, let's do it." Marlowe laughed and grabbed Nora's hand as they jogged the half mile through a thin layer of snow to the Bend.

Silvery ice lined the edges of the swimming hole, but the center was churning. The Bean rarely froze over.

Marlowe and Nora spent several minutes deciding how many items of clothing to take off. "Obviously, we have to take off our boots and coats, but is it better or worse to jump in with shirts and jeans on?" Nora wondered.

"Our jeans might be too heavy," Marlowe pointed out. "Once they're wet, they'll weigh us down."

She remembered a summer long ago when Nate pushed her into the Bean fully clothed as a joke. She wasn't scared until she tried to pull herself to the surface, and her sneakers held her back, like weights around her feet. She made it up, but for a brief moment, she was terrified.

"I think underwear is best," Nora said. "We'll just have to get dressed with our dry things quickly and run."

Marlowe nodded. "Agreed."

Their squeals and whimpers of excitement echoed off the water's surface as they rapidly stripped down, tossing their sweaters, shirts, and jeans in a pile, until they were standing together in bras and panties.

Marlowe felt a burst of self-consciousness about the shadow of hair peeking out from her underwear, but Nora didn't care. She had her own hair. She'd once confided that she hated shaving down there unless she absolutely had to. For swimsuits and whatnot.

Marlowe ventured to dip a toe in the water.

"Big mistake," Nora said. "It's best to just jump and do it quick."

Marlowe looked back. Nora's skin was already purple with cold.

"All right." Marlowe took a breath. "No more thinking, we jump together."

"I'll jump when you jump."

Marlowe counted them down. "One, two, three, go!"

They dove headfirst into the current. The rush of water was nothing like swimming in the summer. It wasn't painful at first—it felt amazing. As Marlowe pushed her head through the surface, she felt energy spread over her skin, as if her body had come alive.

Only after another second did Marlowe feel the cold. Her chest suddenly felt as if it had caved in, and she let out a scream of mingled joy and pain.

"Holy shit!" Nora yelped. "Oh my God."

Her hair was plastered to her head, the blond streaks turned dark by the water. They paddled back to shore as quickly as possible, their teeth chattering.

"That was amazing," Marlowe cried.

"My lungs." Nora pressed a hand to her chest.

"Yeah, mine too."

They yanked on their jeans, the thick fabric catching on their wet skin. Then they threw on their shirts and shoved their feet into their boots without bothering with socks. They scooped up their coats and ran.

"I feel like I'm gonna die!" Nora screamed as they sprinted across the Flats, the cold air biting at their skin.

"Why do I have the urge to jump back in?" Marlowe gasped.

"Because you're a lunatic!"

They scrambled into the gully and then climbed out, half stumbling to the top of the Rise, and then the Gallagher barn was in sight.

"Almost there!" Nora yelled.

A second burst of adrenaline kicked in, and Marlowe felt as if sparks were flying from her fingertips as they ran down to the cow fence and launched themselves over. She landed in a crouch and set off running again. Her feet were going numb, but surely hypothermia took more than ten minutes to set in.

They banged through the front door of the Gray House and kicked off their boots.

Henry poked his head out from the kitchen. "What the heck?"

"We jumped in the Bean!" Marlowe yelled. "It was *freezing*."

"But amazing!"

Glory looked like she might scold them, but she laughed instead. "You girls are crazy! Now hurry, go get some dry clothes on before you turn into icicles."

Within minutes, they had dashed to the girls' room, torn off their wet clothes, and yanked on dry shirts and sweatpants, too cold and used to each other to be precious about nudity. They ran back down to the fire and pressed themselves up against the screen, lips purple but stretched into smiles.

"It felt so good," Marlowe said. "Like my skin was buzzing."

"I almost want to do it again," Nora said.

"Brave girls." Enzo winked. "French ladies douse their faces in ice water every day to make their skin glow."

Henry did not hide his jealousy as he stomped about swinging his long limbs. He had finally hit his growth spurt and had shot up by several inches, but he still acted boyish at times. He hadn't joined them on the walk. With Nate away at college, Henry was hesitant to believe the girls were capable of cooking up exciting activities on their own.

"You should have gotten me before you did it!" Henry said.

Marlowe laughed. "We couldn't stall, we had to act!"

She pulled her long hair over her shoulder and leaned over the fire so that the flames could dry her freezing, wet strands. Nora did the same thing, bending over and throwing her locks upside down so they dangled above the screen.

"Don't burn yourselves," Glory said. "I don't want to have to put out a fire on your heads."

Frank wandered in from the study. He smiled at them drying their hair by the heat of the fire and recited a line from one of his favorite poems: "You may see their trunks arching in the woods, years afterwards, trailing their leaves on the ground. Like girls on hands and knees that throw their hair before them over their heads to dry in the sun."

# SUNDAY

## DECEMBER 2, 2018

# THIRTY-TWO

Ascending the staircase from her room, Marlowe squinted against the early-afternoon light spilling through the kitchen windows. Her head throbbed—a dull, manageable ache—but she steadied her breath. No room for nerves now.

Henry was making lunch for the kids when he noticed her.

"Mom and Dad went to town?" She could see their car was missing from the drive.

"Yes, they just left." Henry flipped a grilled cheese in one smooth motion, the bread sizzling in the butter. "Don't go in the study—Steph and Constance are wrapping gifts. It's top secret."

He turned and winked at Kat and Dolly.

"Where's Enzo?" Marlowe asked.

"He's resting upstairs," Henry said. "Would you ask him if he wants lunch? He can come down, or I can bring it up to him."

Henry fit so easily into the role of caregiver. He had been carrying half of Enzo's meals up to him on a tray. He never seemed uncomfortable or ashamed when Enzo took forever to chew one bite of food, or when Enzo spewed out sentences that didn't make sense.

Marlowe turned toward the stairs and made her way slowly to the spare room.

She knocked gently and pushed the door open to find Enzo propped up in the twin bed, a book on his lap.

"Marlowe." Enzo's eyes crinkled as he smiled.

The room was painted in a shade of light blue. A large window faced the North Field, framing a massive oak, bare branches swaying in the wind. In the summertime, the leaves would crowd the glass, making the room feel like it floated among them.

"Henry wants to know if you would like to come down for lunch." Marlowe stood in the doorway, examining the shriveled man. "But you look comfortable here."

Enzo chuckled, his thin frame sinking deeper into the pillows. "Henry once told me he'd like to die in this room. What a thing to say."

She tried to return a smile but couldn't quite manage it. "Enzo, I want to ask you about my friend—Nora. I know you remember her."

He frowned, lines deepening around his eyes. "I was so sure that bear would kill her. Kill you all. That's why I had you gather the stones for the wall. Turned out well, didn't it?"

"Enzo," she said again in a bracing voice. "Do you know where Nora is?"

Enzo made a strange humming sound, fingers tracing the worn pattern on the quilt. For a moment, she thought he hadn't heard, but then he looked up, his eyes bright as if he'd been struck with a memory.

"Can you find the Bend in the Bean? You children should run along and hide at the Bend."

He smiled at the old joke, and Marlowe tried to suppress her frustration. Enzo didn't know what year it was. He didn't know who was still a child and who wasn't. Or maybe he did, and this was his way of dodging.

"Lunch?" Marlowe snapped. "Do you want to come down for it?"

Enzo blinked and opened his mouth, as if wildly confused by Marlowe's question. More confused than when she had asked about Nora, she realized.

He turned his head from side to side, scanning the room, suddenly alarmed.

Marlowe felt a spasm of guilt and pity for the old man.

"I'll send up Henry," she muttered.

"Henry," Enzo whispered, seizing on the one name that brought him comfort above all else. "Henry is a good boy. Such a good boy."

Marlowe left him to his babbling and headed back downstairs.

In the kitchen, she accepted a plate from Henry and sat down at the table with the kids. She watched Henry's shoulders rise as he briskly walked up to Enzo's room.

Marlowe was still replaying her conversation with Mike from the previous day when Kat sat ramrod straight in her chair, palms flat against the table. It was as if Marlowe could see her young ears pricking forward, attuned to something in the living room.

And then Marlowe heard it too: the crunch of car wheels over gravel.

It must have been a visitor. Nate was in Hartford, Stephanie and Constance were wrapping presents in the other room, and Frank and Glory had gone into town not long ago.

Everyone was still, and then Kat was tumbling over her chair, running toward the side door, Marlowe at her heels.

"It's the detectives," Kat said, gasping.

Henry pounded down the stairs, his eyes wide. Marlowe saw the tightness in his jaw.

As Marlowe swung open the door, she saw Ben Vance striding up the drive, tall and straight-backed. But it was Ariel behind him that sent a flurry of anticipation up and down her spine.

She had a small, arrogant smile on her face. Not an expression Marlowe had seen on Ariel before. She always had a difficult time reading Ariel, but this one was unmistakable—not merely smug, but confident.

"Good afternoon," Ben said.

"Hello." Marlowe held the door, Henry a shadow behind her. "My parents aren't here."

"That's all right." Ariel's eyes were fixed on Henry. "We came to talk to you. Both of you."

It was too cold for a walk, so they stepped into the kitchen.

As the children were shooed away, Marlowe knew they would eavesdrop. Ariel seemed to know it too, but judging by the sly look in her eyes, she wanted them to overhear.

Henry cleared the empty plates and straightened all the chairs as the detectives sat. Marlowe put on a kettle of tea.

Once seated at the table, Ariel and Ben across from Marlowe and Henry, Ariel pulled out a small notebook. She flipped through the pages covered in a tiny illegible scrawl.

"Your brother is still in Hartford?"

"Yes," Marlowe said.

"We would have liked to talk to all three of you at once." Ariel shrugged.

"He's due back in a few days," Marlowe said.

"We can't wait that long." Ariel cocked her head, like a curious bird examining a worm. "It's a funny thing, this case. Years and years with nothing—no answers. But now, suddenly, it's coming together."

"You've had a break?" Marlowe asked.

"Not quite a break." Ariel glanced at her partner, who nodded in agreement. "Like I said, things are just starting to come together."

Ben leaned forward. "We know this has been rough on your family, but we really just need your help to nail down a few final details."

Henry nodded, resigned to more questioning.

"Thanks. This won't take long. We just want to make sure there are no discrepancies. Marlowe, that night, it was you and Nate who ran out of the house first to look for Nora, right?" Ben asked. "Everyone else stayed inside?"

Marlowe nodded. "Yes, that's right."

"And Henry, you followed?" Ariel asked.

"Yes, they went outside first, but I was right behind them. We thought it was just one of her jokes." Henry linked his fingers together on the table and leaned over his forearms. "But when I heard them yelling her name with no response, I ran outside too."

"So, to confirm, there continued to be no answer, and then what happened?" Ariel's finger tapped a page of her notebook.

"We started to get scared," Henry said. "Our parents woke up, and we were looking for flashlights and pulling on our shoes to go look for her."

"And you went down to get Enzo, correct?"

There was a pause, nearly imperceptible, before Henry nodded. "Yes."

"Did Nate send you down there, or did you go on your own?"

"I don't—I don't remember." Henry stared into his hands, as if he was really trying to recall.

"Marlowe, do you?"

Marlowe shook her head. "I remember Henry going to the stairs, but I don't know who told him to."

"You didn't go down alone, right, Henry?" Ariel asked.

When Henry delayed his response again, Ariel tipped her hand. "We know you went down there with your friend," she said. "We spoke with Liam."

"Yeah," Henry relented. "Liam went down with me."

"And what happened once Enzo came upstairs?"

"We called the Millers and then started looking." Henry exhaled; his eyes glazed as he recalled the witching hours spent out in the fields. "We took the flashlights and spread out. Nate and Marlowe and my parents crossed the street and checked the barn, Liam and the others checked the garden and around the house, and me and Enzo headed back into the orchard to see if she was out there. It was so dark, we couldn't see anything."

"That's part of the core issue, isn't it?" Ariel nodded in sympathy. Marlowe had a sudden urge to grab her younger brother's arm and tell him to be careful. Ariel wasn't nice. She was pretending. Drizzling honey over the table and enticing him to drop his guard before she struck. "I'm sure you've both thought it: She could have been out there, unconscious, in the hayfield, hidden in the tall grass or under some leaves or sticks, tucked away in the barn. Isn't it possible that she was there and you didn't see her?"

"Yes," Henry whispered. "Or whoever took her could have driven away before we realized she was gone."

The kettle started to whistle, startling Marlowe. She'd been caught up in a state of déjà vu—Henry and her at the table, being asked to relive that night again, as if twenty years hadn't passed. In some sense, maybe they'd been stuck here all along. Ariel leaned back, unphased by the piercing sound. Marlowe stood and went to remove the kettle from the stove but neglected to offer anyone tea.

"Do you think you missed something that night, Henry?" Ariel asked.

An edge crept into Henry's voice—he'd returned to the present too. "Not that night. We thought—I thought—there was just some misunderstanding. She had fallen or maybe was hiding. Or something. I truly believed we would find her."

Ariel spoke again. "What was Enzo wearing when you went to get him in the basement?"

Marlowe froze.

"His pajamas." Henry said. "He was sleeping."

"So you opened the door, and he was in bed, and he got out of bed?" Ariel asked. "In pajamas and slippers? Something like that?"

"I'm not sure exactly what it was like." Henry was a lawyer again. He knew to never agree with a detailed question. "We knocked, and I think he opened the door."

"But he was in his pajamas?" Ariel asked.

"Yes," Henry said. "He had just gotten out of bed. He had just woken up."

"Do you remember the color of his pajamas?" Ariel was on a trail, and Marlowe had no idea where it was going.

Henry shrugged. "Light blue shirt, maybe? He wore the same stuff for years."

"Just a shirt? Was he sleeping in boxers?"

"I don't know." Henry's right shoulder was rising, inching closer to his ear. An old habit when he was nervous.

"You don't remember if his legs were bare or not?"

"I think he was wearing flannel pants. Like I said, I can't be sure, but I think he was."

"And no shoes?" Ariel asked.

"No, but he put some on," Henry said. "And a jacket. So we could go search."

"Right." Ariel relaxed into her chair. "The thing is, Liam remembers it differently."

Marlowe didn't move an inch.

"Liam told us that Enzo opened the door as soon as you knocked. As if he had already been awake. And Liam remembers that Enzo was wearing boots. Liam could tell us the color, size, shape of the boots. And he says Enzo already had on a jacket and pants."

Henry froze, as if the weight of the moment had physically pinned him to his chair.

Brierley had pressed Liam, hoping for something big that could crack the case wide open. But maybe Liam never had the whole picture. Maybe he had only fragments, a sliver of something that seemed so incidental it didn't even bear mentioning.

And that tiny detail had just exposed Henry's lie.

Ariel's gaze sharpened. "That's a pretty big inconsistency, Henry."

Henry leaned back, affecting calm, but his jaw was twitching. He didn't yell or rant. Instead, he whirled toward Marlowe and held his hands up. "They're twisting things around. It doesn't mean anything."

But Ariel kept her foot on the gas. "It's not just Liam's statement. We went through the old case files again. Turns out, a piece of evidence wasn't properly examined. A bracelet that belonged to Nora." She let that hang in the air. "It was collected from her house during the initial investigation for the bloodhounds, but no one thought to DNA test it back then, since it wasn't found at the crime scene. So we had it examined with new technology. And guess what?"

Henry's knuckles whitened on the edge of the counter.

"Enzo's DNA," Ariel said, gratified. "On the clasp."

The bracelet? Marlowe's mind was racing, trying to make sense of it. She struggled to picture what it looked like. And suddenly it came to her: a silver-embossed antique bracelet Nora had picked up at a pawnshop, on credit she'd made from trading in Frank Fisher's sterling letter opener. Marlowe vaguely remembered when Nora showed up wearing it the spring before she disappeared. She remembered Henry looking askance at Nora's newfound interest in baubles. But Marlowe just marveled at the piece as Nora spun her wrist and told her in private where it came from. So it hadn't all been school supplies and other essentials.

That still didn't account for why Enzo's DNA was on it. Nora hadn't been wearing it that night in June, not if it was found in her bedroom. No memories of Enzo and Nora interacting that spring surfaced. The idea felt impossible, but the words hung in the air.

"That's . . ." Henry said, his voice catching. "That's just not possible."

"The lab says otherwise," Ariel said without missing a beat.

Ben spoke up again, low but firm. "It's enough for probable cause, Henry. Combined with Liam's statement, Enzo's odd behavior that night, and the lie you just told us about what he was wearing. That's a pattern."

"I'm not talking to you anymore without a lawyer present," Henry said.

"Fair enough," Ariel said. "We don't really have any more questions anyway."

"Henry." Marlowe whispered her brother's name. She would be furious if he'd known something all this time. If he was hiding something from her.

"You're not talking to them without a lawyer either," he said.

Instinctively, Marlowe looked over Henry's shoulder at the two detectives.

"It's fine, Marlowe, you don't have to talk to us." Ariel's mouth curled up in disdain.

"We need to see him," Ben said.

"He's upstairs resting," Henry snapped.

"We'll wake him." Ariel's voice was cool. "We're placing him under arrest for suspected involvement in Nora Miller's abduction."

Placing a hand over her chest, Marlowe opened her mouth to protest but found no words. The detectives were already moving toward the stairs.

Henry slammed his hand on the granite counter. "How dare you. You have nothing concrete—just scraps and theories!"

"Henry, why was he wearing boots?" Marlowe was ashamed of her plaintive, wailing tone. But she felt her world slipping away from her. "What did Enzo *do*?"

"Nothing, I swear. He didn't do anything." His eyes were wide with manic confidence. "I told them there was a man in the woods, I told them over and over, but they never believed me. Enzo said they never would believe me."

"That's just a story, Henry," Marlowe said. "You believed it when you were young; you can't still believe it now."

"There's an old house in the woods," Henry said. "I can't explain now, but I found it with Nate. There was a man living there the night Nora died—that man was living in the woods."

Marlowe closed her eyes. Her brother didn't realize how crazy he sounded.

Moments later, the detectives returned with Enzo in between them. He looked dazed but calm. His eyes met Henry's first.

"They say I must go with them."

Henry rushed forward. "I'll be right behind you. It'll be all right, we'll get a lawyer. Don't say a word until then."

As they led Enzo out, Kat and Dolly burst in from the yard, voices overlapping in a chorus of questions that no one answered.

Marlowe stood frozen, watching Enzo disappear through the front door.

"You believe me, right?" Henry said. "She was here all the time—there are a million ways his DNA could have been on her bracelet. They're just trying to make this fit. They don't care about the truth. They only care about their careers."

She wanted to believe him. Detectives always had a broader agenda, and solving this cold case would be a significant bargaining chip for their next career moves. But Henry didn't seem interested in the truth anymore either; he was looking to obscure it.

The office door swung open and Stephanie burst into the hallway clutching her phone, her face pale. Constance followed with Frankie in her arms.

"The sheriff's department showed up in Hartford," Stephanie said. "They're bringing in Nate for questioning."

Marlowe heard the car door slam shut and the detectives' cruiser idle out of the driveway. And then the room fell silent. It felt like the ground beneath the Gray House had cracked open and sent them all plummeting into endless darkness.

# THIRTY-THREE

Henry paced the living room, barking into the phone, his shoes thudding over the patterned rug. He'd been dialing law offices since the detectives left. When he finally hung up, he'd secured a top New York lawyer, already en route to Poughkeepsie.

Marlowe stood frozen until Henry turned to her, and she dropped into an armchair, fingers gripping the edge of the floral brocade.

"What happened to Nora?" she asked.

Henry sighed and raked his hair back. "I've always wanted to tell you."

"Then tell me now."

"I don't know what happened to her." Henry lifted his hands to reveal his palms, helpless. "But Enzo, he used to walk at night. Sometimes he'd go out, just to keep an eye on things. And he knew about the man in the woods."

"Mr. Babel?"

"No, not Mr. Babel." Henry sank onto the couch across from her. "That was a story. This man was real."

"You saw him?"

"Glimpses," Henry said. "I never spoke to him."

Marlowe shook her head.

"There's a house in the woods. Past that rusty car. If you follow the old stone wall. I know you never walked that far. It was old and run-down, but someone was living in it back then. Nate and I found it and poked around. I know someone was living there."

"And what about Enzo?"

"He knew, and it made him nervous. Like the bear," Henry said. "He was worried about us, so he took walks at night. Just to keep an eye out."

It sounded like a story spun too many times, but Henry seemed to believe every word of it, and she felt a pang of sadness as she watched him lose his grip.

"I told Brierley about the man," Henry continued. "I told him. But he thought I was making it up. Enzo said they'd never believe me. So I shut up. It only made us look worse."

The hired help, their protector, with his charming accent and warm smile. Enzo told Marlowe to drink the whiskey, so she drank it. And Enzo told Henry to keep quiet, so he did it.

"So you think this man took Nora?"

"I don't know. I never knew. But it wasn't us. It wasn't Enzo."

"They think it was."

"Of course they do," Henry scoffed. "They want a clean ending. Villains in a big house. It makes a good story."

"They arrested him, Henry." Marlowe rose to her feet. "They must have something."

"Circumstantial," he snapped. "The boots, the bracelet. It's thin. They can't charge him on that. Enzo will have a lawyer with him soon. I can't even venture a guess as to why they want to talk to Nate again. This is basically harassment. But Nate's gone willingly to answer their questions, and he can leave at any time. They won't get anything out of either of them."

"But is there something? Something you don't know."

Henry was silent, his head falling. "I don't know. Maybe Nate or Enzo hid something from me. But they're family. And I'd never believe they were responsible for this."

His curly hair fell over his forehead, like a sheep's wool hanging over its brow. Finally, he stood up. "They can hold him for twenty-four hours. I need to be there when he gets out."

"I'm going with you." Stephanie emerged from the kitchen, clutching her phone and her coat. "Frank and Glory are on their way home."

In an instant, they were gone, and Marlowe was left with her own spiraling thoughts. Henry was loyal. That was why he had swallowed the story of a man in the woods—hook, line, and sinker. That was why he was driving to Poughkeepsie to catch Enzo when he stumbled out of the questioning room.

If what Henry said was true, then someone else was out there. The decision came sharply to her. Heart pounding, she grabbed her coat and headed for the door. One way or another, she needed to see that house. She needed to see if Henry's story held any truth.

Her breath clouded the air as she cut through the apple orchard, boots crunching over the brittle crust of snow. By the time she cleared the orchard and was past the bottom of the North Field, she was winded but didn't stop. A narrow path snaked into the woods, steep and uneven, carved with streams and hidden roots. The incline would take her to the main stone wall in twenty minutes, then another trek along it would bring her to the rusted car. Uphill. No path once she had to follow the wall, just snow-covered brambles and rocks.

She checked the time: just past two. Not long before sunset.

Marlowe's legs ached, and her lungs were raw. She always prided herself on not obsessing over exercise like her sisters-in-law, but now her lack of cardio was punishing her. Stephanie could probably sprint this path. Breath came in short, shallow gasps, and her thighs burned as she pushed up the slope and reached the first stone wall, the one they had scavenged rocks for all summer. A right turn would take her to the top of the North Field and then to another path that intersected with the woods just up the road from the Gray House. That was the route Nate used for the wheelbarrow loaded with stones, hauling them across the street, behind the cow pasture, and straight toward the Flats. Not an easy distance, but Nate was strong, with toned arms and long legs. Only Marlowe was delusional enough to think Nora hadn't noticed.

Marlowe veered left, toward the wall that crawled deeper into the woods, higher up the ridge. Prickers from overgrown bushes clawed at her coat as she climbed. There was a time when it felt like a short distance, but now it seemed to drag on interminably.

When she reached the split in the wall, where one branch of it veered deeper into the trees, she paused. The snow thinned under the forest canopy, but the wall was harder to see now. She gazed down the line and saw that in some places, the stones had completely disappeared. The trees watched her as she scanned the path ahead. Somewhere beyond that wall was the car. And past that, the house.

She thought of Enzo slumped in a rigid chair in Poughkeepsie, desperately confused. Nate would be sitting with his arms crossed, leveling the detectives with a bland stare. If he knew anything, it would remain locked deep inside him. But Enzo? He'd crumble under the pressure. If he knew anything, he might let it slip without even realizing.

Marlowe stumbled over a root and caught herself against the wall. Again, she was struck with the thought that her memory was failing her. Was this really the way to the car? Or maybe she'd evinced an astounding lack of curiosity, a desire to never leave her safe harbor so strong she had erased the route from her mind.

Then she saw it—the rusted car, blackened and rising from the patches of snow.

It didn't seem to have aged a day since she last saw it, though the forest had filled in around it. The wheels were buried now, swallowed by dirt and snow and debris.

She circled the hood, hands brushing the cold, dented metal. In the summer sun, she and Nora had once crammed into the front seat, laughing.

Past the car. That was what Henry had said. Marlowe checked her watch again: nearly three thirty now. She had to move quickly. The trail beyond the car was barely visible, but she followed it. The incline decreased to a gentle slope for a while, and then, tucked between two pine trees, a roof sagging under the weight of the latest snowfall, and the lichen-covered siding of a house.

The cottage was small, only one story, its front door hanging off the hinges. The windows were smashed; jagged shards of glass gleamed in the fading afternoon light. How was it possible she'd never come across the house before? She thought she'd explored every inch of this land, or perhaps that was the hubris of youth.

Somewhere far away and out of sight, the sun was sinking fast. The top of a narrow brick chimney had crumbled, and bricks were scattered on the ground. The place looked deserted, but someone had lived there once. There must have been an old dirt road leading to it ages ago.

Marlowe stepped closer and all went quiet around her. She told herself nothing within the house could shock her—even if there was a bear or a body or Nora herself sitting cross-legged.

The door creaked as she pushed it open and she sucked in a breath. The floorboards had been torn out, revealing a sunken pit filled with stacks of old newspapers, neatly tied in bundles, arranged like someone had been preserving them. They filled every inch of the space, from where she stood in the doorway over to the crumbling stone fireplace.

She crouched at the nearest pile and brushed away dust, squinting at the faded ink. April 2004. Years after Nora disappeared. Someone had placed them here long after the search ended—someone who was living in the house. Or hiding.

A creak echoed from the sagging roof, then the scurrying of small paws. It couldn't have been anything larger than a raccoon, but Marlowe bolted anyway, down the slope and back toward the stone wall. Her feet slipped on snow and leaves, branches slapping at her arms, as she scrambled past the car.

As she reached the familiar path and the intersection with the first stone wall, she slowed, gasping for breath, hands on her knees. The woods had dimmed into a fragile twilight. Soon it would be pitch black. But she knew this wall. She had picked over every inch for days on end. It was *hers*.

And then—a sound. A sharp rustle, leaves crunching under deliberate footsteps. Too heavy to be an animal. Marlowe whirled around, her heart in her throat. A figure stepped out from the trees. She could see the edge of a brown jacket and heavy boots.

"Who's there?" Marlowe stumbled backward and tripped, falling onto her backside.

She pushed herself up into a squat, and then the man was on her, in a blur of movement. She kicked, clawed, but she was pinned beneath a massive torso, his weight crushing her into the dirt. His breath was hot, reeking of beer, his face wild and flushed.

"Where is she?" he snarled.

Marlowe's vision blurred with tears, but his voice was clear as day. "I don't know, Damen—I swear."

Damen Miller shook her, and her head slammed against the ground. Pain shot through her skull. A rock was digging into her back, and she was pinned to the ground again.

"I always knew," he growled. "Everyone said it wasn't your family, but I knew. I knew it was you."

Tears poured from the corners of his eyes as he held her wrists tighter. Marlowe gasped, chest heaving, panic rising like a cresting wave. She had to get free.

She bucked her hips upward and managed to drive her knee into his stomach. He grunted and loosened his hold just enough. Marlowe twisted out from under him, scrambling on her hands and knees, but he grabbed her coat and yanked her backward.

"Please, Mr. Miller," she sobbed.

He froze. Marlowe sucked in a quivering breath and pulled away. He let her go this time.

That name. "Mr. Miller." Just as she'd called him as a kid. Nora's dad. The man who used to drive them to the diner, who bought them ice cream at the county fair.

His hands trembled and he crumpled to his knees, eyes widened in horror at what he had done. Marlowe pulled herself to her feet and staggered a few steps away. When she looked back, Damen Miller's shoulders had deflated. His gray hair was mussed, and he looked like he didn't have the energy to stand up. Marlowe was tempted to go help him.

"Go home," she whispered. "I won't tell anyone about this."

Damen didn't seem to hear her. He just buried his face in his hands and wept.

Marlowe turned and ran down the slope, back toward the orchard. The sun had set by the time she emerged from the woods. She brushed the frost and leaves off her coat and pulled twigs out of her hair, but her jeans had mud stains on them. The Gray

House glowed in the distance, each window a perfect square of warm light, illuminating the kitchen, the hearth, the Christmas tree.

It was a sanctuary. A haven. She stumbled forward, heart still pounding, tears hot on her cheeks, and ran for home.

## THIRTY-FOUR

The color was drained from Marlowe's face, and she moved through the living room like a wraith, her coat unzipped but still draped over her shoulders. Murmurs emanated from her father's study.

"Marlowe, is that you? Are you all right?" her mother called, leaning around the doorframe.

"Yes," Marlowe replied curtly on her way to the kitchen, while carefully masking a limp.

"Does she want to talk?" She heard her father's distant, gravelly voice.

"No, not now," Marlowe said.

Her parents would only echo Henry's refrain: We've done nothing wrong. The lawyers will protect Nate and Enzo. In an armchair near the fire, Constance sat with a book open in her lap, but her eyes were fixed on Marlowe.

Crossing the kitchen, Marlowe slipped behind the counter and squatted, her legs still aching from her frantic run through the woods, and plucked a bottle of whiskey from the cabinet. She poured a generous amount into a glass and downed half in one swift gulp, ignoring Constance's wide-eyed gaze. Clutching two cans of ginger ale from the fridge, she gathered the bottle and glass in her other hand and headed for the basement.

There, after refilling her glass, she pulled out her phone and dialed Charlie Beacon—the neighbor from up the road who lived closer to Damen. He had been a newcomer decades ago, long before the Fishers, but was now considered a local.

Charlie picked up after one ring.

"Hi, it's Marlowe Fisher. I need you to check on Damen Miller tonight." Marlowe paused as she considered how much to divulge. "He's been having a rough time. Just call if he's not there."

"Of course. I'll walk over to his place in a bit," Charlie said.

Hanging up, Marlowe took small comfort in the unspoken rural code: Neighbors watched out for each other, sharing warnings even over small mishaps.

God, she hoped he made it home. She hoped he didn't collapse in the woods.

Returning to her drink, she crossed the room and shut the door behind her. There was a moment, Marlowe knew it well, in between a drunken stupor and a total blackout—a rare moment of clarity when she saw things for what they were. The only time she was able to know the truth. And she was going to find it.

She mixed the ginger ale with the whiskey and then sank into the armchair by the window, taking a long swallow and staring at the blackness outside. Had it been this dark the night Nora disappeared?

As she took another long sip of her drink, the legend of Rip Van Winkle came to her. There was a nearby bridge over the Hudson named after him. As the story goes, he was a Dutch farmer who wandered off into the Catskill Mountains one day and met a stranger who gave him liquor that sent him into a deep slumber. He slept for twenty years and awoke to a changed world. His wife was dead and his children were grown. Yet faint remnants of the past were still recognizable. Marlowe mused that perhaps twenty years was the perfect measure: long enough for dramatic change, but not so long that all traces of what once was had vanished.

She imagined Nora returning to the Gray House, marveling at a renovated kitchen yet finding solace in the unchanged hearth. Nora would shake her head and laugh about Henry's graying hair, and she would tease Nate over his protruding belly.

And then she would turn to Marlowe with a gentle smile.

"At least I'm back now," Nora would say. "I just slept in the woods—took a sip of a strange drink and fell asleep."

Squinting through the darkness, Marlowe chugged the rest of her drink, already planning to switch to the hidden bottle of red wine in the closet once the whiskey had fully eased the tension in her head and the soreness in her body. Damen Miller's attack, his clumsy pursuit of revenge, had forced a reckoning she could no longer ignore.

Another swallow confirmed it: She didn't need to face more harsh truths or painful memories tonight. As Ariel had warned, overthinking was the enemy; all she needed was a stiff drink to quiet her mind. She wasn't a violent drunk like Damen. No, Marlowe was a wise drunk.

But she couldn't stop the barrage of fragmented memories from surfacing: Pete Gallagher's anger, Harmon's desperate claims implicating the Fishers in Nora's fate, whispered secrets of family guilt, and the small details that spoke louder than words—Enzo's boots, Henry's adamant belief in Mr. Babel, Nate's skepticism about Henry's stories. That night, Henry and Enzo headed back to the apple orchard while she and Nate dashed to the Gallagher barn, which made more sense now. They knew the mysterious house was in that direction. That was where their thoughts had gone.

Meanwhile, Marlowe and Nate stumbled across the street, breath ragged in the night. Their parents made for the pasture. It was Nate who'd checked the loft. Marlowe could remember his shadowy form slipping into the barn. She had stood at the sliding doors, calling out over the fields but glancing back at Nate as he climbed the ladder, quiet as a mouse. He had poked his head up into the loft; she remembered him shining his flashlight, and then he'd come down. "Nothing," he had said. "Nothing up there."

The next day, the hounds tracked Nora's scent and then ran to the trash bin. And then they ran right to the barn, where the trail went cold.

She remembered it all.

Marlowe made herself another drink. Later, her mother knocked on her door. Marlowe opened it, meeting Glory's knowing eyes.

"Rest tonight. Tomorrow we are a united front."

Marlowe's sluggish mind could offer only silence. Glory's quiet departure up the stairs spoke volumes—as if she didn't care, as if they had all resigned themselves to letting her drown her sorrows in a bottle, dulling her senses until the pain receded.

If only they knew. When she drank, the truth became clear, but she could never hold on to it. That was why she would never be a great artist; she was brave enough to face reality only when too inebriated to hold a pencil or brush.

As she sat on her bed with her knees drawn up to her chest, drink in hand and feet freezing beneath her, a lump rose in her throat. Visions of long-ago sleepovers with Nora flooded back: whispered secrets shared between the twin beds and the giddy rush of warming limbs as they kicked playfully under their duvets. These were moments she'd never recapture. Because they were together.

A familiar release came with the right amount of drink. She let the tears fall down her cheeks as she heaved in silence. Curling up with her head spinning, she wished for an endless sleep—a twenty-year slumber, maybe even forty. She hoped that when she woke, the whole world would be changed.

# THIRTY-FIVE

**BONFIRE**
**Sunday, May 24, 1998**

Nate pounded into the kitchen in grand spirits. He had just finished his first-year finals at Princeton and was home for the summer.

"Marlowe, Nora, start gathering blankets and snacks for the bonfire," Nate said.

Marlowe rolled her eyes, but she knew she and Nora would do as he said. She had missed Nate's authority while he was living on campus. It seemed he had missed bossing them around as well, because he spent the whole day piling up sticks at the top of the slope behind the orchard, near the edge of the woods, for a massive Memorial Day bonfire.

They rushed through dinner, and then Nate and Henry ran off to start the fire. Marlowe and Nora picked up a pile of blankets and a container of cookies freshly baked by Enzo, and Glory handed them a large thermos full of lemonade as they headed out.

"Get it burning for us, and we'll stop by," Frank hollered after them.

Marlowe and Nora moved through the orchard, the trees forming an archway of apple blossoms. The sky was cloudy for the season, but up at the top of the hill, a thin line of smoke was rising.

Nora had gone quiet and sulky the way she sometimes did, and Marlowe was at a loss for what to say. Marlowe had been busier that year, staying in the city on many weekends because her mother had found an oil painting class taught by a real New York artist that met on Saturday mornings twice a month. Marlowe had resisted at first, but after one class, she knew she had to take it.

Nora never complained, but Marlowe felt she had been neglectful.

She looked up ahead at the towering stack of sticks. It was over six feet tall and ten feet wide. "Oh my God, Nate really outdid himself this year. The bonfire is going to be huge. The perfect start to our summer." She smiled over at her friend.

They sat down on the logs Henry had dragged out of the woods and watched as Nate scurried around the fire, adjusting sticks and coaxing the flames. It took some time, as some of the wood was damp from spring rains, but slowly the mountain began to heat and crackle, and the flames started to lick at the night air.

"That's what I'm talking about. It's going now," Nate cheered, applauding his efforts.

"More sticks!" Henry yelled excitedly.

Nora's odd mood evaporated as she and Marlowe threw on more sticks, shrieking when the sparks flew up at them. The clouds had parted and the darkening night sky was crystal clear. A cool night breeze twirled in the flames, making them dance. But the heat of the fire was getting so intense that none of them needed the blankets they'd brought out.

Frank and Glory came up as promised. "Well done, boys," Frank commended them. "It's one of the best bonfires we've had in a long time."

Glory circled the fire, nudging the ring of stones around it. "You just better make sure it's out before you come in," she reminded them, before taking Frank's arm and returning to the house.

At its full apex, the bonfire transformed into something from a different time. It burned tall and bright, a massive torch. Marlowe and Nora pretended they were witches and danced and pranced around the crackling flames. Nate and Henry laughed at their silly pretend play, but they didn't care one bit; the fire was magical.

On nights like these, Marlowe knew why people said the Hudson Valley was haunted. She knew why stories of demons and mischievous fae folk had persisted in the Berkshires and the Catskills for so long. As recently as a decade before, there had been stories of strange happenings near the old Sheffield Bridge, the wooden structure that spanned the Housatonic River.

Most of the time, Marlowe did not fear the supernatural. She didn't deride such stories, but she didn't obsess over them either. But with the bonfire blazing up into the night, making the trees stand black and tall around them, Marlowe knew those stories to be true. She knew them to be part of the fabric of the land.

Witches flying above the trees to convene with the devil in some far-off meadow? Why not? Cows opening their mouths and speaking? It didn't seem out of the realm of the possible. She knew there was power in the mystery of this place. She'd felt it when she and Nora made their own mischief when they were younger, sneaking into the Gallagher hayloft and painting their brand on the cows. She felt it again now, building in the flames.

Nate declared that the bonfire was so amazing, he was going to stay out all night. "We'll watch the sunrise!"

Marlowe readily agreed, rejoicing in the four of them together again, side by side on the log, passing the lemonade back and forth. But by an hour past midnight, she was fading. The fire had become so hot that standing too close was almost painful. Her eyes were scratchy from the smoke and starting to droop. She longed for her bed.

Henry was dozing off already, his head lolling on Nora's shoulder.

"I don't think I'm going to make it all night," Marlowe said. "Are you ready to head in?"

"Oh, stay just a bit longer!" Nora begged. She shook Henry's arm, jostling him awake. "We're almost there."

Marlowe laughed. "We're nowhere close. It's going to take hours for this to burn down. But you can stay if you want—I'll take Henry back."

And Nora stayed, alone with Nate.

Marlowe wasn't annoyed, but she thought it was strange. Nora and Marlowe were usually a unit. If one of them went to bed, the other followed. But then, Nora was excited about the bonfire, enthralled by the idea of staying up until dawn. Nate swore he pulled all-nighters once a week in college, and Nora hung on to all his stories of toga parties and wild nights with her eyes wide and eager.

As she and Henry stumbled down the hill to their beds, Marlowe remembered how the girls in her class thought Nate Fisher was the boy of their dreams. It made Marlowe laugh, given that she knew none of them had any real chance of dating Nate. It was baffling, actually, how girls seemed to like him. Nora was just as immune to Nate's charms as she was—they were more like siblings than anything else.

At the bottom of the hill, Marlowe turned back once and caught her breath at the sight. The flames reached as high as the trees. Sparks rained down around the pit like stars. Nate and Nora were not visible; there were only shadows flickering about.

"Maybe we should go back." Henry yawned. "We're going to miss it." But Marlowe felt spooked by the way the land seemed to shift and whisper in the dead of night. She quickened her strides back to the house, dragging Henry along.

She slept deeply that night, without dreams or nightmares. When she woke, it was almost nine in the morning. Nora was in the spare twin bed, her hand tucked beneath her smooth cheek, the daisy-covered quilt pulled tight around her. And, once more, all was right.

# MONDAY

**DECEMBER 3, 2018**

# THIRTY-SIX

Marlowe swung her legs out of bed and stumbled toward the bathroom. Her mouth was dry and coated in a sour, sticky film, and her head throbbed.

Coffee, she needed coffee.

But first a shower. She stepped in before the water finished warming. The shock of cold sharpened her senses and distracted her from how sick she felt.

After her shower, she pulled on black jeans and a gray turtleneck, trying to compose herself. It wouldn't be enough to convince her mother. Then again, maybe Glory would be too worried about Nate and Enzo to consider Marlowe's fragile state.

A united front. Today, they were supposed to be a united front.

Frank and Glory were in the kitchen, their heads bent over their coffee and newspapers, as if it was any other morning.

"Have you heard from Poughkeepsie?" Marlowe asked.

"Nate left last night, and he stayed at a hotel with Henry and Steph," Frank said. "Enzo was kept overnight, but they're letting him go now."

Her father's voice was tight with anger. How humiliating that his son was tangled up in this mess, his presence requested at the police station when he could have just been questioned at home.

Marlowe didn't understand why Nate had agreed to go into the station, when he didn't have to. Ariel and Ben had said something to encourage him to show up. Nate probably did so out of pride.

The more she thought about it, the more she felt that Ariel and Ben just didn't like Nate. They demanded that he come in just to scare him. Not because they thought he would confess.

And if Enzo was being released, that meant their evidence didn't stick—the bracelet, the boots, his testimony. None of it.

Marlowe poured a few drops of milk into her coffee.

"You just missed a ride to town for breakfast," Glory said. "Constance took the kids to the diner."

"I'm not hungry." Marlowe sank into a chair.

"Marlowe, do you realize these detectives are just playing tricks?" Her father's voice was gentle and soothing now, as if he saw her pain. "They're picking at us to see if there's a weak link with something to tell, but there's nothing. Nothing at all. We don't know what happened."

Marlowe stared across the kitchen at her father. When she was a little girl, she thought her father was the most handsome man in the world. It was always jarring when Marlowe turned toward her father, expecting to see the hale and healthy man from her girlhood, and saw instead his wrinkled skin and white hair.

And his hands. It was Frank himself who had told her to look at a man's hands for signs of his health. He had pointed at a picture of Bill Clinton in a newspaper.

"He's sick, age has caught up with him," Frank had said. "He used to have big strong hands, but look at them now. Look how thin and frail. That's the sign."

Frank's hands were now even worse than that. The fingers were thin and gnarled, and it took great effort for Frank to lift them from the table to grip his mug.

Glory pursed her lips and looked at her daughter. "Remember, a united front."

"I know, I understand," she said. They would never forgive her if she let on that their only daughter was harboring doubt.

An hour later, Henry's car pulled into the drive. Marlowe opened the front door and watched as Henry and Enzo got out of the car and walked toward the house at a glacial pace. The hours spent in an interrogation room had been unkind to him. He was pallid, and his clothes were rumpled.

When they reached the door, Marlowe stepped aside. She didn't look at Henry; her gaze was fixed on Enzo.

He looked lost. He had been confused over the past few weeks, but he had always known where he was and whom he was with. He had known he was at the Gray House with Henry and Marlowe and Nate. He had been confused only about the year. But now he looked at Marlowe as if he didn't recognize her.

"I lived in Manchester for a time," he said. "Only a short time."

Glory brushed past Marlowe to take Enzo's arm, and he stared at her as if he'd never seen her before.

"Here, Enzo, let's get you up to your room."

As Glory and Enzo made for the stairs, Henry's voice rang out from the kitchen. "They badgered him for hours, the lawyer said. Demanded his entire life story, and now he's all muddled. He keeps spouting random fragments."

Clearly, Enzo's mind was far more deteriorated than they'd realized.

"The lawyer said they have nothing, absolutely nothing. Just random details and old memories. An anecdote about boots. An old bracelet of Nora's that Enzo could have picked up and returned to her after she left it here," Henry said. "It was barely grounds for arrest in the first place. None of it would hold up."

"Where is Nate? Is Stephanie with him now?" Frank was entirely sanguine.

"Yes, they're right behind us, driving back," Henry said.

"Snow is on the way, could be six inches," Frank said. "But they'll beat it."

The kids would be excited. The snow would keep them occupied with sledding for at least a day or two.

Henry's voice dropped to a lower register, and Marlowe knew they were talking about her. Frank would tell him that she had drunk herself into a stupor but was docile this morning. Marlowe didn't need to eavesdrop to know.

She crept up the stairs and stood in the shadows of the hall outside the spare bedroom.

"I was born in Italy; they did not believe it, but I was," Enzo was saying.

"Yes, I know, of course." Glory's tone was distracted. She was only half listening.

"Then Paris and then England, only for a few months." Enzo laughed then, and it was a dry sound, like dead leaves rustling in a fall breeze. "You know in England, they call stone walls cairns. A cairn. Yes."

"Here you are, just lie back." Glory's hands were probably occupied, fluffing pillows and arranging the covers over Enzo's scrawny legs.

"But then I went back to Paris. No other city can compare."

Sudden tears stuck to Marlowe's eyelashes. She used to cling to every one of Enzo's words about late-night meals in tiny restaurants tucked beneath old buildings, and long walks along the Seine. She and Nora used to perch on the kitchen stools, elbows on top of the counter, while he cooked dinner.

"Tell us about Paris," Nora would say.

And Enzo always obliged.

"The lights are like nothing you have ever seen," Enzo would say. "They glow as if they are touched by fairies."

Nora and Marlowe planned out their future trips. They made lists of all the places Enzo mentioned. The Notre-Dame Cathedral and the Champs-Élysées and the Louvre were on it, but also the smaller, obscure streets and restaurants Enzo could rattle off the top of his head.

When Marlowe finally got to Paris, she did a painting for Enzo. It was a view of the Seine on a June evening, with the lights gleaming atop a line of lampposts that seemed to stretch on forever. Enzo sobbed when she gave it to him.

When Enzo paused mid-memory, Glory interjected. "Just close your eyes for now, and I'll bring you up some tea later, all right?"

Enzo was silent, and Marlowe could picture him blinking up at Glory, questioning exactly who the old woman was and why she was bringing him tea. Marlowe wondered if her mother resented the fact that she was stuck caring for two aging old men.

And then his memory wheel started up again. "It was July when I first saw New York, and I could not believe the heat."

Marlowe didn't bother to hide as her mother emerged from the room. Glory closed the door with a tight click, her mouth set in a thin line of anger as she regarded Marlowe.

"They broke him," Glory said. "His mind is gone."

Glory stomped downstairs, her loafers flying over the steps as she made a beeline for the kitchen. Marlowe plodded behind, thinking of Paris, but she froze halfway down the staircase.

Cairn. Enzo said that stone walls were called "cairns" in England.

Only they weren't.

It meant something else.

A sudden moment of clarity brought her straight back to her college anthropology class, the pen gripped in her hand as the professor, a charming Brit, talked about burial rites.

"You'll see these all over the United Kingdom," he'd said. "Piles of stones to mark significant locations or graves, or in some cases, the stones cover the actual bodies. Some societies buried the dead in rocks instead of digging into the soil. Sometimes it was a necessity, especially for soldiers or travelers, but other times it was the tradition."

Her professor had shown a variety of pictures. The piles could be elaborate, or simple mounds. They could be stacked high into the sky or feature tall rocks upright like pillars. But they weren't stone walls. They were different from the walls that bordered sheep fields and marked property lines. Stone walls were just stone walls. A stone wall was not a cairn.

Somewhere in his addled brain, Enzo had seized on something that made sense.

The detectives wouldn't have caught on during his babbling about Europe. Maybe only Marlowe understood. Hadn't she asked him the day before where Nora was? In his own way, Enzo had answered.

*Find the Bend,* he'd said.

# THIRTY-SEVEN

Marlowe fled the house before anyone could stop her. Snow started falling in light flurries as she passed the Gallagher barn.

Her trek the previous night had been painful and plodding, but the walk in the opposite direction, over the Rise and to the Flats and the river, seemed to pass in a blur. She continued upriver, away from the Bend and where Harmon had been killed, toward the swamp.

Marlowe stopped when she reached the stone wall, pausing to take it in. She had been content when it came up to her shins, but Nate had insisted on building it higher. It wasn't like they were keeping livestock fenced in, she'd argued—so what was the point?

"Aesthetics," Nate said.

Higher and higher it went as they carefully placed each rock—and shouted in frustration when a section caved in—until it reached Marlowe's stomach and was a yard in width. They had made sure to build it a few steps from the edge of the swamp, where the earth was solid. Nate envisioned it stretching for forty yards or so before stopping where the river coursed out from the swamp. Instead, it ended abruptly at less than half that length. Still, nothing to sneer at. It was a monument of sorts. Marlowe could remember the dull ache in her muscles, the sweat dripping from her brow at the end of a long day.

Now the stones looked like they'd been there for a century. It amazed her what time and harsh weather could do to something left untended. She reached out and skimmed her hand over a smooth length of the wall.

And then she set herself to the task of gently plucking rocks from the wall one by one and placing them on the ground behind her. It felt like sacrilege to undo the work of that long-ago summer. She remembered how hard they had all labored to arrange the stones just right. All four of them had wanted to build something that would last.

Still, she persisted. She removed the top layer of rocks from a six-foot section at the center of the wall, the discarded stones forming a haphazard pile around her. She had to be quick. If any of her family caught her in the act, she wasn't sure what they would do, but she supposed their reactions would be telling.

An hour later, the section she was working on was down to her thighs, and she saw the sheen of black canvas.

Marlowe's hands yanked at the rocks, and she didn't flinch when a few stones tumbled onto her arm—she just hoisted them away.

There was something in the wall that Marlowe had not put there. She'd been present for every second of its creation, and none of them had included a black canvas tarp.

After another layer of rocks was gone, Marlowe could grip the canvas. She started to tug on it, and bit by bit it emerged. She had the strangest urge to be gentle, as if the thing in the tarp could still be hurt by rough handling.

Marlowe worried she would need a knife to cut through the tarp, but it turned out not to be wrapped very tightly. Before she pulled it all the way out, she was able to unravel one side to reveal dust and debris surrounding frayed and faded denim. Part of someone's blue jeans. And a deteriorating black wellie that had once gone on a small foot. And beneath that fragment of cloth, a bone.

She started to tremble. Tiny needles were pricking every inch of her skin.

It was Nora. It was Nora in the stone wall.

Marlowe always thought the attacker must have come from behind and hit Nora on the back of the head. She would have had to be rendered unconscious right away, or else they would have heard her yell. She always shrieked when she was startled. Nora's scream would have torn through the air with a vengeance. Everyone would have heard it.

But she hadn't screamed that night, because she hadn't been startled. Whoever was waiting for her at the trash cans had not surprised her.

Nora knew her killer.

Marlowe knelt at the ruined section of the wall, staring down at the partially exposed tarp for what felt like an eternity.

The snow started to fall harder, and she thought about staying still and letting herself get buried. She'd freeze to death, right next to Nora, as it always should have been.

She pulled at the tarp a bit more, revealing more bones and black muddy grime, which she realized with a flip of her stomach were the decomposed parts of her best friend. It didn't take long for a body's soft tissues to liquefy. She knew that from her anthropology classes too.

If the ground was too hard to dig, rocks did a good job of keeping a body protected. And, in some cases, hidden in plain sight. Whoever had done this had been careful. Nora was perfectly encased in stone.

The world fell silent, until the sudden sound of footsteps and heavy breathing echoed from behind her. She looked up to see Nate's dark figure crossing the Flats, his head rising and falling as he approached her.

Marlowe had a small rock clutched in one hand. She didn't know what she planned to do with it. Not that she was feeling up to any kind of physical altercation. Not after the previous day.

By the looks of him, Nate wasn't prepared for a fight either. The purple half circles under his eyes and his rumpled appearance suggested he hadn't gotten much sleep. Part of her, the part that could somehow dismiss the bones beside her, was glad to see him. She had missed him—and his composure, all his confidence—this past week.

When he reached the wall, his face was as rigid as the scattered stones.

"So, she was here." Nate's words fell heavy on Marlowe's bent head.

"You knew." Marlowe's voice cracked. "You knew this whole time."

"No, I didn't." Nate didn't seem to care if she believed him or not. He seemed exhausted with it all. "Enzo never told me where he put her."

"Why?" Marlowe dropped the rock. "Tell me why."

"She said she was pregnant."

"So you *killed* her?" Marlowe would have lunged at Nate if the wall hadn't been between them.

"I didn't kill her," Nate snapped. "I was a kid, I asked for help."

"You told *Enzo*—"

"I told Dad."

Marlowe went still. She couldn't picture it. She supposed everyone said that when someone they knew and loved committed a heinous act, but it was the truth.

At this point, she could imagine Nora and Nate in each other's arms, up by that bonfire on Memorial Day. Nora creeping down the hall in the middle of the night to meet Nate in the spare room. Nora and Nate keeping their delicious secret until it turned too risky. Nate panicking.

But her father, a man of law and justice and logic, ending a teen-age girl's life—a girl he had watched grow up. The thought was more appalling, more unbelievable than the bones at her feet.

Marlowe glanced behind Nate's shoulder, expecting her entire family to suddenly appear in a line. But the field behind Nate was empty.

"It's just me," Nate said. "I told them I needed to clear my head. Henry said you walked toward the Gallagher barn, so I followed you. I always knew you would figure it out one day."

"Dad, he wouldn't have." Marlowe's words came out in gasps. "It wasn't her fault she was pregnant! She didn't deserve to die for that!"

"She wasn't an idiot, Marlowe!" He glared at her over the wall while white snow gathered on the top of his head. "She could've prevented it and she didn't! She was manipulating us!"

"*You* could have prevented it!" Marlowe shrieked. "If it mattered that much to you. If you were smart!"

"I didn't *know*."

Marlowe turned away in disgust. "You *knew* you were having sex with her, and if you were going to do it, you should have been responsible."

Nate was silent. A look of bewilderment filled his eyes.

"I thought you realized." Nate blinked. "It wasn't me. Nora and I—no. Marlowe, she was sleeping with Henry."

The bottom dropped out of Marlowe's world. She collapsed against the wall.

"I don't know anything." Marlowe sobbed. "Please, Nate, tell me what happened."

Nate stepped over the wall and stood before her. "Open your coat. I know you left your phone at the house, but I want to make sure you're not recording."

Marlowe's jaw dropped. "I'm not."

"You don't know what those detectives put me through," Nate said. "The things they said about you. They said you had already figured it out and that you told them everything. That you were helping them gather the evidence they needed, so I might as well confess." Nate hung his head at the thought.

In truth, Marlowe didn't have any evidence, but she had given the detectives enough for Ariel to spin convincing lies.

Marlowe reached for her zipper and undid her coat. She flipped her pockets inside out. Then she stood up and lifted her sweater to reveal her pale stomach. She tugged at the neck to show her bra with no wires attached.

"I didn't think you would." Nate kicked at the ground before sitting down beside her. It was a poor excuse. "Why did you look here?"

"Enzo," Marlowe said. "He was babbling about a cairn, which I knew was a pile of stones used in burials."

"Jesus." Nate ran his hand through his hair, his touch melting the snowflakes.

"I don't think he said it to the detectives." Marlowe zipped her coat back up to her chin. "He had a good lawyer."

Marlowe stared straight ahead. She needed to know. She would get the information first, then decide who to hate. And how to be angry.

"Tell me, please."

"You remember how she was, how easy it was to love her. She was funny and brave and *alive*." Nate spoke softly. "And Henry had always been smitten. Since the moment they met. For years, he followed her around like a lovesick puppy."

Marlowe shook her head. It still didn't fit. Yes, Henry had trailed after Nora, but that was his way. He was always trying to tag along.

"He followed you too," Marlowe said.

"It was different." Nate shook his head. "I guess they were only a year apart, but she always seemed much older than him. Or rather, I guess Henry seemed so young."

Henry was almost fifteen when Nora died. How long had it been going on? Marlowe shivered. It was difficult to imagine Nora with Henry. Nora knew how young he was, how he was the baby of the group.

"I think when she set her sights on him, he didn't stand a chance," Nate continued with his weary tone. "She probably didn't have to try very hard."

"You make her sound like some seductress."

"And when you thought it was me, weren't you ready to paint me as the seducer? The older college guy. Are you telling me it wasn't the same with her and Henry?"

"They were closer in age."

"Never mind their ages—she did it for a reason. She wanted power. She wanted control. She had that with Henry."

"How long?" Marlowe asked.

Nate stared down at her quizzically. "I always wondered if you knew or suspected. Or if you didn't want to know."

"I didn't know," Marlowe said. "And if I ever started to wonder, it was always you and her."

Nate shook his head. "I never would have done that."

Marlowe believed him. He would have seen it as a betrayal of his sister. Nate had a code, and he stuck to it.

"I think they started sleeping together the winter before she disappeared, during my freshman year of college." Nate crossed his arms and turned back to the river. "Henry didn't tell me until the beginning of May, and only because he was terrified. I was visiting a friend that week, and he called me during his school lunch from a pay phone in Manhattan because he was scared to call from the apartment. He was crying. I've never been more furious in my life. He was fourteen and she had just told him she was pregnant the weekend before. Can you imagine how overwhelmed he was?"

"Probably just as overwhelmed as Nora finding out she was pregnant." Wrapped up in the thoughts that occupied her young mind, Marlowe had been blind to it all.

"I don't know if she was." Nate shrugged. "I've thought about it over and over, and part of me thinks she made it up. To get money or a promise from Henry. He thought he was going to have to marry her. He asked me if it was possible to do that at his age." Nate broke off, as if remembering the absurd phone conversation and getting a renewed burst of frustration.

Marlowe opened her mouth to defend Nora, but no words came out.

"She just wanted to be a part of our family," Marlowe said. "I always thought she was."

"You were a good friend to her." Nate's voice twisted with fury. "Better than she deserved."

Marlowe glanced down at the wall. "She's dead, Nate."

"I know I shouldn't still be angry at her," Nate said. "But I am."

"What did you do?" Marlowe asked.

"I told Henry to stay calm and not tell anyone, I was going to help him. And then I told Dad," Nate said. "I took the train into the city and went to his office and told him everything I knew. And he just sat there and listened. He told me not to do a single thing.

Not to change my plans, and not to say a word. He told me he would take care of it. And that's what I did.

"It sounds so bad now, after what happened, but I swear, I didn't think it would go this way. You know Dad. I thought he would find a rational solution. And I think he really could have, if things hadn't gone wrong."

If Marlowe hadn't thought the same thing, she would have chided her brother for being so delusional. If anyone could come up with a reasonable, airtight plan, it would be their father. So why hadn't he?

"You could have talked to her," Marlowe said. "She might have listened to you."

"I thought maybe I should, but I was young too, and I was scared for Henry," Nate said. "I didn't have any experience with a girl until I was a senior in high school. And I felt I had already failed by not telling him what he needed to know."

Nate paused, running over those strange twists of logic. He and Henry had been riddled with anxiety, Nora had been hoarding secrets, and the whole time, Marlowe had thought it was the start of another summer, just like all the ones that had come before.

"When she didn't come back that night, I thought maybe she had been driven away by someone, off to a clinic or something." Nate shrugged. "I found out later that Enzo had tried talking to her the week before, and it went badly. That must have been when he touched her bracelet. He confronted her again in June. It got physical, and she fell, hit her head. There was nothing he could do."

With sudden clarity, Marlowe recalled a conversation with Enzo when an injured bear had been roaming the woods. He'd said it himself: Animals backed into a corner fight with everything they have. There must have been a major struggle. Nate was being generous to call it a fall.

"Did he hide her in the loft?" Marlowe asked. "I remember you climbed up there."

"It was dark and I was panicked. Henry was too. We were both out of our minds. That's why Enzo took him away—to calm him down.

"It was hours later, after we had searched and the Millers had called the police, when Enzo told me I could never say a word about it. He told me there had been an accident, but he'd taken care of it. And that Nora was gone."

Both Marlowe and Nate instinctively glanced at the wall.

"Dad repeated the details later, vaguely, but he never told where she was," Nate said. "Enzo must have moved the body out here just before dawn. When we were all in the house, and we thought he was resting in the basement. He must have worked like a madman, pulling the stones off and then replacing them."

It was a strange thing to consider, how hard Enzo must have labored.

"Henry never knew anything," Nate said. "I'm sure he suspected, but he never knew anything concrete. I made sure of that. He believed what happened between them was unrelated to her disappearance."

"Because Enzo told him some nonsense about a stranger in the woods," Marlowe said. "So Henry could believe whatever gave him comfort."

"Doesn't he deserve that?" Nate asked. "He didn't do anything wrong. You two are the only innocent ones here. Don't think I don't know that."

Marlowe didn't feel innocent. She felt stupid and angry and hurt and ruined. But not innocent.

"Why now?" Marlowe asked. "Why tell me all this now?"

Nate looked at her as if the answer was obvious. He nodded at the tarp. "You know where the body is. You could turn that in, and we'll all be guilty. I figured you should at least know the truth before you decide."

"You could move it."

Nate scoffed. "I'm not touching it. And if anyone asks, I'll say I knew nothing about it."

"And if they run DNA tests on it? And she was pregnant?" Marlowe didn't know what could be recovered from a body in this condition. "Won't they be able to see who the father was?"

Nate shook his head. "Maybe. Maybe not. I don't think she was ever pregnant. I think she was playing a dangerous game."

"You just tell yourself that to make it a little less painful."

Nate was telling the version of the story that made sense to him. He was giving the details that painted Henry as a victim and Nora as greedy and manipulative and grasping. She may have wanted to control Henry, and she may have made rash decisions, but that didn't make her a criminal.

"I don't think I ever realized how hard it must have been for her to leave the Gray House after the weekend was over," Marlowe said.

"She loved it," Nate said. "Too much, I think."

"I wish I had realized."

"We're all selfish when we're young." Nate stood up and looked back at the stones where Nora lay, to indicate who he thought had been the most selfish of all.

He moved to the stones Marlowe had tossed on the ground and picked one up, grunting as he bent his knees. He placed it on the tarp.

"I'm putting them back for now, and then I'm never speaking of this again," he said. "She's not going anywhere. Not if it's up to me, anyway."

Marlowe watched as he continued picking up the stones, so much slower than he had when he was young.

Then, as if by instinct, she began working at his side.

# THIRTY-EIGHT

The snow was coming down in heavy drifts now. As they neared home, Marlowe could sense Nate trying to think of what to say next. There were still loose ends to tie up. And he was meticulous.

"Please don't tell Henry," Nate said. This was what he had cared about. He had gotten into this whole mess trying to protect Henry.

"Do you really think he doesn't know?" Marlowe asked.

"He didn't want her to die. No one did."

"That doesn't mean anything now." Marlowe knew Henry. He had been protected since birth. By the life they all shared, and by his older siblings.

"Liam never knew," Nate said. "That was what stopped Brierley from getting to the truth. Henry never told Liam about his thing with Nora. Liam might have been scared or suspicious, but he didn't have anything to point to."

"Except Enzo's boots."

Nate shook his head, his eyes cold and calculating. "You already know that won't stick in court. All the evidence—if you can call it that—doesn't mean anything. The detectives' only hope was to try to break me or Enzo, but they failed."

"So there's nothing, then. Only what we know."

Nate stopped walking, and Marlowe paused beside him. They looked up at the Gray House.

"Not unless you give them something," Nate said.

Marlowe waited for his arguments. Enzo was dying. Their father probably wasn't far behind. This might be Frank's last Christmas. And with his death would come his will. Nate didn't have to say it. He didn't have to voice the selfish questions Marlowe was already asking herself.

She would lose it all. If she told the detectives where Nora was, she would lose the Gray House and her family and her home. And for what? To send Enzo to prison for the few years that remained of his life? To implicate Frank? To devastate Glory? To break Henry's heart?

Nate didn't say any of that. He didn't tell her what to do and why she should do it.

He looked back at the Gallagher barn, the snow falling so thickly they could barely make out the red structure. "Nora seemed to think we were going to leave her behind. We wouldn't have. And if she had waited, who's to say she and Henry wouldn't have ended up together in the end? It would have been nice, I think, if that's how it worked out."

She thought of Glory, a girl from a dirt-poor dairy farm who married into money. She was a good wife. Nora could have done it too. Marlowe was briefly repulsed by the sentiment. It wasn't fair that Nora had to play any sort of game in the first place.

"Stephanie doesn't know?" Marlowe's words came out slowly, as if she were speaking in a dream. "And neither do Henry and Constance?"

Nate shook his head.

"But Mom knows," Marlowe said. That was never a question. Glory Fisher saw all that went on in the Gray House. If Frank hadn't kept her informed, she would have easily pieced it together on her own.

Nate nodded. "And she'll take it to the grave."

Glory was more acquainted with the hard truths of life than anyone else in their family. She probably hadn't batted an eye. Perhaps it was unkind of Marlowe to think that, but she had seen her mother receive brutal news several times before with no more than a quick nod.

Marlowe started walking again. Nate stood still for a moment before lengthening his stride to catch up. She grabbed the door handle and looked over her shoulder.

"I won't promise you a thing."

There was something approaching admiration in her brother's eyes, as if Marlowe had finally stood up for herself. A modicum of power she could hold on to for the rest of her days. A ghastly consolation prize.

The lights were dim in the living room, but Marlowe could hear Constance and Glory putting a meal together in the kitchen. She turned and walked downstairs to the basement without a word. Standing at her open closet door, she stared at the bottle of red wine tucked behind her shoes. She told herself not to do it. Try something else.

Then she opened the bottle and filled the glass by her bed.

Nora was brave. Nora never gave in to people just because they were older. That was why she ended up dead.

She could imagine how it had happened now: In the early hours, as everyone waited for the police to arrive, Enzo had crept back to wherever he'd hidden the body—the barn, of course, but they hadn't found her in the dark—and carried her to the wall, while Frank assured the Millers the police would find her, and Mike Cameron threw up in a bathroom, and Liam sat silent and terrified. While Marlowe tried to remember every last thing Nora had said and done the day before.

Marlowe cried then. She cried for Nora, and she cried for herself. Nora had been right in front of her, all this time, and Marlowe never knew. Or maybe, like Henry, she never really wanted to know.

Truthfully, Marlowe had not spent all her time thinking about Nora. Unlike Damen and Jennifer Miller, with the immovable yoke of grief atop their shoulders, Marlowe had eventually managed to stare away from the void. At first, it was for only a few hours here and there. Then the hours turned into days. And the days turned into weeks.

She felt more guilty about the relief than she did about Nora's death itself.

Now was her chance to go to the detectives. She could tell them everything. She could make it right.

But would they believe that she hadn't known? How had it been possible for her best friend to be sleeping with her little brother right under her nose? The rest of the town already suspected her and her family. Main Street would be ablaze with gossip. Everyone would be disgusted by her. Because of her last name, because of who she was, because of what she had done and what she had failed to do.

She had dug up the body. And now she was part of it.

She would be part of it forever.

# THIRTY-NINE

Enzo didn't come down for dinner. Glory reported that he was sound asleep in his bedroom. Stephanie murmured that she was just happy the unpleasantness was over.

Marlowe quietly ate her soup and sipped her wine. When the meal was over and everyone started to clear their plates, she remained seated by her father. He reached over and patted her hand.

Marlowe looked into his pale watering eyes, and she saw his grief.

"I love you, my Marlowe." Frank's voice rumbled with age and exhaustion. "I always will."

It was a promise and an excuse. He did what he did because he loved his children. And he would not stop loving her, no matter what she did.

How could Marlowe not be touched?

"I know," Marlowe said.

As the children discussed which movie to watch, she drifted upstairs. Enzo's slumber was light. He blinked awake as soon as Marlowe dragged the chair across the room to sit beside his bed.

"Henry?" Enzo murmured. But then, his eyes focused. "Marlowe."

"I went to the stone wall," Marlowe said. "The cairn."

Enzo's sagging mouth gaped open in shock, but then a small moan escaped his lungs. He was relieved. At long last, she knew.

"It killed me to see you walk by it," Enzo said. "To sit on it. It killed me."

"Did it?" Marlowe couldn't keep the wry twist of sarcasm from her words.

"You want to know." Enzo spoke softly, his head tilted to one side. "You want to know about that night."

Marlowe didn't dare to breathe. After days of confusion and non sequiturs, Enzo seemed to be lucid. She considered that, all this time, maybe he wasn't as confused as he let on. Maybe he had been desperate to tell the truth. He was just waiting for the right moment, and here Marlowe was, presenting it.

"Are these my last rites, Sister Marlowe?" Enzo cackled then. "You know, I was raised Catholic, back home."

He wasn't just raised Catholic. Every Sunday, Enzo had left them to make breakfast for themselves, and he had driven to St. Joseph for Mass. Occasionally he would take Henry with him.

"Tell me," Marlowe said.

Enzo closed his eyes and leaned back against the three pillows that Henry had most likely fluffed and arranged. He clasped his hands over the quilt that lay atop his stomach.

"I wonder if she loved him, but what does one so young know of love?" Enzo's accent was a gentle lilt around his words. He always found that strange and soothing cadence when he told stories. "There is one thing I regret."

"Just one?" Marlowe had to keep reminding herself that this old man, the man who had cared for her and her brothers, had cooked them countless meals and done their laundry, was actually a murderer.

"I knew about it before, and I did not tell anyone. I did not stop it." Enzo shook his head in remorse. "Not even your parents knew. They were so busy that year, they didn't come up on weekends much, you remember? But I saw them once, at dawn, you know." Enzo widened his eyes as if the time of day was the shocking part of the story. "Henry loved to sleep in, the lazy boy, but there he was, in the gray light before sunrise, walking with Nora in the apple orchard. I was up early, and I wouldn't have seen them, only I slipped out to sit in the garden for a bit. Tucked outside the basement, I could see just a sliver."

Marlowe knew exactly the spot where he would have been sitting. It was the chair right outside her basement room. The corner of the house blocked most of the orchard, except for the very edge. They wouldn't have seen him, not if they were up there with each other.

"Nora looked like a child of the morning. She turned to Henry, and she smiled, and she was lovely, the loveliest thing I had ever seen." Enzo's tone grew heavy, and his pale eyes were damp. Marlowe didn't move an inch. She wouldn't weep for him.

"Henry adored her," Enzo continued. "I knew that. She was easy to adore, wasn't she? I always thought, Marlowe is the smart one, and Nora is the charming one. And both of you were beautiful, you know. You may not have realized it at the time, but you really were." Enzo's mouth closed, and it seemed to retreat into the sagging skin of his jowls. "I knew it was scandalous, but I suppose I also thought it was romantic. I am European, you know."

It was a poor attempt at a joke, but Enzo meant it. He had assumed the best in Nora and in Henry, at least that morning.

"When your parents told me what she said to Henry, about being pregnant, I was shocked." Enzo bowed his head. "And I was ashamed. I was supposed to watch over all of you. And despite what

I saw that morning, I really thought it had gone no further. Henry was so young. Nora as well."

Marlowe watched him in stunned silence. She couldn't believe how sharp his memories had suddenly become. All the muttering and disorientation—if he wasn't outright inventing it, he was certainly exaggerating slightly, letting it be all anyone noticed over the past few days.

Enzo cleared his throat. "I tried to talk with her first—to let her know that we could help her. This was a few days before that awful night; you were painting on the lawn, and she came inside for water, and I saw a chance," he said.

Marlowe had held tight to the memory of those few days over the years, cherishing their final adventure together, spotting that injured bear, rejoicing in their escape. At least she had been rejoicing. When Marlowe's back was turned, Nora had been confronted. The bear must have been the least of everyone else's worries.

"But it did not go well. She became animated within moments, and I tried to calm her down, which only made things worse. When I reached out to steady her, she locked arms with me. That's when that bracelet broke; the old clasp caught on my hand, nicked me. She picked it up and ran off. When I told your mother how it went, she decided that she'd speak with her instead. She was confident in her abilities. She just wanted to talk—to tell Nora that the adults knew, and we were going to handle it."

So Nora knew that Henry had gone to his family for help, and she likely assumed Enzo's confrontation would not be the end of it. Still, she never shared any of this with Marlowe. And now the truth was worse than she could have imagined. The thoughts flooded her all at once, making her chest tighten and her vision narrow: It wasn't Enzo in his boots at the trash cans. It was her own mother.

"Glory spotted Nora from an upstairs window, then slipped downstairs and through the living room while the rest of you were chattering. It was too loud to hear the side door open and shut. Your mother couldn't sleep with the noise. So she walked across the lawn to reach her. Nora was mad at Henry for telling his own brother and asking for help." Enzo shook his head, the corners of his mouth downturned.

"Your mother had a plan. Whatever the situation was, your parents would pay for a procedure, plus a little extra for her troubles. It was the kind thing to do."

Marlowe closed her eyes, and she saw Nora, standing alone in the dark. She saw her confusion and panic fade into raw fury when Glory approached and offered her money—paying her to go away, when all she wanted was to never have to leave.

"She leapt at Glory," Enzo said. "Like a bat out of hell. She clawed and scratched, and your mother only meant to get her off so they could calm down and talk like rational beings. I'd seen that fury in her when we spoke. I should have known it wouldn't end well." Enzo lifted his head, entreating Marlowe. "Please believe this, if nothing else. Glory only meant to push her away, but Nora fell backward."

"She must have pushed hard," Marlowe whispered. "You saw it?"

"No." Enzo sighed. "Only afterward, when Glory came down to the basement to explain what she'd done with her."

Marlowe's eyes widened in horror. Right beneath Marlowe and the others, as they laughed and joked, Glory and Enzo had been whispering about Nora's body, stuffed into a large trash bin.

"When I was young, if a girl got in trouble like this, you did what had to be done," Enzo said. "You got married, or the baby was sent to the church orphanage. But your father, he said this was for Henry. So Henry could still be a child. And if Nora really wanted to keep it, your father would never have forced her. He would have helped her do whatever she wanted, but he would have always made sure Henry didn't end up paying for it. He and Glory would have raised that child themselves, but he would never have let it cost Henry. *Henry* was still a child."

There was no argument against that. If she had become pregnant at fourteen, she would have wanted her parents to save her from bearing the consequences alone. She couldn't begrudge Henry.

"I stepped outside while Glory changed her clothes. I checked her pulse, but it was no use." Enzo hunched his shoulders in a small shiver. "She was dead. So I dragged the bin to the Gallagher barn. I put it in a stall, behind a trough."

Marlowe brought her hand to her mouth. A sharp, churning wave of nausea made her break out in a cold sweat. Glory had once boasted about finding the best animal-resistant trash bins on the market. The lids had an airtight seal, locking in the scent of discarded food, and a latch that snapped closed, making them bear-proof. The highest quality: There would never be so much as a squirrel getting into the trash. Nora's slight frame would have fit easily into those large bins. It was a hopelessly grisly thought. Marlowe fought to breathe as she was assaulted with the image.

"I kept thinking I would be caught, that you would come looking for her, but I had time." Enzo furrowed his brow. "You told the detective back then she had been gone ten minutes before you and Nate went outside, but it was so much longer, almost half an hour."

Brierley had said it over and over: Teenagers are so emotional. So dramatic. And so selfish. They had been wrapped up in their own revelry that night. No one heard footfalls as Glory crept out of the basement and up the back staircase. Marlowe hadn't been able to admit to anyone, least of all herself, that Nora had been gone for a long time before anyone noticed.

"Your father was devastated. Truly devastated," Enzo said. "I ran back to the house and slipped in the side door and up the stairs to their bedroom. Glory had already woken him up."

How had Glory told her husband that she'd killed a girl? However she phrased it, Frank would have understood that Glory always did what had to be done.

"Your father didn't want to believe me," Enzo said. "He wanted to check the body, but I swore to him she was dead. I had never seen him like that. So lost and distraught. I promised him I would take care of it. I promised Glory." That would have been the vow Enzo stuck by. Frank was his employer, but Glory ruled their domain. And she'd come to him for help.

"I went back to the basement as fast as I could," Enzo said. "That was when I heard your yell." Tears fell from his eyes. "Marlowe, it broke my heart. I have never—I could never forgive myself for what I hid from you."

"Don't Catholics believe God forgives everything?" Marlowe whispered.

"Only when you truly repent." Enzo turned his head to look out the window. There was only blackness scattered with the falling snow. "I do not know if I ever have. I did not do the right thing, did I? Or, rather, to me, the right thing was to protect Henry. And your parents. And you, in a way."

"By hiding the truth from me?" Marlowe gasped. "By making me live with this, by making me wonder for years what happened to her?"

"Do you think you could have stayed here after that?" Enzo's voice turned hard and brittle, his tears gone. "I would have gone to jail, and your mother would have too. Do you think Nate could have returned to college after that? Would you and Henry have just gone back to school like nothing happened? Your father would have been disgraced. He would have had to go into hiding. And the

Gray House—you would all have had to leave, or this town would have burned it down while you slept.

"I could only have repented that night. I could have turned myself in and taken the blame. You could have said it was crazy Enzo, and no one else. But I didn't, and after that night, it was too late. Besides, it was not all my fault, was it?"

Marlowe leaned against the back of her chair. She felt tears streaming down her cheeks.

She wanted to argue with Enzo, but she couldn't. Every word he spoke was true. As soon as Nora was dead, the path was set. He made his promise, and he would uphold it for the rest of his days. He would protect the Fishers, and they would protect him.

"Henry came to fetch me, and he was so scared," Enzo said. "And when I went upstairs, you were terrified. You wouldn't stop moving about, opening and slamming doors, as if she was hiding in the closet. Your father couldn't take his eyes off you."

Marlowe struggled to remember the actions of her mother and father that night, but she had been consumed by her own panic. At least now there was an explanation as to why her father seemed so slow to call the Millers, only to embark on a wild search in the dark and then, finally, call the police. He had been buying Glory and Enzo time. For Glory to wash her hands, hide her clothes somewhere they'd never be found, even with a search team.

"Nate knew something was off. He looked at me once, and he knew. So I did not worry about Nate. I took Henry first. I took him back toward the orchard, and I told him to stay calm. He asked about the man in the woods then. The man I had seen trespassing. I let him believe it was the stranger. I let him convince himself of that."

"Who was he? The man in the woods?"

Enzo looked up, as if surprised that Marlowe would care about the false story he'd fed to Henry. "Just a strange man camping out.

I assumed he was some kind of vagrant. I don't really know. Henry told the police about this stranger, but they never believed him," Enzo said. "I told him not to push it, or they would think he was hiding something."

For a man who had not planned this, and who was supposedly riddled with guilt, Enzo had navigated the situation with remarkable skill. He had given Henry a bone to distract him but made sure Henry kept quiet over it. He had left Nate in the dark but made sure Nate knew enough to keep his mouth shut. Marlowe wondered again what he had gotten up to back in Italy, France, and England, and why the Gray House seemed to be the only place he could never leave behind.

"After searching with Henry, when we all went back to the house, I walked away again," Enzo said. "There were so many people, it was easy. I got a tarp from the gardening shed, and I went back to the barn and dragged the bin across the fields, to the wall. It was grueling, but the wheels made it somewhat bearable. It was the wall in the end. It seemed fitting. She had built it, after all. I still do not know how I pulled those stones away. I only know it hurt. Every second was painful. I rebuilt the pile as the sun was starting to rise. I prayed for her. It might make no difference, but as I moved the rocks, I prayed over and over."

"And then what?" Marlowe asked.

"I took the bin back to the barn and hosed it clean," Enzo said. "But what did I know? I could not wipe everything clean, right?"

He did well enough. Hosing it off in the barn had kept any scent or strands of hair *there*, not by the wall. The Flats were too far for anyone to go looking there on the first morning, and then the summer rains would have washed away all traces of her.

"I thought it was over when they brought in the hounds," Enzo said. "I had done my best. I would live with whatever unfolded. But the dogs stopped at the barn."

"They're not as good as people think," Marlowe murmured. "And the bin would have prevented a trail of scent."

Animal-resistant. Just as Glory had bragged.

"What happened to the bin?" Marlowe asked. Could it really have been simply returned to the roadside? Had she walked by Nora's mockery of a coffin every day for years?

"Glory handled it," Enzo said. "I do not know when or how, but she got rid of it. She kept that to herself to be safe, I suppose. In case I told, I would not have been able to tell everything."

As if Enzo ever would have betrayed them. Glory wasn't the type to trust others, though. She would have wanted to take care of the most damning evidence on her own.

Enzo slumped his shoulders then, exhausted from telling his story.

All the details had been inside of him. He remembered every moment of that night. Marlowe thought of the faraway look Enzo had whenever the detectives showed up. All his old phrases from bygone times. She finally saw just how wily Enzo had been when it came time to face the detectives, and even Henry. Enzo had played it well, emphasizing what people might expect from an aging man, knowing Henry would comfort him, and that Henry would unwittingly add to the facade of infirmity in his dotage, because that was Henry's way. He had the biggest heart of all of them. Nora had seen that.

With a jolt of recognition, Marlowe understood why Enzo was finally dropping the act. He had won. He'd passed his final test with the detectives, babbling random phrases for hours, as if his mind were full of holes and fragmented half memories. He'd done his part, fulfilled his obligations. Now what happened next was up to Marlowe.

Marlowe stared down at him. "You know I can't forgive you."

"Of course." Enzo gave her an odd smile. "You can kill me if you like. You can take that pillow and hold it over my face, and I will not object. I will be glad, really, after all this. You deserve that revenge."

Marlowe glanced at the pillow nestled against his side and then back to his placid face.

"You will not do it." Enzo sighed, and it was a sound of utter peace. "Because you are Marlowe, and you are good."

Marlowe rose to her feet so fast, the chair scraped back with a harsh sound. It didn't seem to disturb Enzo in the slightest.

Glory was waiting in the hallway, arms crossed, leaning against the door to Nate and Henry's old room. She had heard every word.

"Was that true?" Marlowe whispered.

Her mother didn't deny it. She nodded, unflinching.

Marlowe and her mother had the same thick hair and the same wide-set brown eyes, but no other resemblance. Marlowe was taller, as Tom Gallagher had once predicted. But Glory was stronger, both now and then.

"She fell badly," Glory said. "I was trying to get her to stop fighting me, and she stumbled backward."

An accident. Or something resembling one. Marlowe searched for her rage, but it was gone, back in the room with Enzo, who had been following orders to save his family.

"I put the trash in the other bin." Glory stood up straight. Her hands dropped to her sides. Hands that had once picked corn and milked cows and typed up legal memos and fought with an innocent girl. "Before I did anything else, I picked up that bag and threw it out."

Glory blinked a few times, as if she might cry over this one small act. The only thing she could admit to.

Of course she put the trash in the bin. Glory Fisher kept an impeccable house.

# FORTY

**THE BEAR**
**Sunday, May 31, 1998**

They would have slept until lunch if Enzo hadn't sauntered into their rooms clanging an old cowbell and literally startling them out of their beds.

Marlowe could hear Nate yelling from down the hall. "What the hell, Enzo! It's summer. I can sleep all day if I want to." Marlowe and Nora were rubbing their sleepy eyes in their twin beds and burst into a fit of giggles when Enzo put Nate in his place.

"Rise and shine, young master. Just because you're at university now doesn't mean you can waste this beautiful day. Get up or there will be no breakfast for you." Whenever Enzo raised his voice, his Italian accent became more pronounced, which tickled Marlowe all the more.

The four of them piled downstairs, where a hearty breakfast of bacon and eggs awaited, along with Enzo's homemade bread and jam. Marlowe watched Nate get up and pour himself a large cup of coffee, while the rest of them filled their glasses with freshly squeezed orange juice from the pitcher on the dining table.

It was early, and unlike last summer, when they set out each morning to build their wall, none of them had a plan for the day. Nora sat with her chin in her hand, swirling her fork around her scrambled eggs. She wanted to swim, she had told Marlowe last night. Marlowe glanced out the window. No clouds, and it would get warmer by afternoon.

"There have been rumors of an injured bear in the woods," Enzo announced. "Shot in the leg, I heard."

Nate's ears perked up, but he continued to slurp his black coffee.

"You must be careful if you go out wandering today. Stay out of the woods. The bear will be vicious, if you come across it," Enzo continued. "A wounded animal backed into a corner will lash out with everything it has."

Marlowe looked up at him. "We understand, Enzo, thank you for telling us."

With no particular goal in mind, the four of them found themselves back at the wall later that morning, surveying the work of the previous summer. It was, in fact, a feat that they had managed to haul so many stones out of the woods and build such an impressive structure, a new wall that looked as though it had been there for ages.

"We could extend it farther," Henry ventured. Nora shot him a sideways glance.

"Ugh, no one wants to keep building the wall, Henry," Marlowe said. "Let's just go down to the Bend. I want to sketch for a bit and then we can swim."

But when Nate said, "Maybe we should go look for that bear," they all knew the decision had been made.

As they crossed back over the road, Nate told them they had to move quick so Enzo wouldn't spy them dashing up the North Field's hill and into the woods, flouting his orders. So they ran, and Marlowe's face was coated in sweat in no time. Nate outstripping them was no surprise, but Henry pulling ahead of the girls was new. He had gotten faster.

Marlowe and Nora were still several yards behind, leaping over the tufts of cut hay, when the boys vanished into the trees.

"Wait up!" Nora shouted.

"Keep up," Nate snapped over his shoulder. "And keep quiet, we'll never find it if your shouting scares it off."

Marlowe glanced at Nora's face, twisted with annoyance, as they jogged after the boys. For a moment, Marlowe considered stopping and telling the boys to go off to one of their dumb old forts—she and Nora would devise their own fun. But then Henry slowed, glancing back at them, his eyes apologetic.

"College made him a jerk." Marlowe rolled her eyes, inviting Nora to tease Nate behind his back instead of glowering.

"He's always been one," Nora muttered.

When Henry and Nate paused on the edge of a grove of pine trees, Nora and Marlowe caught up. Marlowe worried over Nora's mood until Nora put her hands on her hips and asked, as she had a hundred times before, "What's the plan?"

"Walk lightly, on the balls of your feet," Nate said. "And keep your eyes peeled."

They slowly paced the land, peering into the shadowy foliage for signs of the bear, their ears tuned to any rustling that might give its location away.

In the end, the bear didn't rustle. The bear made no secret of its movement at all. It lumbered on heavy feet right out in front of them, giving their hearts a jolt for a second time that morning.

They froze in place. Whatever Nate had planned to do when he found the bear had obviously flown out of his head the moment he was confronted by its mass of black fur topped with a long snout and dark eyes.

Until that very moment, the bear hadn't been real. It was just a rumor. Marlowe never expected they would actually find it, or she never would have agreed to go searching. She thought the true wilderness was somewhere other than where they roamed on foot from the house. They made up stories all the time about witches and hermits, like Mr. Babel, hiding in the woods. But nothing that would ever hurt them.

The bear's size was alarming up close, no more than a few strides away. It stepped toward them, and that was when they saw its back foot dragging on the ground. Its back leg was twisted and warped. A bullet was lodged in the muscle. It would never walk right, but it was still massive, with sharp claws and teeth.

Marlowe felt a keening moan of despair rising in her throat. She had the strangest urge to wail and tear at her hair, like a grieving widow.

It was a strange feeling, to both fear and pity a creature.

Nate moved first. He grabbed Henry's T-shirt and yanked him backward. With his other hand, he reached out and pushed Marlowe in the stomach so she stepped back onto Nora's toes.

He spread his arms out wide so that he was between them and the bear, blocking its path.

"Run," Nate whispered. "Run and I'll distract it."

Nate was a hero, plain and simple. It was something Marlowe knew too well to ever resent. He not only looked the part, with his tall, athletic build and dark curly hair, but lived the way a hero would. He simply did the right thing. He led the group with only occasional tyrannical bouts. He took responsibility for their victories and their losses.

Nate had gotten them into this; it was on him to get them out. Even if it meant sacrificing himself. If it had come down to a fight between her brother and a bear, she might have bet on Nate. "Run," he said again.

But Marlowe couldn't turn. None of them could.

Instead, Nora, Henry, and she linked arms and started to back up, like crabs with their claws hooked together.

Nate rocked slightly on his feet, as if about to lunge forward, when Nora let out a shriek that ripped through the air. Nora had a scream that could shake mountains, and she could never control it. Whenever Henry jumped out to scare her or she saw a garter snake in the garden, she shrieked. It was high and piercing and raw.

She hadn't been thinking of the common hiker's rule about making yourself big and loud to scare away a bear on the trail. The scream had simply been building up inside her since the moment she'd laid eyes on the animal, until it was yanked out of her chest by some unknown force.

The shrill sound pierced Marlowe's eardrum and seemed to send shock waves through the woods.

The bear flinched as if it had been physically hit. With a bark, the bear fumbled backward on its injured foot, its eyes brimming with pain and confusion.

As soon as Nora's scream tapered off, Marlowe opened her mouth to fill the silence, shouting at the bear to get away. Henry joined in, his boyish shouts ringing loud and clear.

The bear turned and ran with its heavy gait, crashing through the underbrush and out of sight.

As if one single unit, they spun around and bolted on trembling legs back toward the Gray House. This time, the boys didn't outpace them; whether they slowed down or fear gave Marlowe and Nora a newfound speed, Marlowe couldn't say.

They didn't tell Enzo or their parents about the bear. Instead, they spread out a blanket near the garden and played cards, read books, and made up jokes at each other's expense, giggling over their primal fear within safe proximity of the house until Enzo called them in for the next meal.

That evening, when they were back in the city, Frank got word from a neighbor: The bear had been found near the road, dead. There was no longer a risk lurking in the woods. But Marlowe's thinking had been permanently altered. She wouldn't be able to wander into the woods alone anytime soon. She no longer knew what might find her out there.

# TUESDAY

**DECEMBER 4, 2018**

# FORTY-ONE

The snow exceeded forecasts, muting the noise of the world around the Gray House. Seven inches had fallen overnight. Marlowe lay in bed, listening to the children's ecstatic yelps above her. She waited until they had rushed through breakfast and tumbled outside for sledding.

Then she rose, dressed, and gathered up Brierley's notes—his musings circling so close to the truth and yet never quite landing on it—and slid them back into their envelope. A sleepless night had left her with one resolution: Whatever she did, she would do it today. No room for someone else to make the choice for her.

Upstairs, Nate sat with a book by the fireplace.

"I'm going out to do some shopping." The lie came smoothly; her blithe tone might have convinced anyone else.

Nate only nodded. "Have fun. Hope it's not too crowded." Then, lowering his voice, he added, "I'm not going to beg."

Marlowe yanked her coat zipper up. "I wouldn't appreciate it if you did."

"The Gray House," he said. "It will be yours, you know. He's going to leave it to you."

There it was. The offer on the table. Just as her father had once taught her when negotiating a contract—if you're prepared to walk, they'll offer you more. It was the only way to get what you were worth.

She saw the years stretched before her. She had time. She was healthy, after all.

"All or nothing," Nate said. He picked up his book, eyes already drifting back to the page. "Good luck with the shopping."

Marlowe turned on her heel and stepped into the cold. The snow lay in drifts, crystalline and untouched. The sky had cleared into a brilliant blue. Some roads wouldn't be plowed, but once she reached the main route, she would be fine.

She cranked the heat in the car and pulled out of the driveway.

As she drove to Poughkeepsie, her mind wandered. Her mother would disapprove. Glory would tell her to focus on the road, on the black ice waiting to send even experienced drivers into tailspins. It was about an hour's drive to Poughkeepsie. Brierley's notes lay beside her in the passenger seat. She had to return them. If she didn't, Ariel would come to fetch them, and Marlowe no longer had any use for Ariel's house calls. But she wasn't yet sure if she would hand over everything. The key to the entire case. It wouldn't take long. A simple instruction: Go to the stone wall by the river. All they needed was the body.

Or she could outline the entire story: The details of the final year of Nora's life. The message passed from Henry to Nate to Frank to Glory to Enzo. The truth about Nora and Henry, and the pregnancy that no one could agree was real or not.

If it had been real, there could have been a child. A lump rose in Marlowe's throat as she imagined a child with Henry's curls and Nora's blue eyes. She pushed the image aside. Either way, that child was long past saving.

But who exactly would be saved if she told Ariel the truth?

Not her parents.

Not Marlowe. If she spoke, she would be dragged down with the rest of the family. She would lose the Gray House. The land. The river. She would lose everything.

And what about Nora? What good would vengeance do now?

A small part of her, somewhere deep down, was mad at Nora. For the betrayal, even though she had lived all these years without the pain of knowing. And it wasn't just Nora. Henry had betrayed her. Nate. Her parents. Enzo. Every single one of them. She could betray them in return, or she could choose another kind of revenge.

Nora had done nothing wrong. She had just been a desperate girl trying to shape a life.

So why couldn't Marlowe give her justice?

Something twisted inside her, warping her breath. Her head spun. She scanned the signs up ahead. The turn onto the Taconic State Parkway was close. A Stewart's loomed in the distance, and Marlowe pulled into the parking lot. She sat still, hands gripping the wheel, waiting for the lightheadedness to pass.

When she turned to the passenger seat, she saw the faint outline. She inhaled, filling in the gaps with every detail she could think of. Nora appeared in Marlowe's mind—not the fifteen-year-old girl frozen in time, nor the thirty-six-year-old she would have been now—but late twenties, the age when she would have been most alive, most herself. Her blond hair was darker but still gleamed; her clothes fit well.

"The whole house?" Nora raised an eyebrow. "*And* the land?"

"There'd be a fail-safe," Marlowe said. "A clause in the will. A way to push me out if I turned on them down the road."

"But you would own the majority? The house, the barn, the river?"

"You can't own a river," Marlowe said. "Not really. You can't own flowing water."

Nora tilted her head, considering. "You'd have everything. Everything you ever wanted. Everything I ever wanted."

"But they killed you," Marlowe said. "And they would get away with it."

"And I'd still be dead," Nora said, flippant as always. "No matter what you do." She shrugged. "But they wouldn't have the Gray House, would they? That doesn't sound like getting away with it to me."

Nora turned her blue eyes toward Marlowe and smiled. That knowing, teasing smile that had always made Marlowe believe in her friend's invincibility. It made Marlowe believe in herself, as if she was bestowed a slice of Nora's luminosity, simply by proximity.

"Take it, Marlowe," she said. "Take it all."

Marlowe wanted to tell her—wanted to say that she didn't have to die. That if she had asked, Marlowe would have given her anything. She would have run away with her. She would have let Nora sleep on the floor of her dorm room.

She never would have left her behind. Ever.

But Nora hadn't known that when she was fifteen.

And now she was gone.

What was the point of making promises to a ghost?

After giving her name to the receptionist, Marlowe waited in the empty lobby, the envelope clutched tight against her chest. Outside, bells chimed faintly over the hum of Christmas music.

Ariel appeared around the corner, dressed in her customary black blazer. The sleeves were too long; the fabric looked cheap. If she ever made it out of the backwoods, maybe she'd invest in something sharper.

Marlowe stood and held out the envelope without a word.

Ariel stared for a moment before reaching out to take it.

"Thank you for giving it to me," Marlowe said.

"I don't really want your gratitude." Ariel studied Marlowe.

Marlowe had to play stupid. It was second nature by now. She had spent years believing her own ignorance—what was one more conversation?

She lowered her head. "I don't have anything else to give you. I'm sorry."

Ariel scoffed. She'd long since abandoned any pretenses of mutual respect or decency. "Seriously? You're just gonna toe the line? Dance to your brother's tune?"

"I don't know anything." Even to her own ears, the words rang pitifully.

Ariel shook her head. "You know something. You have to."

"But I don't."

Marlowe found fragments of steel in her spine as she straightened against the weight of Ariel's scrutiny. She wouldn't be pushed around anymore; she wouldn't let Ariel yank on her strings. She was not the criminal here. Ariel could curse Marlowe's name forever—it wouldn't change a thing.

Ariel exhaled sharply. "This isn't the end."

"It is for me."

Marlowe could have dared Ariel to comb through the Gray House and the land on her hands and knees for all she cared. But silence was better.

She turned for the door, and Ariel didn't stop her.

"I believed you, you know." Ariel's parting words hung in the desolate lobby. "When you said you wanted her found."

Marlowe stopped. "I truly did."

Then she stepped out into the cold.

# FORTY-TWO

**NORA**
**Friday, June 5, 1998**

Laughter bubbled up in Marlowe's chest as Nate swaggered about the kitchen, reenacting their shock at encountering the bear the weekend before. He downplayed his own panic, of course, but Marlowe allowed it, as he told the story well. His words came out louder than usual. She glanced down at the half-empty beer bottle in her hand. The glass was cool and comforting. The beer itself made her gag at first, but she had gotten used to it. Nora leaned against Marlowe's shoulder, and Marlowe grinned at her friend's flushed cheeks.

Nate's friends from college arrived earlier that morning, and Nate led them all on a romp, showing his friends the view from the top of the North Field before they went for the season's first swim in the Bend. Henry's friend Liam joined them as well. A full posse.

It was hot earlier, but the evening was mild and long, and Enzo dragged out the grill so the boys could make hot dogs and hamburgers.

Her parents and Enzo had gone to bed hours ago, but Marlowe, Henry, Liam, and Nora stayed up with Nate, Mike, and Luke. Nate had bought plenty of beer, and everyone was at least a bit tipsy. Marlowe's eyes seemed more attuned to the light after her first beer. She itched to paint the kitchen bathed in a golden glow. She wanted to capture the vivid blue of Nora's jeans, the soft green of Nate's sweater.

They'd spent the first weekends of the summer finding their groove, adjusting to Nate's return from school, but now Marlowe thought this summer might be the best yet. She would buy a new bikini at the Saperstein's in Millerton, and then she and Nora would drive to the lake and then something would happen. A great romance. They didn't have licenses, but Nora's dad had taught her how to drive and given her permission to take his car on short journeys. Mr. Miller was much more relaxed about that sort of thing than Marlowe's parents were.

"All right." Luke held up a deck of red cards. "Here's how you play."

He launched into a rundown of the rules of a complicated game while dealing out the cards.

Nora shook her head. "You're making no sense."

"He's drunk," Nate teased.

"Tipsy." Luke held up a finger.

Across the table, Henry and Liam stared up at the college boys with blatant hero worship. Marlowe wasn't immune either. How was it that they seemed so much more grown up than her own classmates?

She and Nora had mostly just listened to their banter all night. Nate's roommate Luke was tall, with dark hair, and had the kind of smile that made girls go weak in the knees. He was funny too, and he regaled them all evening with hilarious stories about college life. About how he and Nate were conspiring to win favor with the upperclassmen in the best eating club the following year. He told stories of leaving parties at daybreak and somehow making it to class by nine.

Nate started plucking the empty bottles off the table and putting them in a bag.

"We better take this trash out or Mom'll pitch a fit," Nate said. Nora set her bottle down and stood up.

"I'll do it." She grabbed the top of the bag. "You guys cooked and Marlowe did the dishes, so it's only fair."

Nate relinquished the bag with a wink. Henry leaned forward and tapped Nora's nearly full bottle with his finger. Marlowe swatted his hand away. He was already red-faced and too loud; he didn't have to filch Nora's beer. But Nora gestured that Henry was welcome to it. He grabbed the bottle and took a swig, smiling smugly and shrugging at Marlowe, as if to say, *Sorry, Mar, overruled.*

"Let us know if the coyotes are out," Nate said. "Mike and Luke might want to howl back at them."

Nora smiled and rolled her eyes. "They don't howl, they *yip.*"

Then she gave a jaunty wave and lugged the trash bag out of the front door and into the darkness. Marlowe felt a low, buzzing current in the room as she took the last sip of the beer. Her eyes were drawn back to Luke, the way he kept running his hand through his dark hair, and she wondered if she would even know how to make a breezy movement, a playful gesture, or a joking quip, the way Nora seemed to do so naturally when it came to boys, even her brothers.

Nate pulled a bag of chips out of the cabinet. Marlowe, suddenly hungry, got up and grabbed some bowls. They would have to wash them before bed to avoid comment from Glory, but everyone was ravenous.

"You're up, Marlowe," Mike called to her from the card table. "Your brother sucks at this game. Maybe you'll show him up." The game involved throwing cards down on the table and smacking the pile if a certain suit was on top. She and Mike both lunged for an ace of clubs so that their hands fell atop each other, and she flushed. He pulled at her fingers, trying to insist he had been first, and

Marlowe felt a thrill. She playfully elbowed Mike while flicking her eyes to the side in a coy glance. It was easy to flirt, she suddenly realized. There was no secret formula, no mysterious riddle.

Nate laid out the plans for tomorrow: a late breakfast at the diner, and then a long walk through the woods, followed by a picnic by the Bend. Henry suggested they go to town to see a movie, while Liam nodded eagerly.

Mike dealt out a new hand while reminiscing about a college play he had acted in, which set Luke off.

"If bad acting were a sport, you'd be a gold medalist, man," Luke mocked.

"Hey, I got cast, didn't I? Anyway, you know I just did it to meet girls." Mike laughed, only slightly defensive.

Marlowe felt a lull then. A feeling of boredom almost, the card game no longer of interest. She blinked and realized that Nora was taking an unusually long time.

"Where's Nora?" she asked.

Luke let out a little laugh, his eyes sparkling. "She went to take out the trash, don't you remember?"

Marlowe didn't even respond; she just swung her eyes toward Nate, who had gone still, his brow furrowed. Henry stood up. All three of them knew with certainty that she had been gone for too long.

They wouldn't put it past Nora to come up with a prank. Maybe she was trying to scare them. But that felt wrong; she would have acted by now, banging her palm against the window and giving them a fright.

"Get the flashlight," Nate snapped at Marlowe.

She stumbled out of her chair and ran to the closet without hesitation.

Nate burst through the door and into the night.

"Nora! Are you there? Nora, where are you?" Nate yelled.

Marlowe staggered onto the lawn. She shivered as her bare feet hit the damp ground. The screen door banged open again as Henry followed. She flicked on the flashlight, and the yellow beam bounced across the lawn, which seemed even larger under the shadow of darkness. She pointed the light toward the road, illuminating the trash bin, tall and isolated. Nora wasn't there. Marlowe's gut turned sour.

"This isn't funny." Nate's voice cracked a bit. "If this is a joke, stop it now."

"Nora, please come out now," Henry yelled in the direction of the trees.

This wasn't Nora's type of prank at all, Marlowe realized. It was too blunt. Nora's jokes had subtlety and an edge of slyness to them.

"Nora?" Marlowe called. "Nora!"

When there was no answer, Marlowe's heart surged in panic. Nate started running toward the road, and Marlowe followed, but she knew Nora wouldn't be crouching behind the bin.

"Did you hear a car?" Nate asked.

Marlowe shook her head. "I don't know."

The road was just far enough from the house, and if a car's lights were off, it would have been easier to remain unseen.

Marlowe spun in a circle, trying to light up the surrounding area, but it was useless. The flashlight just made the shadows of the trees more pronounced, the darkness beyond deeper.

Next to her, Nate made a small choking sound and turned in a slow circle.

"Let's go back to the house," Nate hissed. "We need to go back to the house and—and figure this out."

"We need to get Mom and Dad." Henry's voice sounded especially boyish, forever the baby in their pack.

Marlowe turned away from her brothers and yelled into the night. "NORA! NORA!"

There was a beat of silence, and then the name returned from somewhere in the distance.

It was the echo. Sometimes Marlowe and Nora would sit on the lawn during lazy summer evenings and shout, "Hello! Who's there? Hello?"

And laugh as their voices, dim and twisted by the distant hills, returned to them: *Hello! Who's there? Hello?*

Nate grabbed Marlowe's arm and dragged her back to the house. His breath came out in heavy gasps, but Marlowe wasn't scared for her own safety. Nora was gone. She had vanished into thin air. Marlowe's foot banged against the porch step, and the pain cleared her head.

"We need to call 911."

"Let's be reasonable about this thing," Nate said.

Marlowe almost clawed his eyes out. Nothing about Nora taking the trash out and disappearing was reasonable.

Her parents staggered into the kitchen in their pajamas and robes, awoken by the shouting. When Nate explained, they agreed with him. No need to panic.

Marlowe ran from the kitchen to the coat closet, swinging the doors open. She stomped upstairs, checking the girls' room, in the unlikely scenario Nora had been hit hard by a few sips of alcohol and had decided to go to sleep.

Henry and Liam ran down to the basement to wake up Enzo. He was a deep sleeper, but he would be useful once he was awake. He knew how to navigate a crisis.

Frank commandeered the phone, calling Nora's parents first. It took two tries to wake them.

Nora's parents jumped in the car as soon as they ascertained what was going on. The whole lot of them gathered up all the flashlights in the house (two good ones, and one with a dying battery) and spilled back onto the lawn.

Nate and Marlowe ventured toward the Gallagher barn, while their parents moved into the pasture and Jennifer and Damen took the road, shining their flashlights into the fringes of the woods, screaming her name. Enzo and Henry wandered out into the orchard and woods beyond, covering every possible direction. The others stayed near the house; they didn't know the land, and someone needed to be there in case Nora came back or tried to call.

The Gallagher barn loomed dark and silent. Marlowe ducked behind Nate as he swung open its sagging doors, terrified that some monster would leap out. Some ghost or ghoul, witch or hermit—one they had dreamed up themselves, conjured somehow with their chanting around the bonfire. Or the fiendish bear, come back to get them after all. The inside of the barn was silent as a tomb, the air stale and dusty.

"Nora?" The beam of Nate's flashlight bounced down the stone aisle. He jogged to the ladder and climbed up to the hayloft.

"What do you see?" Marlowe called up.

"Nothing. She's not here."

Marlowe tried to choke back the tears that were already flowing down her face, obscuring her vision, as she ran by each empty stall in the barn and checked the small office, just in case.

She and Nate ran out of the barn and into the cow field. They jogged upward, swinging their flashlights in wide arcs. Near the back fence, Nate stopped and stared into the blackness.

"It's too dark," he said.

Marlowe stared out beyond the fence, squinting at what she knew to be there but could not see: the swamp, its silty passageways impossible to tackle without full sunlight.

Back at the house, no one suggested that Nora was playing a prank anymore. Something had gone very wrong.

Damen Miller got back in his car to drive slowly up and down the road, farther than he could go on foot, searching for any sign of her. Enzo announced he was going to climb to the top of the North Field, just in case Nora had gone for a midnight stroll. They had done it before, to take in the sight of the Gray House bathed in starlight or to watch the sunrise. The night was cloudy, but still the North Field offered the best view of the surrounding area.

Glory ushered Henry and Liam upstairs. Nate and his friends sat in a silent circle in the living room, staring at their feet.

"Jennifer," Frank said, looking down at the table. "Is there any possibility she ran away?"

Nora's mother didn't answer; she simply stared at Frank, her face full of bewilderment. In that moment, it seemed eerie that her hair was the exact shade of blond as Nora's, only straggly and matted in the back from sleeping. Her pupils were dilated, flickering with desperate yearning, as if she hoped she might still wake up from this nightmare.

"She didn't run away," Marlowe cried. "She'd never do that without telling me."

Just past three in the morning, they called the police. Frank made the call, while Marlowe sat, drained and defeated, by the empty fireplace.

Her parents walked her up to her room to try to get some sleep, but Marlowe sat alone at the table, her drawing supplies scattered around her. There was something out there, if only she could capture it. But she'd never been able to draw the landscape in its true essence; there was no technique able to illustrate the invisible. As the night faded, her eyelids grew heavy and painful.

She woke with a jolt, just as the sun's first light cast a glimmer on the dew-covered grass. She ran outside and scanned the lawn. The darkness had gone, but there was nothing in its place. No footprints to follow. No scrap of a clue. Nora was nowhere to be found. She was gone.

Marlowe stared at the ugly trash bin by the side of the road. Just one bin; the other was missing. She chided herself for not taking the trash out herself. It was her mother who demanded such constant cleanliness, after all.

"Marlowe, come on," someone shouted at her.

She turned back toward the house as Glory, Frank, and Enzo emerged with Damen and Jennifer; the boys, exhausted and spooked, trailed out behind them.

"Spread out," Glory said. "Twenty paces apart and we'll walk in a line. That's how a search is meant to be done."

Marlowe ran to join the line as her family started to move across their land together, toward the smaller hayfield beyond the lawn.

Marlowe walked by a copper-colored tractor parked on the edge of the field. She inhaled the sweet smell of waving hay ready to be cut. It was, to her, the most beautiful scent, better than roses or lavender. Clean and fresh and light. After the Gallagher brothers were all gone, Frank kept the fields active. Farmers from neighboring communities came to mow at the beginning of the summer. In exchange for their work, they got to keep the hay.

The grass was tall now, as Marlowe moved through it, searching. But soon the tractors would come through with their Haybines. The large rotating spikes cutting the tall green grass down in large swaths and flattening it.

In another few weeks, the grass would dry to a golden brown, and the tractors would appear again to rake the grass into windrows and eventually bale the hay into squares to be piled atop wagons and stored away in barns. The land, with its own rhythm pulsating through seasons and generations in an endless cycle. Nora would be there to witness it, as always. The hay could not be baled without Nora; it simply didn't make sense.

Just then, Marlowe remembered a story the Gallaghers had told her and Nora one summer evening, after the first cut, when they were poking around the parked equipment. Tom warned them to be careful, the blades were deadly. And then Dave told them about the fawns. The does hid their newborns in the tall grass after giving birth in the spring. Entirely helpless, the tiny fawns with their delicate white spots spent their infancy hidden in small nests in the grass, until they were able to walk far enough on their own to forage in the woods with their mothers. Every year, when it came time for the first cut, a half dozen fawns were slaughtered in the field by those Haybines. "A bloody day," they'd called it.

"You see," Tom said, "the white spots on a fawn are meant to help them blend in with tall grass and hide from predators. Those spots resemble speckles of sunlight shining through the trees, so their natural instinct is to freeze in the face of danger and become invisible. Only, us farmers can't see the little things either from up on a tractor. It's a sad thing. Makes their deaths all the more inevitable."

Marlowe squinted into the dappling sunlight and walked farther into the field, using her forearms to push the grass away from her chest. She had better eyes than those old farmers did. She would find Nora, like a fawn in the grass. She would search for the glint of those tiny white spots for as long as it took. She would never stop.

# ACKNOWLEDGMENTS

I owe so much to so many people who helped me, in ways big and small, to create this book. I'm grateful to my agent, Steven Chudney, who saw the potential from the start. My wonderful editors Coralie Hunter and Jordan Blumetti put such care and expertise into this novel, and I learned so much during the revision process. It is due to these editors that *The Gallagher Place* was able to become what it is. I also want to thank Zibby Owens, Kathleen Harris, and everyone else at Zibby Publishing—they have made this experience truly special and thrilling.

Countless others have provided me with feedback and support. Maggie Walsh, Rachel Xiao, Gracie Rittenberg, Grace Dietshe, Bobby Doar, Laura Casarez—you all read early versions of this novel, and the fact that you took the time to get through the whole thing means the world. My fellow writer and sister-in-law Katie Doar has been loyal and true for all the ups and downs, and Rocío Elenes has been my port in every storm. I'm grateful to my parents and all my aunts and uncles for their endless encouragement, as well as my grandparents for giving me the most wonderful place to grow up—which also happened to be the perfect setting for a murder.

Finally, to all the people who believed in me when I said I wanted to be a writer—I cannot thank you enough. None of this would have happened without that belief.

## ABOUT THE AUTHOR

JULIE DOAR grew up in the Hudson Valley with her family. After graduating from Rice University, she worked as a Starbucks barista by day and a ghostwriter by night. She currently teaches middle school English at a charter school in Brooklyn. *The Gallagher Place* is her first novel.